WATER, SLAUGHTER EVERYWHERE

Mark Rasdall

CONTENTS

'...You lock the door
And throw away the key
There's someone in my head but it's not me...'

From *Brain Damage,* Pink Floyd

CHAPTER ONE

"So, our laddie in the lake refuses to sink without a trace?"

It isn't so much a question as a statement of fact, accompanied as it is with a slamming down on the saucer of a half-full coffee cup whose beans remain grounded, remembering from bitter experience not to try and bounce over the edge.

Detective Chief Superintendent Rupert Hunter-Wright doesn't do 'no progress.' He assuredly does not do 'no effort' as voiced by one Barry Jones on Facebook that morning. Frustration he can cope with, but falsity needs to be actively dealt with, and fast. 'No information' quickly becomes a void into which conspiracy theories somehow become 'news' with absolutely no data to back them up.

DI Harcourt has known for some time that this summit meeting was coming but even the stairs leading up to 'death row' (as the senior officer suite is known by everybody below) seem to have gained several new flights since he last had to climb them. He doesn't need to see the cracks in the aforementioned saucer to know that his superior's patience has been well and truly fractured.

"We carried out a thorough investigation prior to

the coroner's verdict, sir," he hears himself mumble ineffectually.

'Shout, shout, let it all out' Hunter-Wright hears his inner voice urging his DI to man up; not for the first time.

"Speak up, man!" He roars back. "Why then is the boy's father announcing to the world that we're doing nothing to find the murderer of his son when forensics and your best friend Jenny Graham could find no evidence of foul play, and even the local rags had to reluctantly accept that it was just a tragic accident?"

"Dr Graham leaves no stones unturned and..."

"I'm not looking for reptiles, Inspector, I want to know why this hasn't been satisfactorily put to bed."

"Barry Jones is a very angry and very vocal man, sir."

Hunter-Wright simply stares back at him.

Harcourt continues tentatively. "His son Gary..."

"Barry, Gary; what is this: a Bee Gees reunion?"

"No, sir. But Gary was the apple of his father's eye and so..."

"Spare me the metaphors, Inspector. I don't care if the father was once known as William Tell. He clearly still needs reassurance that his son did die as a result of a drowning accident, even though it's been, what, nearly four months? At least he had a body to bury; many parents don't even get that!" He seems to reflect for a moment before bellowing further: "There is no new information because there is no active investigation.

I cannot deploy police resources because a father is unable to come to terms with his grief, tragic as it all is."

"Family Liaison are still in touch with the family, sir."

"Handy that! Get Flowers over there; no, send Taylor. I want action, not fancy words. Get her to firm up that if any new evidence comes to light casting doubt on the original verdict, we will of course investigate with all guns blazing."

"Possibly not using that particular idiom though, sir!"

Harcourt's limp grammatical attempt at defusing the situation is far less effective than that of a bomb disposal expert. He flinches as the door is slammed behind him. The number of stairs taking him quickly back to earth seems to have been fixed during his 'interview.'

***

Moira Ahern is gazing out over the water. Unsurprisingly, it having been her 'home' for more than five years now, she looks without seeing. At first, she would circuit it several times, each time expecting to hear the soft, familiar purring of engines in the distance. Her thought was that by turning her back on the parkland behind her hut, she would not see them coming - like a boiling kettle that isn't observed - rather feel them approaching before her ears confirmed it. But there was only ever a silence broken by natural forces.

The late autumn sunshine highlights in a series of news flashes the tiny beating wings of flies that dive and settle on the calm surface, some on short breaks as the plentiful fish below head up to the surface for quick snacks, others for longer, though still precarious stays.

What had he said? 'Water gives us life but can just as easily take it away again and watch us as we float away, quite lifeless.'

She considers again the Nivaši: mythical water spirits from her childhood stories - from her roots - who lived in golden houses at the bottom of lakes such as these. The males had horses' hooves and red hair streaming behind them as they too reached up to grab unsuspecting humans, dragging them underwater and imprisoning their souls.

'Don't say a word,' he had also told her, firmly and with the conviction of a rational man, 'Then all will be well.'

***

DS Gabrielle Taylor takes in the hills climbing inexorably upwards to her right, seemingly determined to meet the low-lying clouds that have made Worcestershire their home for several days now. Away to her left, a vast rural panorama leads her past green and brown fields - dotted with farm buildings and small industrial units - and the Three Counties Showground, to Broadway Tower and the Cotswold Hills in the distance.

The cream Victorian villas of Malvern are, of course, a far cry from the terraced streets of Birmingham where she grew up but she remembers from a long-ago history lesson that it was the opening up of the railway, initially from Worcester to Malvern Link in the mid-Nineteenth

Century, that had brought so many of her compatriots from the Black Country to the spa town in the first place, and helped to make it famous. Many of those visitors were industrialists who so enjoyed the clean air and space (never mind the supposed health benefits of the spring water itself) that they stayed to build many of the buildings that still define the town today.

The road towards Ledbury is taking her even higher, making her feel slightly giddy, before she gladly spots her destination to her immediate right - a large and ornate building, clearly based on a classical villa with giant columns supporting the roof over a grand entrance at its centre, and several large oval windows interrupting the whitewashed walls to either side, at perfectly symmetrical intervals.

A black Land Rover with blacked-out windows is parked over to one side, like the latest shiny model on a dais at a motor show, or a dark, almost Satanic presence balancing things out against the unblemished white building before her.

The multiple grey-white stone pots both surrounding the perfectly manicured lawn and lining up outside the door, like small children forming lines in the playground after the school bell has tolled, are empty now, bar the occasional green splashes of perennial shrubs. Taylor considers her tiny 'courtyard garden' where she has spent a small but very relaxing part of her Sunday planting daffodil and tulip bulbs, along with the odd (more expensive) hyacinth. Since when has she become a gardener?

Considering that she might well be being observed

on CCTV (small black cameras have been installed 'sympathetically' just below the guttering delineating the divide between the second floor and attic bedrooms) she adopts a pose and stride pattern far more confident than how she is feeling inside. She passes purposefully between the central columns and espies an old-fashioned circular doorbell button embedded in the stone wall. She presses it, half-expecting it to be for decorative purposes only, but is surprised to hear distant chimes that are far more electric than mechanical.

A very tall, solid-looking man, in an open-necked white shirt with elaborate gold cuff links, and pin-striped dark trousers, eventually opens the dark arch-shaped wooden door, far more akin to that of a church than one meant for mere people.

"Yes?" He barks at her like a guard dog, but his accompanying poise and haughtiness are so pronounced that he must be the butler.

"DS Taylor, sir; I phoned earlier."

He doesn't even look at the warrant card she holds up, merely standing silently on one side as she passes from one world into another.

The hallway is clearly meant to confirm a casual opulence suggested by the outside approach, yet one obviously finely detailed and minutely choreographed in its execution. Again, painted almost universally white and of double height, she hears her scuffed shoes clatter along a polished, white marble floor with occasional brown swirls - like polka dots that have unexpectedly melted in a cake mixture. By contrast, her hallway at home is a slalom course of 'useful' bags, walking boots (which very occasionally get to experience the world beyond her front door) and an array of broken umbrellas.

Her guide is already heading towards one of the opulent archways in the far corner. Taylor isn't easily intimidated by wealth. From an early age, her father had always encouraged her to 'look first for the quality of the cotton, not the label stitched on to it later.' The trickle of water from a marble (or plastic?) fountain can be heard to one side - most likely provided by 'natural mood' sounds from a Spotify playlist thinks Taylor mischievously. Just look closely and you will see more Argos than Aphrodite.

"Your colleague is in the kitchen at present, I believe."

She assumes he is guiding her in that direction but knows too that highly polished shoes can be misleading.

After passing two occasional tables along the dark passageway, with fussily ornate lamps occasionally providing light if not illumination, he stands opposite an open doorway and waves her in with a dismissive gesture, rather like a traffic policeman prepared to commit no further energy to the task, before continuing his journey into the gloom without even glancing back to see if she has followed his unspoken directions.

Natural light is mercifully flooding in from huge, oval windows and Taylor appreciates that they have just walked along a corridor to the right-hand side of the front door and have now arrived in a large room towards the front of the house.

The marble floor has passed her abruptly on to the much more utilitarian grey-coloured stone flags which are warmer and altogether more inviting to one of such a lowly station in life. They may have been the original flagstones from one of Malvern's more historic sites, or, equally, they could have been transported from one of the many builders' yards in the area. Either way, under-floor heating is indisputable.

WPC Tina Bewin, plump, middle-aged and perfect for the family liaison role she has held for the previous six years bustles over to her like the mother hen she could have been.

"Good to see you again!"

"You too. It's been a while, hasn't it?" Taylor always feels calm when Tina is around, even when they have crossed paths in the most distressing of circumstances.

"Probably for the best!" Brewin acknowledges, raising her eyebrows slightly.

"How are things here?" Taylor takes in the fabulous open-plan space featuring a smart white leather settee at one end, a highly polished black table and matching tall dark chairs and then a dizzying array of black and chrome high-end appliances making up the kitchen proper. "I didn't expect them to have a kitchen/diner, to be honest?"

Brewin shakes her head, smiling knowingly. "And you'd

have been right. This is just a 'family space.' There's a (very) formal dining room on the other side of the house but it's much darker as it faces the hills. Occupational hazard around here, apparently: by three o'clock in the afternoon you're having to put lights on in a lot of the rooms to see what you're doing."

"I think you might mean uplighters!"

"Believe me, nobody lights up a room when they enter it in this house, contrary to what they'd like you to think."

"Grief?"

"Partly. The daughter - Gary's sister - rarely leaves her bedroom. If I had a daughter of that age, I'd take a bit more notice of what she's up to in there - just to be sure, you know. Especially after what happened."

"And the mother?"

"In pieces. She still can't get her head around it."

"Her son dying or the way that it happened?"

"Both. Today's the first time I've been over for nearly a month but not much has changed, to be honest."

Taylor instinctively likes Tina Brewin - as everybody does - feeling absurdly grateful that she was able to meet her at the Jones's residence, even though it's what she's paid to do.

"And the father: Barry Jones?"

"He is more angry than sad I would say."

"That's why I've been sent - to try and reassure him that..."

Brewin looks beyond her, expertly interrupting her in mid-sentence. "Hello, Cerys. Shall I make that coffee now?"

Taylor turns to see a woman, possibly in her late 'thirties, slowly, almost deferentially enter the room. It is as though she is the guest, not the policewoman. Taylor's first observation is that Cerys Jones is strikingly pretty. Though much too pale and with dark lines below each eye to accentuate the lack of colour, she nevertheless has a beautiful face, partially hidden by a lush mane of platinum gold hair.

Of medium height and with a blue woollen dress hugging a near-perfect figure, she could have stepped off a high-end magazine cover and yet seems strangely at one in a kitchen where gleaming copper saucepans hang on wall hooks, and only a partially sliced loaf of bread on its Scandinavian pine board indicates that life has continued here.

At the woman's nod, Brewin starts to head over towards a chrome Italian espresso machine that Taylor knows (from an ill-advised wander with her mother around the John Lewis store just off Birmingham's New Street at the weekend) costs more than a third of her monthly salary.

"This is Detective Sergeant Taylor, Cerys, from Worcester City CID."

"Gabby! I'm very pleased to meet you." Taylor extends her hand which is touched lightly by the woman - more a vaguely encouraging tap of two tennis players between points in a doubles match than a welcome, but not a cold dismissal either. The woman still hasn't spoken though.

She heads silently across the room and Taylor follows, sitting on one of the dining chairs which is facing the settee Cerys sinks into. Brewin brings over a tray of small white China coffee cups along with the requisite brown and white sugar cubes in silver (plate?) jars, silver tongs and small silver spoons. She passes cups to both women before settling down alongside Cerys who quite perceptively relaxes as she does so.

"Thank you for seeing me today, Mrs Jones," Taylor begins, tentatively. "We felt it necessary to reassure both you and your husband that, although it is a matter of record that the coroner ruled Gary's death to be the result of a tragic accident, we will be keeping the case on file so that, should new evidence come to light, we will, of course, investigate it with all of the resources at our disposal."

Cerys sips at her drink before placing the cup carefully on the side table between her and Brewin. "It's not going to bring him back though, is it?" She speaks so quietly that it is little more than a whisper. "My husband had to identify the body. It was my son. I suppose I was hoping for there to be some doubt, some hope…"

"Once again, we are so sorry for your loss." Is that far too late in the day? Does repeating the stock phrase just prolong the bereavement process? Taylor isn't quite sure how else to respond.

"One of the last things I did for him was make coffee."

If anything, the voice is fading further. Brewin pats her

hand gently, then fills the void before it can widen. "As we've discussed, memories and associations with times and places - and different activities - will continue for some time. If you can, you need to allow them to form and play out in your mind. If you suppress them or try to bury them completely, it will take longer to accept them: to come to terms with them."

"I will never be able to do that - 'come to terms' with him not being here anymore; not walking through that door."

"How is Mr Jones bearing up, if you don't mind my asking?"

Both Cerys and Brewin recoil at the same time, the latter regaining her composure much more quickly as befitting her special training for this job.

"He has gone right into himself I'm afraid," Brewin offers, "I'm not sure he'll speak to you."

"Preferring to air his views on Facebook you mean?"

There is no flicker of recognition from Cerys. Taylor wonders if she is so highly sedated that social media - central to so many lives - has moved (probably quite therapeutically) to the periphery of her vision.

Brewin moves quickly to close down any difficult conversation. "We can go and see him if you like; he's just down the corridor."

Slightly mystified, Taylor follows her to the end of the same corridor she'd left earlier.

A silver glow makes a triangular shape on the wall

opposite an open door. Taylor considers that the room might contain an aquarium as there is no sound as such from within. Stepping into the room she quickly comprehends that what light there is comes from a series of three large computer screens, arranged across a vast glass desk forming a right angle to the door. The well-built man who had let her into the house is perched, seemingly precariously on a black swivel chair, gazing at the screen to his right. Taylor can make out only flickering numbers in various gaudy colours but these seem to fascinate the man who is plainly not a butler and never has been.

"Mr Jones?" She ventures.

Without speaking, he looks up momentarily then quickly down again in a well-practiced gesture of disinterest.

"Mr Jones. I was asked to visit you today to reassure..."

He looks up again and stares directly at her.

"Not by me you weren't! I did ask the police, openly and without ambiguity, to do more to find the killers of my son - but they failed. Then they sent me you! I shan't ask again."

"I just wanted you to know..."

It is as though she isn't even present in the same room as him. He has a closer affinity with the faces that might occasionally appear in windows on one of his screens. "I very much doubt that I am ignorant of anything which you might consider to be useful knowledge. I am also entertaining some very important clients later." With this he turns back to the numbers that are the subject - the only subject - of today's lesson, not words.

Taylor understands the implications of what he is saying. She has experienced such reactions on numerous occasions before. She also turns away and quietly leaves the room, and with only a fleeting goodbye to Mrs Jones and her colleague - similarly recruited to protect the public - she lets herself out. If only she really could, she thinks, gathering pace as she heads back down the hill.

***

The calculus exercises seem to have spread further down the page than she remembers, as though an invisible hand is adding to her problems - making them even more difficult to solve.

She knows that this is ridiculous of course. Besides, these aren't problems for her they are merely tests. She's been working privately at higher levels than the curriculum has so far demanded. Integration might always be a bit of an issue for her, but not calculus, not those kinds of figures.

She can't go to sleep. It isn't that she doesn't want to or that sleep won't come quickly. She can feel all the familiar mental and physical processes shutting down in readiness.

What was it like for him? That question is never far from her mind. Far from the lights being switched off one by one, in more or less the same sequence, he was plunged into darkness. Everything must have short-circuited almost immediately.

It is the evening's conclusion to what has been another fairly warm day for the time of year, and yet she shivers. She grabs the old, multi-coloured blanket from her bed - the one her Granny Agarwal had struggled so long to make for her before dispatching it and, her work on this earth finally completed, dying before the international couriers had a chance to deliver it.

She'd never had the chance to say 'thank you' directly but whispers it most days. She knows that Granny is listening: what else is there left for her to do?

If anything, this just makes her feel worse, thinking about one so precious who rarely saw anything bad in anyone. She hurls the blanket back onto the bed. What can she do about it? Every morning she wakes up and arranges the pieces of the puzzle into a picture of the recent past she feels comfortable with, one with definite edges and the slightest hint of blue sky. By evening, the clouds have rolled in again and her world is indistinct, fragmented.

Sleep harbours no refuge for her. The sun does not provide its comforting nightlights of pinks and oranges over calm, resting seas. Pirate ships are waiting out there, just beyond the horizon. Closing her eyes is their signal to anchor their filthy boats on her: gnarled, calloused hands crawling over every inch of her body, fetid breath creeping up her nose and terrible, terrifying noises booming in her ears.

Opening her eyes used to make them go away, all of them. Not anymore. No, she cannot possibly sleep.

***

16

Daniel Reed is sitting at the round table in one corner of his small garden. Though there is much less strength in the sun now, it is still warm and bright enough for him to require the 'aqua green' sunshade as cover. Sitting on one of the similarly coloured garden cushions, he nevertheless cannot settle down to the job at hand.

He has been commissioned to proofread a debut novel about a woman who reaches back into her past to try to 'find herself.' The writer is just 28 years old and it is not only her lack of experience with words and phrasing that jars his senses but her lack of experience so far in life that makes her prose so stilted and cliche-ridden. Grammatically the book is clumsy. As a plot, it fell over after just a couple of chapters.

He surveys the largely empty pots and tubs around what his wife always called the 'courtyard space' being delineated from the strip of lawn by a series of terracotta paving slabs. Almost colourless now, he remembers when they were first laid many years previously: bold and seemingly landed from on high (well, from a greater height than the two men who had sweated many hot drinks over the project one summer morning). 'Like an unexpected flash flood of orange peel,' he'd suggested. She hadn't liked that and assured him firmly that the colour would fade over time. And it has. They both have.

He gets up to make more tea: his fourth though it is barely mid-morning. Perhaps he'll take her second cup up to her? She worked hard yesterday, clearing up the debris of that summer's blooms. Dried and brown and withered now, she had carefully replaced the dead and dying with the hope of new bulbs below the surface amid the expectation of one more bountiful spring.

Just a few months earlier, they had discovered that Charlotte was suffering from an illness called Pick's Disease which would lead to the gradual disappearance of her world through dementia. Her doctor wasn't quite sure where on the 'spectrum' she currently showed up. ('The research isn't that advanced yet, I'm afraid.') Lately, she has been calmer - keeping herself busy with small things. 'Manageable bites' the neurologist had suggested, before dismissing them and rushing home for his roast dinner.

Or is all of this just quiet resignation? Never would he have ascribed such a word to the feisty lawyer he had married and lived with for so long. A gentle breeze blows down from the Cotswold Hills to the southeast. Maybe she is just afraid too? Fearful of the infinitesimal changes that in most people's journeys through life remain unnoticed.

***

"Where is she?" Colin is becoming more agitated. They're getting used to it now. He never used to be like this. Gary had once described Colin as more laid back than a hammock. They had all laughed about it then. They used to laugh a lot.

"She'll be along. Stop stressing, yeah!" Barbara tries to sound reassuring and lights up a third cigarette in seemingly as many minutes. Right arm firmly propped on the table before them, she holds it above and slightly behind her right shoulder, her similarly searching eyes thankfully hidden behind dark glasses which always see the light of day.

They could be sitting outside a cafe in the South of France but, instead, they are perched under a sunshade at a table on Worcester's Cathedral Square at the southern end of the High Street. Not that there is much sunshine around.

"Remember when we discovered skateboarding on here?" Janice tries to break the icy atmosphere or, at least, to re-engage with Colin. "Until Gary went into the glass window of Pizza Express that is!"

She'd hoped for giggles or at least smiles of recognition at the distant scene they'd been such a part of. Instead, they just ignore her. Colin, especially, ignores her.

Barbara tries to fill the uncomfortable void. "My dad told me that there used to be an alleyway over there," she waves vaguely in the direction of the Travelodge in the corner of the square, "He said it used to run behind the Next store with a little row of shops on either side. He played a live set outside one of the pubs."

"I thought Next had been there for years." Janice again.

"Only about eight or nine I think." Barbara smiles condescendingly at her 'friend.' She merely tolerates Janice in public; it serves to make her feel much more 'cool' and 'out there' in contrast to the home-spun dork who had latched on to Colin and wouldn't let go of him. Even he seems to have concluded, finally, that he's bought a lottery ticket that will never win.

"While we're at it, my father said there used to be a

church here." Colin has relaxed a little and is seemingly oblivious to the unarticulated bitterness between the two women.

"Duh! What's that over there?" Barbara points at the cathedral towering over them and everybody else.

"No. I mean, yeah, but this was a different medieval church – St Michael's I think he called it. It stood right next to the old cathedral church.

"Safety in numbers I suppose." Barbara isn't interested in buildings, especially not church architecture.

"How does he know about stuff like that?" Janice sees another opportunity to grab Colin's attention.

"He said he learned it in History at school. I think the fact that he can still remember it makes him feel less old somehow."

"It gives me the creeps, all of it."

"History, right?"

"Religion – or the man-made version of it." Barbara is not one to be goaded by Colin, by anyone.

"Do you wanna hear something particularly creepy, then?" Colin seems to be enjoying all of this for some reason.

"Go on." She sighs theatrically.

"This area where we're sitting was the original graveyard of St Michael's. There have been sooo many accounts of people hearing unexplained voices right here, even visions."

"I don't believe in ghosts either. More likely due to the bars on that side of the square." Barbara is strident but pale, nonetheless. "There she is!" She adjusts the black bandana unnecessarily over her closely cropped, auburn hair, before smoothing her jeans and briskly rubbing non-existent hairs off the front of her thin white blouse.

If the movement had been designed to attract Colin to her ample breasts, it fails. He gazes at the pretty Indian girl approaching as she half-skips, half-runs, childlike, past the site of the music shop once operated (and occupied) by Edward Elgar's father.

Her dark hair partially frames her lovely face which had once been a picture of innocence. She makes to sit down next to Colin who quickly removes his jacket and hangs it over the back of his white chair.

"Coffee?"

"Lovely. Thanks. Chai if they have it."

"I shall go and consult with Mr Starbuck!"

As Colin heads into the adjacent coffee shop, the others survey the newcomer, each with their peculiar brands of jealousy. Barbara resents the fact that Zoya appears to have no sense of style and yet is indisputably the candle lighting up every dark space; Janice because she wants to be stylish and cool like Zoya but knows that this will never happen.

"There we are, ma'am." Colin places a white cup in front of the new arrival. Calmer still, he appears to have regained his stature and the summer suntan less faded.

"Thanks. Sorry, I was a bit late. I offered to help Dad in the shop. There were some outstanding bills to be dealt with."

"Not a problem, we were just wondering where you were, that's all. The wheels of commerce stop for nobody!"

Barbara looks more closely at Colin and takes in the tiny beads of sweat on his forehead. It's only ten thirty in the morning, there's no sun to blame, and Starbucks is hardly known for piping-hot drinks, even when 'eating in.'

"How's your dad's business going?"

Like Colin's interested in that! Barbara considers, maliciously; deliciously.

"It's been a bit of a struggle with the weather and everything. Although we always expect rain during British summertime, it's still disappointing." Zoya, perhaps aware of Barbara's antipathy, is addressing Colin directly.

"I thought everyone read the news online these days," Barbara takes a long drag and blows smoke in Zoya's direction.

Zoya moves her head backwards and tries to wave the offending fumes goodbye. "Not by any means. Dad still has his regulars, although tobacco sales have fallen away, obviously."

The pointed remark isn't lost on Barbara, even as Colin giggles a little too loudly. Perhaps he is trying to diffuse the tension after all.

"The real problem though…"

Each of them moves slightly closer and could probably have heard a proverbial pin drop on Cathedral Square as Zoya continues her story.

"… is that Dad's newsagent shop - and the three others in Hereford, Cheltenham and Stroud - were taken over by a company based in Hong Kong: Chans. He didn't even know about it until the signwriter appeared one morning. Old Mr Brannigan had been in talks with them for ages, apparently, and forgot to talk to Dad about it."

"Doesn't make any difference whose name is on the door though, does it? I mean your dad's still got a job?" Barbara doesn't do sympathetic - especially not with Asian shop owners who many of her own father's lounge lizard mates blame for the unemployment situation in Worcester, the rest of the country and indeed the rest of the world outside of the sub-continent.

"Well, actually, it does." Zoya stiffens but through anger, not fear. "He is now effectively managing a franchise whose owners have no interest in him, the work he has done for so many years, or his position in this city's community. They are the investors behind a news app - '24 Ours' I think they've called it - which they want people to buy to read breaking content digitally. It might not affect Dad's older customers, but it means he'll find it almost impossible to build new relationships with people wanting to buy newspapers.

If they don't come into the shop, they won't buy

anything else either. The new owners just want to use the shop - his business - as publicity for their digital product and he's now got to stock it with all kinds of leaflets and advertising material which will take up the space used to sell sweets or drinks or crisps."

"Tragic." Barbara sits back, not really that interested in unhappy endings.

"It is. Especially as they've increased their monthly fees too. He's under real pressure and I worry about his mental health which is why I'm helping him whenever I can; just being here, you know, even if I don't have anything much to do."

"Don't tell me: he's suffering from 'anxiety.' Barbara inverts the last word with her fingers in the air which barely moves between them.

Zoya takes yet another swipe in her stride. She's used to it, but won't run away from it either. She doesn't usually run away from anything.

"Many people are. They just don't know how to deal with it. They prefer to internalise everything in the hope that if they don't say the words out loud, then, somehow, they won't spell anything bad."

Not for the first time Janice admires the way Zoya articulates everything properly. She supposes it is maybe an Asian thing. She's only met Zoya's father a couple of times, but he has spoken to her in perfect English on each occasion, albeit so softly she has barely been able to hear him. Zoya's texts are hilarious in their grammatical perfection.

"Isn't writing things down the opposite of rubbing them out?"

Barbara thinks she is being so clever. Maybe one day she'll appreciate that quoting snatches of song lyrics is no substitute for original thought. It must be her father's influence, Janice decides.

Zoya quite rightly ignores Barbara, and yet Janice notices a slight, almost sparkling movement of her eyes belying the dark, puffy patches all around them; a dilation of her pupils suggesting that she has turned her attention to something - or someone - else.

"Can't he get out of the contract early?" Janice cannot bear any kind of injustice, but her pointed glares at Barbara go unnoticed (or unacknowledged).

"Not for three more years. If he tries to do so before then, he'll have to pay all future franchise fees due to them. He doesn't have that kind of money, so he's stuck. It's a worry for the whole family. A very unpleasant, smarmy man called Jonathan Preen visited him last week - one of the new owners I guess - and didn't listen to any of Daddy's concerns. He told him the world was changing and that news now travels much faster than it ever did before. If he didn't pull himself together quickly, he'd just be yesterday's papers."

"Nobody in the world." Barbara completes.

"Sorry?"

"Oh, nothing! It's an old *Stones* song. My Dad used to play it."

"I'm sorry to hear about all this." Colin leans closer to Zoya. "How have you been - apart from being concerned about your father, quite understandably?"

Janice notices the Indian girl's subtle but definite shift backwards in her seat, rejecting intimacy as she sips her tea. Intimacy with Colin at least. If only he'd talk to me, she stares at him. Like he used to. That's all I want, and all he needs.

"I've been a bit all over the place, to be honest." Zoya's voice is barely a whisper, and they all lean forward again, as one, to try and hear her above the chatter of others sitting near to them or walking across the square (or below it). "I'm still getting the nightmares and mum had to change the bed again last week."

"I've been changing my own bed since I was thirteen," Barbara sneers in response.

"To remove the various body fluids?" Zoya silences her. They all heard that.

"It'll get easier." Janice unexpectedly hears her inner self being expressed out loud and wonders what explanation the second year of her Psychology A-level will have for it.

"Will it though?" Zoya looks her straight in the eye for apparently the first time; an uncomfortable look from one also in need of comfort.

"Just stay cool." Colin offers, although, again, Janice notices him breathing more heavily than usual.

"I wonder whether we shouldn't just…"

"No!" Colin is generally alarmed now. "We shouldn't. We all agreed."

***

Alex Crown has returned to her desk with a 'fresh' cup of coffee from the vending machine. It already looks as though it should be coming out of the other end of her body, even as she sips it, but there must be some caffeine in it; surely that will help to kick her system into action. If only she could do so simply by flicking a switch like the one on her console in front of her.

She turns slightly in her seat to look out on to the landscaped gardens beyond the ancient windowpanes. A team of gardeners, armed with wheelbarrows, are tidying up the flowerbeds - removing the last of the summer wallflowers. It's that time of year. It's a beautiful spot and she knows how lucky she is to work here. Most of those who left school with her, more than two years ago now, are either working 20-hour contracts in supermarkets, taking 'courses' that will lead them nowhere, or meeting up in groups to aimlessly wander around the city centre.

No, she knows that she has a structure to her life that they crave. It may not be what she wants to do long-term, but it will do for now and it's only a quick hop up the M5 from the family home. Not for the first time she considers how Hindlip Hall could ever have been considered a home. It's much more like a museum, and yet it is less than two hundred years old, being rebuilt after a fire on the site.

Alex has always been curious, if not academically

gifted. Her 'research' has more to do with basic nosiness than citations and bibliographies. She has read up on the original house that stood here from 1575 and the even earlier timber-framed manor house which preceded it. It was famous for the owners - the Habingtons - being involved in the Babington plot (she'd double-checked the spellings to ensure she'd got them right) to put Mary Queen of Scots on the English throne. Thomas Habington was the godson of Elizabeth I and was spared the fall-out from the plot. He subsequently adapted the Hall to contain priest holes which were then used to hide fellow Catholic recusants after the Gunpowder Plot some twenty years later.

Some people court trouble, Alex considers, much like many of those same names who come up on her screen day after day, week after week. Her reverie is interrupted by the flashing light signifying a new emergency, the latest incident in the county's history.

"Good morning, West Mercia Police, how can we help you?"

"Is that the police?"

"Yes, sir. How can we help?"

"Are you the local police?"

"This is the West Mercia Operations and Communications Centre. Can you tell me the nature of the emergency please?"

"It's my wife. She's gone missing. I need someone local though, so that I can show them where to look."

"Have you tried dialling 101, sir, or contacting your

local police station?"

"It's closed down. I thought 999 was the number to call."

"Only for emergencies, sir…"

"It is an emergency for me. I can't find her. I've walked right around the lake, and she isn't there."

"I can put you through to a local call-handler, sir. They will be able to help you. Please hold the line."

The line goes dead.

CHAPTER TWO

Even as he walks along the third-floor corridor Gordon Clay can hear his wife shouting from two floors below. He can even work out what she is saying - commanding him to do - but insubordination at a safe distance has been his preferred route for years now.

He's quietly let himself into three bedrooms already that morning. There's been no realistic expectation of any kind of hedonistic diversion (although some of their older female guests have quite often brushed long, bony fingers through their wafer-thin hair far more than has been necessary) but the relative silence and peace of an empty hotel room provides a delicious escape from the corridors of power.

He has almost escaped once more before he is stopped in his tracks by Colonel Honey-Comb. Celia in Reception had gulped loudly and unavoidably when the Colonel had informed her politely but firmly that it was a double-barreled surname, its effect compounded by the seriousness with which he drew attention to this vital information about himself. Presumably an unfortunate or rash re-naming decision, or marriage – or perhaps both – lay in the past, although there appeared to be no sign or even a mention of a Mrs Honey-Comb.

The waiting staff instantly renamed him – quite anonymously of course – Mr Plain and/or Mr Chocolate-

Covered (hyphenated, of course). Here in the narrow corridor, Gordon is well and truly trapped. Too late to retreat quickly (and probably into the grasping hands of his wife) and too rude to even contemplate passing the gentleman without making conversation. Gordon is many things to many people, but he is invariably polite.

"Good morning, Colonel, I trust you are heading down to lunch?"

"I may go for a light lunch elsewhere today, Clay. Had a good scoff at breakfast you see!"

"Right, you are; well, please do not let me stop you."

"I wouldn't."

"Wouldn't?"

"I wouldn't let you stop me."

"Quite."

"Although I would like to clear up a detail from last night's briefing."

"Briefing?"

"Are you perhaps a little under the weather today, Clay? You seem to be experiencing great difficulty with your hearing."

"No. Not at all, sir. I can hear you perfectly. Now, what was the matter you needed clarifying?" He can hear his wife in the distance, surely at least a floor nearer now, maybe little more than a vacuum cleaner lead away.

"The name the Britons gave Malvern. What was it again?"

Gordon now recalls the late evening chat in the bar over a single malt whisky the Colonel had seemed determined to single-handedly age, given its longevity in the glass he gripped tightly in his hand for well over two hours. He replies quickly: "The Ancient Britons (never *Britains* of course) may have given Malvern its name - 'moel-bryn' meaning 'the bare hill' - but it was altogether more sophisticated capitalists who put the town on the map."

"Indeed! Well, can't stand chatting to you all day. Things to do and all that. Maybe an update later?"

"Quite possibly!" He makes a mental note to avoid the bar that evening for as long as he can persuade Malcolm to cover for him. Malcolm has no conversation of course, but then again, he is only employed as a kitchen assistant.

The Colonel marches to the end of the corridor and disappears around the bend at the end of it. Mercifully, most of the other guests have already checked out by the prescribed noon deadline.

Gordon quickly enters number 32, cracking his head on the lintel as he does so. Rubbing his temple vigorously but refusing to let out the yelp of pain that has reached his lips, he curses himself inwardly for once again forgetting to duck when entering rooms.

He checks that the cleaning detail has done precisely that: paid attention to detail. Apart from one missing container of Germanic body scrub from the bathroom accessory set, all is fine. Not a major misdemeanour.

For the first seven years of the hotel's existence, they had stocked luxury products from *Crabtree and Evelyn*, as found in other 'high-end' hotels such as the Hilton bathrooms they had once frequented together. However, two years ago, Patricia had been seduced - only metaphorically, obviously - by a visiting rep from a German company, who had persuaded her that the *Gesund!* range would be much more exclusive.

Gordon had argued in vain that it was only exclusive because nobody had ever heard of it and surely a more romantic, Latin-sounding alternative would be preferable? For him, *Gesund!* conjured up images of deathly white, large-boned Aryan men and women standing in line behind neat piles of white towels, before dutifully heading off (probably following two blasts of a whistle) to take their prescribed cold showers.

Gordon now sticks to the details rather than the 'look and feel.' It's safer that way. There are rarely any surprises or shocks - which follow the narrative of his married life - and the worst 'faulty' check he has ever come across is an unemptied wastepaper basket - clearly just forgotten in the desire to stay on timetable. He doesn't need to follow the maids around at all but finds that infinitely preferable to being followed by his wife.

The king-size bed is made perfectly with just the correct amount of 'timeless' ivory counterpane allowed to hang on each of the three sides. The pillows have been gently plumped and left perfectly in position atop each other. They do not go in for multiple piles of rectangular 'casual' pillows which, to his mind, simply form obstacle courses to be traversed before getting down to the main event - be it sleep or sleep-inducing.

The room is decorated in a simple, classic style: unfussy but with the correct details in place. Table and bedside lamps whose switches are easily found (rather than requiring the tracing of endless wires across carpets or hidden behind heavy furniture), jars of teabags and loose coffee in abundant supply (rather than the regulation two sachets per person), and several packets of digestive biscuits. Many of their guests are at an age where digestion is a problem solved only by 'dunking.'

He allows himself a brief smile as he recalls a stay in a 'posh' hotel in Richmond-on-Thames some years ago. A large rosy apple had been placed on a side plate on the 'credenza' along with a silver knife. If such pretension promised rarefied treasure for ordinary travellers to aspire to, the maggots that wriggled and tumbled out of the fruit when sliced open revealed the abundant danger of not being in control of every situation.

He crosses over to the window, its lock sealing it open at the required one-centimetre gap he specifies in the *Operations Manual*. This gives just sufficient room ventilation without ever becoming an unwanted draught. The Malvern Spring Hotel does not have air conditioning. Its Grade Two listing would make that almost impossible to get past Planning, and totally impossible to get past the bank. So, they must do what their ancestors who lived and worked in this town did: use their ingenuity to prosper and thank the Lord for some of the oldest and hardest rocks in the UK.

Although the healthy qualities of the water captured in the rocks' fissures and then sprung on humanity at more than 60 litres a minute were lauded over 400 years ago, it was the Victorians and then the doomed Edwardian generation who used the natural resource on the doorstep to create a spa town that would bring visitors from all over the country and beyond.

The town is still popular with tourists, even if curiosity has largely replaced cure as the main reason to visit. Their hotel (and it is very much a joint enterprise because that's what it says on the Deeds) is more modern. Built after the Second World War, initially as a grand, private residence, its stone facade is solid rather than spectacular - which fits the hotel's *Mission Statement* perfectly: 'to quietly serve before being called upon.'

Gordon has always been proud of that guiding, proactive principal. His wife never mentions it; possibly because he came up with the wording rather than her. Even now he can hear movement behind him, but it is the flickering images in the corner of his eye that are burned more permanently on his retinas than anything he might see through a hotel window.

***

She had expected the night to pass slowly and badly as a result.

Colin is never going to let her go; that much is clear to her now. Whenever she closes her eyes, she sees him: his harsh, demanding voice in her head has permanently replaced the gentle, comforting commentary of her father. She will never be able to escape it.

She had thought the best approach was to try and deny it - all of it - and the memory would gradually fade. Hadn't Colin himself told her this was the only way of dealing with it? Her mother had also told her something similar, hadn't she? Would she have come to the same quick conclusion if she had heard the whole story though?

It hasn't worked and she cannot do this any longer. The peaceful sleep that came after several hours of writing proves to her that she is doing the right thing. He said as much this morning, insisting that she has no time to lose, not if she wants to do the right thing: the only thing she can do.

Zoya looks out of her bedroom window for one last time and sees her mother directly below, pulling the front door closed and walking slowly up the High Street towards the Post Office. She doesn't have long now - neither of them does.

She clutches the handwritten sheet of paper to her chest as she says her silent prayer, before attaching the tape to it. Her words - their words - are in a safe place now. Maybe they will be discovered one day and be understood; perhaps they never will.

She has no choice. Whereas she felt slightly better in the night - a little relieved even - now he pushes her forward, roughly, all the time reminding her of her obligation to others, to him. She must be strong and face her destiny. There is no going back; no going home.

***

Claire Reed gazes up at the monumental stained-glass window at the far end of the chapel building. Even from where she is sitting, just inside the main door, the image dominates all else. It is of St Anselm in simple grey robes, clutching a large gold, embroidered book - presumably the Bible - slightly above the heads of several other figures to his right. The extras are dressed in bright, multi-coloured tunics and appear to be arguing with Anselm. It is the simple message that words in a book are all the tools that you need in an unequal argument which first grabbed her and has resonated with her ever since.

It was in this building that they had their induction two weeks ago, and, away from the new sixth form chatter about GCSE grades, career paths and boys (mostly boys) she has quietly researched the eleventh-century Italian monk whose name is carried by the college she has now become a part of. Anselm had risen to become the first Abbot of Bec in France which became a seat of great learning (hence the college's adoption of his example to be hopefully followed) and then Archbishop of Canterbury.

The latter post had been awarded after much discussion and disagreement with the then-English King William Rufus. This recruitment process simply reflected a wider debate which was raging across Europe at the time over who held the ultimate powers of appointment of such officials: church or state.

Claire loves History and is keen to find out much more

about the Concordat of Worms and the results of other early English power struggles with European bigwigs. She hopes that Uncle Fergus will be able to help her too. Like her and Dad, he usually has his head in a book, and he was delighted to hear that she was taking History for A-level, as well as English of course and, to a lesser extent, Religious Education.

It is her second RE class that she is waiting for. Miss Butcher had spent their first by way of asking the five of them about themselves - either through academic curiosity or basic nosiness (she isn't sure which yet) and then talking at length about herself. As with Anselm, they had learned a lot about the early period in her life during which she had 'found herself.' Claire now finds herself waiting for her tutor who is already late.

The door opens and a small, mousy girl tentatively enters the room, jumping slightly as the door bangs shut behind her. It is Sarah. She nods almost deferentially in Claire's direction - like some kind of tangential genuflection - then comes to sit down beside her, on one of the five wooden chairs set out in a semi-circle with one other in front of it.

"I've just passed Luke and Bee," she half-whispers, "But no sign of Miss."

"Probably stroking her ego!' Claire responds naughtily. She likes Sarah but, even at that early stage, finds her a bit wimpish. Challenging convention seems like a much better plan than acceding to reverential acceptance. Even from such a distance away, Anselm seems to be winking in agreement.

"I've just had Maths." Sarah appears to be even warier now.

"How did it go?"

"OK. We're going to be focusing on calculus first, which I did a bit of before, so it's not too terrifying."

She smiles at the last word as if being ironic, but Claire suspects that she probably isn't - at least not entirely.

"Strange combination: Maths and History?"

"Especially if you throw Economics into it too…"

"Oh, my God! That really doesn't add up."

"My father is keen that I prepare for some kind of career in business. I suppose History is just my easy option. It will still be worth it if I get a good grade."

Claire smiles sympathetically. "I know what you mean. I'm hoping to do Psychology at Uni. It's a real pain that they don't offer it here. English is my fun subject. I'm not sure it's going to help me understand how and why people think as they do though."

"Oh, I don't know. Stories reveal what people think about themselves and their places in the world, don't they?"

"Wow. Very profound. You should be studying philosophical ideas not equations."

Sarah laughs softly. It is a nice sound, but the joy does not reach her eyes which remain in a fixed stare, sad even.

Their conversation is interrupted by the two others arriving: a boy and a girl.

"No Jane?" Sarah seems to be more confident with numbers.

"She's dropped it!" The boy, Luke, stretches long legs in front of them all, "She said her timetable was far too full once she got down to it. She's just going to concentrate on Music and Drama instead."

The door opens again and, without even thinking about it, they each sit up a little straighter. They may no longer be called 'school students' but they still need to be schooled by a teacher.

***

Edward Mills is sitting in his old leather armchair by the window, gazing out over the race. Scuffed and lined now, the chair is a great example of comfort without any intrinsic financial value. Not everything needs to be counted in those terms he muses, except that he remains on the lookout for new pieces. Old habits die hard, and even older if you've ever been an antiques dealer.

The dependable ticking of the mantelpiece clock provides the constant rhythm that has been part of the drawing room background since he bought it some five years ago now. He still jokes with Daisy that it probably helps to keep his blood pressure in check. She in turn still laughs at his jokes, as only one who found her true life partner long ago would do. He glances sideways at the photograph of them both on their wedding day.

How young they were and how overwhelming the day had been! A private ceremony at St Martin's followed by a lovely lunch at Claridge's. So many of the guests that day had been colleagues from the Service. He wasn't in touch with a single one of them now; not since he stopped serving in fact.

The clock is a lovely example of Hamley's work at Warwick Place in the early 1800s. This piece - a George III - had been valued at £2,500 but he'd got it for just £2,000. It was probably worth more than double that now. Dated between 1812 and 1815 he has always been amused by those years' association with Napoleon's decline and ultimate defeats. The clock may have been ticking on that particular Empire, but it is still going strong after more than two hundred years.

He's always stressed to his granddaughter how lovely objects can also be marvellous tools for remembering stories from the past. Indeed, Janice had been keen on pursuing a course on the History of Art at one point; he's not sure whether she is still interested. Perhaps more pertinently, neither is she.

She has been rather listless lately - unable to settle down to anything. Daisy tells him not to worry, that it's just a teenage thing. He can barely remember what it felt like to be a teenager, though he does remember the pressure to conform - perhaps that's always been the case. He remembers wearing a garish purple tank top and bright blue jeans with flared bottoms, not that it helped him to fit in. He has never really 'fitted in.' He spots a tiny gold thread on his mustard yellow corduroys and removes it carefully, before returning to his treasured copy of Kafka.

The ring of the doorbell brings him up to date with technology. His neighbour from just down the road, Oviya Agarwal, is standing on the doorstep. She is wringing her hands and her eyes confirm the urgency of her call far more than any doorbell could have done.

"Hello, Edward. I am so sorry to bother you." The diminutive lady in front of him has always been so polite and deferential; so much so that he has often chastised himself for inadvertently (and entirely unconsciously) presenting any kind of superiority - geometric, social or racial.

"It's no problem at all, my dear. How can I help you?"

Her dark eyes, usually so wonderfully vibrant, are clouded by the night, although several hours of daylight remain.

"Have you seen our daughter?"

"Not today I'm afraid. Is she not at college?"

"I texted her Biology teacher. Apparently, she didn't turn up for her lesson today. That is so unlike her; in fact, I don't think it has ever happened before."

"Perhaps she got involved in some other project which overran…"

"Possibly. I've been in touch with two of her closest girlfriends who each told me that they hadn't seen her since yesterday lunchtime."

"But she was with you yesterday - in the evening I mean."

"Oh yes."

"And all was fine? Nothing she appeared to be concerned about?"

"No, not that I can think of. She's still a bit stressed of course; well, we all are, but no more so lately than on any other day. I think she's gradually coming to terms with it."

"I'm sure there's nothing at all to worry about then." Edward tries to sound soothing, but Daisy would have been so much more convincing.

"I'd invite you in but I'm afraid Daisy is in town." Once a gentleman, always a gentleman, he considers, though he does long to help even as his helplessness eats away at the formality that he wears like a good suit.

"I understand; it's fine. I might give the police a ring though, just so that they are aware."

"That she's missing? I'm not sure they'd classify her as that for at least 24 and maybe even 48 hours - but if it puts your mind at rest, it would be worth doing. What time does your husband get back?"

"Usually not until around seven but I've phoned him and he's closed early. He should be back soon."

"Good man. Like I say though, I'm sure there's nothing to worry about, though I can understand you worrying."

"I suppose you might be right," she nods her head, but they both know that it is only a physical affirmation. "We have all been a little jumpy lately - I imagine it has been the same for both of you. I have probably got things well out of proportion. As you say, she probably got focused on something and forgot about everything else - everyone else."

Edward acknowledges the slight bitterness to her conclusion with a gentle nod before returning to his armchair and the passing of time.

**

Flowers is visualising Rob, sitting up in his dressing gown for the first time in a few months, nodding thoughtfully as the image of Coleridge's doomed crew, dying of thirst, is conjured up in his 'Rime of the Ancient Mariner.' Ian Flowers understands though that for him it is far more than just an image or words from a poem. For Rob, the roll of a dice resulting in one man existing as the property of Life-in-Death resonates daily, while others can choose to bemoan their Fate.

They both enjoy the poetry of the Lakes Poets - even at breakfast time. It helps Flowers to get through the day ahead - to deal with whatever the haves and have-nots have devised to get ahead of their fellow human beings - knowing that Rob will be longing for his return, even if it is late into the night. Words and pictures can then take them even further away, but at least they will remain sitting side by side.

As he passes over the M5 flyover and skirts past Spetchley Gardens, he considers (as he often does at this point in the journey to work) how so many people will today drive too fast, often dangerously so and without due care and attention to others to arrive at their destinations ahead of them. He recalls his mother telling him years ago when they were out practising between driving lessons, that it was 'better to be a few minutes late in this world than a few minutes early in the next.' Rob would have loved just being able to drive.

He parks his car carefully and walks into the station, purposefully climbing up the utilitarian grey steps to the CID floor: not poetry in motion, more getting into character and acting out the role the lanyard around his neck tells the outside world he is expected to perform.

The DI's office is empty, but he notes that a new figure is sitting next to DS Taylor at her desk, her back to him as both of them stare at the PC screen in front of them. Flowers quietly takes in the shiny blonde hair and a seemingly elegant figure dressed in a grey, woollen jacket over a cream blouse. However, when the newcomer, on sensing his approach, swings around in her chair to face him, he cannot help but smile broadly, ridiculously, and regrettably.

The woman from the hourglass steps out and holds out a small, but perfectly manicured hand. "Hello. I'm DS Linda Farren. You must be Ian?"

He isn't normally caught off guard in such situations but, with some effort, tries to concentrate on her pretty face and not her beautifully rounded figure, with the result that he appears to be staring at her intensely.

Shaking the hand firmly (but not too firmly as that would suggest either a traditional male need to dominate or the grasping fear of being out of control of the situation - neither of which apply to him), he simultaneously hears a somewhat distant voice acknowledging her very real presence. "It is, yes. Acting DS Ian Flowers. Welcome to the team."

What is the matter with him? Women do not usually have such (if any) effect on him. With some difficulty, he sits down on the chair at his adjacent desk and swings around to address them both. Gabby Taylor is smiling broadly - knowingly - just behind the new recruit.

"Thanks. I'm looking forward to it. When you say 'acting?'"

Flowers hears a fairly incoherent and not a little detached voice answer her perfectly reasonable question: "We don't have a constable on the team at the moment and I've been acting up to assist Gabby – DS Taylor, that is. Of course, that might all change now that you're here!"

"What happened to your constable?"

"He – that is to say, DC Hanrahan – is off sick at present; has been for a few months now. He was helping his father-in-law to prepare a base for a new conservatory (at his house, not Hanrahan's) when he slipped over and broke his leg. The concrete was going off so speed was of the essence I think and it may have made the initial injury worse by them trying to lift him too quickly.

"His wife said he hadn't been that hard for ages!" Taylor offers with as straight a face as she can manage.

They all laugh and Flowers relaxes a little, glad to get it all out.

"I'm sure we'll do just fine as the 'three sergeants.' All

for one..." Farren smiles at the joke or is at him? Is he the joke? He detects a similar West Midlands intonation to Taylor's, even before she explains that her last post was at Selly Oak but that she wanted to be part of a city force, within a fondly remembered rural area where she and her family used to come camping when she was younger.

"Well, we certainly have our moments here!" Unfortunately, garbage continues to spill from his overflowing (and much too open) mouth before he manages to control himself, and remember who he is and what he's supposed to be doing there. "There's a lot of petty crime, of course, often fuelled by drugs and homelessness which is preyed upon by operators from quite a lot further away - much of it over county lines. Having said all that, it's a friendly and welcoming city - more like a garden city I suppose - and being close to the Malverns and the Cotswolds it gives us quite a rounded patch, wouldn't you say, Gab?"

Taylor turns her serious face on for the first time that morning. "It is, yes, though I'm not sure that anything much in Malvern is particularly 'normal.' The villagers out beyond Upton can be a bit strange too, but I think that might be due more to them being so regularly flooded than any great genetic defect."

All three laugh ironically.

"Anything much happened since yesterday?" Flowers asks of Taylor, still trying not to focus all of his attention on the lovely Linda.

"Control has passed through a call reporting a missing

woman from Pickerton which we need to follow up on, but other than that…"

"Report writing it is then!"

He grins at them both and is rewarded by a gorgeous smile from Farren and an eye roll from Taylor, who turns back to her but not before another little aside. "I said that you could do with an extra pair of hands with the filing - we've all had to help each other out for what seems like ages now. They've also promised us a DC but we're going to have to continue to muck in for now."

"I'm at your service whenever you need me!" Farren takes up the theme. "I'm always happy to get my hands dirty."

Flowers nods his appreciation enthusiastically but doesn't trust himself to speak, which, for a man who loves beautiful words so much, is rather like being constipated.

***

Charlotte Reed looks at the disappearing countryside around her – literally, a three-hundred-and-sixty-degree view over slopes falling away. The tower is just behind her: partially forming a wall between her and the morning sun and causing her slight form to create a much larger shadow of herself. Perhaps she has been eclipsed? Not for the first time.

She has read about Lady Coventry's late eighteenth-century desire that a 'Saxon' tower be built on this beacon site to assess whether it could be seen from her home in Worcester, 22 miles away. Capability Brown -

that man so capable that he seems to appear in the histories of every grand house she has ever visited - was responsible for its construction and passed the test. Not bad for someone called Brown.

What it must have been like for a woman with so much money that she wasted it on falsity, purely for her own amusement, Charlotte muses. And what had the word 'work' ever meant to her? She had worked hard, really hard, just as her father had shown her. But where had that got them?

Either of them? Charlotte can feel the familiar rise of anger within her. It happens much less often now, but its perniciousness is still easily and instantly recognisable.

An image of her former colleague - Amy Whiteman - flashes up in front of her, although it must be a spirit presence as she died some years ago. Manipulative and spiteful, her 'partner' in the law firm had made Charlotte's life hell: necessary fallout from the Scottish woman's ruthless ambition to get to the top. Well, Charlotte is on top now alright, but something isn't right about it: the view is clouded and not by clouds.

She hadn't thought about Amy for years. She had managed to successfully bury the petty quips, the two-faced false praise and the double standards. Had Lady Coventry been like that? Nasty and vindictive to those at home who were starving during the Napoleonic Wars, while she spent her precious time and money on a folly?

The 'therapy' sessions she had been to over the last

couple of years had not helped much. The specialist doctor had attempted to reveal every layer of truth, like an onion being unpeeled, and with lots of similarly accompanying tears. He had certainly been determined in his mission on her behalf although she had managed to not give Amy any more depth than she merited - in life or death. However, having previously managed to largely remove that woman from her everyday consciousness, the regular discussions, quite apart from being therapeutic, had only served to allow all these thoughts to resurface: to become a waking focus for a tired lens. Examining them has made them only too real again, and you cannot bury reality nearly so easily.

She recalls one particularly toxic incident. A potential new client had visited their smart, modern offices just off Fetter Lane. The 'client' was technically three different people. A Mr Goater - tall and avuncular, belying his sharp suit and immaculate manners - and his smug assistant, Miss Gooding, equally tall and similarly dressed, but without the breeding. At the last moment, a third member of the client's team arrived: Mr Hendricks. Mr Hendricks was a junior, having successfully navigated a work placement while at university. He was smaller, chubbier and a bit spotty. Miss Gooding made sure that he was aware of such shortcomings even as he idly gazed at her and her alone.

The problem with the meeting was that Charlotte had been asked to set it up and manage it, with Amy Whiteman also in attendance as this was a client from the financial services sector whom they were keen to entrap. Because of the late and unexpected arrival of

Mr Hendricks, there were only four chairs in the office: comfortable grey office chairs that were also extremely heavy. Amy had seized on the opportunity to demean her colleague, declining to call 'Resources' to find and bring in an extra chair from another meeting room down the corridor, instead belittling Charlotte in front of the client team and demanding she put the situation right immediately.

Unfortunately, the other meeting room was also busy, so Charlotte had to go down to the floor below, locate a spare chair and then wait for the lift to bring it back to the meeting room she had vacated at least five minutes earlier. As she struggled to wheel it up to the central table, sweating profusely - with Mr Hendricks standing and watching on - she heard Amy announce in a very loud voice. "Have no fear, Mr Goater; this is precisely why our Senior Partner, Mr Brainsfoot, has insisted that I take charge of this meeting and any subsequent dealings between us.

If Miss Gooding was visibly amused by proceedings, Mr Goater was not. The firm did not get the business and Amy saw to it that Charlotte very publicly took the blame. To argue back would have been political (and financial) suicide and simply make her appear to be 'protesting too much.'

She can see a small trail of hikers - backpackers, judging by the orange, tornado-proof baggage they are carrying on their assorted backs - heading down for the 'nuclear bunker tour.' Some chance that same baggage would have had if the Cold War had heated up a few degrees like the whole planet now seems to be doing.

More than 300 metres above sea level, on a clear day you are supposed to be able to see 16 counties from up here. No wonder Lady Coventry could make it out via the uninterrupted view from her comfortable drawing room chair. An early autumn mist is clearing slowly, burned to near nothingness by the sun - at least nothing that can be seen, just seen through. Perhaps this is what she is now to become: a body without substance; no secrets. A personality that is soon to be transparent.

The leaves on the trees below will soon be falling, the Black Mountains of Wales growing darker with each icy, pointing finger of winter. Footprints in snow that will then melt, taking away all traces of her very existence. She shudders and wraps her old, blue cardigan more tightly around her. This action momentarily unbalances her, and she stumbles slightly, just as the voices reach her from somewhere below. She feels slightly woozy, close to the edge.

A tall man is running towards her menacingly, his eyes fixed on her. He is dressed in a dark coat over blue jeans. Somewhat incongruously he is also sporting a clerical collar. It offers her no reassurance. Terror has her in its grip and what reason she has left quickly assesses that flight is an easy victor over fight. Someone is shouting. A few of those backpackers who haven't yet disappeared over the horizon have turned to stare up at the drama now unfolding above them.

Is she the lead character or just another victim? She urgently needs to get away, but where can she go? There is nowhere to hide, nowhere. She knows this. Amy Whiteman knows this. She stumbles again as she backs away from him and then she is just falling, falling.

***

Kate Shelbourne gets the call just after eleven. She was supposed to have been covering a new Council initiative in Pershore that lunchtime, hence her still being at home. The 'Reimagining of the Georgian High Street' would have to be left to somebody else's imagination.

She washes her plate and mug before drying each and placing them back in the smart kitchen cupboard to the right of the 'designer' sink with the plug that seeps more water than it secures. The items of crockery must have known their places as well as she did: long periods of darkness before the opportunity to shine and be briefly useful came along again. Most days were the same. Not terrible; just the same.

She smooths her grey trousers and pulls her fingers through dark, shoulder-length hair, still in good condition - still hers. She catches herself in the mirror by the front door. A slightly plumpish middle-aged woman looks out at her as she always does - as she seems to have done forever and a day. She isn't unattractive, but neither does she seem to attract anyone's attention these days. Perhaps it's better that way, although a few photographs to remember fewer solitary days might have been nice.

She still kisses the family portrait by her bedside before she settles down each night. Just her as a little girl and the people who had once looked after her; loved her. Nobody else saw her in the way that they did - presumably nobody ever will now. The only other image in the house is of her beloved Granny Vera, taken when the two of them were on holiday in Switzerland, just before Kate started at the paper. It's a lovely picture of an old lady with a coffee cup in hand and a smile that no amount of caffeine could have made broader. Kate sighs. It's been more than ten years now since she left; still, she catches herself thinking of things she wished she had said to her, never doubting at the time that she would have plenty of time to do so.

Gran had loved this three-bedroomed house on the outskirts of Evesham. She'd often stayed with Kate, who'd delighted in making up the bed for her, arranging small vases of fresh flowers by the bedside, remembering how much she loved the natural scent of roses and lavender. Now three bedrooms were two too many. Gran had spent hours sitting in the conservatory at the back, straight through from the sparse but comfortable lounge. There wasn't much to see through the large expanse of glass though - just a small patch of lawn with borders that she helped Kate to plant and weed every summer. Gran saw beyond the pane though, way beyond, as older people often do when there is so much to look back on if not forward to.

She purposefully straightens the cushions on the settee where she had been lying with her iPad, checking her emails and, of course, the latest news feeds from the West Midlands and further afield. Kate has always been curious, wanting - needing - to know what was going on in the world around her and why. Apart from a mother of two being stopped on the M5 after dutifully heeding her Sat Nav's advice to head in a northerly direction on the southbound carriageway, and another local farmer claiming that there wouldn't be enough food in the shops following Brexit, all seems reasonably calm.

This call has changed all that though. Of course, she shouldn't view any incident more compassionately when it concerns the death of women rather than men, but she does. Another little piece of her dies inside too. She does a quick, final check of the tiny kitchen and lounge. Nothing is out of place. Why ever would it be?

She parks in the Diglis Hotel car park, which is much busier than normal for a weekday out of season and walks briskly down to the towpath. The ugly, white tower blocks from St John's on the other side of the river peep through the trees spotting, as she does, the police cordon just to her right, at the bend in the river where the spire of St Andrew's and tower of All Saints churches appear to be just a few inches apart, though they are on different banks of the river. If that is an optical illusion, there is nothing illusory about several uniformed police officers, the blue and white ticker tape and two figures in white outfits ahead of her.

Behind her, the diagonal white painted stripe reaching down to the water's edge signals the junction of the river and the start (or end) point of the Worcester and Birmingham Canal. Two further officers have cordoned off Diglis Parade, preventing any more walkers or cyclists joining her, or them.

While not exactly a flashback, she has witnessed a similar scene in her mind ever since she was a young girl. The details are different, or at least blurred, but always there is a river: reassuringly tranquil on the surface but assuredly deadly below.

She takes in the scene before heading along Kleve Walk towards it, the dark, gnarled branches of elm trees in their familiar Y shapes framing a different kind of nature entirely. Bizarrely she can recall a story about new elms being planted near the South Quay fountain which were supposed to be resistant to Dutch elm disease.

A small crowd of onlookers dressed mainly in multi-coloured anoraks below grey or greying hair has already gathered on this side of the tape. She can see a similar and growing group on the other side, down towards Brown's restaurant. She quickly spots DI Martin Harcourt stripping his feet of protective plastic coverings. Just behind him is DS Taylor, talking to a tall man in uniform. Harcourt holds his hands up to his eyes to shield them from the midday sun, before appearing to recognise her and, ignoring the voyeurs with their worthy airs and unworthy presence, walks the few steps in her direction.

"Kate."

"This looks bad, Martin. Can you tell me anything about it?"

"You're quick off the mark?"

She isn't sure if he is accusing her of something (perhaps it's just a police thing) or simply making an observation: a pretty fair one as it happens.

"A friend contacted the news desk."

"Handy?"

"Well, you never forget your friends do you?" She replied testily.

"Are you able to give me the name of the friend?"

"Of course, it's not exactly privileged information, is it? Nancy Gutteridge. She works part-time at the Diglis." She flips her head towards the hotel just above them. "Nancy was preparing tables for lunch and happened to look out of the window; saw activity down below here. A middle-aged woman had become very agitated, and a crowd quickly gathered around her, joined soon after by two policemen. That's when she called me."

"The first witness on the scene would be the woman in distress that your friend observed, Harcourt confirms. "A Miss Miranda Ann Clackerton. She volunteers for the local swan project - helps protect their environment, feeds them when other food is scarce and so on. We'll need to talk to Nancy as well." Harcourt looks directly at Kate. "First witness statements are often critical in cases such as this, however minor."

"That shouldn't be a problem; if she's gone off shift, she only lives a few doors down in one of the terraced houses by the river. You know, with the brightly painted front doors. Hers is number 4A: purple. It's the first one you come to going in that direction which has had its front door raised - because of the flooding. Not that it's been a total success: she's still fighting an insurance claim on her ruined carpets from last winter. You confirmed that a body has been found."

Harcourt tuts, almost imperceptibly, but she is trained to interpret body language - professionally at least. "No.

I didn't but, yes, we have a body of a woman." His reply is grudging, but there is something more to it than that. "She was found in that nettle bed down there, partially hidden, which is presumably why the swans hadn't yet shown any interest in her. That's a small mercy I suppose."

"Had she drowned?"

"We're assuming so but waiting for Jenny Graham to assess it - her."

Shelbourne can see now that Harcourt is visibly distressed. She instinctively places a hand on his shoulder. He doesn't attempt to move it.

"I don't suppose this ever gets any easier, does it?"

"Not for her it didn't!"

Seeing Taylor walking towards them, he does move now, twisting around gently to face his colleague.

"Hello, Kate." Taylor looks past him, acknowledging the older woman. "We only ever seem to meet at the worst of times!"

"Nature of the jobs I suppose." Kate smiles. She has always liked Taylor - well, both of them - because they don't ever try to dress anything up. What you see is what you get, unlike many of the people they have to interview, she supposes.

Harcourt is making to move back to the crime scene - if that's what it turns out to be.

"Have you managed to identify her yet, Martin?"

He half-turns, but sufficiently enough for her to see watery eyes in the sun's glare.

"We have, yes. The Press Office will be in touch." With that they both turn and quickly walk away from her, leaving her with the truth, but not the whole truth.

**

Linda Farren crosses her long legs, aware that several of her male colleagues are similarly dotting the i's and crossing the t's in the forlorn hopes that their attention to detail will make her notice them, even impress her perhaps.

The Ops Room is filling up quickly and she is pleased to see DS Taylor enter, quickly spotting her new colleague and taking the seat next to her. "The Detective Superintendent is going to lead on this today but then he'll hand it down to DI Harcourt to follow up; so, just listen to what they have to say and we'll have a catch-up afterwards."

Farren smiles both her understanding and thanks.

Rupert Hunter-Wright marches into the room just afterwards. Farren finds herself sitting up straight, noticing that most of the other detectives are doing precisely the same. She met the Super when she first arrived and has heard his booming voice many times since. She hears it again now.

"Right. Thank you, everybody. I'm not going to beat about the bush on this one. We have this morning recovered a young girl's body from the River Severn, just along from Diglis. The exact location is in your notes, along with the initial Scene of Crime photographs. The pathologist - Dr Graham - is examining the body as we - I - speak. Initial findings do suggest that the cause of death was by drowning and do not suggest any other kind of foul play. However, it is of course, most unusual - unlikely even - that a young girl would simply walk or fall off the towpath and drown in broad daylight. We will await her detailed findings.

DI Harcourt and his team will be leading the investigation. For those of you who haven't yet met her, DS Linda Farren has just transferred to us from Selly Oak. Please make yourselves known to her. It goes without saying that DI Harcourt's team has been under-resourced for some time. I hope that this new appointment will go some way to redressing the balance.

However, if she'll forgive me," at this point he allows himself to look directly at Farren over the no-nonsense spectacles just about clinging to his enormous head, but he does not linger over her as others have done, "The main reason I wanted to have a few words today is that there will no doubt be speculation that this tragic death is somehow linked to the equally tragic drowning of Gary Jones in the late spring. As yet, there is nothing whatsoever to link the two, though I know that DI Harcourt's team will be all over every inch of grass on this one - or should I say every fathom of water.

You will know that Gary Jones's father has been very vocal about his son's death being neither accidental nor the result of an intended suicide. The coroner ruled it as accidental, so that is the way it stays unless new evidence suggests otherwise. Is that understood?"

Affirmative nods confirm his stance, rather like a room full of 'Moonie' candidates at their first induction meeting, thinks Farren, who has studied a lot of background material on the 'Unification Church of the United States.' A previous case she had worked on in Solihull had suggested that increasingly aggressive Moonie recruitment practices were taking place outside the local pubs late at night. The rumours had proved inconclusive, with the police only detecting the usual drunkenness, prostitution and other demeaning ways in which women's lives were rendered hopeless by men. Still, Farren is determined to make a difference and produce a body of evidence that is not the one they see first when gauping at her so lasciviously: even if she needs to go to the moon and back to do so.

Hunter-Wright is continuing, his feet planted firmly on the ground. "We will not be re-opening the Jones case as a matter of course, though there may well be pressure on us to do so from the outset. People do not do well when faced with the unexplained. They tend to substitute their own fantastic theories in place of facts, egged on by the loud and the ignorant - often both - who do so purely to sell stories. We are not about happy or tragic endings, though, sadly, our starting points are normally the latter. You all joined the force to seek out the truth and provide justice for the victims of crime; everything else is hearsay. I hope that what I say is clear."

More nodding and shuffling of papers accompany this call to arms, as the Detective Superintendent leaves the room as abruptly as he entered it. Several members of his immediate entourage jump to their feet, struggling to keep up with the great bear of a man who is, nevertheless, still nimble on his feet.

***

"I just don't understand what she was doing up there in the first place - on her own."

"One minute she was there, the next she'd gone; disappeared."

"And Uncle Fergus said she was running away; running away from him?"

"That's what he said, yes. I don't think she was though - not really. She was certainly running away from someone, but I don't think she knew who he was. What I mean is: I don't think she was running away from him because of who he was, just that she felt afraid for some reason. He could have been anybody, or any man I suppose."

"And yet he just happened to be there?" Claire Reed knows that she sounds way too aggressive, but it was a shock to hear that her mother had been 'brought home safely' by her holier-than-thou uncle. She'd expected an evening of saints being persecuted, not the other way around. Her bag of school stuff lies at the foot of the stairs, where she'd dumped it a few minutes earlier before heading into the lounge to find her father making hot chocolate for her mother who is apparently lying peacefully upstairs, 'recovering' from that day's adventure.

"Thank goodness he was. A happy coincidence I suppose. He said yesterday that they were coming over to Honeybourne to see Auntie Lucy's cousin and that they'd drop in here at some point. I guess they decided to go for a walk up to the Tower first."

"So, he talked her down?"

"I don't think it was quite as dramatic as that; besides, if you were relying on your uncle to talk any kind of sense into you, you could be waiting up there for a very long time!' Daniel laughs at his daughter's solemn face, but she doesn't smile - not yet.

"She did recognise him, though, eventually I mean?"

"There was a group of people who'd headed around the other side of the hill, in case she fell. They'd calmed her down by the time Fergus caught up with her. I think she did know who he was then, yes."

"We could have lost her!"

He folds his arms around her, the tears don't come right away but he knows they've made an appointment with her eyes. "I think we might lose a little bit of her every day, and we have to be prepared for that." He speaks softly, and gently, trying to bring her some comfort. "It won't be incidents like this that catch us - and her - out; not if we look after her properly. It will be the small differences that creep in that separate who she is now from who she once was. We don't know how long that will take - it could be years."

"Must be very frightening for Mum, not knowing when these things are going to happen but with all the experts telling her that they definitely will. Not knowing how long she has to live with it - with us."

"It must be, but she has us here to help her to adjust to it."

"What about us? Who's there to help us? I'm sorry, that sounded selfish, didn't it?" She pulls away from him slightly.

"Not selfish, just concerned, and quite understandable. If this was a book, we'd get to know the answers to all these questions sooner or later - depending on the quality of the writing, of course!"

She knows he is trying to make light of her worries, certainly not her mother's disease, and rewards him with a lop-sided smile of sorts. "It's not a story, though, is it? It's real... much too real."

"And the reality is that we simply don't have those answers; nobody does yet."

"Do you think this is the start of the next phase, like the doctor said would happen?"

"I don't know the answer to that either - I'm not even sure the doctors themselves would be able to tell us."

"But she is becoming more confused?"

"I'd say a little bit forgetful, rather than confused but, hey, don't get too upset. I forget things all the time; we all do." He reaches out for her and gives her another hug, holding her close to him, feeling her relax at last."

"All the same, we're going to have to be more on it aren't we?"

"I think we already are. I honestly didn't get any sense

that she was planning to go out. Like I say, her brother was due to come round, and she was looking forward to seeing him, or so she told me earlier this morning."

"Maybe she forgot that he was coming?"

"You could be right. I never close the door to my study these days, but I still didn't hear anything. She must have crept out like a mouse."

"I think mice normally creep in when you're not looking, Dad."

They do laugh then. Each nervously holding on to their forlorn hopes for normality.

***

Harcourt beckons DS Farren into his office, bidding her to close the door, whilst pretending to attend to some vital communication on his screen which is staring expectantly at him rather than her.

It is another email message from his wife, Debbie. She is planning a weekend away with three of her new 'friends' from the gym. Fit4You is no better or worse than any other gym he has come across, although he did make some discreet enquiries about it before she enrolled there. He has only met one of the ladies - 'glam' with no eyebrows and fewer inhibitions than he would have liked.

Debbie had invited him to join them for a quick drink after work - which was nice of her, he acknowledges now, but no more successful for it. He'd furtively texted Taylor and asked her to phone him back with an urgent call to action. She'd done so promptly, and he'd escaped.

He doesn't feel proud of it, and it isn't something he intends to make a habit of - that wouldn't be fair on Debbie (or Taylor) - but he'd spent a long afternoon in court that day, and listening to further petty nonsense into his evening was just too much to bear.

Nevertheless, he does feel uneasy about her going away, especially as it's a 'City Break' in Dubrovnik. He's never been there but an Englishman's natural wariness of all things 'over the water' has kicked in, much as he tries to deny it. Thank goodness they don't live in Liverpool as he'd no doubt be imagining a Wirral full of seediness and vice: or is that just Birkenhead?

He replies to confirm that he will pick up her currency on his way home and closes down the Gmail window. He now turns to Farren who is sitting quietly, patiently.

"Sorry about that." He smiles before adding enigmatically, "Just needed to finish something." He also knows that it isn't his wife's forthcoming trip that is bothering him the most. It's the visit to the riverbank that morning, seeing her like that, all alone and lost. If he is presently unable to do anything about his marriage, he can surely provide help or seek hope for people who are suffering from losses elsewhere.

He can understand of course why Farren has attracted so much attention - especially among his male counterparts - because she is certainly attractive. To him, though, she remains a welcome addition to his team: a depleted team which has been working (expensive) overtime just to do little more than stand still. He has heard very good reports about Farren's natural inquisitiveness and determination, coupled with sound organisational skills that make him optimistic she will need little handholding. Everything else is superfluous.

He taps a light green Manila folder on his desk. "This is the file on the Gary Jones case. I want you to read it and get up to speed quickly. DS Taylor will give you any other background you need. Keep quiet about it though. As the Super mentioned earlier, we do not necessarily think there is a link between the girl's body we discovered earlier today and Gary's death. However, I want to be ahead of the game if things prove to be different. Do you understand?"

"Completely, sir." Farren nods her head, gets up from the chair, takes the folder and makes to leave.

"Oh, and Linda!" He stops her in her tracks.

"Sir?"

"I'm sorry that this might prove to be a very upsetting case for you to begin your life with, here with us."

"Not your fault, sir; somebody else is responsible for causing this woman's untimely death, not to mention the upset they've left behind. Do we have a name, sir?"

"We do. Her name was Zoya Agarwal."

CHAPTER THREE

"So why is Barry Jones adamant that his son's death was anything other than accidental." Farren is sitting across from Taylor.

"Firstly, Barry Jones is an absolute piece of work." She shivers at the memory of their recent encounter. "He seems to have tried very hard to build an image of himself and no doubt his 'professional' reputation that he'll do anything to defend - or deny."

"Sounds a bit harsh?" Farren is staring at her, trying to understand where the sudden anger has arisen from.

"Sorry. That did sound a bit one-dimensional, didn't it? I don't doubt that he was devastated at his son's death and that may well be fuelling his behaviour now, but his absolute conviction that the death was no accident is about much more than the point-blank refusal to accept the truth we often see in bereavement. It feels to me that basic denial is only part of it - it's more like an obsession. You know, when you have an answer to a question and, even though it's the wrong answer, you keep trying to make the question fit?"

"And Mrs. Jones?"

"Quiet. Lost. Unable to communicate."

"Which might change?"

"Hopefully, with time."

"And there was just one son, I understand?"

"Which is also part of the problem. He was not just the only boy; he was the golden boy! This wasn't just on his father's say-so either. Everyone we interviewed described Gary as likeable and full of fun. There's a daughter, but she doesn't seem to get much of a look-in. I suspect it's the same with the mother. No, Gary appears to have been the life and soul of the party if you'll pardon the cliche"

"Pardoned! Oh, thanks." Flowers places plastic cups of tea in front of them both before returning to his desk.

"So, nobody had a bad word to say about him" That, in itself, is suspicious, don't you think."

Flowers wrinkles his nose, as they all do after a single sip of the hot liquid. "I agree that perfection rarely comes in human form."

"He's a bit of a poet in his spare time I'm afraid." Taylor smiles at Farren.

"Oh, no. Just an admirer of beautiful words. That's all."

Flowers' face is colouring as he protests.

Farren comes to the rescue. "I love great writing. When I'm not on duty I usually have my nose in a book."

"Really?" Flowers' excitement gets the better of any attempt to hide his enthusiasm at this unexpected announcement. "We'll have to get together for a chat sometime."

"We will. Yes." Farren does not blush, only grins at them both. "But back to the case. Jones's friends - there are four of them I believe. Did none of them raise any doubts about Gary, concerns for his behaviour?"

"No, they didn't," Taylor consults her notes, "They all said pretty much the same thing: that Gary had waded out alone towards the middle of the main Pickerton Lake. They had each shouted to him to come back but he just kept on going."

"Why 'the main lake?' Are there others?"

"There are three in total." Flowers hands Farren a large-scale map of the immediate area, but the one Gary died in is the largest, and deepest."

"Could it have been a suicide attempt that went wrong... or right?"

"Again, his father is especially adamant that Gary would never have considered such a thing. The others each backed him up on this. Gary had everything to live for and appeared to be living life to the full. As I said, nobody could find anything bad or even mildly controversial about him, so it's hard to imagine him becoming isolated or depressed. He was well-liked - loved even - by seemingly everyone he came into contact with." Taylor sits back in her chair, as mystified now as she has been throughout the case's development.

"So, the witnesses - the four friends - confirmed that he seemed to get into difficulties and started thrashing about in the water?"

"They did."

"And there were no other witnesses to the incident?"

"None that we could identify at the time or who have come forward since (and there's been plenty of coverage in the local press as well as a mass of activity on social media - most of it unhelpful, as you can imagine). It was early evening and not a particularly pleasant one, so less likely that there would have been anyone else walking around the lake at the time. Certainly, none of our four reported seeing anybody else."

"Could Gary have had some kind of fit - an undiagnosed medical condition?"

"It was a line of enquiry the DI was keen on at first." Taylor leans forward again. "However, the pathologist was quite clear that there was no evidence to support it, and his medical records were standard for a boy who had just turned eighteen."

"No liver or lung damage yet from alcohol or tobacco you mean?"

"Or worse." Taylor nods.

"The other four rushed out to him and managed to drag him back to the shore, whereupon the other boy attempts mouth-to-mouth resuscitation," Farren consults the notes in the file, "Colin?"

"He does. But to no avail. Janice Mills dials 999. The ambulance arrives shortly afterwards. Jones is pronounced dead at the scene."

"Tell me about this Colin; not every teenager knows

how to do mouth-to-mouth, or was it something he'd seen on *Casualty*?"

"Colin Pearson." Flowers offers. "Seventeen at the time of the accident, though he's just turned eighteen. He went to Worcester Sea Cadets where he learned basic life-saving skills. The paramedics in attendance said there would have been so much fluid in Jones's lungs by the time they got him out of the lake that it would have been a fairly futile exercise. Dr Graham - the pathologist - concurred."

"At least he had a go though?"

"He did. He was also the most upset by it. The three girls were too, of course, but Gary had been Colin's best friend since childhood. It was only later that the five of them started knocking around together. Colin looked a lot like Gary - similar build, same fair hair - so people often assumed they were brothers. They could easily have been for all the things they did together, holidays with each other's families and so on. I guess for Colin especially it was like losing a family member."

"I read that there was some bruising on the victim's neck - quite pronounced."

"There was." Taylor again. "Consisting of several different patterns. The pathologist was very interested in this, but it seems that Gary's head hit some rocks, just before they managed to get him out of the lake. There is a rocky outcrop which runs right around that side of it. It was a gravel pit originally; only filled with water about ten years ago.

They would also have been gripping his neck with some

force from below. When under severe duress like that, you would tend to hold too tightly for fear of the head going under the water again; you wouldn't have the foresight to be gentle like trained medical professionals might have been. All of this is consistent with Dr Graham's findings, although, of course, bodies in water for even a short time do tend to distort the exact bruising record."

"She also made some notes in the classified section on the first aid given?"

"She did. She considered whether, in the understandable stress of the moment, Colin Pearson inadvertently pressed down too hard on the body, causing even more bruising to the back of the neck - particularly as they laid the victim out on the bank of the lake which at that point also consists of mainly exposed rocks and very little grass to provide the body with any give. The clear impression we got was that there was utter panic down there."

"They were - are - only teenagers." Flowers's voice is grim. "Seeing the lifeblood literally seeping out of one of your friends, right in front of you, must have been horrific. To think that you could have been making matters even worse by your actions is too much to bear."

"That's why DI Harcourt asked her to keep those observations out of the public record, accessible only by professionals on a need-to-know basis. Colin Pearson was in bits. Reading or hearing details like that was unlikely to have helped to put him back together again."

Farren nods slowly and quietly, picturing the terrible

scene, as they all are. "Do we know what caused Gary to get into difficulties?" Her voice is little more than a whisper.

Taylor exchanges glances with Flowers before responding. Even as trained police officers, and now detectives, they each work much better with compassion than the kind of blunt carelessness often used as the lead instrument in the Hunter-Wright investigation toolbox. Farren should fit in just fine.

"There is an extensive reed bed, just below the surface. It extends away from close to the centre of the lake to the northern edge. Gary entered the lake from the southern bank. The others confirmed that he would have known about it - as they all did - but that he just went out too far. He might have become disoriented as it was dusk and night was falling quite quickly. There was also extensive cloud cover so it would have seemed even darker."

"Was Gary in the Sea Cadets too?"

"No." Flowers replies. "But he was a strong swimmer. They all are. They'd been going down to the lake together for some time. Two of them live very near to it. Sorry, one, now."

"Just to finish then. Gary's legs must have become ensnared by the unseen reeds below the surface, and he couldn't break free from them - at least not by himself?"

"Which is the point at which the other four heard him thrashing about in the water and leapt in to try and rescue him, yes." Taylor nods again.

"And they comprised Colin Pearson and the girls: Barbara Flint, Janice Mills and Zoya Agarwal."

"Correct." Taylor looks from Flowers to Farren. "And then there were three. We need to pay a visit to Zoya's parents."

***

At that precise moment, Janice Mills is walking slowly along the left-hand bank of the River Pick. She isn't alone, although in the daytime the voices that have been swinging on the synapses in her brain are mercifully quieter, whispers even.

Colin Pearson is to her left. He is in no rush - doesn't want to rush her - but his question lingers unerringly in the late afternoon autumn air.

It's almost like they are back to where they were, just over a year ago. They'd held hands then, of course, though Grandad didn't like it; didn't, doesn't, really like Colin if he is as honest about this as everything else. People wouldn't know. He's far too polite and well-mannered, but Janice knows, as does Granny.

Not that Granny would say anything either. She is the kind of lady who smiles problems into submission; wears them down with good intentions. Janice can't remember her being any other way, even though her mother broke her heart all those years ago.

Well, there's nothing for them to worry about, now. Everything's changed.

"So?"

Ah yes. He's still there, still wanting answers from her.

"I've been sleeping badly if you must know."

"You make me sound like one of those police officers."

"Then don't behave like one. How do you think I've been? Zoya's dead!"

"I know. I know." He does her the courtesy of remaining quiet for a few minutes, though she suspects it's because that's what people do (eventually) rather than what he prefers.

They reach the turn in the river where they would normally leave it to head through the break in the trees and down the narrow track to the lake. She wants to hurry past it, but Colin stops, turns and stares, while she walks slowly on.

"It seems so long ago now." She hears him mutter.

"Not for me it doesn't," she retorts without making any attempt to spare his sorrows, which she doubts are genuinely felt. "It could have been last night, as far as I'm concerned."

He catches her up quickly and takes her hand, roughly like a pursuer, not gently like the lover he has never been.

"You must let it go, Jan, all of it. Gary isn't coming back; neither is Zoya. You have to accept this."

"Aren't you at all worried? You seemed a bit stressed the other day?"

"Worried?" He steps back again, dropping her hand.

"Yes. Worried - frightened even."

"What is there to be afraid of? She was the one who walked headfirst into the river; nobody forced her to do it. It was her decision, nobody else's. The papers said there was no one else anywhere near her when she did it."

His protests sound too loud: too heavy to be carried for long by the calm air all around them.

Could it be that he really is worried? Janice is unsure. "You used to be able to talk to me, share things with me. I know it's not quite the same now, but we're still friends, aren't we?"

"Of course, we are. I'd never do anything to hurt you."

A bit late for that, she thinks, miserably. Or is it a bit early? She has no idea where that idea came from. It is as though someone has opened the top half of her head, swung it back on an invisible hinge, and popped the thought inside before closing and sealing it again.

"I'm not like him, Janice." Colin is continuing. "I thought I was - for years I wanted to be. Everybody did. I don't know how I could have been so stupid..."

"I'm still the same though. I haven't changed. I'm still here."

"I know you are and, well, we just need to stick together that's all. Just like we agreed."

"That didn't help Zoya though, did it?"

He doesn't break stride in his response, as though it's

a well-rehearsed move. "I don't think anything - or anyone - could have saved her."

"It's just that I seem to see her everywhere around here."

"It's only in your imagination, Jan. Look, she lived here, and walked where we're walking now. It's completely understandable.

"Is it?"

"Of course, it is. You know it is. Besides, Zoya wouldn't have wanted you - or any of us - to be unhappy. It would have been totally against her nature."

"So would taking her own life. You know that as well as I do."

"But she did. Facts are facts."

She can hear his voice rising again. She hasn't so much struck a nerve as hit it with a blunt instrument.

"Why did she do it then? What made her do something that she knew would upset all of us and destroy her parents?" Tears are streaming down her face now. "What's going on, Colin? What's going to happen next?"

He begins to walk forward again, slowly, letting her fall in alongside him. His shoulders are hunched, his head bent slightly forward like an athlete stretching for the winning tape. Except he isn't running; refuses to do so... yet. They can get as worked up about it as they like. So can the police for that matter. There's nothing for them to find now. The water has taken care of that.

"Say something, Colin, please?"

He'd almost forgotten that Janice was there. But she is there, and she has a voice. "Look, there's no connection with what happened to Gary and Zoya. They were completely different people. Who knows what bombs were going off in Zoya's head?"

"She seemed well enough the other day!"

"Worried about her old man, though, wasn't she? They were a close family. You know that. You spent more time with them than any of us. Zoya loved life but hated any kind of injustice. Maybe it just got too much for her to bear?"

What he is saying is true but it brings her no nearer to a universal truth she can believe in. She has tried to replay the image of them all sitting outside in the square - when Zoya was still so full of life - but it's a quite different picture that is projected in front of her each time she closes her eyes, longing for darkness.

"She was very upset about all of that. She often talked to me about it. She even became embarrassed when she thought she was dumping on me, even though I kept telling her it was much better to let it all out."

"That's the kind of girl she was." His manner is gentle now, conciliatory. "Which is why we all loved her so much."

Janice can't believe he said it. Though he might have intended his words to inject healing and well-being into her soul, they are like so many barbs, stabbing her all over again and again with their poison.

"Well, we all know that's true, don't we?" She cannot

help herself. Her face is flushed now, but no longer in sorrow. She turns to face him and is gratified to see him shrink a little in front of her. "Perhaps Zoya had you on her mind too; forever in her head." She spits out the venom, like a flying doctor in the outback attending to a patient who has been bitten by a poisonous snake. "But not in the way you think she did. Remember what you did to her - to both of us - because I won't ever be able to forget it either."

***

"Sir! DS Flowers catches himself on the corner of his desk in his haste to reach the DI's office. Another bruise for Rob to complain about, he grimaces. "We've got the footage back from the lady who found the body in the Severn. Remember, you told us to expect it."

Harcourt exits his office at a more respectable speed, but still with a degree of urgency befitting the evidence he is eager to see. "She said she was filming the swans on her phone at the exact point when the girl headed into the river."

"Coincidence?" Flowers still finds himself speaking out loud before first considering his rank. He blushes before continuing. "What I mean, sir, is, if she was filming the swans on the river, why would she catch our victim on the towpath?"

"Well. Firstly, the swans do look for food on the mainland sometimes. They walk as well as swim you know..."

"I'm sorry, sir, I didn't think."

"Yes, you did. Relax. You do sometimes over-think things but that's far better than not considering them at all. Don't try too hard. When DC Hanrahan finally gets back I want to see you put in for the Sergeant's exam, OK? No going back then."

"Yes, sir."

"Good. You also make a good point and relevant in this case. Miss Clackerton is a volunteer with the local swan project. Given the sheer number of swans that nest here - though God knows how with all the tidal changes - the group was set up to try and improve their habitat and make sure they have enough to eat when all the visitors and tourists go home, especially in the winter - not that they should be feeding them anything at all."

"I remember the Worcester News picturing two hundred or so that were floating along in the car park in Newport Street during the floods last winter!"

"Exactly. Miss Clackerton had bought a food bag of floating pellets from the cathedral shop before heading down and placing them in the river, just along by the railings leading up to the Basin. You have to put them in the water itself so that dogs can't go after either the food or the birds; it also means that swans can drink with the pellets at the same time - helps the digestion."

"You're very well informed, sir. I didn't have you down as a nature lover."

Harcourt smiles in response. "I just like to understand better the environment in which we work, Constable. Makes it harder for people to pull the wool over my eyes, though, of course, they continue to try. We weren't sure if we were at a crime scene or not - it still could be a tragic accident - so I couldn't authorise or officially confiscate Miss Clackerton's phone, but asked her to forward the video to the digital team there and then, which she did. It seemed very dark to me. I wanted our people to brighten it and enhance it if they could."

"Still a bit murky, sir" Flowers has hit the Play button on his PC screen, "But easier to view on here than on a phone."

They study the footage - which lasts about forty-five seconds - several times.

Harcourt has been bending over the screen but stands again now. "So. What do you see?"

Flowers is a little flustered, guessing that this is some kind of trick question. After all, they've both just been playing and then rewinding the same film together. "I see a young girl heading along the towpath from the Diglis direction, sir. She isn't exactly running, but she's certainly walking very quickly. She's getting closer and closer to the river as she gets nearer to us (Miss Clackerton) before suddenly veering straight off the towpath and into the river. I hear a scream - either the victim or viewer - but don't see the girl again, not even her head bobbing up in the water. It's like Virginia Woolf in the River Ouse."

"Enlighten me."

"She filled her pockets with rocks and stone, sir, and simply walked straight into the river and drowned."

"Suicide?"

"Brought on by bouts of madness according to notes she left behind, sir."

"Except I don't believe that this was the same."

"Sir?"

"She certainly walked straight into the river of her own accord; there was without a doubt nobody else on the riverbank with her at the time. She turned to look behind her as if to confirm that, and the guys have certainly enhanced the film sufficiently for all of us to agree on it."

"Absolutely."

"And yet, it doesn't fit with a deliberate act of suicide. Firstly, you'd do it under the cover of darkness wouldn't you - without people around to see you and try to stop you?"

"Miranda Clackerton didn't exactly dive in on this occasion, sir?"

"That's because she told us she couldn't swim. She immediately stopped filming - as much through shock as anything else, I should think - and phoned 999. You'll need to pay her a follow-up visit. She was probably still in delayed shock when she gave us her initial statement."

"Will do. But you don't believe that she or we witnessed a suicide, sir? An accident perhaps, given that nobody else was around: maybe she just lost her footing?"

"It doesn't look as though our victim tripped or misjudged her closeness to the river, does it? She got to the end of the railings between the towpath and the river and then just walked straight down the bank and into the water. It's as though she was following a different path which she could see as clearly as the actual path.

But, no, it doesn't feel like suicide to me. I think you would somehow do it with the assurance that this is what you knew you wanted - had - to do. She seems more distressed than resolved. You can see that on her face rather than resignation. If you'd reached the end of the road, so much so that you just wanted to end it, surely - even in the darkest moment of your life - you wouldn't rush to do it?"

"Unless you were afraid that you'd change your mind, sir? You know, commit the act before you lose your nerve?"

"Possibly. Suicides generally come about though after days, weeks, and sometimes years of anxiety: ongoing battles in people's minds without really knowing who the good and the bad guys truly are: who the real enemy is. This looks much more of the moment to me."

"Maybe something just clicked in her head at that precise moment in time?"

"And yet she was all alone."

"But she didn't believe that she was alone, sir? 'The voices in my head, which I used to think were just passing through, seem to have taken up residence.'"

"Enlighten me again."

"Elizabeth Wurtzel: 'Prozac Nation.'"

***

Kate Shelbourne has parked her car at King Street's car park this time, needing first to buy some butter fudge from her favourite sweet shop on Worcester's High Street. Everyone needs a sugar hit from time to time, she considers, half-smiling to herself, especially at times of stress. Her friend Nancy knows all about that.

She then walks down the cobbled alleyway to one side of the cathedral, joining Severn Street before approaching the gentle incline up to the Diglis Hotel. She takes in the blue plaque by the main entrance. It had been presented by the Worcester Civic Society to commemorate Benjamin Williams Leader who was born in and lived at this his former family home.

Quite a family too, she recalls: Benjamin's father, Edward, had been chief engineer for the Severn Navigation Commission - set up to make the river navigable - and also a keen amateur landscape artist who counted John Constable among his friends. Benjamin's brother - also called Edward - was knighted following his work first on the Bridgewater Canal and then for his pioneering designs for the Manchester Ship Canal.

Benjamin himself had spent time with his father and famous friend on sketching trips and become a landscape artist in his own right, changing his name to Williams Leader as he felt there were too many competing artists with the surname Williams at the time.

If only it were that easy, thinks Kate, to distinguish yourself from others just by changing your name around. Talent no doubt helps but, for many, the label they see first is the one that sticks, no matter what success might follow.

First registered as an Inn in the 1900s the hotel describes itself grandly as 'The Country House Hotel in the City' and, stepping into the familiar surroundings of the hotel's lobby, Kate is transported to a world of yellowing flock wallpaper and the rather stale smell becoming of a National Trust pantry. Having said that, she has always enjoyed meeting people here because it is different, and rather splendid in its timeless way. The magnificent grandfather clock that stands on guard in the main hallway sees to that.

Kate pops her head into the bar to check that her friend is not there. It's mid-afternoon so few patrons remain, with the two barmen in their regulation black shirts too busy clearing and cleaning to curry favour with an unexpected newcomer. She turns back towards the dining room - more like a private conservatory, with magnificent views of the river below - and finds Nancy sitting on a comfy sofa between the main food and drinks areas.

She is dressed in a casual green jumper and blue jeans, checking her iPhone for messages. She looks up as Kate approaches and promptly puts the phone on the occasional table beside her, below a small bookcase of books that nobody has ever read and, likely, never will.

That isn't the point.

"Blue and green?" Kate smiles at her friend.

"I know. I know." Nancy stands to kiss Kate on the cheek: a proper kiss, no air involved.

"Sorry if you've been waiting long; I got held up by a man with a small revolver."

"What!" Nancy is genuinely shocked. "Are you OK?"

"Of course. Oh, I see." Kate chuckles. "It did sound a bit too real, didn't it? Well, it is - was. A story in the paper about a hold-up at a newsagent in town. Just coming through as I left the office."

"Was anybody hurt, do you know?" Nancy sits back down again.

"I don't believe so. The police were on it quickly - presumably with several vans of uniforms, firearm offices and a helicopter circling overhead." She sits down opposite, smoothing her navy blue suit as she does so.

"You look nice, as usual."

Kate enjoys this most about her friend. There is never any underhand meaning to what she says, no competitive streak that so can so often be fuelled by comparison with others, breeding either vanity or jealousy. What you see is what you get (well, almost).

"Thanks. I got this blouse from Marks's. When you get to my age you begin to find clothes in there that you would previously never have spent the time looking for!"

"Suits you though. Who cares where it comes from?"

"Thanks again. What time did you get off shift?"

"Just after three. They always find me something to do at the last minute. Life as a waitress I guess."

"Regular work though. And tips?"

"Less so now but, yes, plenty during the summer. I might even be able to afford a little holiday next year."

"Wouldn't that be nice?"

"You could come with me if you wanted to."

"I don't think that would work - nobody of your age wants their maiden aunt friend hanging on."

"Rubbish. You don't look or act like that and I could use the company."

"Thanks for a third time. Now, this is about you much more than it is about me. Have the police interviewed you yet?"

"A DS Flowers is coming round at five."

Kate checks her Fitbit and sees that it is already three twenty-five. For all her rushing around, the watch rarely displays an updated step count: just the time. "OK. Well, I won't keep you long and this is off the record, obviously, but you shouldn't hold anything back from the police either. It may be something and nothing, or what you saw could be vital in their enquiries."

"Do you know this Flowers chap?"

"I do. He has a disabled brother - cerebral palsy I believe. Devoted to him. I know his boss, Martin Harcourt, better. They're good people."

"Makes a change!"

"I know you won't have a lot of faith in any of them, and I do understand why."

"And I won't ever forget that you were there for me when they weren't."

"I'd do the same thing today; you only ever have to call. I assume there's been no sign of Joey?"

Nancy's silence causes Kate to lean forward. One of the barmen approaches to ask if either of them would like a drink, eyeing Nancy a little scornfully, as though she should have packed up along with her uniform.

Kate waves him away then lowers her voice. "He hasn't been round again?"

Nancy wrings her hands, almost imperceptibly, and looks away slightly, as if the image in her mind will dim if she doesn't face it head-on. "He came around very late on Saturday night. Banging for ages until I had to answer the door. The neighbours were already awake judging by the number of upstairs lights that were on."

"Money, I presume?"

Nancy nods but doesn't vocalise her reply.

"What did you do?"

"I didn't give him anything if that's what you mean!" She is uptight now and does face Kate. "It was the same as usual. All nicely, nicely until he realised he wasn't going to get cash or anything else, then he…"

"Did he hurt you?"

"Only by saying he'd be back."

"Do you want to tell the police; or would you like me to?"

Now there is a look of panic on Nancy's young, unlined face, like a hairline fracture in a pane of glass. "No. No, please don't. I can handle it; him."

"Just remember, I'm at the end of the 'phone and, if you ever change your mind…'"

"Thanks. I'm sure he'll get fed up with it eventually, hiking over here."

Kate strongly doubts it and resolves to check in with her even more regularly in future. She continues quickly though, knowing that Nancy needs to get home. "The young girl you saw on the riverbank - the one they're coming to you to talk about - you saw her walk straight into the river?"

"I was in the dining room, putting out the cutlery when I saw a movement just outside the window there. I think I noticed her because she was walking so quickly, almost running. I thought at first that she was late for an appointment with the older woman who was bending down by the river."

"Miss Clackerton. She was placing food in the water for the swans."

"Ah. Well, that explains why she didn't immediately get up when she saw her coming then - you know, to greet her. The older lady almost turned her back on her, then turned around, in a half circle I suppose, with her phone in her hand. It became clear then that she was taking a video."

"Of the swans?"

"I guess so, yes. Several of them were swimming right up to her. I'm not sure if they can smell the food?"

"Me neither, but no doubt the police will be on it. What happened next."

"The girl - the younger one - got closer and closer to the bird feeder and then veered off to the left, straight into the river."

"Did you see her struggling in the water?

"No. Nothing. The nettles or reeds - whatever they are - might have obscured my view from here anyway but, no, I never saw her or any part of her after that."

"And what did Miss Clackerton do?"

"She screamed, but she didn't move; it was like she was rooted to the spot."

"It must all have happened so quickly; terrifying for her. Not what you'd expect to see when you come down to the river to feed swans."

"Or maybe it was the boy who was right behind the girl."

"Boy?"

"About seventeen or eighteen I suppose. Blond hair."

"Was he chasing the girl then? Did he touch her, force

her into the river?"

"I didn't hear him say anything to her and he certainly wasn't close enough to make any contact with her before she went in, but there is one thing."

"What's that" Kate acknowledges now that she has been holding her breath, waiting for the tension that has built up in the tiny room to be released.

"When the girl looked behind her and saw that he was still there, I could see by the look on her face that she was absolutely terrified."

***

The words hang in the air, but they aren't hers. Unlike the old and old-fashioned radio in its scratched, brown casing in the corner of her room, she isn't just a transmitter, but an increasingly unwilling receiver too.

Her father introduced her to the joys of radio before she even went to school. Or so she remembers (and so he reminds her often). Yes, she has her iPod, though she streams more and more these days, and yes, she builds playlists like everyone else in college expects her to do - especially because of Dad - but there is something much more of the moment about her treasured radio.

It isn't just that it's 'live' or alive in the sense that she may not have previously heard a particular song or artist, or known of their existence. It's the sense of not knowing what she's going to hear next: only the DJ knows the answers to that, nobody else.

This has always been part of her make-up: adventurous, wanting - needing - to explore the world around her. At first, it was the undulating Worcestershire countryside when a large group of them would head out of town and, their parents suitably immersed in coffee or probably coke, she and the other children would explore woods and old, abandoned barns and other dwellings, seeking out signs of life... or death.

It all comes from Dad of course, though her mother has always tried to convince her (or herself) that she too is a free spirit, a creative spirit somehow. But she isn't like them.
Nobody with a recycling bin timetable on the kitchen wall is like them.

They'd continued to do this as they got older and left the parents at home to barely notice their return. They'd hike up into the Malvern Hills because of Gary, but increasingly in Worcester itself. Bars and warehouses bore witness to new sweat from different bodies. The urban landscape holds no fears for her, and there is still coffee or coke for tea.

She's always told herself that she is seeking inspiration for songs that she might record herself like budding photographers looking for new angles on old subjects. But nothing came to her. Not inspiration nor new music. That much is certain: the radio will never be playing her songs back to her. Maybe she is more like her mother after all.

It's even worse now. Not only can she not think outside of the box, but she can't even remember where she left it. Textbooks occupy the floor where CDs and pieces of notepaper containing random words or lines once 'spoke to her.'

She hasn't opened any of the books yet; they stand in columns like sentinels guarding her future from her. Concentration left on the first train out of Shrub Hill station, and it has left her stationery, unable to think in either straight or curved lines.

The words play on an endless loop in her head, sometimes it's as if he's saying them from in the room itself. Beside her, speaking, scratching, gouging out her skin with them. Only the screams make them stop.

***

Miranda Anne Clackerton looks out of her kitchen window towards the Old Gilding House, sympathetically fused with the similarly modern apartments of her neighbours, although the darker brown bricks of the old warehouse buildings do give them away. You don't have to be a student of architecture or even look too closely for cracks to work that out.

Miranda has been trying to work things out for seemingly the whole of her life. She runs a hand through her short, grey hair and then smooths her chunky yellow cardigan for the umpteenth time that afternoon. There are no crumbs, of course. Miranda doesn't do crumbs or any other kind of mess. Everything in her tiny home is neat and ordered and comfortable - 'in good shape' as her rather suburban mother might have remarked. Miranda herself has always been rather shapeless: 'no vital statistics to speak of' as her mother often did say. Nobody has ever said anything to the contrary.

She is content here, that much is unarguable. Brown not beige, she likes the way the old porcelain works, including the Throwing House and Slip House further along have been preserved. Presumably, this is exactly how people perceive her: preserved in an adequate and functional state, but having never been gilded?

It is entirely in keeping that she should occupy a flat which overlooks a utilitarian past, rather than the canal on the other side of the block, which might have offered an altogether more romantic view of life passing by - and possible escape routes.

She quickly espies the detective, reassuringly whole against the low, soupy sunshine. He is walking slowly towards the main door below. He looks very young: like the son she might have had, getting to grips with his first job. He isn't doing anything to disguise the fact that he is seeking - detecting - the correct building; and why should he? He doesn't need to act covertly because she is under no suspicion. She must keep reminding herself of that, though a delicious ribbon of excitement has tied itself around her chest. Perhaps it's the anticipation of having a visitor?

Flowers introduces himself. He's taller than he looked from the window, though perspective was never her strong point - or maybe she's just shrinking physically as well as mentally?

"Coffee?"

"That would be lovely. Thank you."

She leads him into the lounge as, having an open-plan

arrangement with the kitchen, he can continue to talk to her while she prepares the espresso machine.

She watches him looking at the spines of the many books that line the whole of one wall.

"You have a great collection!"

The word conjures up the last moments in the school she'd taught at for over thirty years. They'd pressed her erstwhile colleagues for money, presenting her with an expensive cut-glass vase as a result and in celebration of her retirement (and probably getting rid of her at last). The symbolism of the cold, empty vessel had not been lost on her.

"Thank you," she bites her lip as she rather unkindly finds herself being surprised that he reads.

"I enjoy reading poetry too!'

"Wordsworth?"

He turns towards her. His fresh-faced demeanour is a canvas so like those of the many students she has painted her own grudging picture of life upon. Those that can, write and paint. Those that can't...

"How did you know?"

"Oh, as an English teacher of many years, one gets to know." She tries to make her comment enigmatic but it sounds sarcastic, prickly.

"I find his work very therapeutic."

Then why doesn't he run a 'Friends' book stall in the main reception of A&E?

"'On Westminster Bridge' is one of your favourites I expect?"

"Actually, no." Bless him. He shuffles forward clumsily on her expensive Italian sofa, as though he was in a metallic booth in McDonald's. "The 'Ode on Intimations of Immortality' has preoccupied my mind quite a lot lately! I plan to move on to Coleridge next."

He is expecting her to comment - question the context of his reply even. Naturally, she will do neither.

"Interesting." She remarks disinterestedly while completing the coffee preparation and presenting two tiny white cups to the glass coffee table she perches behind, facing him.

He reminds her of those fresh-faced 'fellow' students who had paid for a weekend's 'creative playwriting' course in Scarborough some years ago. They'd spent the whole time trashing Shakespeare or getting trashed. Most of their 'knowledge 'appeared to have been gleaned from a film. She'd tried to defend him of course, but admiration had not bred any original thoughts or skill with words of her own. She'd escaped to the beach whenever possible - long, lonely walks by the sea. A body of water hiding seemingly infinite possibilities in its depths.

"Do you have a favourite poet?"

"No more than I have a favourite colour. Now, you wanted to talk to me about more important things than poetry I imagine?" She knows - hears for herself - that it's all going wrong. Perhaps it always has done.

"I'm sorry," he looks resigned to the task at hand. Doesn't she know that feeling? "We just wanted to clarify a few points in your statement."

"Points or commas?" She is trying to lighten the mood with wit and charm, but it just sounds grand and superior.

"Did you teach locally?" He is so much more respectful.

She pushes her glasses up her nose, which she does far too often. The dark, square frames were supposed to be a new look for her. In reality, they are much too heavy and they often make her head ache. "I did. English. At Blessed Benedicts. Things changed though. Education is not what it was."

What a stupid comment. Learning is nothing if not fluid.

St Anne's had been a challenge at first, but she had seen her future, even then, as an independent woman of intellectual repute; an ascendancy founded on such an Oxbridge base camp. At the end of her second year, they had admitted men for the first time. Her academic reputation had already been rocked by the levelling out of other, equally bright and bitchy women. Her social self-esteem was fatally holed by men's ignorance of her, and her of them.

"You needed a change?"

Most of her life and especially after spending twenty-nine years nurturing little empathy for either her fellow staff or pupils whose parents' money aspired them to greatness. "I did, yes." She slowly pulls up her grey, woolly stockings, not expecting him to notice, which he doesn't. His focus is elsewhere or on someone else.

"I set up as a consultant and went from there." Except that it didn't take her anywhere. Yes, she moved into the centre of town, hoping for an exciting urban lifestyle, punctuated with juicy commercial tutoring projects that only her unique set of skills could be matched with, but volunteering and feeding swans is what she now does.

As if to acknowledge the failure, the young detective says nothing in response, just retrieves a regulation notebook and chewed pen from his scuffed, 'leather' folder.

She still reads of course: literary fiction (occasionally) and crime thrillers (often). It is the latter that has been consuming her since witnessing that unfortunate girl heading directly into the river. This is Miranda's opportunity to be part of history - maybe even change it.

The detective - young but real - is ready to commence the interview. "Can I start by asking how often you feed the swans?"

"Can I start by replying that, as I told the Detective Inspector, probably just once each week? As volunteers, we operate a rota system but cover for each other at additional times when necessary."

"And do you always feed them at that part of the river, or do you all move around to different feeding points?"

"I rather think it is the ducks that move around,

depending on where they can find the most food; however, I suppose we humans do act similarly." She is being pompous and silly.

He continues questioning her in the same deadpan voice, as though the answers she is giving him are superfluous. Perhaps he has noticed after all. "But you would agree that you know this part of the river well?"

"Like the unfortunate liver spots that have started to form on the back of my hand, yes. I stroll along it often - sometimes early in the early morning and often later at night when all the lights come on and transform the towpath." Why does she need to embellish her answers, so? 'Often' is enough, surely?

"Did you see anybody out on the river itself that morning?"

Is this a trick question? In summer there are plenty of boats to be seen, but she can't recall seeing any that day. Apart from that girl, she can't remember seeing much of anything else. Still can't.

"Not that I recall."

"You're sure about that?"

Who does he think he is? "Quite sure. Thank you."

"Only we've been able to ascertain that there were several small craft on the water, just beyond the location in question: pupils from King's School undergoing basic rowing tuition."

Ah yes. He is a police officer. Nobody else uses words like 'ascertain,' much like 'inclement weather' seems to be the preserve of railway station announcers these days.

"I didn't see or hear anybody else." Her mouth is slightly dry, but the coffee is far too bitter. He has left his refreshment too.

"Have you ever seen the young lady in question before?"

"Possibly. One passes so many young things, or they hurtle past me on their bicycles. I spend more of my time trying to avoid pushchairs than I do on surveillance activities."

"We have an eyewitness report which suggests that the victim was being followed, chased even?"

"Not to the naked eye she wasn't! Nor was there anyone else within several metres of her according to my camera. And we both know that the camera never lies, Sergeant."

They both know that it can and often does. She needs to calm down. He mustn't see that she is becoming increasingly uneasy.

"And you couldn't have been mistaken about this? The... person couldn't have ducked down out of sight when they saw you filming?"

"Behind what? There is nothing grown by nature or constructed by man by the river at that point to hide behind, and the old wall up to the cathedral runs all the way along the other side of the path. Unless this person of whom you speak managed to reconstitute him or herself as lime mortar I fail to see how or where they could have disappeared to."

Flowers draws the collar of his jacket up against the late afternoon chill. He quickly passes the site of the old medieval church of St Peter the Great which gave its name to this parish and city suburb stretching south of the centre. History gives him little comfort - it never did - nor does the Old School House, though it is much more modern, dating from the 1850s. He doesn't need lessons from the past when lifelong learning proceeds to confirm his place in society's hierarchy.

Miss Clackerton represents exactly the kind of patronising, self-righteous example he was expected to look up to (but never reach) at school. It was this and this alone that had made his school years so unbearable. He had hoped that a recently found love of verse that had sprung up in his life, surviving the cold winter of schooling, might enable scholars like her to eventually see him as more than just a policeman. Of course, they didn't, and wouldn't.

He arrives back in Mill Street where he'd parked, not knowing whether cars could be parked in the new, posh quarter that has arisen from the ashes of kilns and potters' wheels. The charming, terraced houses curve down towards the river as though seeking water after a long climb. Flowers knows how they feel, unsure now whether the attempted ascent was worth it.

***

He hasn't been down to the lake since it happened. He's not even sure why he is standing there beside it this afternoon. It's been windy for the last few days and some of the leaves are already falling; each yellowing carcass finally losing its grip on a thinning oak tree and entering its descent with a final, defiant rotation into the water on the far side - helpless but at least avoiding a copper-coloured fate. There is barely any breeze, but when the wind does change, family and friends must necessarily be left behind. He shivers, though the autumn afternoon is unseasonably warm.

He watches the birds flitting from branch to branch of the trees overhead. The swallows that kept him so amused in the spring have left him now. Everybody does, eventually. The homes they built in the spring have suffered from the subsidence that only nature truly understands. A magpie hops along in front of him. He tries to remember the old rhyme: 'one for sorrow... ' A bit late for that now.

He won't see her this afternoon. He knows this of course. Still, he had felt drawn to the place they share; the secret place where nobody else can see them; would never dream of finding them. She has stuck to her promise. The question now is for how long can he do the same - flirting with his own, inexorable descent into the water's depths? Despite everything, and no matter how much he continues to hate himself for it, he still longs to be with her. A sorrow that mere water could never part him from forever.

***

Detective Sergeants Taylor and Farren head into the tiny hamlet of Pickerton, on the eastern slopes of the Malvern Hills and neighbour to the larger nearby village of Welland.

"Nice, individual houses," Farren looks around while Taylor concentrates on the road and the possible cyclist or (hopefully, black) cats that may cross their route, "There's certainly money here."

"Not in the Agarwal's case though, I shouldn't think, unless it's family money," Taylor recalls details from the briefing document she'd read the previous evening. "Nadin Agarwal runs a small newsagent's shop in Worcester: part of a chain which has recently been taken over. He's of Indian descent but a British citizen and, according to the background checks, moved out to Pickerton about eleven years ago. Nothing else out of the ordinary to report."

"And Zoya's mother?"

"Also, British. They'll have been married for nineteen years in December. No other children, which makes this even worse for them."

"And us." Farren pictures the father as a well-built, quite aggressive businessman who works every hour provided for him, while his diminutive, dutiful wife waits in the house for him to come home, whereupon she will attend to his every need. These are terrible racial stereotypes of course and she curses herself silently, still turning slightly towards Taylor to make sure she hasn't given away any non-verbal clues.

Living on the edge of Birmingham all these years has coloured her views on other cultures and the patriarchal way in which family units normally operate. It isn't healthy and certainly isn't balanced or fair. Another reason why she needed to move away from that area - before the shading became impossible to rub out.

"I assume Family Liaison are in position?"

Taylor shakes her head. "They arrived while the DI was confirming the bad news, but the family preferred to be on their own. He wasn't sure if it was their way - 'gentle Hindu dignity' he described it as - or if they were still in shock. Certainly, they wanted to grieve in peace.

"Not much peace coming their way I'm afraid - even after we find out what happened to their daughter."

"The boss said they're lovely people. His name means 'Lord of the Rivers.'"

Farren castigates herself, and not just because the irony is not lost on her.

They draw up outside a pretty, black and white timber-framed cottage with tiny windows, almost covered to one side by a secondary wall of green ivy.

Two white-painted front doors face the road and the left one is opened almost immediately as if those behind it could sense it was safe to do so.

It is Nadin Agarwal who stands in the doorway, a diminutive man with thinning hair over a beautiful face. His wife quickly comes to join him. Of similar slim stature, she shares his bright, brown eyes, wide open but seeing less than they used to.

They exchange greetings in the tiny hallway before Nadin leads them around to the right into a small, snug lounge. An open fire flickers and crackles to one side. Though the autumn days are not yet chilly, Farren knows (with an even greater sense of guilt now than before) that the chill in the hearts of these beautiful people will never be extinguished by mere flames.

She and Taylor sit in comfy grey armchairs on either side of the fire, facing the couple who perch on the edge of a battered old settee that has probably been in this room for as long as they have lived there.

"This is nice and cosy." Taylor offers.

Oviya Agarwal smiles in appreciation. "We could only afford to buy a semi-detached house, though it is significantly nicer than the flat we lived in when we first married."

"How long have you been here - in Pickerton?" Taylor continues, hoping they haven't noticed her hasty qualification.

If he has, he is polite enough not to show it. Nadin answers quietly. "We moved out some thirteen years ago. It was important to my wife and me that we got away from Worcester, especially as ..."

The detectives watch as she takes her husband's hand in her own and squeezes it gently. After a moment she completes the meaning of the sentence with one of her own. "We were blessed with the birth of a daughter and did not wish her to grow up in a city environment as we had both been forced to do."

"Are you both from Worcester, originally?" Again, Taylor is treading cautiously.

"Please do not worry about hurting our feelings," Nadin

replies, kindly, looking directly at Taylor. "They are as fleeting as raindrops. They will stop eventually and dry up to the point when we can almost forget what it was like to be soaked. I think that you will understand this?"

Taylor nods her understanding, only able to whisper. "Yes. Yes, I do."

"My wife's family originally came from the beautiful city of Chandigarh up in the Punjab, in the north of India. Her mother was a famous sculptress, though Oviya is too modest to admit it."

They exchange friendly glances before he continues. "I was lucky enough to meet her one winter's day when calling into my local cafe on Angel Place for my morning coffee. She had just got a job there and still had her coat and hat on! They had…"

"Run out of takeaway cups" the two of them chorus before he continues. "So, I offered to take it in a glass and bring the glass back later. It has been full ever since."

For a few moments, the sadness lifts from both of their faces. Perhaps, one day, it will stay that way, Farren hopes.

"I come from a family of entrepreneurs, you might say. Our ancestors lived in Sindh which is now part of Pakistan. Before the Partition in 1947, my grandparents had the wisdom to move along the coast to an Indian city called Jamnagar in Gujarat. My grandmother was a seamstress; well-known for her gold embroidery, while my grandfather had served in the British Indian Army. Things had become difficult for him, and it was decided that my father should move to England where he could seek to prosper in peace."

Farren is humbled by this gentle man who nevertheless remains so proud. "And did he? Find peace I mean?"

"Well. He found my mother!"

There are welcome smiles on all of their faces, but they don't last for long.

Nadin continues. "He worked in the car industry in Birmingham - latterly at the Longbridge plant - but, like my grandparents, I suppose, he saw that all was not well, so moved us to Worcester where he opened the newsagent's shop. It was not easy for him; there was a lot of pain. When I got older, I advised him to let a local man called Brannigan buy it, once he agreed on paper that my father would earn a salary to continue to run it. He was reluctant to let it go but then I took over his job gradually so that he could retire in peace."

"He must be very proud of you?" Farren notices that Taylor has gone very quiet.

"I hope that he was, though he was never quite able to show it. Thank goodness he is no longer here to see what has become of us."

Farren leans forward to gently reassure him. "We are so sorry for your loss, and that we need to intrude on you at what must be a really difficult time for you both. Believe me, if it wasn't necessary, we would not be here."

"We understand this," Oviya sounds so much more reassuring, almost serene, "You have your jobs to do, and we appreciate that you are just trying to help us."

"Thank you." Farren feels that she can now move on, even if they cannot. "I'm sure you've been asked this already, but was Zoya unhappy or distressed over anything: college perhaps? It's a difficult age for many teenage girls."

Nadin visibly flinches at the word 'teenage' as though she has thrown it at his face, like a stone.

Oviya answers for them both, calmly but with tears in her eyes. "We are a very open family, Sergeant. We have tried to learn from the restrictions of our elders, however well-meant they were. Nothing was considered off-limits and, because Zoya was an only child, there were no secrets within our little family. If Daddy or I had something to say to her, we would do so, right there and then. She was no different. We would have known if there was something wrong."

"She didn't do social media?" Taylor seems to have got past whatever it was that was troubling her. They both know that this question is rhetorical though as the police have found no social media profiles for her.

"No. Nothing like that." Oviya wrinkles her face.

"She caught up with her friends in real life!" Taylor smiles but it is not returned.

"If you can call them that."

"Why would you say that?"

The older woman hangs her head slightly. "I suppose it's nothing. Just an uneasy feeling we had about them. Janice seemed like a nice, quiet girl but Barbara was just the opposite. Zoya used to say that she was the one who was fun to be with - full of life - but we weren't so sure. As for those boys..."

"Colin and Gary?"

She shakes her head almost imperceptibly. "Gary could do no wrong but, you tell me, where do you find a boy like that? Nowhere. Everybody has their faults - especially at that age."

"And Colin?"

"He was quiet too. In Gary's shadow, I suppose. I didn't like the way he spoke to Janice, especially as they were supposed to be good friends."

"In a relationship you mean?"

"Whatever that means these days!"

"Did Gary and Barbara come here a lot?"

She looks up at that and Taylor can see that her eyes are blazing. "To our humble place? Of course not. Gary Jones wouldn't have lowered himself. I doubt if his father would have permitted it either. No, they mostly met in town. Zoya would take herself there on the bus. Janice came round here occasionally, and she and Zoya would go off for walks through the woods."

"And down to the lake." Farren senses there is more to this uneasiness than Zoya's mother has so far been prepared (or able) to uncover.

"Yes, to the lake. Of course. Why wouldn't they?"

"It was quite safe?"

"Unless you waded into it all on your own, as Gary did, and then couldn't get out."

Nadin comes to his wife's rescue. "The real point is that we didn't like them hanging around in Worcester; people assuming they were just yobs with nothing better to do. Zoya was a good girl with a great future. She was so much better than all that."

Taylor takes in the small television set in the corner, dwarfed by rows and rows of books seemingly climbing every wall. Her own father would have been impressed by traditional values continuing to buck whatever trend was seemingly current for the next week, day, minute...

"Did she keep a diary, do you know?"

"Why would she need to do that?" Nadin looks up at Farren. "Diaries are for secrets, aren't they?"

"Or a nice place to write down your memories, so that you don't forget them: something to look back on later maybe?"

"It is not healthy to look back. Only forward," Nadin is speaking so softly that all three of them are straining to hear what he is saying. "In our religion, samsara describes our understanding of death and rebirth. You are always moving forward towards one or the other, depending on where you are in the cycle."

"And Zoya believed this too - despite her studying sciences?" Taylor is still trying to be sensitive but also keen to establish whether a scientific, rational mind might have been overtaken by spiritual forces taking her down an altogether different path.

"Zoya had no problem in accommodating science and religious belief." Again, Oviya is polite but firm. "Her sole aim in life was to preserve it for as long as humanly possible."

"Before karma completes the action that is intended," Nadin adds, tears pouring down his face.

Farren needs to get out of here, out of this room at least. "May we look in Zoya's bedroom please - it's purely so that we can get a better feel for the girl she was."

The past tense seems much too present. The two of them rise to join Oviya as she quietly leads them up the tiny staircase to the first floor, comprising two bedrooms and a small but spotlessly clean bathroom. Nadin does not join them. They wonder if he has been able to step foot in this room since his daughter died, or perhaps he is frightened of not being able to leave it again if he does.

The room is tiny, occupied by a single bed and bedside table along one wall. A small desk sits in front of the window. Moving over towards the light, Taylor sees that it looks out over a small but well-tended lawn surrounded by flowerbeds whose recent occupants have also been taken, making room for those hidden bulbs below to flourish once more in the spring.

There is a physics textbook next to a laptop but no other books or, indeed, bookshelves. Nor is there any sign of music, not even a clock radio. Donning gloves, Farren begins pulling out the desk drawers while Taylor opens the small wardrobe in the opposite corner. Everything is tidy, with no sign of anything out of place.

Interestingly there are no 'party' dresses or outfits for a 'night out.' Farren remembers fondly getting ready with her sixth-form friends for a trip to some late-night club in Birmingham, only to wish she was back home again almost as soon as the taxi had dropped them off. The fun was in getting ready; the pain was in getting away. "There's no sense of the girl beyond the school student here," she whispers, "Everything is so... regular."

It could be that Oviya has tidied everything away. That would be a common first phase of the bereavement process, but Taylor does not believe that to be the case here. She thinks the state of the room is precisely the one it was in when Zoya last closed the bedroom door.

"Nothing out of the ordinary in here," Farren whispers again, "But we'll let tech have a look at the laptop in case there is anything - deleted or otherwise.

As they descend the stairs and make to leave, Taylor notices a beautiful pen and ink portrait of a young woman on the wall at the end of the hallway, just along from an ornate-looking mirror. She hadn't noticed her image when they'd first entered.

Nadin reappears beside her and notices her looking at it.

"Zoya." He gestures sadly with his head, before turning back to his wife and announcing proudly: "My daughter captured once again through the special talents of my wife, long after she'd released her from her body. Once Zoya had straightened the mirror here (every morning it seems!) she used to lay her palms on that image before she left for the school bus. It became a kind of silent 'thank you' to us and to the higher being that did so much more to make her the lovely girl that she was."

***

Harcourt hasn't slept well - again. He is vaguely aware of being awake in the early hours and then again at just after 5.00 when he needed an early trip to the toilet, after which sleep has eluded him completely. He has noted that these trips are becoming more regular as his internal plumbing system becomes more irregular. At least he hadn't woken Debbie at 5.00, avoiding the regulation interrogation and insistence that he go to see a doctor (and stop waking her up so early in the mornings).

If he wanted to collect pills, he'd go to Boots. He doesn't and won't. He isn't sure whether it's an age thing, which would be far too worrying to even contemplate further, or stress over the case: two bodies now and no obvious motive or evidence to work with. It might even be subconscious stress over Debbie going away this weekend or even the meeting he has arranged with Kate Shelbourne later this evening, while Debbie prepares for action with Pilates.

Farren is at her desk, as usual. He makes a mental note to try and get in even earlier - maybe at the end of the week when Debbie is away instead of lying in bed making a pointless effort to go back to sleep.

"Good morning, sir." Her mouth issues the words cheerfully but he notices that her eyes are tired; not sleepy, tired.

"Morning. Everything alright?"

"Yes, thank you."

"Settling in OK with the others?"

"No problems, sir. It's a nice team to be part of."

"And yet?" He decides to tackle the issue before it has a chance to grow (and before the others get in).

"Sir?"

"There seems to be something troubling you. Forgive me, I'm a detective."

She returns his smile.

"Everything's fine, honestly."

She's lost her mojo a little though. He instinctively knows that it's more than the 'new girl in school' effect wearing off. "You can talk to me at any time you know."

"I know that sir."

"Is it the case? You visited Mr and Mrs Agarwal yesterday, I believe?"

"We did. As you can imagine, their world has fallen in on them."

"People say that it gets easier, but it never really does."

"Are you referring to them or us, sir?"

He sits on the chair at the desk next to hers. "Both, I suppose. The difference is that we are trained to be professional in how we deal with it. No parent is taught how to deal with the sudden and unexpected loss of their child."

"Continuous Professional Development?"

"That's it. Except that it isn't continuous, is it? As with the victims and their families, there is no smooth path or process. Everything in life comes in fits and bursts, whether they be happy or sad ones."

"They were such lovely people, sir. I had imagined them - their family set-up - as quite different and I hate that."

"We all suffer from perception bias from time to time, no matter how hard we might try to avoid it. The important thing is to always separate the easy - some might say lazy - backstop of stereotyping from your gut instinct: what you see; what you hear, what you feel. Never confuse the two. The one is not the same as the other. Go with your gut every time. It will rarely let you down."

Although others might, he thinks darkly.

Thankfully DS Flowers arrives at that point, with DS Taylor just behind him.

With a final reassuring smile at Farren, Harcourt turns in his chair to greet the rest of his team, as they sit dutifully at their desks close to hers.

"Thanks for getting here in good time. I must brief the Super shortly but wanted to make sure I hadn't missed anything before I do. I've read each of your reports and my summary of our enquiries this far would be that we have done our due diligence on each of the key witnesses but aren't much further forward than that." He hesitates before concluding: "I may not put it in precisely those words.

Smiles abound followed by Taylor's voice. "Techies are due to report back later this morning on Zoya Agarwal's laptop, sir. They had a cursory look at her browser history and stored files but nothing excited them initially."

"I've not seen many excitable tech people in my time," Harcourt exclaims in a dry tone, "Unless it's a new virus that literally makes them eat their words of course."

Flowers laughs out loud then. He immediately surveys the faces of his colleagues to see where on the self-conscious scale he has pitched it. He counters the inevitability of it by cantering forward. "Did you find anything interesting at the Agarwal's house?"

Farren answers him, fixing him with a stare that he finds unnerving. "Apart from her parents, you mean?"

Taylor reads more into her enigmatic reply than Flowers does. Her colleague was very quiet throughout the return trip to Worcester. She jumps in. "Being quite overcome by grief, of course, there seemed little that her parents could add to Zoya's profile. A diligent student who worked hard in her subjects. Obviously, there's much more to her than that, but not sure how far it would help our investigation. They're adamant that they'd have known if there was anything wrong - if she'd been worrying unduly about college or friends. She certainly didn't seem to have any enemies as such."

"Probably because she kept clear of social media and the bullying that evolves from playground to public platforms," Farren adds. "I'd have been surprised if Zoya hadn't been the target of some abuse, most likely fuelled by jealousy."

"Can you elaborate on that?" Harcourt turns back towards her.

"Just that she seemed to have been very studious - which is by itself often enough to torment those who cannot or choose not to apply themselves in the same way. Also, judging by the picture her mother had painted of her, as well as the photos that were placed around their lounge, she was very, very pretty."

"Brains and beauty!"

"And outwardly self-confident too. Either she looked the other way when bitchy girls - and believe me, I've met a lot of those in my time - made comments about her; or maybe they didn't. Maybe she was the archetypal golden girl who everybody wanted to like and be like?"

"As with Gary Jones?" Flowers interjects. "Nobody had a bad word to say about him either!"

"I don't like this." Harcourt sits upright, hands together in front of him on Farren's desk. "I could understand someone targeting a 'goody goody' if you like, especially if they were suffering low self-esteem themselves, quite apart from some kind of psychological imbalance. You get what I mean?"

Each of them nods in agreement.

"But though they seem to have been liked by their peers and adored by their parents, they were from quite different backgrounds - different communities. Yes, I know that they 'hung out' together as part of a social group but that doesn't make them any more similar, does it? We see disparate clusters of students from the university heading into town all the time - the only thing that seems to glue them together is that they are at university."

"So, what you're saying is why would one person target two such different people?" Taylor asks.

"Or are we looking for more than one perpetrator?" Farren qualifies.

"If indeed we are looking for any such person?" Harcourt shapes his fingers into an arch before flattening them out again. "It's very confusing, isn't it? On the surface, these could both just be accidental deaths - as per the coroner's verdict on Gary's."

"Not suicides then?" Taylor continues. "Barry Jones is as convinced that Gary would never even contemplate something like this as Zoya's parents are. I appreciate that no parent wants to ever admit that this could be the case (or that they missed the signs) but, quite apart from it being totally out of character, neither of them could think of any reason at all why their children would be so desperate that they could see no other way forward."

"It's a silent killer though, isn't it: suicide?" Farren offers. "People can feel lonely, isolated - anxious even - yet they appear to be entirely normal to those who think they know them best. A little quieter than normal maybe, but everyone still blames hormones for it at that age, don't they?"

"I believe you're right." Harcourt is staring at the wall opposite, and way beyond it. "Sometimes the structure of repetitive action - the mundane and minutiae of the day-to-day - is the safeguard that anxious people need just to get up in the morning."

"But unless we find something written down which we can use as evidence, or some other person comes forward to corroborate a suicidal state of mind, that theory has no legs for either victim," Taylor concludes.

"We don't want to go down the unexplained route again though. It's too much of a coincidence, surely, that two people who were ostensibly friends - who spent so much time together - should both accidentally die within a matter of a few months?"

"Not only that, sir, but when I spoke with Nancy Gutteridge she was adamant that she saw someone following Zoya Agarwal along the towpath that day. And yet Miranda Anne Clackerton is equally certain that Zoya was quite alone." Flowers reaches for his notebook and, after flipping through several pages, reads 'There was nowhere for anyone else to hide along that stretch of the riverbank when I looked up. If someone else had been present I am certain that I would have seen him or her.'

"And I guess she is as reliable a witness as we're likely to get?

"Yes, sir. Cold and clinically so."

"You didn't like her?"

"I didn't warm to her, sir, no. Let's just say that some women of that age like to dress to look as though they're twenty years younger; in her case, she looked at least twenty years older because of it. Shabby chic with ripped skinny jeans and very noticeable hair isn't usually meant for pensioners, is it?"

"Harsh!" Harcourt is nonetheless vaguely amused by Flower's observation and the real reasons behind it."

"And Nancy?" Farren asks.

"Slightly more difficult to read; deeper if you like." Flowers checks his notes again. "I did find her a little unworldly, to be honest. It wasn't that I didn't believe what she was saying, just that she was, well, unbelievable in a way."

"But she has no motive for making up such a story, does she? Harcourt doesn't want them to get into one of Flowers's lyrical puzzles - certainly not Farren who's only just joined the team. "I'm seeing Kate Shelbourne shortly. She was the one who put us onto Nancy, and she knows her much better than we do. She might be able to give us something more. I may also be able to head the press pack off for a short while. If there's one thing they love to feast on more than a bent copper it's a confused one. In the meantime, I think we should visit the remaining members of their little group: Colin, Barbara and Janice. Starting with Colin."

As he stands, it's as though he has set off an invisible beam - the 'magic eye' they used to call them - because his desk phone immediately begins to ring.

Harcourt walks wearily into his office and picks up the receiver.

"I'm sorry to ruin your evening, sir," the friendly but

firm voice of Sgt Tim Roberts, one of the station's oldest desk sergeants greets him, "But a Mr. Jones is here in Reception. Says he has to see you urgently... he's in quite a state of agitation, sir, and I believe him when he says his name really is Mr Jones."

The last few words are almost whispered and Harcourt smiles even as his eyebrows knit together in a familiar frown. It isn't the first time that his long-standing colleague has cupped his hand around his telephone downstairs to vainly try and achieve a little discretion.

"Tell him I'll be right down." Harcourt sighs.

***

"What further proof do you need, Inspector?" Barry Jones has reluctantly placed his large frame on the much smaller plastic chair behind the wooden table of the interview room. There is nothing else in there apart from a second chair occupied by Harcourt. Jones had taken some considerable persuasion to sit down but, once it finally dawned on him that the policeman wasn't remotely intimidated by either his physical presence or superior (and beautifully enunciated) words of wisdom, he had parked himself angrily and momentarily.

"We are still gathering evidence, sir."

"You know very well what I mean! The fact - **fact** - that another one of their group has now died."

"I know it can be difficult not to make connections in cases like this, Mr Jones, and especially given the timing, but we have nothing at this stage which indicates that the two deaths are connected."

"So, you're going to pronounce this as another accident, are you; or is this perhaps another completely out-of-character suicide?"

"You knew Miss Agarwal well?

"Not 'well,' no. But of course, I knew her. She was a friend of my son."

"Would you have said that she was a person likely to take her own life?"

"I wouldn't have said so, no, but who am I to make an assessment such as that? When someone is so full of life, why would you suspect them of wanting to be consumed by death?"

"Quite so. It still does not mean there is a connection though: that someone else was responsible for either of their deaths - that crimes were perpetrated. I know it would make it easier for you if there had."

"Drowned. They both drowned. I don't believe in coincidences any more than you do: not if we're each doing our jobs properly." The sweat on Jones's forehead glistens freely under the strip lighting that is usually meant to enhance facial movements which those helping with enquiries often tried so hard to control.

Harcourt remains impassive in the way his experience over the years had taught him to be. Mostly it worked but sometimes emotions got the better of him. This is not one of those times.

"What line of business are you in, Mr. Jones?"

"What?"

"What do you do for a living?"

"I haven't the faintest idea what this has to do with anything, but, 'for the record,' I am a financial consultant. I trade online for a select group of clients - each of them high net worth individuals."

"A stockbroker then?"

"How quaint. Do you think you should be putting a telephone call into 'The Yard?'"

Harcourt pretends to ignore the man's arrogance, not to mention his sarcasm. He has found both attributes to be excellent character flaws when it comes to revealing truths. "And do your clients 'consult' you, or do you manage their portfolios without intervention, because you are the expert; because you know best."

"I'm not sure I like your tone, Inspector."

"I don't know what you mean, sir. I was simply trying to learn more of the way you do things, handle things."

"Whatever for? I hardly think you'd ever be in the market for my services."

"Quite so, sir, I agree with you about that." Harcourt is pleased to see that massaging this big man's ego has diffused his anger somewhat, and even more satisfied that the sweat remains unabated. "Dealing with stress for one thing. Timing and decision-making must be paramount in your job, especially given its hugely competitive nature."

"It does require a degree of calmness, certainly, though I would add that conviction - belief in one's decisions - is more important."

"And yet, whenever we have met you seem to be the opposite of calm: full of anger, in fact."

Jones stands and roars his reply from on high. "What do they feed you people, on? An early-learner diet of psychology for beginners which few manage to graduate from? I've just lost my only son for Christ's sake. That's just a little bit different to making money for other people."

Harcourt ignores the obvious fact that nobody makes money for other people alone. He remains seated, happy to look up at the froth exploding from Jones's contorted, angry mouth. "And did you 'consult' with your son, sir?"

"About what?"

"About everything… anything?"

"What are you implying, you insolent little man."

"I'm not implying anything at all, sir; just wondering if you discussed things with Gary to the extent that you would know for certain what was on his mind. Equally, if he had told you something that you disagreed with, I suggest that you might have been less than conciliatory, judging by the behaviour we have all witnessed thus far."

A huge fist finds itself being slammed on the table. Had anyone been foolish enough to accept the offer of a drink, it would now have been tracing the long-ago grain of the living tree.

"By God, Harcourt, I sincerely hope you never have to 'witness' the kind of grief a parent might have to suffer; you'd know then how unpredictable one's reaction can be."

Harcourt watches silently as Jones walks steadily across to the door and practically wrenches it off its hinges before exiting and leaving him quite alone in the cell-like room.

CHAPTER FOUR

She has no idea how long she's been lying there for, in the quiet, in the dark. Without putting on her glasses she can't read her radio alarm clock, strategically placed across the room from her bed so that she'd have to physically get up to go over and turn it off. Old habits die hard while a little piece of her dies each day; slowly, it seems.

She has woken suddenly from a dream because she was struggling to remember the name of a male character in that dream, and the action had reached that excruciating climax where she had to introduce him to someone else. Dry-mouthed now, she can nevertheless feel her heartbeat begin to settle down.

There are no signs of real life from elsewhere in the house. She remembers her husband working quite late. He has recently bought a softer, foam-based pad for his keyboard to sit on and keep down the noise of his typing strokes to a minimum. She hasn't the heart to tell him that the landing light coming on suddenly outside her bedroom door is what wakes her each night when he tiptoes up the stairs to his bed.

Now she pictures her brother's face; the increasingly pronounced crease lines bending away from his nose in the way that a willow tree's branches first spread outward - almost defying gravity - before heading down towards the ground below. Down to earth. Their neighbours in Merton had planted a willow tree - just a small one - which soon flourished next to the stream that ran across the far edge of their garden. Her mother had always worried about that stream flooding, but, of course, hadn't dared to raise the issue with her father.

She feels the familiar rage from within. It's been much better lately, just as they said it would be. But it's still there. If not just under the surface it isn't too far below it either. A slight headache is forming again, but it is the prickling skin on her arms that cautions her to be careful.

Father. Seemingly always tired of the world until it grew weary of him. Even by an early age, Charlotte had become profoundly aware that there were usually two sides to most stories. It wasn't that she necessarily gravitated to the 'victim' or the underdog, but she did want to hear their side of things. This wasn't just frowned upon by her father (and mother, desperate to 'keep the peace') but actively discouraged by the health and safety valve in her head.

However, it remained a major driving force in her heading towards the law and a fairer justice system; that and not wanting to be owned by anger as her father had allowed himself to be. Shouting at the moon was never going to stop it from rising or pulling in the tides that eventually overwhelmed him completely.

How shocked Fergus had looked when he stood over her on Broadway Hill. What had he expected? Her arms dutifully folded across her chest: a sign of the cross? She had stumbled, fallen, yes. But she wasn't a fallen woman praying for forgiveness from his god. She had lost her way back down the hill, but she wasn't lost. Not yet. Not like her poor mother.

A light comes on across the garden from their house. A security light, she supposes. Possibly the cat or even a fox. She often hears the mangled screams of the young animals. Or are those screams just in her head? What had Fergus's wife called them? 'Cub Shouts!' Daniel had laughed out loud at that. Charlotte hadn't. She can't remember whether Lucy is dead or not.

She tries to arrange the evidence in her head: 'for' and 'against' as she had done practically every day of her working life. She hasn't seen her sister-in-law for a very long time; or was it yesterday? The major problem in her life now is that nobody has published a book on dementia, because nobody can remember the beginning.

***

Colin Pearson scratches the blemish on his forehead as he yawns and stares across at the houses opposite yet again. It isn't the only blemish on his character, just the most visible one. Unless you count his feet. Great useless pieces of meat that could never kick a ball in the intended direction nor move to the right position from which his grateful arms could thrash a tennis ball back over the net.

He's had the dream. No wonder he feels the total opposite of refreshed. It seemed so, so real, as it always does. He knows it isn't - can't be - but still.

The houses all look the same to him, though he knows

that the Warndon Village area is probably one of the nicer parts, despite the way Gary sneered at it each time he came over. He quickly tries to think of something else, anything else. He watches the cars pass slowly through the estate on their way to the shops, the supermarket, or even the library if old people still did that. A white Skoda slows down and eventually parks outside their house. A white man and a younger, black woman get out and head towards the front door.

The doorbell is like an alarm bell ringing in his head. He can feel himself sweating already, walking slightly forward towards his bedroom door and then back again to the window. Entries but no exits, each of them. What should he do? Should he feign sleep or illness? Not with his parents - that's never going to work. Stupid. Stupid. Think Colin. You're good at that... usually.

"Colin!" His mother's voice no longer provides him with any comfort. "Colin. Could you come down for a few minutes please?"

A few minutes, or a few hours. Maybe longer. Maybe forever. He has imagined this since it happened; played out the scene in his mind until it did so of its own accord on a loop he cannot pause, let alone stop. Should he have jumped out of the window when he saw them arrive, or maybe made a dash for the back door of the kitchen and taken his chances with the Alsatian on the other side of the fence?

Even as he notionally considers those lost opportunities, he knows that is not what they are at all. Where would he have gone - who could he have turned to next? Besides, any earthly attempt to escape this hell he has been living in would merely draw attention to himself. That's the last thing he needs now. Not that he ever wanted it, craved it like Gary did.

He can do this. He can handle this; needs to deal with it. He and Gary had been known as 'the invincibles' hadn't they? He wipes his head on the crumpled towel he had previously flung onto the end of his bed, pulls on a sweatshirt then immediately takes it off again. That would just make him feel even hotter, and sweat more.

"Colin?"

Alright. Alright. He checks his face in the mirror, immediately wishing that he hadn't, before slowly heading for the door. Is this the door into the rest of his life, one he'll never be able to walk back through again, into his past?

Harcourt gratefully accepts the mug of tea presented to him by Marion Pearson and lines it up clumsily on the edge of the wooden coaster on the glass coffee table in front of himself and Taylor, using his index finger to prevent the single brown dribble from making it to base camp.

"Is your husband's GP practice nearby?" Taylor has continued talking to Colin's mother, while setting down her cup accurately and without spilling any of her drink.

The wonders of multi-processing Harcourt thinks, enviously.

"Just over in Barbourne, close to Gheluvelt Park. Takes him about twenty minutes if the traffic isn't too awful.

"I've often wondered where that park got such a strange name from?" Taylor is trying to keep her on side by talking about non-threatening issues that are a stage removed from her, Colin and Zoya.

"Oh. I think they were going to build a park there anyway but, after the First World War ended, decided to dedicate it as a war memorial. Geluveld is a Belgian village where, in 1914, our own Worcestershire Regiment prevented a German offensive from breaking through the British lines. More than thirty people died and over a hundred and fifty were wounded I believe."

"The First Battle of Ypres," Harcourt adds.

"Quite, Inspector. They rightly praised the heroism of our troops, but I've always worried about the level of death involved in any war, let alone those who are scarred for life as a result.

"You had relatives fighting over there?" Harcourt can already tell that she did.

"My grandfather was caught up in the French action at Verdun. Thankfully he'd avoided the Somme earlier in the summer though. He'd been sent home at the beginning of that year with a leg injury, before being sent back. He never spoke to my Granny about the things he'd seen, although I suspect he continued to see them until he died - when I was just a small child.

"You work at the Royal I believe?" Taylor brings her slowly forward more than one hundred years, but back to the reality of 2017.

"I do. Yes. I'm a radiologist. I've been there for four years now. It's a split shift today so I'm not due in until two."

"Busy I expect?"

"Always. But you get used to it, unlike the trauma nurses. I couldn't work in A&E. I couldn't do your jobs either." She smiles - seems almost relieved - as though she's just let out a big secret."

"I suppose we get used to it too, though we really shouldn't." Taylor looks across towards Harcourt who silently nods his agreement. "Every case is different of course, but you do find yourself able to cope a little better, perhaps without even acknowledging the fact. Unless it's particularly gruesome of course."

"Or mystifying!" Harcourt offers, at which, perversely, both women seem to relax a little.

Taylor continues. "Today's visit is purely routine. We know that they all met up recently and just wanted to check with Colin how Zoya had seemed at the time."

She stops talking abruptly as a tall, blonde boy enters the room from their left. Harcourt perceived Colin coming down the stairs, slowly, one very deliberate step at a time.

"Ah. This is my Colin. At last!" The protective mother sitting opposite and smiling introduces her son, while the adult woman announces: "This is Detective Inspector Harcourt and Detective Sergeant Taylor. They're here to ask you some questions about Zoya."

Both having stood to shake his warm, damp hand, the detectives settle back into the comfy sofa, while Colin seats himself on what looks to be a far less comfortable high-backed chair close to Marion.

An early sign of contrition wonders Harcourt. The teenager is certainly not what he had expected. In his mind's eye, he had pictured a self-confident college student, displaying all the arrogance of youth and with no doubt total disdain for authority. Colin is not that person. He looks unkempt - like most boys of his age, to be fair - and very, very nervous; frightened even.

"This shouldn't take long, Colin." Taylor kicks off, as they'd agreed in the car. "And there's absolutely nothing to worry about."

Harcout watches the boy for any signs of relief, of pressure lifting. But there are none.

His colleague is continuing, leaning slightly forward as she does so. "We're just trying to build a clearer picture of the last few hours of Zoya's life."

The boy has shrunk back into the chair but has found the wooden frame unyielding, unforgiving perhaps.

"Colin is still very upset about his friend's death," Marion senses it too then, "So soon after poor Gary."

"How did you find out about Zoya's death, Colin?" Taylor isn't about to do sympathy; certainly not until they understand better the cause behind the cause of death.

"It was all over College." He responds softly, almost imperceptibly glancing at his mother. For moral support or something else?

"You must have been very upset - her being a close friend?" Harcourt knows they need to keep up the momentum before the mother inevitably intervenes.

"I was. Yes." He is suitably remorseful, but his eyes are seeing and saying something else. Harcourt can't work out what it is yet.

"Presumably you wanted to know what happened? Didn't want to trust to idle gossip?" Taylor again.

"I texted Janice. Her grandfather knows – knew…" He stops. Confused by his response or maybe for effect?

"Go on." Harcourt is slightly gentler now, seeing that Marion has finished her tea and is paying full attention.

"He knows Zoya's mother quite well. Janice came back a few minutes later and confirmed that Zoya had killed herself."

"Is that what Janice thinks? That Zoya took her own life?"

"Well, there's no other explanation is there?" The boy is practically gushing sweat now, and his voice is breaking.

"Not at the moment, no," Taylor has also read the warning signs about the mother's likely response.

"You saw her the day before?" Harcourt phrases it as a question thinly disguised as fact.

"Yeah. In the Square. We don't, haven't seen each other much since Gary died."

"You don't bump into each other at college?"

"Not often. We're all doing different subjects, besides we've had the summer holiday…"

"You're doing Economics and Business Studies. Is that right?"

"And Media Studies," Marion interjects proudly and yet quite incongruously in the context of the conversation they are having, and why they are having it.

Taylor now tries to cover him with kindness which Harcourt is pleased to hear. "Did Zoya seem upset about anything; anything at all that you can remember - that might be useful to us?"

"Only about her old man! He's been having some difficulties with the shop. Some know-all guys have bought the owner out and are giving him a hard time."

"She talked about this when you met up?"

"She did. Yeah."

"Anything else?"

"Not that I can remember."

"Does Zoya strike you as the kind of person who might want to take her own life?"

"No. Never. Yet everyone now thinks that she did."

"You felt the same about Gary too."

"I did; do. Yeah. Gary's death was a total accident, but we were all coping with it OK. You know. As well as we could anyway. I don't see how Zoya could have just accidentally walked into the river. She must have walked along that towpath a zillion times. It's completely different." He looks across to his mother for moral support, for an escape.

"Where were you on the morning that Zoya died, Colin?"

"At college. Like I said. I'd just come out of Economic... had a free period."

"Like Zoya must have had?"

"I don't know. You'd have to ask..."

"Inspector!"

Here it comes, thinks Harcourt before grasping the nettle. "The others were there too - in the Square: Janice and Barbara?"

"Yeah."

"Inspector..."

He ignores her. Stunts the protest before it can be articulated, knowing he doesn't have much time left.

"Did they notice anything out of the ordinary - about Zoya I mean."

"You'd have to ask them?"

"It must have been hard," Taylor notices the boy clamming up, as her DI has, "So soon after the death of another close friend."

"Just as I said, we were coping. Helping each other through it I suppose. I don't know what was happening inside Zoya's head though. I'm not a shrink. I don't understand what could have happened. All I do know is that neither she nor Gary would ever have wanted to end it all: they both had everything to live for - just as we all do.

***

Just a few minutes later, Marion Pearson does indeed decide that it's high time she safeguards her only son - for now at least. They are back in Harcourt's car.

"He only let us get so far before the shutters came down!" Harcourt closes his door and places the key in the ignition. "He seemed terrified. Did you see his face when he first walked into the room? I thought he might faint on us."

"Must be tough though." Taylor nods in agreement. "If their little group was as tight as we're being led to believe, it's been blown apart, hasn't it? I mean, two deaths in the space of just a few months."

"I obviously wouldn't mention this to the Super but I can't help thinking there's a connection somehow - way beyond them all being friends of course."

"I think I'm with you on that."

"The suggestion or keeping it from Hunter-Wright."

"Both." She smiles supportively. "Colin Pearson was one very unhappy individual, but I had the strangest thing notion that, even as we were questioning him, he was seeing something quite different - and I don't mean Zoya walking into that river."

"And you know what else was missing? This I find even more remarkable after losing two of his closest friends."

"Anger?"

"That - although I thought he did get a bit edgy towards the end - but, no, I was thinking of sadness. He might have had longer to come to terms with Gary's death I suppose although Gary was supposed to be his best friend. But I got fear rather than full-blown grief."

"Happens in different ways, though, doesn't it?"

"Perhaps he's developed a kind of immunity to it." Harcourt sounds no more convincing than he is convinced. "The three of them stared death in the face and the only way to stop it staring back at them is to close their eyes."

"Or their eyes are wide open, wondering who's next?" Taylor engages gear and they move off, if not on.

***

'I remember
How the darkness doubled
I recall
Lightning struck itself'

Hunter-Wright is lying on the sofa in his 'den.' Miriam had suggested long ago that they turn one of the rooms into a 'music room' where he could indulge himself without interrupting whatever serial trash she was watching on the television.

Television's 'Marquee Moon' is crashing out all around him. Miriam is out anyway so there's no chance he'll be asked with increasing degrees of irritation to turn the volume down.

He's always loved the song, especially the extended 12"

vinyl version currently being played on the battered record deck on the far side of the room. He's always seen it as a warning against taking success too seriously but equally finds himself dwelling on the many small reminders of its demise.

As the turntable arm lifts itself with the familiar audible jolt that all record collectors knew so well and re-positions itself for a well-earned rest to the right, the landline rings, as though the whole scene has been choreographed by Tom Verlaine directing the video of his song.

"Hunter-Wright." He glances at his digital watch in the gloom, noting that it is just after eight.

"You asked for an update, sir, but I was unable to connect with you earlier."

"I was out."

"Evidently, sir."

"Can this not wait until the morning, Harcourt? Unless there's been a breakthrough?"

"It can, sir, and no, there hasn't. I was about to leave, but thought I'd try once more."

Hunter-Wright is feeling tetchy, not just at the monotone delivery of his DI, or the less-than-subtle way in which he's trying to ascertain his whereabouts that afternoon. It's more that the mood has been broken - and for no good reason it would seem.

"How did it go with Colin Pearson and his parents?"

"Just him and the mother, sir. The father is a GP - he

was at his surgery. We haven't spoken to him yet. There seems to be no need to at this stage."

"Go on," Hunter-Wright has turned on the small, red arc lamp he acquired from the 'Pop Art' exhibition at London's Royal Academy some years ago and is on his knees looking in his shelves for the Clash's second album: 'Give 'Em Enough Rope.' A conjunction in bad taste? Possibly. An excellent album, nonetheless.

"The boy seemed afraid, sir. Everything about him spoke of fear and this was proved when he got quite uptight about Zoya."

"Could be grief? He's only young, after all."

"Not that young, sir. He'll be off to university next year."

"Yes, but young in terms of having the capacity to deal with grief yet. He has just lost two close friends in disturbingly quick succession!"

"DS Taylor and I felt that he would have opened up if we'd pushed him a little more, but the mother was having no more of it."

"A natural parental reaction, Harcourt." He waits for that unnecessarily poisonous little dart to hit its target. "The boy hasn't done anything wrong, as far as we know, and wasn't under caution. I'm not surprised the mother was defensive on his behalf. You asked about his whereabouts I assume?"

"Of course. He has a foolproof alibi."

"Whatever are you suggesting?" Hunter-Wright smiles as he takes the familiar black circle out of its inner sleeve.

If Harcourt has spotted the irony, he doesn't dwell on it. "He was at college at the time. We'll check it of course, but, as you rightly say, he's not a suspect."

"So, the 'sighting' from…"

"Nancy Gutteridge, sir."

"Quite so. Did her rather ethereal description match that of Colin Pearson at all?"

"Partly, sir, the build and blonde hair were probably right, but the description was so sketchy. Besides she was looking from behind this so-called pursuer."

"Your point being?"

"Colin Pearson has quite a distinctive birthmark on his forehead - that would have been a much more significant detail, even if his alibi is proved to be false."

"She might still have missed it, though, at that kind of distance."

He hears his colleague blow out his cheeks and knows that it has been a long day for all of them.

"I think you're clutching at straws, Martin. There is no evidence of foul play in Zoya Agarwal's drowning, and we have to assume that this Nancy's description was somehow flawed - especially as Miranda Clackerton is probably a more reliable witness, being closer to the action and seeing it face-on. She is adamant that she saw nobody else?"

"Nobody, sir. Flowers found her a bit prickly, but she has

no reason to lie to us and hers is, as you say, perhaps a more robust account of what happened."

"Don't underestimate grief in her case either, though: watching someone die right in front of you is a shocking thing to witness, especially as there seemed to be no obvious motive behind it. The unexpected can throw everything we previously assumed to be true right out of the window.

"Indeed, sir. Nobody we've spoken to so far, though, will entertain even the idea that it could have been suicide."

"But we have no evidence to the contrary or anyone else with any kind of motive to harm her!"

Hunter-Wright hangs up and, as 'English Civil War' blasts against the walls of his comfortable home, he looks out into the night. Time has passed and there is no moon. It isn't *New Wave*, it's the same old tide that washes in and washes out again without cleaning anything. Making things clearer. How he wishes it would, just once, deposit a different body on the beach, so that they would finally know for sure, instead of forcing them to face the unknown each long day.

***

Harcourt spots the journalist as soon as she walks into the pub; not because of his professional ability to spot journalists long before they even think of going into print or because he has been focused on the doorway since he arrived, but more because he's the only person seated in that part of the pub.

Kate looks first into the sparsely populated bar area:

three men with one opinion between them. She quickly turns right into the 'lounge' where he is sitting in a quiet corner of what is little more than a snug - but one where he can easily be seen.

He hadn't expected The George in Lower Spetchley to be so quiet - even on a weekday evening - and is a little unnerved that their conversation might now be overheard should any other customers decide to join them. Neither does he want to keep his voice especially low, or whisper, which is the furtive stuff of lovers who should not be left alone in the same room together.

His phone call with Hunter-Wright was typically enigmatic and unhelpful though he had felt the need to update his boss. Perhaps he had needed to assuage the guilt he had felt since arranging to meet with Kate, though this has been tempered by seeing his wife begin to pack her weekend bag that morning.

Initially wary of the journalist - probably out of an instinctive desire for self-preservation as a policeman - he has nevertheless come to appreciate the very real value of working with her rather than cutting her out, as some of his senior colleagues might have preferred him to do. Getting information out into the public domain has always been part of it, of course, but she has also more than fulfilled her side of the bargain by giving him the time to investigate new leads she and her team have uncovered, or at least sufficient time before presses have rolled (or, more likely these days, digital boxes on a screen have been clicked).

He hadn't wanted to get involved with Debbie's packing (that way madness lies, or at least one person getting mad) but couldn't help remarking: "There's a lot of smart clothes in there just for the one weekend."

"You may be perfectly content to switch between your cheap work suits and nondescript 'off duty' stuff, Martin, but I like to have options in my life!"

"Options?"

"The ability to choose a different dress or top, depending on where we're going, or what we're going to be doing. It's a girls' weekend away: you can't plan for these things, just need to have alternatives to hand if you need them."

"I see."

"No, you don't. You can detect crimes every day of the week, but maybe you're not as good a judge of people as you keep telling me you are."

He disagrees but maybe this is only the case within his professional world; a world in which he spends far too much time - perhaps chooses to? "Or maybe I keep some judgements to myself?" His reply sounds weak. Is weak.

"That's a pretty cheap response."

"Why are you getting so upset?"

"I'm not upset but you clearly are. You don't want me to go away - you never do - and you're getting all uptight about it."

"I'll just miss you, that's all."

"No, Martin. You'll miss food on the table and clean clothes in your chest of drawers. It's only for a weekend;

there is a limit to the number of pairs of socks you're likely to need."

"It's not like that at all!" He tries not to raise his voice, but the element of truth in what she is saying is making it increasingly difficult.

"It's exactly like that." She is much cooler, cold even. "I spend whole evenings and weekends on my own and how often do I complain about it? I know this comes with the territory and I'm well used to it - all police wives need to be. Sometimes, it would be nice to be me, not just your wife. Have a few laughs."

"I'm sorry. I can see why you might want some space…"

"This isn't about space. I don't need space. It isn't marriage guidance. I'm perfectly happy with things as they are: you must know that. I'd just like to go and have a bit of fun now and again. That's it."

She had walked out of the bedroom at that point and Harcourt heard her switching the kettle on in the kitchen - surely the archetypal English response to words coming together to make meaning clear, or subtly failing to do so.

He tentatively lifts a skimpy red dress from the top of her suitcase. Usually, he'd be wearing gloves to search someone's possessions without them knowing! Underneath it lay several pairs of new, silky white knickers and a very low-cut lacy white bra: none of which he has ever seen her wear before.

So, the gloves are off then, he had thought, grimly. But even then, and certainly now after musing on it over most of the day and a couple of beers, he knows it isn't true.

Kate's appearance in a tight-fitting blue dress and almost overwhelming perfume assaults his senses but, after all, she's just there to help him with his enquiries, isn't she?

"Sorry if I'm a little bit late."

They both know that she isn't.

He heads to the bar for her glass of chilled white wine and another pint. He looks back at her while he waits, almost shyly, like a teenager on a first date. Yet this isn't a first date - not even a date at all. They are not young or skinny, either of them. Even if she has learned how to cover spots up, he never has.

She places her phone on the table between them as they toast each other with a rather cheesy 'cheers!'

"You're looking well?" He hates this: social platitudes, small talk. He usually feels awkward in social situations when his voice sounds unnatural, and his words convey no real meaning. He just can't do it. Perhaps this is another reason why he's never been part of the bigger conversations.

He tries to reassure himself that it has always been like this, but he knows it hasn't. He's a detective - trained to deal with untruths: even (especially) his own.

Thankfully, Kate isn't one to mince words. She'd have no job without them. "Thank you. I wish I could say the same for you though."

"How so?"

"Maybe I forgot how tired you always look."

"I'm wide awake now, I assure you!"

She smiles dutifully. "So, this is all very nice, Martin, but no such thing as a free drink, as they say." She glances at her phone again as a text alert comes through, then turns her lovely, wide eyes on him again. "I haven't been in here since last summer - the paper's summer bash in The Gardens. I don't think you were able to make it?"

Harcourt lowers his voice unnecessarily. "I was busy on a case I expect."

"Grace Beech?"

"Almost certainly."

"Did anyone ever find out where she'd moved to?"

"I'm not sure anyone looked that hard, to be honest." He reflects on a case that had confounded them for months before they were able to make the vital link between a child's death - Grace's sister, Julie - and that of one of her childhood friends that spring.

"Off the record, we're drawing - have drawn - another blank: this time on Zoya Agarwal's cause of death."

"Drowning, surely!" She raises her eyebrows lightheartedly lest he should think she is being sarcastic (though she does do sarcasm regularly, and not just with her older dyed-in-the-wool male colleagues either).

"Yes. Yes!" He is relieved that she is keeping it light, but after all, they are talking about a young woman's death. "The coroner is more likely to rule it a suicide as it's hard to make a case for accidental, but they might just fall back on 'cause of death unexplained.'"

"Which you and we, and certainly her parents would hate."

"Presumably less so than suicide in their case though? That would represent a complete character change in their daughter which neither of them had suspected at all."

"Suicide gives a greater sense of closure though. An unexplained verdict is so open-ended…"

"I think they would be crushed by it; not that they haven't been crushed by it already. It isn't just that she was an only child, she seems to have been a friend to everyone with barely a bad bone in her body when she was alive."

"Much like Gary Jones?"

He can see her interest increasing. She is sitting slightly upright in her chair now, her eyes more settled; focused.

"Similar, yes."

"But you don't think their deaths are linked?"

"We have nothing at all to link them, apart from their friendship group. We still have to speak to some of them directly, but I can almost guarantee that there will be the requisite sense of shock and each will be mystified as to why Zoya drowned - as are we. Nobody just walks straight into a river without reason. Even if they've lost it, it's still a reason.

Gary got into difficulty because his legs became entangled in weeds in the lake. His friends couldn't get to him in time, according to each of their statements. There were no other witnesses, and this is entirely consistent with the pathologist's report."

"Will they bring more officers in to help you?"

Harcourt grimaces. "It doesn't always help and, besides, the Gary Jones file is officially closed. The Zoya Agarwal case does not appear to be connected so, no, although we're not getting anywhere, there's no obvious call to action to bring more detectives in to help us out. Resources are tight enough as it is. They still haven't given me a DC – even on a loan basis. It's not as if we're looking for a serial killer. 'Accidental death' is entirely appropriate in Gary's case."

"Unless you're his father."

"What do you know about Barry Jones?"

"Very little, other than he continues to post on various online forums about his son's death; how it couldn't have been an accident and so on."

"You don't know anything about his professional life?" Harcourt takes a large gulp of beer and immediately wishes he hadn't. The unseen air he consumed with it will need to escape somehow. Probably soon and almost certainly loudly.

"Never needed to. Background checks by one of my colleagues on the Barry Jones story did suggest that he's a niche player in the financial markets, dealing only with super-rich clients in established areas. That way there's minimal risk to either his reputation or theirs. Otherwise quite secretive stuff - as you'd expect."

"I would. Uncertainty is for gamblers, not the serious money-makers who have it all worked out on their spreadsheets. They are playing with such large sums they can hardly avoid making a lot of cash each time they invest. He did tell me he was a financial expert after all."

"You don't have to earn a lot to have a lot, though, do you?"

They exchange smiles. It feels good.

"Not good to have a son who goes and drowns without explanation! Off-putting to the lucky few I'd have thought." Kate crosses her short but shapely legs while Harcourt does his best to stay focused on her face.

"Especially given the publicity." He notices that Kate has become pensive; still very much alert but less in the room than she was. He needs to bring her back. "You were brought up around here, I think you said?"

"Yes. In Pershore. I lived with my Gran. Grandad had died when he was still quite young, so I think she was glad of the company."

Harcourt has been trained to read between the lines, especially those written by trained journalists.

"Your parents moved away?" He hadn't appreciated how much he'd lowered his voice until he could barely hear himself speak.

"In a manner of speaking, yes."

He waits, patiently. This he has learned also. He watches the choices pass before her, unseen but not unnoticed - like the smells from favourite childhood meals, or from dusty, dank rooms that have been shut up for far too long. Which will she choose to revisit, if any?

"My Dad was a teacher at the De Montfort; Mum was a housewife: 'homemaker' is today's term, I think. She was always there for me, standing by the wall at the end of each school day, holding my hand tightly as we crossed the road and headed home for tea. Letting me play for a little while before reading me bedtime stories after Dad had left more water on the bathroom floor than in the bath itself!"

Harcourt smiles at the happy family memories from childhood that will be forever preserved, just as they were, in her mind; never to grow dim with age and never to be considered childish. "What subject did your father teach?"

"Maths. Not for me I'm afraid, though he did spend hours on the living room carpet with me, arranging beads and marbles into groups and trying to teach me 'adding up' and 'taking away.'"

"You preferred words to numbers?"

"I suppose I did, but I remember an early school report saying that I lacked imagination in my 'stories.' Maybe I just told it how I saw it, even then."

Harcourt laughs encouragingly but senses - knows - that they didn't all live happily ever after.

"My parents died when I was seven." She leans forward to take a sip of her wine, still looking for courage, for support.

He tries not to stare at an accomplice who has suddenly and unexpectedly become a victim. He hopes the silence will be a sufficient security blanket, both for her to continue, and the unwelcome thoughts now flying through and around his brain to remain unspoken until or unless invited.

"They were involved in a car crash."

"Were you..."

"I wasn't in the car, no. I was at home with the childminder, Sarah. They were returning from the pictures: 'Beverly Hills Cop' would you believe?"

He can believe it. Of course, he can. Everyone at primary school had persuaded their parents to take them to see it. He is propelled back to Cambridge - Cambridgeshire - but it isn't as if the hapless Eddie Murphy can come to his rescue. Nobody can.

"They were hit by a petrol tanker. Head on."

"I'm so sorry, Kate." He leans forward, then immediately back again, not sure how she wants him to react. Perhaps she is telling him now because, as a detective, she'll know he has heard equally tragic stories. Inhabited them himself. Trusts him to be able to deal with them without becoming immediately emotionally invested?

"The driver was from Poland. It was late at night and

the police think he was confused by their headlights. He swerved directly into their path. The car went into the Avon. They didn't get out of it."

He doesn't feel tempted to ask about the driver or a young girl's formative opinions of others. That is for journalists, not policemen. The truth is his Holy Grail and that alone - however horrific the endings so often are.

She seems to understand his silence though. "It's fine. Gran gave me a wonderful childhood and I'm not one of those 'what if' women who spend their lives looking for answers that would make no difference anyway. The death was judged to be accidental - a 'tragic mistake' the judge wrote in his judgement, which I saw years later. The driver went back to Poland, and I just hope he was able to come to terms with it as I did."

"That's very magnanimous of you in the circumstances." The assurance in his voice is not matched by what he is feeling inside - like an actor taking direction unconvincingly. He hasn't come to terms with anything, not really. Is this the moment to meet her halfway emotionally and tell her that he understands; really and truly understands? Needs to tell someone?

She misinterprets the struggle playing out on his face. "Some accidental deaths are just that, Martin: accidental. If there is a higher being then only they can understand the timing, the place and the characters involved; like a fiction writer, I imagine. It has made me determined to make the most of my life though, and to help others to do the same because none of us know when that life is going to change - or end."

"Your Gran must be very proud." Safer ground.

"She was, yes. She died eight years ago, but she lived to see me settle down in a job, and buy my own flat."

"And live your life!"

"That too. It might not be the life many people think it is, but I know how lucky I am. I've met enough people to know that for certain."

Again, he wonders if she is waiting for him - for his truth. He finishes his beer, but it doesn't fill him with the courage to elaborate. How he wishes he was as strong as she is. "I've only ever seen you surrounded by friends and colleagues! I doubt you spend much time on your own."

"You'd be surprised." She laughs. Not loudly but he senses that she is seeing the dawn again at the end of a long and troubled night.

"I would. I'm guessing you have lots of good friends."

If she's looking for that 'me too' response, the moment has passed. He regrets it but there it is. Back to work, again. He smiles.

"And one of those – Nancy - can you tell me anything more about her?"

"Very little I'm afraid." She answers immediately but they could have been words on a screen from an impersonal online chatbot. He's still lost her - the real her - in the ether somehow.

"Only that's one of the bigger mysteries in either case. Gary died in a tragic accident at the lake. Zoya deliberately walked into the river and drowned. Those two facts probably do stand up to scrutiny, connected or not. But we can only act on what we see. What we do not understand is why Nancy reported Zoya being followed and yet Miranda Anne Clackerton stated (and her iPhone footage confirms) that nobody else was present at the time."

"I can see why you're drawing blanks."

She is a little more direct now, but the conversation has become stilted somehow. He decides to try a different tack. "How did you come to know Nancy?"

"I don't know her well."

There it is again, that defensiveness which isn't in Kate's character - or not that he has ever experienced before. "No, but your paths must have crossed at some point. You referred us to her, just after Zoya drowned."

"She's worked at the Diglis for about two years I think."

This is slightly better, even though it sounds much too formal for the setting.

"I first came across her when we ran a story on a drugs raid in Warndon."

"Oh!" He hadn't expected that at all and cannot help letting out a little gasp.

"It's not at all what you think. Nancy's mother also died when she was young..."

He watches her stop for alcoholic reinforcement again, and to seemingly, compose herself. There is a hint of dampness around her eyes - whether because of another tale she is about to tell or an even deeper, much more personal story, he cannot discern.

"On the surface, she's pretty easygoing but lacked any real security. She got in with the wrong crowd; the usual thing I'm afraid. One of their gang - Joey - was already into drugs. It was inevitable I suppose as you well know. Worcester is awash with the problem, not just in Warndon."

He nods his understanding, knowing that to speak now might turn the conversation tap off altogether. Kate's halting delivery is still barely more than a dribble.

"Classic case. Joey got into thieving to feed his habit and some of the others got caught up in it."

"Not Nancy though?"

"No. He (they) forced her to give them money to buy stuff until she'd just had enough. She tried to leave several times, and Joey certainly used to hit her. It was on one of those occasions that we ran our story. The neighbours told the police and he was arrested. It will all be in your records. I don't think your colleagues handled it that well - too much force apparently - and Joey got off with a community order."

Harcourt makes a mental note to look at the file, and also the over-zealous officers who helped this Joey slip through the custodial net.

"But you stayed in touch with Nancy; kept an eye on

her?"

"I try to. Sometimes we go months without speaking, but she knows that I am always at the end of the phone if she needs someone to talk to. You know, needs help. I honestly do want the best for people. Anyway, as luck would have it… no, this is going to sound all wrong. *Sadly*, Nancy's father died suddenly. I suppose it must have been about six months ago now. Definitely in springtime this year. He lived in the little house by the river where your sergeant interviewed her. She moved there and tried to leave all the rest of it behind.

"Tried?"

"He still shows up sometimes, but I'm pretty sure he leaves empty-handed. I don't think he's tried to attack her again, but the threat's always there isn't it? She just wants to rebuild her life and move on. A drowning on her doorstep was probably the last thing she needed."

They each fall silent then, both reflecting on water's life-sustaining and equally murderous qualities.

CHAPTER FIVE

Linda Farren is unsure whether the little cul-de-sac off Pitchcroft Lane is on the up or whether it's always been quite posh and is trying to be a bit edgier these days.

"There are a series of allotments at the end of this road," Flowers briefs her, happy that's it just the two of them at last, "Barbourne Road runs parallel to the river and if we could see past those houses, we'd probably be opposite the top of the race course."

Farren shields her eyes from the late afternoon sunshine but can't quite picture the racecourse from here. She's been for several long walks along the river now but still hasn't got her Worcester bearings.

The small front garden comprises a scruffy patch of grass with two weather-beaten grey wicker seats to the left of the front door, only a crumbling copper-coloured chiminea separating them. Farren spots the little piles of tell-tale ash nearby with correspondingly darker patches of grass. How much of that is down to the heater, she cannot yet guess.

A very old apple tree's branches frame the window on the right-hand side of the small red-brick house in front of them. Turn of the century she would estimate for the house; turn of a much earlier century for the tree. A sudden breeze from the west replaces what remaining heat there is left in the day with cold air. A blast from the future, she thinks, with winter just around the corner. Wind chimes, similarly unsettled, sound their welcome - or is it a warning?

A tall, rather plain woman with greying hair tied back into a ponytail with a wooden pin answers the door. Dressed in a brown painter's smock mostly covering a white blouse she acknowledges their warrant cards with a brief nod and a smile that could have been painted on her face instead of lips and leads them silently to a kitchen at the back of the house.

Skylights overhead have brought in much-needed extra light as the single north-facing window faces quite a high brick wall, separating them from the next house along the street. The kitchen is consequently bright, with light-grey cupboard doors above and below various appliances in primary colours, but also homely with the vibrant green leaves of pot plants and trailing ferns reaching down to books strewn across its surfaces. A single bright-yellow wooden table sits patiently amid the cacophony of colours and obvious activity.

"Are you an artist Mrs Flint?" Flowers glances admiringly at the prints of boats and beach scenes adorning the remaining wall space.

"Valerie please!" She flicks the switch of the kettle on and joins them at the table. "No! I wish I did have some talent in that direction though, do you know what I mean?"

They both nod, somewhat superfluously.

160

She continues, without missing a beat or appearing to notice the knowing glances exchanged by her guests. "My partner - Tommy - is the creative one in this house. He's a musician: jazz mainly, but with a bit of funk occasionally, do you know what I mean?"

Incredibly, Farren does. Less incredibly she is already wanting to move this conversation on quickly but is stopped in her tracks by Flowers, who seems to have made himself quite at home already.

"I love the sea."

"Me too."

"There's something about the light dancing on the waves isn't there? I've never really wanted to go in it or even on it; just being beside it is calming somehow."

"My husband would only agree with you up to a point. He has a distant connection with the Greek Royal Family and has many stories to tell about parties on fabulous yachts and so forth; comes out in his music sometimes."

"Very down with the kids!"

"Does he visit them often?" Flowers ignores his colleague's frustrated response, presumably seeing this somehow as key 'background' information.

Valerie is understandably happy to oblige. "Not now. Crown Prince Pavlov moved to New York with his wife and family. They have an apartment on Madison Avenue."

"Wow! Good for visits then?"

"Sadly, he hasn't seen them for many years."

"What is that you do, er Valerie?" Flowers is undeterred.

"Oh, I dabble in this and that, you know. When one has had a comfortable upbringing oneself, one finds it difficult to find one's mojo sometimes, one's motivation in life. It can be a mixed blessing – do you know what I mean? It isn't that I haven't tried of course. I do think maybe getting my hands a little dirtier at an early stage might have benefitted me in the longer run."

Farren is losing one's will to live, as well as mischievously considering it as an option for their interviewee.

Valerie is oblivious to the fact and almost everything and everyone around her it seems. "I give quite a bit of my spare time to The Arc. Do you know it?"

Farren shakes her head, but Flowers nods enthusiastically. "The children's charity?"

"Well, young people, yes. We have a drop-in centre next to Worcester Cathedral. We offer confidential advice to the kids, or they can just pop in for a chat. A bit like The Samaritans I suppose."

Farren suspects it is nothing like it, but indulges the woman in her delusion, especially as she suddenly jumps up to pour boiling water onto real tea leaves in a large, brown teapot. "Does the church fund the project then? The Arc I mean?"

Valerie looks at her a little pityingly. "I'm afraid not. It's a bit too close to home for them you see. They've tried quite hard over the years to get us moved, but haven't quite managed it. Not yet anyway!"

Flowers is still looking around the cosy kitchen. "It's a bit like coming into a Tardis. I never would have thought the inside of the house could have been like this."

His hostess tips her head slightly and replies nicely: "It's having that vision that makes the difference I think. As I may have mentioned I had a very nice upbringing - lovely houses, well decorated. When I left home, I was determined to recreate some of that, albeit in older, poorer buildings that needed a sympathetic eye, you know."

Farren hasn't the time for this self-indulgence, interrupting him before Flowers has time to join in with her designer reverie. "Is your daughter at home Mrs Flint?"

The simpering smile vanishes immediately. "She is, actually. She's working with Tommy in his studio right now."

Farren watches Flowers's face light up at the prospect of some kind of darkened underground recording facility with lots of switches and bright lights, and then drop again as Valerie sends a short text on her phone, whereupon two figures emerge from a dilapidated wooden shed in the yard just beyond the kitchen window.

Both sniggering, Farren wonders what she has said in her text, as they enter via the back door. Tommy is stocky, not helped by a middle-aged fat belt around his sagging stomach above far too-tight jeans. He is proudly wearing a white 'Freedom for the Few' T-shirt, again exacerbating curves where they really shouldn't be.

His hairline is receding and so, bizarrely, he seems to have cultivated a wide patch of wispy hair at the front of his head, above his eyebrows, then a bald gap before the rest of his thinning, grey hair takes over. It has the strange effect of making him look as though he has some kind of hairy skull cap perched on his head.

He holds out his hand, still smiling. Is it in the genes of this family that they are each compelled to smile benignly?

"Tommy Flint. Charmed to meet with you guys!"

Farren can smell the weed in the air but has little time to reflect before the daughter, Barbara, holds out her hand, grinning (obviously). "I'm Barbara."

Barbara is wearing a thin, very tight-fitting black top over torn-off jeans. Her exposed breasts must be breathless in there, Farren considers. She notes that Flowers, gazing at her (them) rather stupidly, must be thinking along similar lines.

"Thanks for joining us; I hope I wasn't interrupting anything too important." She notes an element of sarcasm that has crept in, unbidden, and quickly seeks to send it away again. "I wouldn't want to interfere with the creative process!"

She smiles, knowing she's made it worse, not better. Only Tommy smiles back at her. Probably stoned, he might be thinking he's on a beach somewhere and has just come face to face with a mermaid, she muses deliciously.

"Not at all. We've been trying to lay down this track now for a couple of days, haven't we Babs?"

'Babs' nods her confirmation. The full makeup on her face is far too rouged and melting slightly: like she's just been slapped. Her reddish hair also clashes with it somehow – maybe that's the effect she planned?

"You might wanna take your bud out?" Tommy addresses the ear nearest to him, hoping she can hear with the other.

As Barbara dutifully removes the tiny earpiece, some kind of pounding electro-rock anthem from within can be heard.

Grimacing at either her choice of music or something beyond all of them, Tommy continues. "It's a kid thing, right? Single buds. I had a trumpeter – 'The Sensational Sebastian Roll' (which is why we called him 'sausage') – who took to wearing just the one. Kept turning the volume up 'cos he was on, like, half-power all the time, right? Went completely deaf. Couldn't even hear the sirens, man."

Farren makes a mental note to avoid Steely Dan for the time being, though it will be hard. "You both love music, I guess." ('I guess?' She'd be ridiculed in Selly Oak for far less).

"Barbara's a wiz on the mixing desk!"

Flowers is utterly captivated by this crazy, arty enclave he has unexpectedly stepped into. Farren isn't, has quickly re-grouped. "We're here to ask you a few questions about Zoya Agarwal, if we may."

Valerie turns her back on them to fiddle with the tea things, such that neither detective can read her face - assess her reaction.

"Poor Zoya. Such a cool chick as well." Tommy's smile has finally been erased by the inescapable rubber of conscience, though in all likelihood he has tried to outrun it often.

He and Barbara sit at the table, with Farren and Flowers following suit. Valerie provides each of them with brown, chunky pottery mugs of tea and then joins them.

"You knew Zoya well." Flowers has caught Farren's eye and isn't about to ask any more pointless questions.

"I've known her for quite a long time, yeah. We met early on at High School." Barbara tries to say the last two words as disparagingly as she can now that she has reached the elevated status of a sixth-form student.

"You were friends though." Farren is aware of Valerie turning uncomfortably in the chair opposite to face her daughter.

"I s'pose. We hung out together, but she wasn't really my type; much too quiet and… safe."

"Safe?" Farren enquires, noting the smirk on Tommy's face this time.

"Yeah. Model student. Always on about life at home in the countryside: a bit boring to be honest."

"Would you have said she was stressed by anything before she died?" Flowers has adopted a softer tone than his colleague.

"Her old man was having problems with his shop; she did say that. I didn't talk to her that much."

"So, apart from being shocked by her death, would you say you were surprised by it? That it came completely out of the blue?"

"The great blue yonder." She waves her hands theatrically. Seeing no applause is going to be forthcoming from her captive audience she continues much more soberly. "Well, yeah. We all were. Especially Colin."

"Colin Pearson?" Flowers has also spotted the way Valerie is staring at her daughter, her head perfectly still.

"Yeah. He spent most of his time with her, especially after Gary drowned."

"That must have been pretty shocking for all of you?"

"It was, yeah. Janice got the worst of it though."

"Janice Mills."

"Yeah. Very mousy. Colin used to call her his sugar mouse and she thought he was her sugar daddy I s'pose."

"Sorry. I'm not quite following. Were the two of them in a relationship?"

"You could call it that, but I think it meant more to her

- a lot more - than it did to Colin. Anyway, everything changed after Gary died."

"Can I ask why you are asking these questions today?" Valerie has decided to break cover. "It's obviously very upsetting to lose one's friends - and so young - do you know what I mean?"

"Of course. We do know how difficult this is, and wouldn't ask if we felt it could be avoided, but we're trying to piece together Zoya's state of mind before the accident..."

"Accident?" Tommy seems to have re-tuned his brain into the here and now. "I thought she drove her chevy to the levy and walked right in?"

Farren is inwardly cheered that her use of the word 'accident' has sparked such an immediate reaction. "We have to investigate all possibilities and accidental death can't be ruled out."

Tommy is most definitely in the room now. "But it's completely different to poor Gary, man. I mean, like his legs got all tangled up... pulled him right under. It wasn't the same with her, was it? Word on the street is that she meant to end it all: to kill herself."

"We can't go into any detail," Farren remains calm, "But would you say that suicide was likely in her case?"

Valerie answers first. "Who knows for sure what goes on in a young girl's mind, Sergeant?" She glances across at Barbara, a little furtively. "She may have been perfectly normal on the surface but, underneath..."

"Again, we're looking at all angles." Farren is intrigued

by the unspoken body language between mother and daughter. "Barbara?"

"I dunno. Not really. You'd be better off asking Colin, though. He never seemed to let her out of his sight."

***

He examines his face in the bathroom mirror. Unsurprisingly, it's still a little flushed, but no sign of lipstick. That's good. He really ought to do something about his hair. Then again, it's an integral part of him, of who he is - like Samson he supposes, and look what happened to him when he messed about with it!

He returns to the bedroom and eventually manages to drag on a pair of old, wrinkled jeans, careful to zip up without pinching his skin, which would have been more of a problem when he had first arrived there that evening.

"I hate it when you get dressed!" A husky voice from the bed causes him to turn round to face her once more.

"Me too, babe."

"It's been much too long."

"All's well now though, hey!"

She laughs. It sounds good, even as he struggles with the as-yet-unspoken words he knows he has to say to her next. "We may have to cool it for a little while though."

"Cool it. Why? What's happened?" She is immediately alert, as he knew she would be of course.

"Nothing's happened, exactly. I just think they might have found out."

"About?"

"She just wouldn't let it go. You soon get a sense of whether people are grasping for clues or know the answers to their own questions already."

"And you don't think she's grasping?"

She knows just how to phrase things, especially at times like this; to twist them slightly, imbue them with a slightly different meaning. Not for the first time, he muses that she should perhaps have been a detective. They of all people must know how to hide the secrets they spend their lives trying to uncover. He'll just have to trust her for now.

***

The disfigurement is an ugly red and almost certain to leave a permanent scar. No doubt the bruising will come out soon and her arm will look as though it's been tattooed with some kind of medieval spear.

To be fair, she might have been better just to drop the pan, rather than try to catch the handle and juggle it somehow. Who does she think she is? Certainly not a sensible person that knows not to put their bare hand into a saucepan of boiling water to test the softness of the contents, before jumping out of the way and knocking it over in the same movement.

She managed to save some of the pasta before mopping up the boiling water on the kitchen floor and throwing the tea towel straight into the washing machine. It doesn't seem to have left a stain on the tiles, nor is there any kind of dent where the pan crashed to the floor like a very determined meteorite.

Apart from the pasta which looks a bit sad and forlorn in its bowl, there's little evidence that anything untoward has occurred - apart from her arm that is. She doesn't know why she is feeling so secretive but would rather the others didn't know. Not right away at least, giving her time to get over the shock. She doesn't want any fuss. She never has done.

As if on some kind of dramatic cue though, she hears a key being turned in the lock of the front door and her daughter Claire arrives in the kitchen a few moments later.

"On your own?" She loves that they still embrace when so many children these days express themselves in such different ways.

"I sent your father down to Tesco for a few bits. I don't need any of them, but I just wanted to get him out of the house, on his own for a bit."

"I've noticed he doesn't go out so much. He used to pop into Worcester quite often didn't he – to meet up with old work colleagues?"

"I'm not sure that happens now, not since Linda - Eddie's wife - died. Do you remember Eddie? He came around a couple of times when you were little. They turned up one Sunday afternoon and stayed for tea; said they were just passing, but nobody just passes by Wood Lench, do they? Dad said they were just curious about where he lived. You know how he always tried to keep his work life quite separate from home."

"I remember him being at work much more than at home. I don't remember Eddie at all I'm afraid."

"Well, you were very young, and I think it may only have been the once. Your father would probably find an excuse not to go out at all these days, even if he was invited. He seems to think I need looking after, 24/7."

"I don't suppose you'd like it if he didn't care so much?"

Charlotte nods dutifully, wondering when her daughter had become so mature in her outlook on life. She knows that Daniel is trying to do the right thing by both of them, but she's not a patient - not yet anyway.

"Did you have a good day, darling?"

"Better than Chamberlain I should think?"

"I'm sorry..."

"Sorry, Mum, just trying to be ironic. We're looking at roads leading up to the Second World War and we've been looking at various speeches and articles calling for appeasement."

"Didn't work though, did it?"

"It didn't stop Hitler from invading Czechoslovakia, no, but it might have bought us a little more time to re-arm."

"So, Neville Chamberlain wasn't all bad?"

"I don't think anyone is all good or all bad."

"I thought it was History today, not Religious Education!"

"Now, that was ironic." She smiles as she heads upstairs to get changed before tackling the pasta which has also been forced to play a waiting game.

Charlotte rolls her sleeve up and runs her hand and lower arm under the cold tap. The skin already looks a bit flaky. Thankfully the temperatures have fallen in the last week or so, giving her a good excuse to wear long-sleeved tops until it has healed. Nobody needs to ever know it happened.

***

He runs past the massive brick entrance arch for the third time that morning, ignoring the open invitation to leave the park. He briefly remembers the cemetery sites in Belgium he and Gary had visited as part of their History school trip a couple of years ago. Gary had pretended to be upset by the whole experience - needing a reassuring cuddle from the ever-willing Miss McLean.

He takes the little bridge over Barbourne Brooke, which runs through the park, avoiding the children's play area. He's no longer a child and there's no safety in numbers anymore.

It's a while since he's been for a run. He and Gary used to do so twice a week - usually up here - on Tuesdays and Thursdays, whatever the weather and regardless of how much homework had been piled on to them. Of course, that was nothing compared to the amount he is supposed to read these days, even when no written work has been assigned.

It all seems a bit pointless now, although he knows he just needs to get his head down and keep it down. Unlike Gary, he has always found it difficult to concentrate for long periods. When Gary was focused on something or someone, nothing was allowed to get in the way of it. Like Gary's Dad. Just like Gary's Dad.

A certain image crops up again, which no amount of breathlessness or muscle fatigue can ever erase. How could he have done such a thing and hoped to get away with it?

'You let me down' a voice nearby reminds him. 'You were supposed to be my best friend.'

He runs faster, his head upright; neck taut with the strain of keeping him on track. He is staring straight ahead but all he can see with clarity is that image from the past.

He knows now where they need to go: the special place. Would Gary be able to find them there, or will they be forever prisoners?

CHAPTER SIX

"I've never met Tommy Flint," Harcourt smiles enigmatically, "but I've certainly come into contact with a number of his associates."

"Sounds dubious, sir!" Flowers has brought over cups of coffee whose progeny is certainly very far away from South America.

"Sounds about right. Nothing serious though. Possession mainly, although there was a bit of aggro at one of their gigs in Birmingham last year I believe."

"Are they a serious band, sir?" Farren feigns surprise.

"Depends on what you mean by serious. They do take themselves seriously, but I'm not sure how talented they are. They play the Upton festival every year and one or two others, but I think they're a party band mainly. The line-ups vary according to who's available at the time I expect."

"Jazz not your thing then sir?" Taylor exchanges a smile with Farren.

"Not really, but decent music is!"

"I'm not sure you'd like Tommy, to be honest, sir. Much too full of himself." Flowers has enjoyed his afternoon out with Farren though, and hopes they'll be teamed up together again soon.

"They call him 'Top Hat.' I used to think it was some kind of street reference to the cartoon character 'Top Cat' but apparently, it's because he looks as though he is wearing a hat, although it's just his hairstyle?"

"His wife's a bit of a hug-a-tree person as well." Flowers offers.

"That didn't stop her making sure we knew about her privileged background though; and his." Farren practically spits out the last word.

"I'm guessing they didn't buy the idea that Zoya Agarwal deliberately took her own life either."

"They were more circumspect than I'd expected, sir." Farren looks at Flowers for confirmation.

"That's right," he gushes, "Tommy was more inclined to think it was deliberate, based on whatever gossip he's been listening to. He certainly didn't want to think it was accidental as in Gary Jones's case."

"The mother and daughter were also a bit odd," Farren adds. "It was as though the mother - Valerie - wanted to keep shutting things down."

"Maybe she's unsure about what's in her own daughter's head?" Harcourt suggests.

"If I were her mother, it wouldn't be her head I'd be concerned about." Flowers smiles, even as he makes what he thinks is a serious point.

"Perhaps Tommy just doesn't like the idea that his daughter might be mixed up in something nobody quite understands yet?" Taylor offers. "Fear of the unknown and all that."

"Doesn't sound like the mindset of a musician!' Farren isn't convinced.

"Maybe he doesn't sound like a musician at all," Harcourt concludes.

***

"No, Gordon, I do not understand it." She has pinned him against one of the ancient washing machines in the cellar's utility area. Old and creaking, they are both in a spin.

"Why are you being so difficult? I've told you time and again that I just like to get out and enjoy some fresh air at the end of the day."

"But so late at night?"

"Especially late at night. I always make sure that any guests are catered for. You know exactly what I mean: 'Just a quick night cap' or 'I shouldn't really have warm milk at bedtime - not good for my bladder' or even 'Pop a dollop of honey in the Horlicks would you, old chap; keeps me sweet.'"

"Yes, I do know all this."

"Well then?"

"You're missing the point?"

"Oh, there is a point to this - this interrogation - after all?"

"Gordon, please do not shout at me."

"Sorry, I thought that's why we were doing this down here: so that our paying guests wouldn't hear the screams that come for free."

"You're getting this out of all proportion - again. I merely asked why you felt the need to go out so late at night, so often."

"I like to walk - feel the fresh air on my face after being stuck inside this place all day."

"So why take the car?"

"You know what: why don't you just call in the police, right now? Go on. The number should be fairly easy to remember. Get them over to check for blood patches in the boot..."

"If I thought they wouldn't find any, I would!"

"What? What are you talking about now?"

"I sliced my finger on the veggie box from the farm shop yesterday, when I was trying to load quickly: bound to be evidence."

"Sarcasm perches rather grotesquely on your lips, my love." He makes to wriggle out from behind her, but her arms are strong. This he remembers too.

"Just tell me if there's somebody else involved; don't let me find out by accident."

"There is someone."

Instead of tightening her grip around him, her arms fall to their sides, useless now in his prosecution or her defence. "Tell me."

"His name is Caractacus."

"We don't have kids, Gordon, spare me the children's stories."

"Not the Ian Fleming invention, the one lauded by Elgar: the ancient British chieftain who refused to give in to the Romans.

"Save it for the guests…"

"Many people think his stronghold was at British Camp, up there on the top of the hill. I drive up there sometimes and look out as he once did."

"You're hardly living under occupation: not even house arrest!"

"No, but from up there I can look down on the world, seemingly all of it, just as it has always conspired to look down on me."

"I think I might cry." He hears the relief in her voice though.

"Just walking along that ridge - especially at night - makes me feel 'relevant' I suppose."

He is speaking to an empty wall; hears only her footsteps as she walks slowly but purposefully up the stone steps, away from him and the inevitability of change every bit as fundamental as the Iron Age itself.

**

They are just to the south of the Malvern Hills and approaching the pretty village of Welland.

Harcourt points to the dark sky ahead of them.

"Now, that's a real Judgement Day sky if ever there was one! The hills themselves look pretty stark at this time of year, but it's like we're heading into the apocalypse."

Farren looks up from her phone and nods. "They should be playing 'Ride of the Valkyries.'"

A smile plays on Harcourt's lips, but it doesn't meet his eyes; they are otherwise engaged. "We're looking for a small, detached bungalow on the left."

"Pretty village!"

"Isn't it? A bit too remote for me though."

"Me too. Those hills would do my head in."

"It is as though they're watching our every move, isn't it?"

"I was thinking more of the traffic jams, especially in the summer."

And the rest of the year, thinks Harcourt, recalling the many times he and Debbie have been stuck in traffic, even when heading up there for a cup of tea and a winter walk. He wonders what she's doing at that very moment. His drink with Kate had been pleasant enough - just colleagues sharing information - but he'd become very melancholy on the taxi journey back into town. Maybe it was the drink?

"We're here, sir. Number 14." Farren takes in the well-kept front garden as they pull in behind an ancient once bright red Ford Escort.

Harcourt observes Bob Drake observing them from behind the far corner of net curtains that are presumably meant to preserve the rest of the living room for the land of the living only.

He greets them with firm handshakes and beckons them inside, offering tea or coffee which they both decline politely. In his late sixties or early seventies, Bob is of average height, thick set with cropped grey hair.

The aforesaid 'front room' as Bob prefers to describe it is neat enough but sparse. The carpet is beige but not too worn; ubiquitous magnolia paint would once have made it feel much fresher than it does today.

They sit together on the two-seater settee, opposite Bob in what is indisputably **his** chair: a recliner in matching grey cloth.

Harcourt notes the distinct lack of pictures or ornaments on the ancient oak bureau that dominates the wall opposite the window. Almost certainly an heirloom, he considers, as it doesn't fit with the rest of the furniture that would have been new in the Seventies.

"Thanks for seeing us," Farren begins, "We believe you first reported your wife missing a few weeks ago?"

"Too right!" Bob's gravelly cockney accent fills the small room. "Nobody bothered to come and see me then, mind." He is perched on the edge of his chair; almost certainly on the edge of something far less secure.

"I've been looking back through our records, Mr Drake…" Harcourt backs her up.

"Bob, please."

"Thanks. Somebody did get in touch and took some details."

"On the phone, yeah." He relaxes a little and shifts his body backwards.

"My colleagues told you that most people return within 48 hours, I believe."

"They did, yeah. They said to get in touch again if I was still worried. Mind you, I heard one of the officers on that detective series set up in Shetland say that the first 72 hours were crucial."

"They certainly can be if the missing person is in any kind of danger. Shetland is a lot smaller than England though."

"There's still plenty of coastlines nearby - well, about an hour to Somerset I suppose, or South Wales. Monmouth?"

Farren isn't sure whether Bob Drake is toying with her (as men of a certain generation still think they have the right to do) or if the games are just playing out in his head. "But you didn't think that she was in danger? You didn't contact the police again?"

"They were alright about it, but I couldn't help thinking I was wasting their time, you know what I mean?"

"So, she came back, safe and well, but now she's gone missing again?" Farren isn't convinced that Bob Drake is telling them the whole truth. There's something about the way he hesitates before responding that has made her suspicious.

"No."

"No? Can you elaborate for us please Bob?" Harcourt can spot a timewaster a mile off, and Bob Drake is less than two metres away.

"She didn't come back; hasn't come back. I'm wondering if maybe she's left me. They normally leave a note though don't they? Besides, she'd never have gone without this - took it everywhere she went."

He picks up a small faded white book with crumpled edges from the occasional table beside his chair.

Harcourt takes it and notes that it is a Bible – albeit featuring only the stories from the New Testament. There are no other outward signs of religion such as crosses on the wall. He quickly remembers that Roman Catholics like to think they have a monopoly on such vestiges.

He looks around the room again and his eyes fall on a colour photograph, about A4 size, of two young men in white shorts and mainly red football tops with white arms, hanging above a door that presumably leads into the dining room.

Bob's eyes have been tracking Harcourt's.

"George Armstrong and me!"

"You were a footballer?" Harcourt knows nothing of the game and has never felt inclined to find out more, but it is an often easy lead into a general conversation that could reveal other more specific facts.

"On Arsenal's books, yeah. Had to be. I was born just down the road from Highbury, in Finsbury Park. We were both twenty at the time that picture was taken. Four years later, Geordie won the Double."

"You weren't part of that team?"

"Never made it. He came down from Durham and made his debut about three years earlier. I played a lot for the reserves but never really got my chance. I wasn't fast enough when I ran or tough enough when I stood still."

"I'm sorry." Harcourt may not be a sports fan but he knows plenty about disappointment.

Drake shrugs his shoulders, as he has probably done for most of his life. "I went into the printing trade, you know when every other fellah you met was called Ron. Gave me and the wife a good standard of living, before we retired out here."

"You're quite a long way from 'home!'" Farren offers.

"We used to come over here for holidays; brought the caravan. Usually in the Forest of Dean but sometimes down in the Cotswolds. This was sort of halfway."

"Can you think of anything that might explain your wife's disappearance? Did you argue for example, or was she upset about something else?"

"Not that I can think of, and I have been doing a lot of thinking. She loved to go for long walks. She'd be out all day sometimes."

"Up in the hills?" Farren again.

"Not really. Her favourite place was just up the road; she used to spend hours walking around Pickerton Lake."

**

"So, that was interesting!" Farren is staring at Harcourt staring ahead.

Without changing gear, he responds. "Something is missing there, and it isn't his wife?"

"You mean his state of mind?"

"Partly. He wasn't worried, or anxious; neither was he frustrated, or mad at us for not getting back to him before now. He and his life seemed completely without any substance or colour, apart from that picture on the wall."

"Do you think the connection with the Lake is significant?

"Could be. We're looking at two drownings already and have no reason to rule out a third."

"And no reason to rule it in either," Farren concludes.

**

Less than five minutes later they are sitting in the drawing room of Edward Mills. The contrast with that of Bob Drake's minimalist existence could hardly be greater. An ornate brass clock chimes the hour from atop an intricately carved sideboard. Tasteful prints of timeless country scenes adorn the expensive Wedgwood blue wallpaper, and a series of white porcelain figures stand in line on one of the deep windowsills, towards which Edward now strides.

"What a beautiful room!" Harcourt appreciates beautiful objects even if their owners are anything but beautiful - or objective.

"Isn't it!" Their host beams as they sink into comfortable armchairs on either side of an unlit fireplace. "Parts of the mill are from the sixteenth century, and this particular room is largely unchanged since my great, great grandfather moved here in 1846."

"I've always been fascinated by water mills," Harcourt is in no hurry to get down to the real business of their visit, "I used to live in Cambridgeshire and visited Houghton Mill on the River Great Ouse quite regularly."

"I'm afraid the River Pick would seem like a fairly minor tributary in contrast with the Ouse, Inspector. Besides, I'd have thought windmills were more the thing in East Anglia - perhaps further up, in Norfolk?"

"Indeed. My wife and I stayed up at Cley Mill, on the North Norfolk marches for my thirtieth birthday and, of course, the road to Great Yarmouth is littered with windmills, many of them sadly derelict now."

"A favourite holiday destination - Yarmouth?"

"Hemsby: a village just along the coast to the north. We used to hire a holiday chalet. It was a different world, and I loved it as a boy."

"It's a very beautiful part of the world too. I know Suffolk better. I have very happy memories of Dedham and walking in the Stour Valley."

"Ah. Constable country. It's like walking through a masterpiece, isn't it?"

"Very poetic, Inspector."

"I wish. I tend to leave poetry to my DS though."

Farren blushes as Mills turns to face her. "Not me, I'm afraid, sir. I wish I knew more about art though."

"You and me both, Sergeant. It's what keeps many of us awake at night, although I imagine you're here to talk about the opaque side of the canvas."

"Sadly, yes, sir." Harcourt sees a fleeting look of confusion on Farren's face and rescues her before she falls. "We're talking to friends, family and close associates of Zoya Agarwal."

"That poor girl!"

Harcourt is caught momentarily off balance. The voice is not that of Edward Mills, being altogether higher and yet softer at the same time. With some relief that he hasn't inadvertently become part of some strange Hitchcock film set, he spots Mrs Mills entering by a side door and, much more importantly, carrying a tray of tea and biscuits.

"My wife, Daisy." Mills introduces her proudly, taking the tray from her.

Daisy Mills sits opposite Farren, who takes in the homely, elderly lady, quite at home in dark trousers, cream blouse and yellow cardigan.

"I cannot imagine what that poor family are going

through. Edward saw Oviya on the day her daughter went missing, didn't you dear."

Mill's face clouds over as he recalls the episode. "She was very worried about Zoya, yes. It wasn't in her nature to go off without her parents knowing where she was. I don't mean in a controlling way, you understand. Zoya seemed just as keen that neither of them would get stressed - at least not over anything she had done."

"A lovely girl." Daisy agrees, tears forming in her eyes. As is her mother, the poor lady."

"Did you know her well?"

Mills too has drifted away from them, his own eyes picturing a quite different, far less tranquil, scene now. "Oviya or Zoya?"

"Both I suppose." Farren is aware of this and instinctively understands that they need to keep him - both of them - on track if the interview is to bear any fruit.

"Well." Mills lets out a deep breath that he might have been holding in for days. "I knew Zoya quite well because she spent a bit of time with Janice, our granddaughter, as I'm sure you know. Because they lived just up the road in the village, they'd known each other since they were quite young."

He pauses while Daisy pours tea and expertly distributes biscuits on small china plates.

"Her parents had brought her up properly - excellent manners and ..."

"Respect!" Daisy helps him, as she has almost certainly done for all their married life. "She was quite old-fashioned in the way that she treated people. 'Proper' as my mother used to say."

"And Oviya?"

"Gentle, like Zoya." Daisy continues. "A little quieter, possibly but she is always well-dressed rather than dressed up; there's a difference!"

"Her name means 'artist.' She has a love of old prints and did some sketching of her own while helping Nadin in the shop I believe." Mills is still reflecting, reflective.

"Was there ever any kind of... trouble experienced by the family?"

"Racism you mean. Come on Inspector, I was in the Service in the early Seventies, tasked with trying to find homes for the many unfortunate Ugandan Asians who Idi Amin had taken a dislike to. I know all about that side of things, I assure you. Not that I think the Agarwal family will have experienced much of it around here, thankfully."

"You were a career civil servant?" Harcourt is bemused.

"You're quite right to be surprised. My father insisted I go into either it or the Diplomatic Service. I don't much care for small talk with despots so stayed at home as it were. I quickly came to realise that doing the job well wasn't the point; it was much more about being the right fit."

"Which you weren't?"

"Not quite, though I suppose I talked a good game. Thankfully my father left me a small legacy and I was able to return to my first love."

"He should have been an antiques dealer for all of his life." Daisy clearly adores her husband and all that he stands for. His History of Art degree was wasted among those who stuck to PPE at Oxford and made fun of him to hide their own silly little insecurities."

"We can't escape history, but we can try to do something about its consequences I suppose." Harcourt can imagine how many silly little dinner parties she has had to prepare for when probably all that she wanted - all they both wanted - was to visit art galleries and exhibitions together and talk about what they'd seen over a quiet drink afterwards.

"Can you think of anything else that Zoya Agarwal might have been concerned about?" Farren is fascinated by the couple (no, really, she is!) but she can hardly write an essay about 'cultural change as reflected through art' in her notebook.

Daisy shakes her head. "It was Janice she spent most of her time with, I'm afraid. Well, not afraid. I mean that it's Janice you'd need to speak to but she's out with Colin at the moment."

"Colin Pearson?"

"Yes. He and Janice go walking quite a bit. They had a little break, but he's here quite a lot again these days. He passed his driving test a couple of weeks ago so drives down in his mother's Mini when she's not on shift. To be honest we prefer it. Too much temptation in Worcester; not, I think, in a good way if you'll forgive me."

Harcourt thinks he could forgive Daisy Mills almost anything, even if he came upon a murder scene with her holding a carving knife dripping with blood. "You weren't keen on a group of them meeting in town."

"Not really, but I never discouraged it either. Like Zoya, Janice is a good girl, always sends me texts to let me know where she is."

"And I've just got the hang of e-mail!" Edward Mills laughs a friendly, self-deprecating laugh which makes them all relax, even though they're murder detectives: there for the saddest of reasons.

"Do you have any idea what they talk about - Janice and Colin?" Farren knows it is a closed question but wants to see the older lady's reaction."

"What do teenagers talk about these days? I suppose I'm thankful that they at least appear to be engaged in proper conversations rather than an exchange of grunts!"

"And they're close? You mentioned they broke up ..."

"I don't think they're close in that kind of way, Inspector." Mills takes up the strain seeing, as Harcourt does, the unmistakable grimace on his wife's face. "After the Jones boy's accident, Colin stayed away from Janice. I thought it odd behaviour, given that she probably needed someone to talk to about it all: of a similar age I mean. She was understandably very upset but couldn't find a way of allowing us to help her.

Rather hid away in her room."

"Can I ask what you made of them - the boys I mean?" Harcourt takes in the older man's comfy cream chinos and rusty-coloured woollen jumper but isn't convinced that all is harmonious below decks.

"Colin was, is, a nice enough chap. A little bit of a rough diamond, you might say. His parents are good people, although I think Colin himself may have been led a little astray."

Harcourt recalls Daisy's previous comment about Worcester. "You weren't particularly sorry when he was on the scene less?"

"Quite so. I don't dislike the lad but, oh, well I'll say it. I think Janice can do better. A lot better. I know they're not together in that sense, but I think you do have to choose your friends carefully - especially at such a vulnerable age.

"And Gary Jones?"

Daisy barely tries to hide an intake of breath. "Terrible what happened. He was so full of life, that one. He could work a room as well - flirted with the people he thought would help him and even more so with those that wouldn't."

"Quite a player then!" Farren can see the door opening, yet they've hardly had to push it.

"He was. You couldn't help liking him. I suppose everyone did. Lit up the room when he entered, that sort of thing."

"I preferred it when he left." Mills isn't trying to be witty or drole.

"You didn't like him?" Harcourt notes that Mills is the first person they have spoken to or heard about who hasn't been entirely under the spell of Gary Jones's alleged charms.

"Or his parents?" Harcourt bridges the gap which has opened up following Edward Mills's silence.

Daisy looks across at her husband who, after a brief but unspoken assent, answers the question. "We weren't keen on the family, I'm sorry to say. Mrs Jones was nice enough ..."

"Far too nice for that man!" Daisy has decided that the words need to be said out loud.

Mills continues. "Mr Jones was always, how should I put it, focused."

"On business matters?" Harcourt shares Farren's optimism that they might glean a lot here, despite the couple's inherent breeding and good manners. It often took a G&T to loosen such people's tongues at first, but not on this occasion. There was too much anger (or angst?)

"Yes. All of that. He seemed to project himself as a brand image rather than as a real person. You know the kind of people? Nouveaux latching on to things in vogue at the time. Or am I being too harsh? They say the right things for the situation they find themselves in, as opposed to what they believe. If Barry Jones thought it would be good for his business, he'd probably entertain the devil to dinner."

"You saw through him?" Farren cuts to the chase, as she has always tried to do. It's often easier that way, and always quicker.

"It wasn't difficult, I assure you. When you have no heart or soul, transparency is all too evident. Even having assassinated the man's character I do feel rather wretched about his loss though. No parent should be burying their child. I simply have no idea how you would come to terms with such an outcome - especially if the death is accidental. I mean, there's nobody to blame is there? Nobody to channel all your anger towards."

"Has Janice always lived here with you?" Farren attempts to channel these thoughts in a different direction - while things are flowing so well.

"She's our daughter Gina's child. An only child I'm pleased to say. No other innocents were caught up in the emotional crossfire between her and her husband, Henry."

"They split up?" Farren is happy to be blunt, knowing that Harcourt's sharpness will be undiminished.

"When Janice was just three years old, yes." Mills is becoming reflective again, but probably in a good way in terms of background information.

"I'm guessing from what you said that it was quite acrimonious?"

"It was certainly that, Sergeant, if not downright unforgivable. Janice hasn't seen her father since. He writes occasionally, but it's as though the letters are from someone she knows of, rather than knows. They could be written down in a storybook and they'd be just as believable as far as she's concerned. She'd have no reason to simply accept gifts (as from a relative stranger), but, similarly, no reason to challenge anything he says either."

"Does he live nearby? I mean, has she sought him out at all?" Farren's radar is covering a wider area by the millisecond.

"He does not live nearby. Not even on the same continent. He moved to Canada in 2010, and forgive me, but the arctic wastes are welcome to swallow him up."

"And your daughter, Mr. Mills. What of her?"

This time it is Daisy who interjects. "Gina is what you might call a 'free spirit.' She went off to 'find herself' when Janice started primary school. She left Janice with us and never really came back, apart from on her sixteenth birthday - quite unexpectedly - and for the first couple of Christmases when I imagine that guilt was still able to prick her."

"We tend to argue when she does deign to join us, I'm afraid." Mills looks unhappy now: a metaphorical dark cloud such as the one they saw earlier has crept into the room and is lingering just below the cream ceiling. "It's not good for her, for us, and certainly not for Janice."

"Did she move abroad too?"

"In a manner of speaking. She lives in a New Age retreat near Machynlleth in mid-Wales."

***

Harcourt has had a restless night again. It's only the second night that Debbie has been away, but, even so, he never seems to settle when she's not there beside him. He doesn't believe that anything untoward is going on - much as he's alarmed by the blurry pictures nevertheless revealing the lack of clothing being worn by her 'friends.' She's sent him various texts describing what they've all been up to - or mostly all - along with assurances (or are they supposed to be reassurances?) that she's having a marvellous time.

It isn't that their marriage is especially intimate, though more than adequate in that area for both of them he assumes, and much more so than a number of his colleagues at work seem to constantly complain about. Perhaps it's the expectation of disappointment that cools the ardour of not just them but their partners too?

It just feels 'right' when she is there with him. She has sometimes misinterpreted this as some kind of male chauvinism for which the police service still provides such an excellent breeding ground. However, apart from when she is being deliberately obtuse for whatever reason, he is relieved to know that she does not see him in that way - and never has done.

The gate banging next door in the early morning wind and rain has not helped matters, although it did interrupt a fairly disturbing dream in which, like the case, there seemed to be no logical or convincing reason why things were happening in the way that they were.

He had found himself walking behind Zoya Agarwal along a fairly high coastal cliff path with a sheer drop to the sea below. Suddenly (and he knew his heart had started racing at this point) she had taken a left turn - except that there was no left turn: no conceivable route for her to take.

He had run towards the point where she had disappeared from view and peered over the edge, whereupon his head had caught up in some kind of material that clung to his neck. No matter how hard he tried to extricate himself - and he must have been rolling from side to side of the bed, thrashing his arms around at this stage (perhaps better that he was alone after all!) - he couldn't do it.

Then, in one of those wonderful warm moments of recognition and relief, he realised that he had poked his head through a canvas being painted by Edward Mills who was standing beside him, smiling. Zoya was not at the bottom of the cliff, her mangled body being pushed around by the waves after all. However, some lingering anxiety was provided by Kate Shelbourne sitting right on the cliff edge, her legs dangling over the edge, reading a book before turning to face him, tears pouring down her face.

At that point he had woken up with a jump, gasping for air. His mouth must have been wide open for ages as his throat was completely dry, his face wet with sweat. He'd need some kind of psychologist or dream specialist to interpret that trail of events; perhaps, while they were at it, they could solve what had quickly become one of the most bewildering cases of his career thus far.

The gate continues to bang. He knows what has happened there at least. The family have two young boys who always enter their house through the side gate leading to a back door into the kitchen. The younger one often fails to press the catch fully home and so, when the wind is in a particular direction or is especially strong, the latch of the gate bangs monotonously against its preferred fitting. Longing to be caught but not quite able to do so of its own free will.

Either the relentless thudding noise or the trauma of his restless sleep has given him a nagging headache. At times like these, he wonders what it must be like to have to get up to a constantly crying baby: how parents ever manage to survive such assaults on their sleep patterns. It isn't something he'll ever experience, of course, unlike the parents of Gary Jones and Zoya Agarwal, for whom the cries must surely never cease.

***

"Down dropt the breeze, the sails dropt down,
'Twas sad as sad could be…"

Ian Flowers glances across at his brother, lying quietly, not needing to imagine the stillness – the morbid silence that has filled so many of his days.

"Water, Water every where,
And all the boards did shrink;
Water, water every where,
Nor any drop to drink."

Rob's lips are dry, but, after several minutes of struggle with the usual, involuntary facial movements, he is able to sip from the glass of water Ian patiently holds as close to his mouth as he can get.

"That tastes so good!" he acknowledges gladly, as though he has just drunk a glass of vintage champagne.

"Mum says your cough's been a lot better today!"

The broad grin and shining eyes confirm that she has indeed voiced this, whether it is true or not.

"Shall we continue?" Ian smiles at the rhetorical question. Rob grows tired easily – even more so these days it seems – but never of hearing Ian read to him. It has been the same since the days when Ian first learned to read, and his brother learned how difficult it would always be for him.

His brother nods his head up and down (and side to side) vigorously as Ian continues to read the unfolding Rime.

"… more horrible than that
Is the curse in a dead man's eye!
Seven days, seven nights, I saw that curse,
And yet I could not die."

They arrive back at the wedding feast at last, although, like Ian's brother, the Ancient Mariner will never know the joys of marriage. Never be able to settle or know true peace, not while they are surrounded by water. Rob is serving penance for something unknown that will always haunt him. No albatross will fall from his neck, no wind will fill his sails for long.

Words fill the void to some extent and, while they may take him away – sometimes far away – Ian is happy in the knowledge that they will always bring him home again.

He watches him now, fighting to stay awake, and places the precious volume of 'English Romantic Poetry' on the bedside table and switches the lamp off. A night light instantly bursts into life, banishing the darkness. Perhaps he will have a peaceful sleep at least. Ian kisses his forehead gently, motionless at last.

**

Detective Superintendent Hunter-Wright has snatched the phone out of its cradle. Mercifully, the noise has now ceased but the voices remain. One of them is speaking in his ear now, hurriedly - urgently. It's happened hundreds of times before of course. He digests the information as quickly as a waking mind can, allowing him to engage with the process and issue the appropriate procedural responses. It also leads him, rather shamefully, to a fleeting sense of relief followed by the all-encompassing despair that has been his sleeping partner for far too many years.

He sits up, dragging an extra pillow over from his right, and hits the M1 button. Moments later a sleepy, almost disembodied voice answers.

"You need to meet me by the canal, just above The Commandery. Now."

CHAPTER SEVEN

Harcourt parks just before the police cordon. It looks as though most of Sidbury has been sealed off. He hurries past the line of stark, grey soldier's helmets, embedded in the side of the bridge, briskly down Monarch's Way to the right of the old Sidbury Gate, and past the Commandery towards the canal's towpath.

He remembers sitting outside this fascinating and ancient building – more than 800 years old – which had been the headquarters of the Royalist army leading up to the defining Battle of Worcester in 1651. Not that Debbie had been especially interested of course. She had been quite content to sit quietly in the sunshine, consuming latte after latte, quite at peace with history coming to an end, and with no desire to re-live it.

They'd watched a canal barge, jauntily painted in blue and red, pass into the lock and then descend as the water poured out of the unseen gate below. He'd been amazed at how deep the lock actually was. Obviously, it needed to be low enough to let the boat continue its journey under the bridge, and on towards Diglis before joining the Severn further down, but still, the lock could probably have contained three such boats on top of each other. More disturbingly, he was reminded of a coffin being lowered slowly and irrevocably into a grave: swallowed until it was all eaten up.

All history now of course. The poor girl who might also have frequented the café - even travelled along the canal herself - had met an earlier destination than either she, her family or her friends could ever have imagined. Every bit as traumatic as any nation-defining battle in which there could be only one of two outcomes: live or die.

He shivers as he ducks under the branches of trees adjoining the path, still wearing their early autumn green. He can now see the stationery blue lights in the near distance suggesting that any traffic planning to come down City Walls Road has been diverted at the Saint Martin's Gate roundabout.

A young female officer in uniform hands him the Crime Scene Entry Log Sheet to sign then wordlessly waives him under the blue and white police tape which immediately gives the scene a far less natural look. It's difficult to be sure in the early morning light but her face seems unnaturally pale. Perhaps she had been the first officer on the scene? If not, she had definitely seen something that would remain a high-definition image in her mind, no matter how many times she tried to switch channels.

A white tent comes into view just beyond a slight bend in the path, blocking out everything beyond it. If only it were that simple, he considers, slowing as he approaches it. At that exact point Hunter-Wright bends his huge head as he exits the tent, not so much out of silent respect, but more in quiet contemplation of what has happened and what needs to happen next.

"Response Officers have the area sealed off and SOCOs are in situ." This is by way of greeting. "Young girl – possibly late teens to early twenties. We await Dr Graham's expert analysis of course, but I see no obvious marks on the body to provide us with a cause of death. With the bloating and colour of the skin, I'd say we're looking at another drowning."

"Who found her, sir?"

"Middle-aged couple out walking early. He has a heart condition so they try and get out when they're pretty sure nobody else will be around; apparently, crowds upset him."

"Must have been a terrible shock then!"

The older man nods. "Medics are keeping a close eye on him. The wife saw something under the water just above the top lock gate. She thought it was a rusty bucket – you'll soon see why – that might have fallen off a passing boat or been chucked in by some idiot. Then they saw that it was attached to what looked like clothing. Thankfully they couldn't get close enough to be able to turn it – her – over."

"Do we have any ID yet, sir?"

"Nothing at all. I've ordered a Missing Person search, but we don't yet know who we've found. Shoes and overalls are in that yellow plastic box. Do take a look."

It isn't a suggestion. Harcourt dons the protective garments – much too late to protect the unfortunate victim, he thinks, grimly – and enters the tent. A photographer, also decked from head to toe in white, moves to one side, revealing the body, mercifully still covered in jeans and, beyond a band of white flesh, a once white blouse that would surely have been far too short or thin, whatever the season.

A mass of copper-coloured hair, strewn out beside her, partially covers her face, but not enough to prevent a sharp intake of breath. From the colour photograph on their incident board, he is pretty sure that the soaking, putrid body lying defeated at his feet was until very recently inhabited by the irreverent, independent spirit known as Barbara Flint.

***

Once again, we are so very sorry for your loss." Taylor hears the words, as Valerie and Tommy Flint do, but they are pointless to her ears – serve no real purpose beyond the required platitude.

Tommy is slumped in an old, moth-eaten armchair covered in some kind of faded *Freedom* throw in once vibrant colours. Valerie sits quite upright opposite him, on a hard chair that Harcourt has brought in from the dining chair. Taylor's eyes keep tracking back to the maroon cushion for some reason, as though that particular detail could somehow be important. Perhaps she is simply trying to avoid the confused, questioning expression on Valerie Flint's face or, worse, the vacant, silent stare of Barbara's father.

"You say that Barbara left the house at about ten o'clock last night, Mr Flint?" Harcourt is patiently trying to not just move the conversation along, but to somehow create a conversation at a time when silence really is as golden as the memories that have climbed into play in the grieving parents' minds.

Seeing that her husband is not going to reply, Valerie steps in. Her voice is hard, not soft; controlled, not wobbly. She will go through the angry phase first, both detectives have detected. "She was meeting Colin – Colin Pearson. I don't know if anyone else was involved."

"Were they planning to go on anywhere afterwards, do you know?" Taylor is as relieved as Harcourt that there has been some response but knows that this new flow could be short-lived.

"She didn't say, but then I didn't ask her. I should have known, shouldn't I? Should have known what her plans were. Do you know what I mean?"

Taylor nods helpfully.

"Was it at Colin's house they were planning to meet, or a bar perhaps?"

Her question is met with silence.

Harcourt leans forward, slowly but with intent.

"Mrs. Flint?"

It does the job.

"She was seventeen for Christ's sake! Of course, she wasn't going to meet him – anyone – in a bar. We – Tommy – introduced her to alcohol at an early age, so that she would get used to it first. The strength of it: do you know what I mean?"

Both police officers nod, each keeping an eye on Tommy

Flint who does not nod.

"Besides which she's still at school; well, college at least. She hasn't – hadn't – even sat her A-levels."

"Could she have got mixed up in something? Maybe fell in with the wrong crowd?"

"That's a bit of a judgement, Inspector. Each to their own, in my view. What you choose to see only from the outside, some of us try to look beyond that; to try and understand what makes these kids tick, you know."

Harcourt does know – only too well.

Valerie Flint isn't so sure. "You people just look to harass them until you lose their trust and then wonder why they don't communicate. They're young souls, uncertain of their futures. Often, they just need a bit of time and space. Let's not forget that."

He doesn't and won't.

"She wasn't in with the 'wrong crowd' as you so distastefully put it. There's no such thing. Groups of kids come together through shared experiences and shared ambitions. Labelling them arbitrarily as 'good' or 'bad' is going to get you and them nowhere; do you know what I mean?"

He does.

"You mentioned alcohol Mrs Flint; was Barbara exposed to any kind of substances…"

"Drugs! Don't be so stupid. She knew all about what they could and would do to her. I daresay others have experimented – it's an age thing – but not Barbara. We would never admit such filth in the house."

Her husband continues to stare at nothing much in the middle distance.

"Why" The affronted mother continues. "Have you found something in her body?"

"We're still waiting for the tox report, but we aren't necessarily expecting to find anything. This is all just background research. We're trying to build a picture of your daughter's last few hours. Anything at all that you can tell us will be invaluable I assure you – and will, of course, be treated in confidence at this stage. We don't even know if we are looking at a criminal investigation or another tragic accident."

"Accident! Perhaps Barry Jones was right all along – about Gary's death I mean. It does seem unlikely that three young people have, on three separate occasions and in three different places, drowned as a result of 'accidents.' Wouldn't you agree?"

Harcourt knows that this is anger talking, but no reply from him is going to diffuse it. Besides this, given the short timeframe, he is increasingly of the same opinion. Most people would and will be.

Taylor tries a different tack. "I know this must be very difficult for you Mrs Flint, but was Barbara close to Colin?"

"Only as friends if that's what you're driving at. Not sure I'd have wanted it to go any further either."

"Why do you say that?"

Both detectives have been waiting for just such a moment – a throwaway line; verbal litter that the person discarding it never expects to be picked up by anybody else.

"Just that Janice – Janice Mills – came to see Barbara, here. It must have been the day before yesterday. She was very upset but don't start asking me what it was about because they went straight to Barbara's room. I could hear Colin's name being mentioned though. From what I could gather he led Janice on a bit of a dance."

"Did she come round often; Janice I mean?"

"Barely at all. It was usually Barbara going out to meet them – either in town or very occasionally down in that Pickerton place. Edge of beyond if you ask me. I think she met Janice's grandparents once, but just once if you know what I mean. She thought he was pretty stuck-up; I do know that."

"And where did Gary Jones fit into all of this?"

"His family used to live next door to Colin Pearson's. They used to go on holiday together when the boys were younger, but I'm not sure they saw each other that often after Gary's father moved them to Malvern."

"Did Barbara and Gary get on?"

"What do you mean by that, exactly?" Valerie Flint's heckles are clearly – and unexpectedly – raised by the question.

"Just trying to work out who got on with who; and who didn't?"

"Barbara adored Gary; everyone did."

"You'll understand that Gary's parents are also finding this hard." Taylor cannot forget her 'non-meeting' with the man.

"Forgive me if I don't show too much sympathy for Barry Jones. His poor wife, yes. Whatever persuaded her to want to spend her days with a man like that I'll never understand."

"You didn't like him?"

"If he was a feminist vegan with a soft spot for Amnesty, I'd still find it tough, to be honest."

"And the others? How close were they? I mean, I know they were all in a friendship group…"

The older woman smirks at Taylor's attempt to use the current vernacular of youth. "I think that particular phrase covers a multitude of sins."

"Enlighten me!" Taylor isn't going to be put back in her (much older?) place quite so easily.

"Just that they all hung out – the five of them – but it wasn't all 'Five spend the best years of their lives together.' Barbara hadn't a lot of patience with them much of the time, especially Zoya."

"Why was that do you think?" Harcourt again. He isn't convinced that this is the tight-knit group that the outside world saw, and most certainly isn't now.

"Barbara got on with pretty much everyone, alright? I just think she found Zoya Agarwal a little bit worthy.

Sorry, that sounds like a terrible thing to say after… and I'm no better, am I? What mother lets their seventeen-year-old daughter go out in the middle of the night without really knowing who else she might have been meeting or when she was planning on coming back?"

"I appreciate it's very difficult…"

"It isn't difficult, inspector, it's unexplained. I would say that's far worse, wouldn't you? The pain might be difficult to bear, but at least we know what it is – what the symptoms of it are. I assume we will somehow come to terms with it, one day, though I have my doubts right now. As to the unexplained, well, we might never know what happened or why it did. You're not exactly making much progress so far, or are you going to tell me differently?"

As she finishes the sentence, tears begin to stream down her face. Taylor leans towards her with a wad of tissues. Tommy's expression doesn't alter; it's as though he is in some kind of trance.

"Be assured that a Family Liaison Officer will be with you shortly Mrs. Flint," Harcourt offers. "To help you through this. I'm sure you're feeling – both of you are feeling – completely raw at this point and I'm so sorry that we have to ask you these questions. You'll understand that time is very much of the essence, and it is so important that we glean as much information as quickly as we possibly can."

"And yet it's just a human construct, isn't it? Time!" Tommy's expression hasn't changed in the slightest, but the words had undoubtedly come from him. "The only thing that's real is what is happening right now; nothing else."

Harcourt is wondering whether this is as penetrating a philosophical insight as it sounds, or whether Tommy Flint is 'away with the mixer' as the lads down at the station would no doubt shorthand his output.

"Where were you last night Mr. Flint?"

"Why on earth do you need to know that?" Valerie Flint has dried her tears or, rather, swatted them away. Her slow burn is getting faster, and hotter.

"It's purely routine and many of our questions today are simply designed to eliminate people from our enquiries and in no way meant to incriminate."

"He was with me all night, weren't you Tom?"

Again, there isn't even the slightest flicker of recognition on the man's face.

"He was working in the studio and then came straight to bed; must have been before midnight as I was reading until about half-past. That's when I put the light out."

"And you said that you're not aware of any problems Barbara might have had. No enemies of any kind." Taylor is not about to be put off by Confucius in the Corner.

"We talked about everything; I mean everything, you know. As a mother and daughter, I don't know how we could have been any closer. I would have known if something was up."

And yet, you didn't know where she'd gone or at

what time of day or night your teenage daughter – your only daughter - was planning to come home, thinks Harcourt, silently admonishing himself for being brutal while simultaneously recognizing that procedure was everything in critical interviews such as these.

***

Lance Pearson had been decidedly underwhelmed when he saw the two detectives flashing their warrant cards in his face. His wife had told him of their previous visit to interview Colin, though the man looks much younger than she had described – or maybe he was muddling it up with someone else. So many faces.

DS Flowers sits opposite him, while DS Farren has sunk into the sofa to his left, notebook and pen ready for action.

"I'm sorry. Colin is in the library. He has an Economics exam at the end of November – nothing serious, just an internal progress thing I think, but he's taking it very seriously."

"Good to hear," Flowers is encouraging, "What other subjects is he taking?"

"Business Studies and Media Studies. Not entirely sure about Business when he's already doing Economics. I would have preferred him to take a science to keep his options open, but he wouldn't be told."

"Does he have a clear plan of what it is he wants to do, or is he just focusing on getting good grades at this stage?"

"Oh no. Colin knows exactly what he wants. Always

has been decisive – more like me than his mother in that regard. No, Colin wants to set up his own media company to handle celebrities: image rights, that sort of thing."

"There must be a lot of money in that, especially these days?"

Farren can see how tired the man is and knows they won't have much time.

"It is, and that is at the heart of the issue. Making money. It's also the point at which Colin and I tend to go our separate ways."

"You were always interested in a career in medicine?"

"No. I was always interested in being happy and healthy; in my experience money usually gets in the way of both those things. Anyway, as a GP I'm not sure if I achieved either." He doesn't smile at the irony of his situation.

Farren cuts to the chase. "We understand that Barbara Flint may have met up with Colin on the night that she died?"

"Possibly. I'm not his keeper."

"I wasn't suggesting that you are, sir, but it would help us if you could remember your son's movements on that evening."

"I got in quite late. We had a budget meeting at the surgery. Nothing serious. We have them every four weeks or so. Anyway, it must have been gone nine when I arrived home. Marion had left me some food in the fridge; can't remember exactly what it was now. Some kind of cold pasta. Sorry, you're probably not interested in that kind of detail, are you?"

He looks up but neither of his visitors gives him any visual encouragement, so he just continues.

"Colin was in because I could hear music coming from his room. I ate my supper and watched some TV before heading up at about eleven. The music was still playing. I shouted 'good night' but got no response. Nothing so very unusual about that. I read for a while and Marion got in just after midnight. I'm afraid she's on shift at the moment so I don't know if she saw Colin or not. I certainly didn't see or hear him leave the house. He would have said 'bye' if so, or some kind of semi-coherent mumble at least."

"You have heard the sad news about Barbara I assume?"

Farren isn't at all convinced that Lance Pearson is as fluffy as he is making out. The man is a doctor for goodness sake.

"Of course. Marion had seen it on the local news. Terrible business. Have you arrested anybody yet?"

Farren ignores the slight dressed up as a question. "Did she ever come to the house?"

"Never, as far as I can recall. I think I met her just the once, when they were all off out somewhere and called in for Colin. Gary was still alive. I do remember that but couldn't tell you exactly when that would have been."

"Gary's family used to live next door we believe?" Flowers goes off-piste.

"They did. Moved about four years ago. The boys stayed in touch. What of it?"

"You – the families – saw less of each other I take it."

"Malvern is somewhat further away than the garden fence."

"But you were close – as families I mean. Did you not holiday together?"

"We saw each other a fair bit, but then we were neighbours! I'd hardly say that camping trips to North Somerset were akin to bonding expeditions to the Kalahari. Besides, it would never have been enough for Barry Jones by then. Glamping maybe, but soggy mattresses in a field would hardly have enhanced his place in the social universe he wanted to star in."

Farren tries to diffuse the situation. "So, coming back to Barbara Flint, you wouldn't have known if something had been bothering her. Colin didn't mention anything?"

"My son either has his head in a book, accompanied by headphones on his ears, or he is asleep."

***

"He didn't have his headphones on that night, though, did he?" Farren remarks as she and Flowers head back to their car. "Not if his father could hear music coming from his room."

"He probably did!"

Flowers looks at her enigmatically.

"Go on."

"Just that he might have had them plugged into something else… somewhere else."

***

Claire Reed is relieved that the bus is on time. She knows her mother was planning to go down to the Tesco at Evesham that evening, and doesn't want her to go alone. It isn't that she doesn't trust her to go, do the shopping, and come back again. It's just that she is so easily side-tracked these days. She smiles inwardly at the reverse psychology of her, a teenager, looking out for her mum. It isn't funny though.

She notices the diminutive figure of Sarah Jones get on at the next stop and head down towards her. She acknowledges Claire with a smile. Beyond that, there is little chemistry between them.

She watches as Sarah sends a text, then leans back in the seat and closes her eyes before a ping makes her jump.

"Sorry!" she mouths to Claire and, then realizing the bottom half of the deck is half empty speaks. "I forgot I'd got my volume turned up!"

"Not as bad as Anthea on Tuesday when she forgot to turn her phone off!"

"I know. I thought Miss was going to throw it out of the window."

"More fun if she'd tried as the window was closed at the time…"

They giggle their way out of Worcester, but, as green trees and fields replace traffic and frayed tempers, they grow silent once more until Sarah offers. "I didn't realise that you lived out this way."

"In Wood Lench, yes."

"My Gran lives in Rous Lench, just at the foot of the hill. I'm meeting my mother there – hence the text to reassure her that I'm on the right bus!"

"How is she doing? Sorry, if that's too personal…"

"It's fine; thanks for asking. Mum's still in shock, I think, and spending a lot of time over here where it's quieter. Dad thinks it's for the best, or at least I think he'd prefer Mum to come over here than for Gran to stay with us at home. They don't get on very well."

"I was so sorry to hear about Gary. I didn't know him, although I saw him around. I remember him giving his Head Boy speech at the beginning of term though."

Sarah appears to be watching the traffic coming towards them as the bus waits to leave the A422 before heading up the hill towards Flyford Flavell. Once the main road has been safely crossed, she relaxes back into her seat.

Claire notes that she hasn't commented on her brother's speech. Perhaps she shouldn't have mentioned it – especially if her mother is still having such a hard time with it.

"It's such a funny name isn't it – Flyford Flavell! Like a place name in a comedy sketch?"

Now it is Claire's turn to relax. She is relieved that no offence seems to have been caused by her thoughtlessness. She grins back. "I thought we were in Black Pear country, not Blackadder's!"

Sarah laughs out loud. "How are you finding History?"

Claire considers that this is a little like asking 'What's Geography going to do next?' or, worse, 'Are words important or impotent?' She smiles inwardly as she hears herself dutifully reply. "Vietnam is such an interesting period isn't it? When the superpowers were flexing their muscles for the first time since Korea, I suppose."

"I remember my brother talking with my father about it – or rather him talking at my brother. He said that the communist invasion set the country back years, but then he is a businessman."

"My dad just thought it was a terrible waste of ordinary peoples' lives over misguided principles of what was seen as right and wrong at the time. Nothing is ever so black and white – just as Miss said. He also said it was easy to judge things in retrospect, but that there were major flaws on all sides."

"Lies, lies and Richard Nixon!"

They both laugh out loud this time, easy in each other's company.

Sarah half turns in her seat. "What does your father do?"

"He's a proofreader; used to work on newspapers.

Mainly fiction now, but occasionally some juicy non-fiction projects."

"Wow. He must be very patient. Needs to show a lot of attention to detail I mean."

"He does, yes. I asked him once whether it became easier if he was engaged in what he was reading or not."

"And what did he say?"

"He said it worked both ways. If he was too interested his brain would make connections more smoothly and fill in the correct spellings and punctuation automatically. Which is not what he is paid to do. On the other hand, when he's bored with it, his mind tends to drift off and then he misses things anyway."

"I can see why he prefers the middle ground!"

"Your father's a financial adviser, isn't he?"

"Sort of. I'm not sure he'd thank you for calling him that, but, yes, he advises clients on where to invest their money. Usually, people who are already rich and want to get even richer."

"Or people who worry about being poor again, going back to where they came from."

"Wow. I can see why you're doing RE!"

They both laugh again, not a silly, giggly teenage exchange, but rather a knowing engagement from two young women on the cusp of adulthood.

The bus stops suddenly alongside The Boot Inn, as though the driver has decided he needs a quick drink before he can go any further. Although it is only 4.30 on a weekday afternoon in late September, the car park is packed. Groups of mainly middle-aged men in ill-fitting shirts, just about hiding a multitude of reasons not to exercise, stand or sit at the benches in the 'garden' below fading canopies advertising exotic beers from further afield. Along with the swallows, those promises have long since flown away.

"Your mum's retired, isn't she?" As the bus (and its presumably still-parched driver) moves off again, Sarah's question is easy to answer, yet hard to fully explain.

"That's right. She was a lawyer. Took early retirement. Dad says it had become too pressurised and came at the right time for her." She isn't ready to say much more until (or if) she gets to know Sarah much more.

"I think my dad thrives on the pressure; says it comes from Grandad."

"Is your grandfather still alive?"

"He is. Lives not far from here, in Pershore. One of those 'gated communities.' Not sure if that's to keep the residents in or the 'riff-raff' out, to be honest."

"Do you visit him often?"

"Hardly ever. He got into some kind of financial trouble, though Dad did OK out of it, I think. Prefers his own company now, especially since Nana died."

"So, it's your mother's mother you're visiting."

"It is. My mum's family lived in a very different

world to Grandpa's. Mum was brought up on a council estate in Tolladine. She trained to be an accountant, but I suppose she saw that an even faster way out of there was with Dad. Her family were from Bridgend originally and probably thought Worcester was an upgrade. Granny still tells me about using the newspaper in the toilet just about every time I see her!"

"She's at that stage?"

"A bit."

Again, Claire would love to share her experience of her mother's strange and increasingly irrational behaviour; would love to just lighten the load a little bit with a real friend. It seems to her such a betrayal to even talk about it with her father, as though acknowledging it makes it just a little bit more real. He is great about it, to be fair, but the hurt in his eyes when they do refer to it is both unmistakable and unforgettable.

They are about to enter Rous Lench village and Claire is still intrigued as to the non-response when she'd mentioned Gary's name earlier. Perhaps it is part of the grieving process still. Clinging on for all its worth like one of those green 'sticky weeds' that persisted in holding on to the arm of her cardigan, long after she'd finished 'helping' Dad in the garden last weekend. She's been lucky not to have had to face death in the eye yet. "Did Gary take after your mum or your dad?"

"Oh, Gary was a Daddy's boy."

The response – or rather the expression of it – is much more strident than she had been expecting. Perhaps that phase has passed, after all?

"He liked the money!"

Sarah has become much more serious now, unsmiling – almost unfriendly too – but with no sign of accompanying or enduring grief.

"He liked what he thought he could buy with it. He presumed he could own everyone – make them do anything he wanted, whenever he wanted it. Never forgetting to smile at the same time of course. That big, fat grin… sorry, this is where I stop. See you tomorrow?"

***

He can hear a woman screaming. Could it be Sheila?

Shards of moonlight occasionally break cover and appear on the lake's surface as the breeze gently blows the water away from him. He crouches down under a small line of trees that runs down to the water's edge. His right knee cracks (they never did sort out that cartilage properly) but probably not loud enough to carry.

He can just about make out the edge of water and land, but the trees and swathes of nettles just beyond them make progress risky. There's probably a path that would take him around both, but he can't see it and plainly can't use his torch.

The wooden cabin is about two hundred yards ahead of him, where the lake appears to bend around to the right, although he can't be sure; can't remember. He looks up but the grey clouds have become even thicker now, a few lower, lighter wisps racing along with the wind.

A splashing noise draws his attention to the far bank. His eyes can't make out any kind of movement to corroborate what his ears have reported back. Probably a bird diving into the lake, its night vision far more attuned than his.

When he turns back to the building which he has been observing from a distance for more than a month now, he sees a shaft of light on the decking. The door is open, just a crack. Though the screaming has, mercifully, stopped now, he can hear the unmistakable sound of voices, arguing. There are at least two people in there.

He holds his breath though the cold logic of day would tell him that he couldn't possibly have been heard from there. And this isn't daytime, it's gone midnight.

He silently urges Sheila to make a run for it – escape from whoever has been keeping her captive all this time and, miraculously, as though his prayers have been instantly answered, the door does open, fully. A woman strides through it and stops at the wooden rail running around the whole cabin at waist height.

She isn't trying to run away; she isn't trying to escape, and she isn't Sheila. He would know her anywhere, even in this light and from this far away and after the thirty-eight years of marriage they would have celebrated together on the Thursday just gone.

A shadow pools behind her. It becomes darker as a much taller, male figure appears. It speaks, or, rather, shouts.

"We're not having this conversation…"

"But…"

"We're just not. OK?"

"It's all happened so quickly, I never thought…"

"You – we – couldn't have known that. We cannot throw everything away now; now that we're so close."

"That's two of them now. There's only two left!"

"Just a matter of time then."

"Joe's going to be in the area soon. He's bound to come here."

"Why is he 'bound to come here? Have you heard from him?" The man is much closer to the woman now, menacingly so. "It's not as if he's been back for years, is it?"

"I just feel it in my bones. I sense he isn't too far away."

"You spend too much time out here on your own, imagining things. Getting things out of proportion."

"I didn't imagine the drowning though, did I? Neither of us did."

"Accidents happen."

"We should have said something at the time. We could have found a way past it, her."

"But we didn't, and you absolutely cannot say anything now. It will be far worse if you do and, who knows, it might not stop the accidents coming."

Bob watches as the man places both arms on the woman's shoulders, pulling her closer to him. Like a spotlight, the moon suddenly lights the scene, and he can see that those same hands are now perilously close to the woman's neck.

CHAPTER EIGHT

Rupert Hunter-Wright watches them file into the meeting room. He's turned the heating up, not just because it's a chilly autumn morning, but because he likes to see them sweat: see who can handle the heat when it comes right down to it.

He notes the heavy, dark rings around Harcourt's eyes. No doubt the man will bleat to him later about how stretched his team is, despite being given a new sergeant, though, admittedly, no new constable to support them as yet or any concrete sighting of DC Hanrahan. Flowers had done a good job in acting up (without acting up) so far and would have to do the grunt work as well for now. Perhaps, if they were all doing their jobs better, they'd get more chance of sleep.

The new one – Farren – looks as fresh as a proverbial daisy. Possibly not working hard enough. As for Taylor, well, she fixed his little quota problem and hasn't turned out too badly. Better than he thought. Not sure why she appears to be staring at him though. Perhaps it's a woman thing; he'd have to ask Miriam later.

They wait for the effeminate one – Flowers. He smiles inwardly at his little witticism. The latest word is that he's a fan of poetry. Fine words no doubt, but unlikely to translate effectively when trying to interpret the special vocabulary spat at them by the scum of West Mercia.

Upstairs are getting nervous – not that they ever aren't when the press is nosing around – particularly as they appear to have made no progress with these cases whatsoever. Like him though, they are loathe to call in extra help, even at this stage. The stigma of their force not being able to solve crimes on its own patch far outweighs any perceived benefits and, even (especially) were it to result in a breakthrough, the slight on their professional capability would be long-lasting. No, that simply wouldn't do at all.

He sits patiently while Harcourt laboriously goes over what they do know, using the whiteboard to illustrate points and people. The man is so dull. Had he been a teacher, truancy levels would doubtlessly have reached an all-time high. There is the usual multiplicity of arrows and lines linking all of it together. Except that the lines are dotted. What they need is solid evidence, not conjecture. Possibilities are all around us. So is love, allegedly.

He stands abruptly and watches with satisfaction as each of them sits up a little taller. "In short then, we have absolutely nothing to go on!"

"Sir, I still don't think we can rule out the possibility of these being isolated, unconnected incidents."

It's like looking back at a Radio Times cover from the 1950s and seeing an unsuitable actor playing at being a detective: a misfit in glorious monochrome.

"You may not have done, but I and most everybody else can. Though it pains me to admit it, I suspect that Barry Jones is going to have an absolute field day."

"Sir?"

He ignores the new one. If she can't understand that then she should go back to Police College. 'I can't stand losing you' fills his head. Except he can. He wouldn't mind not seeing any of them ever again.

"There must be a connection between first a young boy drowning and then two of his close friends following suit quickly, and I do not believe that the common denominator of 'accident' is the clue. Even less so, 'unexplained.' We don't do that here, not on my watch anyway. What is clear is that you have not yet found that link and to pretend that there isn't one is frankly ridiculous."

Harcourt is blushing of course. Well, let him feel it. Let him show it to the rest. Three people have died here. If there's a Holy Trinity of failure, embarrassment and hurt feelings then so be it.

He watches as DS Flowers knocks timidly and enters the room, apologizing deferentially as he takes a seat next to Taylor who gives him a reassuring look. Reassuring?

"Thank you so much for joining us today," he laces this with as much sarcasm as he can muster without exploding. "I hope you've had a well-earned rest?"

"I'm very sorry, sir. I wasn't … I got here as quickly as I could."

"Which didn't include breaking the speed limit!"

"Of course not, sir."

Another blusher. What is it with these apologies for

men? They are employed to solve crimes – protect the public from themselves – not look and behave like clowns. Nobody finds it funny, least of all, him. 'Sex and drugs and rock and roll' would be preferable to the sense and sensibility sitting in front of him.

"So, ladies and gentlemen," he raises his voice now as the air conditioning fans grumble their way into action, "Gary Jones dies in a tragic drowning accident at Pickerton Lake with apparently no witnesses other than the group of friends who were with him at the time – two of whom are now also dead.

Nobody saw anything when Zoya Agarwal walked straight into the River Severn and drowned herself, apart from this Nancy girl who, I understand, is a bit flaky. Claims to have seen someone from a distance that our witness who was right next to the second victim assures us that she categorically did not see.

We have now recovered Barbara Flint's body from the Worcester Canal. Tox is clear and the pathologist can find no injuries consistent with death other than by drowning. There is, as yet no known motive for this. Not for the young lady herself nor from anybody else. We have no CCTV either?"

"Nothing of any real use, sir."

'Real use.' It's either real or it isn't. Useful or useless. He's surrounded by fools while they disguise themselves as wordsmiths. "Explain."

"Well, sir, we do have very brief footage of Barbara Flint walking quickly past the external St Martin's Gate car park camera before a second camera above the

Cattlemarket car park that picks her up again at 8.22 on the evening in question."

"Could she have been arranging to meet a car driver, parked in either one? Got confused as to where he or she had parked?"

"Unlikely, in my opinion, sir. She was walking briskly, as I said."

"Head down? Trying to avoid the cameras, but being caught anyway?"

"Nothing that suspicious, I'm afraid, sir."

"Alone?" Why does he need to drag these things out?

"Quite alone, sir." Harcourt watches his superior shudder, either because of the message or the messenger, he's not sure. "She appears to be talking though. DS Farren and DS Flowers reported that Barbara had an earpod in one ear when they visited the house. She was listening to music on that occasion, but it could just as easily have been Bluetoothed to her mobile."

"She could have been talking with someone on the telephone?" Hunter-Wright's mind is playing a Blondie song in the background, but hanging isn't an option here. Sadly.

"She could, yes, sir."

"Or talking to herself?"

"Also possible, sir, though she isn't gesticulating as such. People tend to use their hands and arms much more when talking to themselves out loud."

Perhaps that's why the Italians are always in such a mess, Hunter-Wright considers, darkly.

Harcourt also appears to be talking to himself, gesturing appropriately towards the street map in front of him. "She walks away from the Cattlemarket quickly; we don't catch up with her after that."

"But there's no mistaking it's her?"

"None, sir."

A thought stirs in Flowers's mind; not yet fully formed but the genesis of an idea at least.

Farren looks reluctantly at Hunter-Wright. Drawn up to his full height in full uniform, he seems more like a prosecuting barrister, summing up events to date for the jury. Except that there is no defendant.

Taylor is trying very hard to be professional – drawing inwardly on all those hours, days, and weeks of training. And yet, she knows she is failing and is doing everything she can to prevent that knowledge from appearing on her face. A big white man: a bully. How can generations of women with her heritage ever really get past that?

Harcourt takes all of it personally of course. He can only explain the 'who' and the 'where;' the 'why' escapes him as it has done for so long now. Innocents also trying to escape yet drowning on their way to somewhere else. Or had water been their destination all along, whether they had known that in advance or not; understood it?

"To conclude," Hunter-Wright's voice has boomed

through each audio chapter leading up to this point, "You have found nothing. Consequently, we understand nothing! We do not know if, in fact, there is anything more to know, or whether any or each of these young people's stories would reveal more, were they still here and able to tell their tales.

I for one do not intend to remain ignorant. My superiors – your masters – are not inclined to accept the seemingly inevitable open verdicts that would be sent down. Barry Jones and each of the other parents need answers and we are going to provide them.

Additional resources from other forces have been recommended to me – even from Scotland Yard itself. I don't need to tell you what that would mean for each of our careers. I also do not necessarily think it would make a real difference in the conventional sense. There is no obvious motive behind any criminal activity in either of these three cases nor the means by which one person has hurt another. If they were flying solo, then so will we – for now.

It is only a hunch, but somebody somewhere knows something, saw something. We need to find that somebody, but it is also clear that we do need help. Extraordinary outcomes call for extraordinary insights."

***

"What was he like then, this 'psychic' that Hunter-Wright wants to bring in?" Farren is back at her desk, though facing the door slightly in case her boss – or his – comes into the room without them realising it. There are just the two of them for now. Taylor volunteered to go on the sandwich run.

"Daniel Reed?"

She nods encouragingly.

"He's not what you'd expect?" Flowers reddens and responds a little too quickly.

"What would I expect?" Farren has noticed this; her interest piqued.

"I mean. What I mean is…"

He is more flustered than normal, even though he has calmed down a lot in the days and weeks since they've been working together. Farren can see though that today there is something – or somebody - else. It isn't just her presence that is so unsettling for him.

Flowers manages to grab an imaginary stick and steer a more familiar course. "He isn't… odd, weird in any way. I thought he would be, you know…"

"Intense?"

"That's the word, yes. Oh, and he's good with words too, although I don't believe he loves them in the same way that I do."

Farren has an instant, and slightly involuntary flashback to her childhood home, the shelves of books; her mother reading quietly in the far corner of the room.

"He's a proofreader – used to work on the local newspaper."

"What does he do now then? Read tea leaves or something like that?"

"Not that I'm aware of. I don't think he enjoys the company of rabbits' feet either!"

She suddenly realises that, if she isn't very careful, her irreverence is likely to make her quickly irrelevant in her colleague's view of her (at least, externally). She doesn't want that. Of course, she doesn't. It's just that she's already met far too many charlatans in her short career for her open mind not to have locked some of its doors. Supposedly empathetic people had too often been exposed as the manipulators they really were. She'd learned that from her colleagues in vice.

"I'm sorry. I thought the use by police forces of people with so-called 'extrasensory perception' – is that what it's called – had been ridiculed. Condemned even?"

"And I think you'd be right. When they found out that Mr Reed was helping us earlier this year, Worcester News ran a headline along the lines of 'Cops go mental for answers.' Nobody needs that kind of publicity, do they?

"I can't believe that the Detective Superintendent of all people went along with it then, let alone actively exposing the force to ridicule again now. I know we have little to nothing to go on with these cases, but still?"

"There was a lot of opposition at the time. Mr Reed had helped the force years ago, working with the previous DCI. He was much like you – and all of us a bit I suppose

– in that he didn't believe it would help but, like us now, was getting nowhere fast. Mr Reed managed eventually to 'see' the location a little girl was being held at, but not before DCI Cummings tried to frame somebody else and, even after the case was solved, never gave Mr Reed the credit he should have had."

"Which, again, makes me wonder why Hunter-Wright would be any different?"

"That previous case was more than twenty years before he arrived from West Mids. I suppose he came in with an open mind and no baggage from it - and the fact that Mr Reed was successful in helping us to link a perpetrator in the present to a then unsolved disappearance from the past must have helped."

Farren has had too much extensive training in police interview techniques - not to mention the seemingly endless days stuck in a psychology 'lab' during her student days - to know when someone is holding something back: usually the most important thing or things.

"I'm sure it did," she continues gently, "but there's more to it than that isn't there?"

Flowers turns away slightly, wordlessly proving her point. Just as she thinks she may have gone in too quickly he turns back to face her. She can see that his eyes are slightly moist but she isn't sure if it's sweat or something else.

"You have to promise me that you will keep this secret" he whispers.

"Of course!" She leans over towards him, but not so much that his mind will head off in a different direction entirely.

"No, Linda. I mean it. DS Taylor doesn't know about this, and I only found out by accident when I found DI Harcourt comforting the Super in his office."

"Comforting?" Now she's properly intrigued but can see that it needs a sensitive approach. Not something she is particularly known for.

"It was during the Julie Beech case after they dug up the remains of her body after all those years. The Super was crying. DI Harcourt kept saying 'You mustn't give up hope. Without a body, there is no ending.' The Super kept shaking his head and saying: 'That's the problem!'"

"What did he – they – mean."

"I went to see the DI a few days afterwards. It was a bit scary, I mean I had no right to see or hear what I did. But I couldn't unsee or unhear it. He was brilliant with me and eventually took me into his confidence. Hunter-Wright lost his son when he was just twelve years old."

"Oh, God! How dreadful."

"I don't think he's a believer – not in that kind of spirit anyway! His son wasn't killed – at least there was never any proof – he just went missing."

"When was this?"

"About a year before he moved down here – partly because of all the upset I imagine. The boy would be thirty now if he's still alive."

"The poor man – well, potentially, both of them. So, each time a Misper case comes up, the Super is reminded of his own 'loss.'"

"Of course. He wasn't allowed to be on the investigating team but their leads ran dry very quickly – much to his frustration no doubt. You know: wearing the jacket but unable to press any of the buttons himself. It supposedly ruined his marriage."

"His wife held him personally responsible for not being able to find their son?"

"At least subliminally, yes. I guess she needed someone to blame when the hope ran out. DI Harcourt told me that she had never wanted to leave Birmingham in case the son – Michael – somehow found his way 'home' again, only to discover that they were no longer there."

"But Mr Hunter-Wright sought a fresh start because of it?"

"I don't know about that. He must certainly have been conflicted over it though, mustn't he?"

She nods. "The pain must have been almost unbearable. And there have been no sightings, here or anywhere else in the country?"

"I think there was a potential in East London, but the Met didn't get very far with it. Other than that, nothing. It helps to explain why the Super cannot leave the unexplained alone though doesn't it? If there's even the remotest possibility of discovering what happened to our victims, then he's going to want to at least give it a try."

Farren nods her assent again, believing in the sentiment, if not the expectation of any kind of success leading from it.

"But you mustn't tell anyone, OK?"

"I won't."

"Because very few people know about it in West Mercia."

"I won't. I promise. You have my word. I do get why he is prepared to try your Mr Reed out, but it's still a big risk, isn't it? Do you think he's hoping to get some information about his son too?"

"I guess that must be part of it, mustn't it? Besides, not everyone was so sceptical about the use of Mr Reed. I think it was the Evesham News that argued that everyone has the ability to see inside someone else's aura: it isn't just the preserve of the psychic even though they may be better trained on non-verbal clues I imagine."

"So, do you believe in all this stuff then?"

"Mr Reed explained to me that this 'stuff' might just be a heightened awareness of something we could all learn."

"I prefer to think I'm in control of my own destiny, thanks very much."

"But the angels and spirits are just guides," Flowers is aware, even as he speaks, that he sounds like an evangelist, "They help to lead you in the right direction. You still have to make the decisions for yourselves. If you take a different path at the forks in the road we all come across, they'll be working to get you back on track again, via a different route. Like a SatNav! This is the basis of all true faiths, isn't it? Even if people believe that their lives are pre-ordained and their destinies decided in advance, they don't know what they are or how they're going to get there."

"You spoke with him a lot then, this Mr Reed?"

"Not a lot, no. The DI spent much more time with him than DS Taylor or I did. I did come to understand though that there isn't just one common 'gift' that people like him possess."

"Oh, it's a gift now, is it?" Farren is trying to remain level-headed, seeing how much Flowers appears to have been taken in.

"Some might call it that, yes; I suppose for others it could be described as a curse."

"This 'common gift' that is so unusual; which one does he have then?"

"I think he called it 'psychometry.' It means he feels things – energy I suppose – from objects, artefacts. The idea of it isn't new: it goes back to the nineteenth century."

"I suppose our resident historian provided that backup."

"DI Harcourt? No, I haven't spoken with him about any of this. Mr Reed says that the essence of it is that every single thing gives off an emanation."

"A what?"

"An emanation: something that comes directly from a

single source. Find the source and you'll understand what happened next."

"I thought the use of psychics had been discredited in the force?"

"Not exactly discredited. Distanced from, perhaps. In the case Mr Reed worked on for us previously, there were no obvious connections. A bit like here. We all suspect there is something, or someone, joining them all together, but we don't yet know what it is. That's where people like Mr Reed might be able to help us."

"Right. And his crystal ball, which in this case is full of rocks, allows him to see into the future does it?"

"Not the future, no, although I believe he did get occasional flashes. He could mainly feel things that had happened in the past."

"Nothing supernatural about that; I used to do the same after a late night out."

***

Harcourt has been trying to cut down on sugar, but not too hard. It isn't that his sugar levels or indeed his BMI is especially beyond the recommended parameters for a man of his age, but he doesn't want it to get out of control again. The blood pressure tablets have certainly helped and his annual check-up in August had been fine, or at least a 'proceed with caution' verdict.

Today is most definitely a two-sugar day. He'd picked Debbie up from Birmingham Airport the previous evening and, thanks to a relatively clear M42 and the roadworks finally being finished on the M5, they had got home just after eleven.

She'd fallen asleep almost as soon as her head hit the pillow and was still sleeping as he'd crept downstairs in the early morning sunshine to make tea for them both.

She is tapping away on her mobile when he returns to their bedroom.

"Everything OK?" he asks, placing her mug between the detritus of phone charger, purse and three packets of peppermints – each half-opened.

"Fine. Thanks. Just making sure everyone got home OK." She clicks an imaginary full-stop (or, much more likely, a 'send' button) and throws her phone on the bedside cabinet, narrowly missing the hot tea.

Harcourt knows better than to ask any further questions at this stage. He's just glad to have her home. He's managed OK of course, but it just isn't the same when she's not there.

"Anything exciting happened while I've been away?"

She's not interested in his answer, of course. It's no different to people wishing others a 'nice day.' In most cases, the sentiment is little more than a platitude. His wife may be attempting conversation, but he can spot closed questions a mile off.

"Nothing of any great interest." He decides not to mention his evening drink with Kate Shelbourne – entirely professional though it was. "Just work, eat, sleep really."

"How about the case: that poor boy and then the girl

who drowned?"

This is more like it, though he is bound to be careful how he replies, even to his wife whom he has confided in so much. "I'm afraid there's been another drowning. Another girl."

There is a genuine intake of breath. "Don't tell me she's from that same group of friends you told me about?"

"She is, was, and, before you ask, we have absolutely nothing further to go on. Nobody saw anything and, with the kind of people hanging out down by the canal I'd be genuinely surprised if they'd remembered anything anyway."

"I remember that group of lads, with their cans…"

"Almost certainly 'progressed' to equally toxic substances by now. The Royal has notified us that A&E is full of drug cases again – mainly spice coming via County Lines."

"Do you think your latest victim was involved in all that?"

"Nothing to suggest it, as such. She was only seventeen."

"Doesn't mean anything these days though, does it? Each night after dinner we'd take a walk along the quay. The number of young people – some of them very young - lying wasted, wearing next to nothing was so upsetting we didn't go out at all on the last night."

"I never really saw you as a 'quiet night in' kind of person!"

Debbie laughs out loud before quickly realizing that it isn't funny at all; none of it is. "So," she almost whispers, deferentially, "You don't know whether these were accidents, suicide attempts or even murders?"

Harcourt is at first affronted that she should lay their dilemma out so starkly, but she's right: they don't. She isn't being unfair or unfaithful to him. Surely that would never be the case. "There's nothing in the two girls' backgrounds, and certainly not in the case of Gary Jones, that suggested any underlying pressures to hurt themselves. Nor were there rivals, enemies as such who might have wanted to cause them harm. As for accidents, we don't believe in the rule of three, even if Gary's was just that – a tragic accident."

"Bet his father's having a field day now!"

"Barry Jones? The latest post on Facebook declared that he's joined all of the dots and come up with a picture of police incompetence, shaded with disinterest around the edges. He's created a page for all of those living in West Mercia who share similar concerns. It's only a matter of time before others do the same and then you've got an active national campaign group aligned against the police. Our Police Commissioner isn't so independent that he isn't worried about how it will affect his own job, which is why he's been bending Hunter-Wright's ear about it."

"And Rupert's bending all of you around a big stick!"

"You've got it!"

"No news, I assume."

"None. It can't be easy for him, especially after..."

"Time doesn't always heal – not completely at least."

She holds his hand gently; sympathetic, understanding. "I suppose grief hits people in different ways: anger and sorrow... different coping mechanisms?"

"I thought you read chic lit on your holidays?"

She lifts her head to look right at him, before quickly realizing from his face that he has issued her with a compliment, rather than a criticism. She returns his smile. "I do, actually, and had plenty of time to read!"

"Not shopping or bar stooling?"

"A bit, yeah, but there's a limit to how much hair and make-up fixes you need in between times. I found myself reading on the balcony a lot of the time."

"Nothing wrong with that!"

"Nothing at all, apart from being a bit lonely and wishing you were there with me." She leans towards him, and he gladly folds his arms around her, beaming inwardly as tiny necklaces of hot tears on each of his cheeks reflect in the early morning sunshine, like treasured jewels.

**

"I don't understand why it's caused so much fuss!"

"Not so much a fuss as a misunderstanding."

"You seemed quite upset about it though."

"Just trying to marry arcane grammatical rules with

modern usage."

Daniel Reed and his wife Charlotte are sitting in the 'Apple Barn' restaurant at the Evesham Valley Shopping Centre, which has almost single-handedly squeezed the commercial lifeblood out of Evesham's historic town centre, much like an apple in a cider press.

It's all horribly contrived of course: a faux 'high street' bisecting 'designer' outlet on the way to the ubiquitous garden centre, which also sells clothes. Five minutes from the picturesque village of Broadway at the gateway to the Cotswolds, it is a popular stopping-off point for coach parties of tourists needing breakfast or lunch to satisfy their appetites if not their curiosity.

He'd been delighted when Charlotte had agreed to join him, even though he had planned just a quick trip down the hill to fill the car up at the Co-op garage. He'd need to make sure he was ready to join the police now, whenever or wherever they needed him.

Charlotte has finished her pastry which cost almost as much as the diesel. "Does anyone honestly care about all that stuff – apart from you of course?"

"And the publisher. It isn't my interpretation, it's theirs."

He pauses to watch as a group of seemingly-anxious and quite sweaty elderly people in various sets of unsuitable tracksuits and anoraks for the unusually mild day - in all colours of the rainbow and those that never should have been created – look around wildly at the empty restaurant before settling in the far corner, well away from the windows.

"Normally, it's the publisher that is more prepared to let things flow. They're tuned into contemporary readers' preferences and it's us who act as custodians of good grammar."

"I'll try and feign interest, but only until I've finished my coffee."

He ignores the sarcasm, almost glad to hear it return in all its subtlety after the biting anger of the last few months and near silence of the last few weeks.

"The 'who's' versus 'whose' argument is unambiguous in general but becomes more difficult when we consider non-humans. For inanimate objects, we wouldn't normally use 'whose' as it is acting as a pronoun 'of whom.' One of the leading characters in my book is a film buff and refers to '...*The Railway Children* whose debut in 1970 the studio marketed as a much-loved classic...'" whereas the publisher has called it out and wants it to be changed to '... The *Railway Children* of which the studio marketed as a much-loved classic...' All we can do as proofreaders is highlight bad grammar – which this technically isn't – but also highlight what we feel is clunky, or superfluous English which I think this is."

"Jenny Agutter!"

"I'm sorry."

"She made her name in *The Railway Children*, didn't she? Red knickers and a hot, steamy environment."

"Not exactly how I remember it," he smiles, "I loved the background music though - and how everything worked out in the end of course."

"It doesn't though, does it?" She places her empty coffee cup on the drab, brown wooden tray which sits on the table between them, separating them. "Always work out in the end?"

"Charlotte – Dotty – we will get through this, I promise."

She laughs softly. "No wonder you loved that film! I can still remember you crying over *Black Beauty* too. You're right; I know we will – get through it I mean – but I'm not sure you'll recognise me on the other side. I barely recognise myself sometimes."

"We're all here for you, Claire especially."

"It's her I worry about most."

"She'll find a way. She's young and she's strong and hasn't replaced either the 'terrible twos' or 'teenage tantrums' with a tick in the 'too difficult' box. She's like I was at that age (probably you too) – inquisitive. She won't stop until she's found out all that she wants to know, no matter how long that journey is."

"It comforts me that the two of you are so close, especially after it being her and me for so long."

"We are. We talk and we listen to each other. Nothing can be more valuable than that."

"You'll miss me just a little bit, I hope?"

He shuffles around in his seat, hoping she won't guess at his discomfort. In truth, he's been missing a little bit of her each day, and he knows that it's a one-way street.

"I will but you're not going anywhere just yet so stop talking like this."

"Not physically, maybe, but my life these days is like a collection of scenes in one of your books. You know, when you begin a story and are unaware of who the characters are or how they are going to eventually fit together around a plot?"

"I certainly do!"

"Well, I sometimes forget who the characters are. I can't recognize them from their names or where they are or what they're doing. Sometimes I can, but when they evade me, I can't just go back a few pages or hit search on my Kindle to remind myself about them, when they first appeared in the story."

"We all do that sometimes, especially if the author is making the book too complex – too difficult to follow."

"I know. I know. As I say, this isn't all the time. I seem to lose people at random."

"You won't be losing me." He smiles reassuringly.

The smile is welcome, but her fears are not assuaged. "Everything is so fragmented and what makes it worse is that I won't be able to get to the end of the book to work it all out, will I?"

He wipes away her tears with his hanky and fleetingly remembers his mother who would have been appalled if he'd ever left the house without a clean hanky in his pocket (shorts or otherwise). "As the last doctor said, we need to take it day by day. Don't worry about the weeks or months."

"Or years? It's good that you're so resilient. You've learned how to be. I know how much redundancy took out of you, especially as you'd found a job you loved."

"You were a fine lawyer too."

"Adequate and usually effective. Not fine. I found that out quite early on and so did they. That's why I became an employment lawyer.

"I think you're being much too hard on yourself."

Daniel sits back, relaxed, which hasn't always been the case over the last eighteen months or so. The doctor told them there would be days, possibly weeks now, of lucidity; nobody knew for certain. Science spoke about phases. He looks up and sees the moon, faint now in the western sky, but still there all the same. On a beautiful morning like this, it's hard for him to believe that anything about her has fundamentally changed or is about to.

She hasn't noticed him stargazing. "I was so wrapped up in my own failure that I wasn't there to help you when you probably needed me most?"

"I could always talk to you."

"Even when I didn't listen to a word you said. I was so angry and irrational all the time I probably didn't respond well to logic – still don't!"

"Don't forget that I wasn't there a lot of the time either. Like you said, there were many long evenings after you'd come home from work, when Claire was younger.

You might have found things much easier if you'd had me around more often if only to explode at."

"Late-night proofing came with the territory. I always knew that. They couldn't print anything until you'd completed all your tasks, could they?"

"I do miss it sometimes. I know it's all changed through technology and everything. Digital assistants are gradually phasing all of us out. But there was something about that daily deadline. It made us all feel alive somehow – that human spirit responding to the task at hand - even though we were usually half dead afterwards. Once the adrenaline left our bodies, we tried to replace it with alcohol. After-work drinks in private bars were never going to work. At least I knew it at the time and didn't go down that path when I left. My liver would have been crucified."

They are interrupted by a sudden crash. The young waitress dressed all in black has dropped a tray of drinks near the table where the elderly customers have congregated. Daniel can see immediately that it was caused by her tripping over one of the plethoras of handbags, rolled-up cagoules and what look like army surplus kitbags, all dumped next to their wooden chairs and forming a physical – and psychological - barrier between her (anyone) and them.

"Imbecile!" bellows a thick-set, bald man of about seventy.

"I am so sorry," the waitress is bright red in the face and bending to pick up the debris of broken latte glasses. "I'll sort this out then get you replacements as soon as I can."

"Damn right, you will!" The affronted would-be sergeant major figure isn't in the mood to be placated, even as he leans over to try and look down the front of the girl's blouse. "Why they can't get decent people in here I'll never know!"

Charlotte has always assumed that whenever they are out somewhere six or seven paper napkins will never be enough, or that invisible 'guests' might join them perhaps? As for sugar, there are more silver spoons on the table in front of them than could be found in Eton. Daniel picks up a large handful of the napkins and races over to help.

"Here, use these," he hands some of the paper over while gingerly picking up the larger pieces of crockery and placing them on the tray. "Don't cut yourself on the glass."

The girl nods appreciatively while the deeply affronted others just sit, shaking their heads or lifting their noses in disdain at the unfortunate scene before them.

"You should let them do that!" Sergeant-major exclaims loudly. "It's what they're paid to do."

"Accidents happen." He responds softly. "Try and show a little kindness."

He exchanges smiles at the waitress who raises her eyes slightly in response; tired eyes that haven't yet seen enough of the good things in life. Daniel moves one of the kitbags slightly to retrieve a piece of glass. As he does so, he looks back up towards the man, seeing him sitting there, quite alone now, looking out of his kitchen window as an ambulance leaves the house for the last time.

Satisfied that everything is now under control, Daniel gets back to his feet and makes to return to his own wife.

One of the elderly ladies eyes him, pityingly, before loudly offering her view of the world to her crumpled companion. "No wonder the country is in such a state. People just don't seem to think that standards matter anymore…"

She is interrupted by a figure looming over them. Nobody has seen Charlotte leave her seat and traverse the floor. She cries out. "Crown versus Gingham, May 21st 1955."

There is a shocked silence. Daniel is the most alarmed of them all, fearing that she is about to kick off or, well, kick.

Charlotte doesn't break stride. "A coach party of old folks were charged with breaching the peace through their unreasonable and potentially slanderous behaviour. Do be careful how you treat other people."

The waitress looks at her as though she might be a modern-day goddess whereas those who had previously been concerned about the state of society are left in quite a shocked state as Daniel accompanies his wife back to their table.

"I assume you made all of that up?" He whispers.

She grins in appreciation. "I never did like gingham dresses and it seemed too respectful to refer to them as elderly! I thought your date of birth was a nice touch too."

Daniel can only beam at her. He hasn't seen that look of triumph on her face for such a long time.

"You wouldn't have witnessed such a slice of real life from behind your desk in a newspaper office!"

He laughs. "It all seems a long while ago now, doesn't it?"

"It does. I wish we'd been right at the time about my symptoms, though." She has quickly become serious again, sad even.

"Thinking it was one of the effects of the menopause you mean?" How he wishes he could hold on to the fading light.

"At least I would have been able to plan things better; knowing within reason what to expect.

"Do any of us know, though? I think reason is an over-rated word."

"Especially if you think that the worlds in which we live are actually absurd. What if our foundations are based on a fallacy?"

"Discovering that is the source of many mental health problems – I read a research paper about it a few weeks ago."

"Or perhaps it is the source of true enlightenment."

"Something a 'progressive' from the 'Sixties might have said!"

She laughs, more to herself than with him. "I think I'm passed the drugs stage now, aren't I? Not much room for future growth… A lot of your time is spent going back in time to get nearer to the truth. For me – and people like me – it has the opposite effect. The further we go back, the more removed from reality we become. I guess I'm just frightened by it. What if I find a version of me in the past but can't then join the dots to form a picture of me in the present? I'd be well and truly lost."

He leans forward to take her hand in his, cool to touch and so small to hold on to. "I had to proof a business book some time ago when the self-styled entrepreneur stated that 'the only thing to fear is fear itself.'"

"Do you believe that?"

"It comes from a universal fear of the unknown doesn't it: a primal survival instinct to be on our guard and assume something or someone is bad, only trusting to 'good' later."

"Probably easier to deal with than being let down later or knowing that you've been totally wrong about someone or something you thought was good at the outset?"

"Maybe. The writer of that book went bankrupt!"

She howls with laughter. "Is that why the police suspect 'everyone and everything'?"

"I suppose so, but it's also far too easy to go through life assuming someone is guilty until proven innocent. Remember that West Indian guy who took his company to a Tribunal because they sacked him after finding out his brother had been involved in the Brixton riots in 1981? All that guilt-by-association rubbish?"

"We won the case though."

"Of course, you did," he acknowledges with a rueful smile, "but do people like him ever really win?"

"Do you think you'll be able to help them this time?"

"The police?"

"I remember that you got on well with that detective before."

"Harcourt? Yes, there's something a bit odd about him but if I can help them to progress the investigation, I guess that's a good thing."

"Terrible. All those drownings. For everyone. They can't be coincidental, surely?"

"You wouldn't think so, would you? Neither as a lawyer or one who reads a great deal of fiction."

"I suppose their suffering was quick – not drawn out?"

"Well, we don't know that. Of itself dying alone - if they did die alone - is desperately sad, isn't it?"

"Yes, it is."

The sudden silence hurts his ears. He looks directly at her face. Quite pale now, he watches the slight twitching of muscles in her cheeks. He sees the woman he has loved for so long perched on the edge: of what, neither of them quite knows.

She is aware of his stare if not yet the concern behind

it. A welcome flush of colour seems to revive her for now. "It's incredible that nobody appears to have seen anything."

"Oh, but they did. They always do. It's just a case of who saw what and when. Now, are you ready to climb the hill?"

"Depends on who's asking?"

***

As Kate Shelbourne hurries down Mealcheapen Street on her way towards the Costa where she has arranged to meet Nancy, she spots the bearded gentleman in a scruffy old green anorak and, somewhat incongruously, yellow beach shorts. He is sitting cross-legged on the concrete pavement to her left.

He has a white, china mug in front of him, featuring a faded picture of The Queen and the word 'Jubilee' in blue letters. She assumes it is a remnant from the celebration five years ago, rather than any realistic forward planning for the one in five years (should Elizabeth II make it that far).

As she draws nearer, she can see that the cup has a crack in it, but not so large as to allow the few copper coins within to fall out. Its owner raises a huge ruddy face towards her and asks her in a broad Scottish accent. "Afternoon hen; could you spare ten pounds for a cup of hot chocolate?"

She smiles back, noting the pockmarks on his weathered cheeks and the callouses on his huge hands.

"Are you importing that particular brand especially?"

He grins. "Oh aye! I have a fleet of ships along the canal there. Self-made man, I am."

She smiles again, simultaneously waving at Nancy who is standing outside the coffee shop.

"Another time, maybe."

"Fine. You'll no make a better investment, though; I'm telling ye."

Leaving him alone, she greets her friend. "Hi. Did you want a coffee?"

"I had one while I was waiting, thanks. How are you? I see you've been tapping up the locals for information."

"Insights, Nancy. Insights!"

Her friend laughs. She looks much too pale to Kate but then Kate does forget how see-through a porcelain complexion can seem.

They head off, down past St Paul's Church and onto the street bearing the saint's name.

As they join Foundry Street, Kate feels compelled to ask the question she would ask easily as a reporter, much less so as a concerned person. "Have you heard from him?"

"No. Nothing at all."

"He hasn't been round at all?"

"No, I haven't seen him since we met last time."

Kate isn't entirely sure if Nancy is telling her the whole truth – it wouldn't be the first time she has held things back – but nothing but the truth is an assumption she's happy to make today, given the call she'd received from her the previous evening. She's certainly less stressed now than she had sounded then. Still reserved though. Still Nancy.

"You said you'd been reading an article about the drownings?"

"Yes. In Worcester News I'm afraid; not yours."

Kate feigns a tone of disloyalty. "I can't believe you'd do such a thing to me!"

It does the trick. Nancy visibly relaxes as the canal bridge leading to Park Street approaches. "I'd heard about it on the radio of course. We have it on in the hotel all the time when the manager's out. Obviously, given what happened to Zoya Agarwal I was interested to know if the circumstances were similar, you know?"

Kate nods her understanding. No extra words are required.

"So..." She hesitates as a twenty-something man in a smart charcoal suit approaches them. Kate notices him looking her friend up and down while naturally ignoring her completely.

"Go on."

"Well, it's not clear is it: whether she just walked in, fell off or was pushed into the canal? Nobody else seems to have seen anything."

"Nobody else?" Kate feels a tingle of excitement.

"I saw the picture of Barbara Flint and it was then that

I realized I'd seen her before – on the night before her body was found." They have reached the bridge and Nancy stops to face the towpath running to the left of the canal. "I'd been walking around Fort Royal Park; just wandering round and round, you know? I was nervous I suppose. The job at the Fownes Hotel would have meant more money; quite a big step up too. Anyway, they'd asked me to go in to meet them later in the evening, once the main rush in the dining room was over, to meet both the duty manager and the restaurant manager. It must have been about half eight?"

Kate watches a small longboat chugging slowly towards them, its movement causing a slight swell on either bank. She has long since understood that if she is to get to the whole truth of events, she has to listen to the whole story first. She can filter out the important bits later.

Nancy continues as if she is no longer there, almost trance-like now. "I took a shortcut along here and was going to cut through, past Kwik Fit. I wasn't in a hurry though. I'd left plenty of time to get my thoughts together in my head. It was beginning to get dark, but I could still see quite clearly.

"And that's when you saw Barbara?"

"She was down there."

"On the towpath or a boat?"

"She was running away from me along the path. I know it was her because she stopped for a moment and turned around."

"To face you? Maybe she'd heard you walking across the bridge?"

"Oh no! It wasn't me she was looking at. She turned to see how far away from her the boy was!"

"The boy?" Kate's throat feels almost completely constricted.

"Yes. The boy who was chasing her."

"You're sure he was chasing her, Nancy?"

"Quite sure. Although it was a bit gloomy, I could see the panic on her face – in her eyes."

"Would you be able to describe him? The boy who was chasing Barbara?"

"Of course, I could… can. He was the same boy who was following Zoya before she walked into the River Severn. I can picture him now - clearly."

Moments later, Kate is retracing her steps back to the car she has parked in Worcester's Cattlemarket. Deep in thought over whether she should tell the police immediately or do a little more investigation of her own first, she hasn't noticed that the Scottish beggar she'd encountered earlier has moved his pitch closer to City Walls Road.

"Now then, good woman!" He hails her as though catching up with a much older friend. "Tell Bono and me: did you find what you were looking for?"

More startled than she might have been had she not been in deep thought since leaving Nancy to make her way back towards Diglis, Kate is quite relieved to see him. "I did, thank you." She drops a ten-pound note into his cup which, incongruously, has even fewer coins in it than just an hour or so earlier.

He looks at her, dumbfounded at her generosity, before trying to stand. "Thank you so much, darlin'."

"Don't mention it. No, really; don't mention it." She leaves him there, drowned out by the traffic thundering past: watching quietly now as people and places pass him by.

It's only money, she considers, and not only can it not buy love; it can't buy a way out of loneliness either. She knows that feeling all too well.

***

DS Flowers has been inside The Royal many times before. He must have visited enough different wards to have qualified for a loyalty card, such has been the requirement to sit with victims or protagonists, listening to what words they can muster up; taking statements.

He has never visited the High Dependency Unit before though. Neither has his mum. This isn't a place where anyone has the right to distinguish between the good and the bad. There are no judgements to be made here - no witness statements to be examined. There are just babies who have usually grown into children or adults, only to fall seriously ill, no matter what nature and nurture have done to them in the meantime.

The plethora of tubes beginning or ending in white machines with rows of multi-coloured flashing lights are familiar of course. He remembers them from episodes of Dr Who when he was a young boy. Had he been lucky enough to have grown up to be a Time Lord, as he and his brother had planned, he'd have whisked all of them away from this place, this period in their lives.

They've been here for the best part of a day now, having been rushed in just after breakfast. Mum hadn't had time to make sandwiches and so his stomach is grumbling over that fact. Not that it matters of course. Very little does when it comes down to it.

He's told the DI of course. He, in turn, has passed on his and the team's best wishes. He's grateful; of course, he is. At the same time, good wishes may make the senders feel a little better about themselves, but they're about as useful as prayers. He gave up on those years ago when the towering priest had loudly chastised him for only having ten pence to put in the collection plate one Sunday morning. Many Sundays have passed since then, though no church has witnessed his presence in any of them since.

Mum is putting on a brave face; just as she did all those years ago when Dad left. Just as she did when Dad finally got in touch again and she informed him politely but firmly that he no longer had a place in her life. The three of them have formed their unique version of a High Dependency Unit since then and, increasingly, provided intensive care for its youngest member.

Rob isn't going to get better. He hasn't moved for

over an hour now, although both nurses and doctor have told them that this is somehow 'normal.' Man-made constructs can preserve only the status quo: the equilibrium of things that are supposed to be so good for us.

Mum is talking to him, asking him what time it is, even though a clock sits up high on the wall opposite, silently counting down minutes, hours maybe? She looks so tired, though it is him that feels it. They'd been woken by his brother having some kind of fit, the likes of which they'd never seen before, and likely never will again.

He thinks back to the previous evening: how they'd read some poetry as usual, nearing the end of the Rime that has so captivated him. Rob had been attentive, concentrating hard on endless, restless seas while simultaneously gazing way beyond both him and the bedroom window across the neighbouring fields spun gold by the setting sun, and up into the shadows of hills.

He had eventually drifted off into unaccompanied dreams where life's edges became softer, and words eventually dissolved into water:

'I pass, like night, from land to land;
I have strange power of speech;
That moment that his face I see,
I know the man that must hear me:
To him my tale I teach.'

CHAPTER NINE

Daniel is acutely aware that the people sitting around him are, to varying degrees, thinking: 'Has it honestly come to this?'

On the cynicism scale, DS Farren – who he's just been introduced to as a new member of the team – is probably at the top end of it. Attractive and seemingly outgoing, he knows that this is much less the case than her colleagues might think. He observes but does not buy the persona she is trying to project.

Quite surprisingly the senior officer – Hunter-Wright – is probably the most welcoming of all of them. Gabby Tylor is as introverted as ever, and Harcourt is merely hanging on to every word his boss is imparting. No DS Flowers.

"So, as you can see, this curious situation has arisen whereby three similar events have no obvious connection to each other, with no supporting evidence as to cause or, indeed, motive." Hunter-Wright looks around to see if any of his officers have anything to add.

Only Harcourt is prepared to volunteer. "We'd like to keep a lid on your involvement, Daniel. That's not to say we don't welcome your expertise and look forward to your working alongside us…"

"Just find the connection!" The Detective Superintendent cuts across him. He has little time for flannel. This Daniel does remember, but it is very different from the officer he worked for (alongside?) years ago – DCI Cummings – who made characters in The Sweeney look like social workers by comparison.

After Hunter-Wright has wordlessly but with maximum impact left the room - all of them (including Daniel) standing to attention as he does so – Harcourt beckons Daniel into his office.

Daniel is reminded of how stark it all is. Several cases must have passed through since he was here earlier in the year, and yet nothing new seems to have stuck. There are still no colour photographs, nor yellowing green spider plants fighting for their parched lives.

"They were keen to bring in another force; West Mids almost certainly."

"Isn't that where the DCI came from – before he came to this force I mean?"

"It is. Don't mind him. He has always been angry – or at least since I came over here three years ago. I believe his father was a policeman too, but it's not something he has ever talked openly about. He certainly wasn't going to have them tramping all over our patch and discovering the clue or clues we've missed so far."

"A rearguard action then?"

"Something like that."

Daniel sees a man, not necessarily tired or emotionally

strained, but not at peace with the (his) world either. He'd picked up on this previously – the damaged aura – but, like so many 'professionals' he had worked with over the years, there was also a defensive ring about them which would require a long and sustained attack to break down. Hunter-Wright is similarly broken. However, this is not why he has been called in.

"The girl – Nancy Gutteridge – whom Mr Hunter-Wright mentioned - swears she saw a boy following Zoya Agarwal before she went into the river. I don't doubt that she believed that to be true but she's not the most robust of witnesses. She was bullied by an ex-boyfriend and seemed to be frightened of her own shadow when Flowers interviewed her. Besides, we also have a statement from the lady who was actually on the riverside at the time – Miranda Ann Clackerton. She was right there and yet she saw nothing."

"Interesting. And your instinct is to go with the older lady who was, did I hear correctly, feeding the swans?"

"It is; you did and, yes, she was."

Daniel looks up, expecting to see an amused face looking back at him, but encounters only insecure eyes, darting continuously from left to right, unable to settle. He decides to try a different angle as a result. The entire team appears to have conjured with the 'did she/didn't she' see something scenario for so long that they cannot burst that particular bubble.

"But all of this began with the death of Gary Jones, which you believe to be accidental - a belief the Coroner has now officially recorded as the cause of death?"

"She has, yes. There wasn't a shred of evidence presented to us or discovered by us that suggested otherwise. I'm a bit 'old school' I suppose in that there's an element of doubt that remains with me after unexplained or 'accidental' murders. The truth is, I have nothing to challenge it with and, if there is anything – anything at all – we're hoping you might be able to provide it."

He hands Daniel a colour photograph of Gary Jones – not one that has been released to the media.

Daniel sees a family portrait of two adults and two children in bathing costumes on a beach with a brilliant blue sea as the backdrop. Unless it's been heavily doctored by Photoshop, it's an image saved for posterity of an unashamedly happy family.

"The girl is the sister?"

"Yes. Sarah."

"I sort of recognize her. I think she may be in the same school year as Claire. We had a meeting at the school at the start of term; I think Sarah may have been there with her mother who I do recognise."

"Taylor met with both of them: Sarah and the mother, Cerys. The mother wasn't able to give us much at all, upset to the point of practically losing her voice!"

Daniel notes that this is rarely the case, though there are numerous motivations for such behaviour to be portrayed.

Harcourt continues, not noticing the other man's

scepticism. "Taylor reported that Sarah was a mousy little thing. Not at all like the father."

"The Superintendent mentioned that Colin Pearson often went on holiday with the Jones family. Not this time then?"

"Unless he was the one taking the photo? Talking with Colin's family, we think that this effectively ended some years ago, when the Jones family moved to Malvern. Gary must be sixteen or seventeen here, so unlikely that Colin had gone with them."

"I see that Gary is wearing a bracelet. A bit unusual?"

"Because?" Harcourt leans forward ever so slightly.

"Well, most kids of his age would wear those kinds of fabric wristbands you see, wouldn't they?"

"Like badges of honour from festivals you mean?"

"That sort of thing, yes. They never seem to take them off, do they? Thankfully Claire is still happy to listen to music in her room rather than a field: up until now at least! This looks like it's gold – or meant to look like it?"

"You were right the first time: it is gold. His parents bought it for him last August. A reward for passing all of his GCSEs, apparently."

"And just over a year later, he's dead! This is just too awful, isn't it?"

Harcourt nods his head. No other response is necessary.

"Has the bracelet turned up? In Gary's things, I mean?"

"As you said, it was never taken off. His parents insisted

on it being buried with him. They couldn't bear to look at it anymore."

"That I can entirely understand." Daniel can't help feeling a little deflated, but there would be more clues yet: other 'artefacts.' Much as he hates that word (it sounds as though it should refer to man-made objects from much longer ago) it does reflect a human loss. It reminds everyone that beyond the rotting flesh, there was once a living spirit here; one which interacted with others, just as they are doing now. He will have time to dwell on this later. For now, he continues. "And Gary was the archetypical 'nice kid next door?'"

"Nobody seems to have a bad word to say against him."

"Don't you find that a bit odd in itself? I mean nobody's perfect, are they? As soon as the press report on the 'nice guys' you know that they're simultaneously hunting dirt to dish out on them."

"You're right, of course, but again, Gary's death does appear to have been accidental."

"Unless you're his father? I saw on Facebook that he's still having none of it."

"He's a very angry man and, you know what they say: the only thing worse than 'no money' is 'new money.'"

"You mean that he has the resources to try to influence the key people! Has the police committee been targeted?"

"They and some senior officers I believe."

"Is it bereavement or real money talking?"

"DS Taylor reported that the mother seems to have taken Gary's death especially badly. Barry Jones: possibly. It might be that he is just angry at the world over what's happened."

"Gary's friends must have found the whole episode hugely upsetting too?"

"Not what they could ever have expected to happen on a late summer's evening in such a peaceful setting."

"It must have been shocking."

"Must have. Yes."

Daniel notices a change of tone in the policeman's voice: less resigned, more questioning.

"What is it?"

Harcourt looks up, knowing there is little he can hide from this man. He'd found that out before and just about got away with it. "The best friend, Colin, has been a significant person of interest to us. Gabby Taylor considered his attitude as that which you'd expect: best friend dies tragically and there's nothing he could do about it, despite his best efforts to revive him at the scene."

"Go on."

"Something DS Farren said has stayed with me. 'Wouldn't you go to pieces in such circumstances? Would you have it in you to then visit your friends who were with you at the time, as he appears to have done, and quite coincidentally (maybe) they too have drowned, supposedly accidentally?"

"Perhaps he found comfort in being with them - talking it through with them? The replaying of a shared experience is quite natural, isn't it? Done collectively it can be hugely beneficial in cases where each individual has experienced something bad, especially something as unexpectedly tragic as seeing your friend die?"

"It's just a thought – a sentiment if you like. We have absolutely nothing to back it up; that's been the problem all along."

"People do react to death – especially sudden death – in different ways." Daniel is excited to meet Colin as soon as they'll allow it but also doesn't want to pre-empt too much. He needs to see the boy for himself. Harcourt and his team have had much longer to think about it all. "Sometimes the mind's reaction is to just carry on, even though the body will give it away sooner or later. Sudden symptoms like heartburn, shortness of breath and so on can come weeks later but they're not 'sudden' at all; it just takes the body that long to give the lie to what the mind is telling it and everybody else. Some of the more usual reactions are to burst out crying for no apparent reason, or to just wake up one morning feeling utterly exhausted."

"Possibly." Harcourt wonders again how much Daniel has pieced together about him. He adopts his 'deeply lost in thought' face which has served him so well in the past. "But if Gary was this fantastic guy – and your best friend since childhood – we might justifiably have expected the body response long before now. Instead, we have an edgy, elusive figure who might even have been one of the last people both Zoya and Barbara spoke to before they died."

Now Daniel is intrigued.

***

"How long has she been sitting here like this?" Daniel is shocked to find his wife in apparent shock, and his daughter not too far behind.

"When I got home from school she was sitting there, with a cup of tea – about half-drunk, I suppose (the tea not Mum!)"

He knows that she is not being flippant, just trying to deal with the shock. "And then you said you heard a crash?"

"I'd gone upstairs to get changed. When I got down here, there was tea all over the floor and pieces of broken china."

"Thanks again for cleaning it all up." He sees a brown stain on the carpet that, no matter how quickly his daughter began the clean-up operation and no matter how much stain remover she'd used, would remain forever a visible reminder of the scene she would play out in her mind from this day forward.

"I wouldn't have left her if I thought she was, you know, going to have a problem. She said 'hello' when I came into the room and seemed to recognise me, but I'm not sure now whether she did or not. She hasn't spoken a word since."

Daniel pats Claire's shoulder gently, indicating for her to leave them. She does so, but he senses that she has only exited as far as the kitchen, in case her mother needs her again. In case her father does.

"Charlotte." Daniel kneels gently in front of his wife who appears to not even see another person, let alone know who it is. Her face is a ghostly white. She is staring, unblinking, straight ahead of her. "Dot!' He tries again, but there is still no reaction.

"Should we call a doctor?" Claire is at the entrance to the room again.

"I'm not sure what we'd be able to tell them, or what they'd be able to tell us, to be honest." He smiles at her, before returning to his wife who appears to be in some kind of catatonic state. "The specialist did say this might happen at some point," he continues softly, "It's part of the disease I'm afraid. The mind cannot process what it sees or hears – or tastes I suppose – and so it seems to shut down, like a PC going into hibernation mode. It's still on but you can't reach it without knowing which buttons to press on the keyboard."

"So, what do we do?" Claire and her father both hear the slight edge that has crept into her voice. She thought she was going to be reading about Buddhism this evening, not dealing with a parent in an apparent trance state.

"We'll have to see if she comes out of it on her own – in her own time; a bit like someone who's sleepwalking when you're advised to not wake them up, just be there to prevent them hurting themselves."

"I thought this kind of thing was months off yet?"

"There's still a lot about Pick's Disease that they (we) don't understand yet." He is trying his best not to be patronising, but at the same time aware that it might come over that way. "They expect there to be broad phases and I think it very likely that we've passed through the first one, but I also think we have to expect the unexpected at any time, as indeed does Mum."

Reminding his daughter of this seems to relax her. She leans over to throw her arms around her father's neck, even as he continues to crouch on the floor. "I'll be happy to sit with her if you like?"

"No." He half turns to look up at her. "Thanks for the offer but you need to go and get on. I'm sure you've got lots to do. I'll see if I can coax some of that chicken into a casserole dish and let you know if and when."

Claire grins her response before he turns his face back to Charlotte. "How did it go 'down at the station' as they say?"

Daniel laughs. "Well, down at the station they seem to have hit the proverbial brick wall on every count."

"Do you think you'll be able to help them?"

"Early days." Daniel is suddenly deadly serious, as though the drowning cases mounting up, coupled with his wife's turn, can no longer provide any space or time for frivolity. "When someone as popular as Gary Jones dies, so many lives are affected – beyond his family I mean. The impenetrable part at present is that there must be some kind of connection between the deaths of Gary, Zoya and now Barbara. I'd frankly be amazed if there wasn't."

Claire stops at the entrance to the room once more and turns slowly to face her parents. "It may be nothing but, according to his sister, Gary was not the 'goody, goody guy next door' that many people say he was."

Charlotte eventually falls gently to one side of the sofa, fast asleep, into Daniel's arms, perhaps still oblivious to his presence, even subconsciously. She no longer has that fixed stare on her face, but Daniel does on his.

***

"Gordon! Come back here right now and apologise!"

He hears, no, feels her words stinging the back of his neck, just as he still hears the snarling directives from his old History teacher – Mrs Leckonby. How he had ever got past that and developed a true love of the subject he'll never know. How he had ever lost his reason in what he thought was the pursuit of true love is an even greater mystery.

"Gordon!"

She's on repeat of course, like a playlist option that's never straightforward. He turns, bright red in the face, but not through embarrassment, more a fury he has rarely allowed to meet his eyes, mouth... face.

"What do you want me to say?" He notes at least seven mainly elderly guests turning towards him from their comfy lounge chairs, trying to restrain themselves just a little but not so much as to miss any of the action.

"An apology would be a good starting point."

He regards his wife, all pink blouse and blotchy, pink-skinned bulk, taking centre stage as usual; her supporting cast hanging off her every word.

"For what, exactly?"

"You were rude to Mr. Beecham. He's waiting for an apology."

The offended man stands, frowning, at the far end of the room, in front of an unlit fire. Somewhere in his mid-seventies, he is slightly stooped in his rumpled white shirt and creased khaki chinos (presumably someone had told him it was a sporty look). If he had anything about him, he'd have reached over to place a hand on the faux marble mantlepiece. If Gordon hadn't been on a lead he'd have placed him in the fireplace and produced a box of matches from behind one of the man's enormous ears.

"I was not rude, darling," he replies, icily and fooling nobody with the labelling, "I was merely responding to Mr Beecham's observation that the hotels in Malvern used to be much smarter."

"I'm sure he didn't put it quite like that." She is having none of it, as per her policy of zero tolerance.

"No, you are quite right as usual. He pointedly looked down his nose at me and declared that I was nothing more than a parrot which had fallen from its perch."

"Gordon," she is whispering now in a tone that holds much more menace, "It happens all the time; has done for years. The customer is always right!"

"Citing grounds of diminished responsibility..."

"Gordon! Enough!" She has shifted deliberately from one leg to the other, like a footballer's feint, but presumably to vary the flow of blood pooling in her varicose veins.

Gordon steps a little closer to the aforesaid Mr Beecham. "He also informed me that we and our little establishment which he has frequented every summer for more than twenty years have become 'old' and 'tired.'"

"And he'd be right, wouldn't he?"

"I'm sorry?"

"No, you're not. We have grown older, and I am tired, that is the truth of it: tired and worn out."

"Not worn down though, I notice."

Beecham feels nevertheless vindicated and raises his wiry frame a little in triumph, though, of course, Gordon towers over him (and almost everybody else). "I told you so." He addresses an empty chair or one containing so small and insignificant a person that Gordon cannot see who or what it is from where Patricia has set up her blockade.

"What has got into you or, more importantly perhaps, what have you got into?" Patricia hisses at her husband like a snake ready to strike. Even Beecham recoils, reverting to his passively affronted stance.

"I'm through with all of this: these patronizing

nobodies, this place…"

"And me? Yes, I've heard it all before, but you always come back, don't you? Why is that?" It is a rhetorical question as he is given no time to draw breath, let alone attempt an answer. "Because temporary accommodation can never be made permanent, or it wouldn't be temporary. Cuckoos do change their tune and fly away but, guess what, the following April they're back again."

"Ah, but are they the same cuckoos?" Before she has the chance to turn it into a more general ornithological debate, he picks up a dirty glass from one of the room's occasional tables and hurls it in the direction of Beecham.

Luckily (for the small group who are seated nearby) it was only a sherry glass, and the shards sound like little more than tinkles as they fruitlessly try to reconnect on the floor. Beecham had ducked in an exaggerated, dramatic fashion and now regains his full height of just over five feet. "Like I said: things have changed here, and not for the better. I can sense it."

***

"He's a what?"

"A psychometrist, sir." Harcourt is as unimpressed by the question as Barry Jones is by his answer. "He can detect energy forces, mainly from objects."

"And you seriously think that some kind of psycho is going to help you… us?" He hasn't even let them inside his house yet, preferring to remain standing in front of them like an angry giant in front of the grand entrance arch, so becoming of Malvern in recent times.

"Mr Reed does have other gifts too, sir."

"What, like Father Christmas!" Jones is dressed immaculately in a charcoal-grey patterned three-piece suit, white shirt and yellow silk tie. Not for him online trading with the camera disabled.

Harcourt is immediately aware of his own cheap, rumpled grey jacket and brown tie with the slightly darker brown sauce stain about halfway down it. (This, of course, was the intention of the man in front of him, displaying his superiority in checks and cheques). Always up for a challenge, he continues calmly. "Mr. Reed has also helped us in the past, with a good degree of success."

"If I wanted help with events in the past I would consult my diary, Inspector. How can this possibly help us in the present and, more to the point, prevent similar murders from happening in the future."

"We still have no reason to think that foul play was involved in Gary's tragic death, sir."

"Forgive me, but I still do, especially now that you have two other supposed 'accidents' on your 'patch.' Isn't that how you people describe your domains?"

Daniel can see that this is heading for the inevitable tie-break if they continue to serve as they are doing. "I can completely understand your frustration, Mr. Jones. You want answers and you've not been getting any, despite the best efforts of DI Harcourt and his team thus far. I may not be able to find a way forward for you and your family either, but I can certainly try to read the clues we do have from a different angle."

Barry Jones bends his head towards Daniel, as though condescending to lower himself to the level of a small child or perhaps a helpless animal, pity written all over his tanned face. "The best efforts of your friend and his team have merely taken us around in circles. I see no angles; no corners to be suddenly turned. Here we are again: the police standing on my doorstep, waiting to be allowed in to 'continue with their enquiries' which now enjoy the benefit of some weirdo. No disrespect, but my son's life was worth rather more than that."

"Indeed. Which is why the police are taking a more lateral approach. Surely anything that can improve the chances of knowing what did happen to your son is worth considering?"

"I have considered it and concluded that it is not only futile but also a sad and desperate indictment of the capability of the local fuzz. I shall continue to lobby for police reinforcements if not replacements. Now, if you'll excuse me, the markets in the Far East are about to open. Life must go on, so we might as well profit from it as best we can. I'm sure you'll understand."

Barely disguising a scowl, he turns and steps back towards the door.

"Just one question before you go Mr. Jones?" Harcourt had expected little more.

Jones turns and glares at the policeman, saying nothing yet speaking volumes.

"The bracelet that Gary wore – the one in the picture your wife furnished us with: do you have it in your possession, sir?"

"I do not. Neither does my wife. We couldn't bear to touch it, let alone part him from it. It went to his grave with him. He will continue to wear it in death as he did in life."

The slamming sound of the impressive door indicates that this Act is over with no further dialogue expected.

***

"He's very stressed about it all!" Dorothy King is a plump woman with straggly, grey hair; around sixty years old, Farren would guestimate. Her woebegone expression hasn't changed since she first entered the police station and was eventually taken to the interview room to begin her testimony. "I do think you need to do something about it."

"We can hear him shouting in the garden at nobody in particular," her husband, Derek, perhaps slightly younger, certainly fatter and far more flamboyant, dressed as he is with a large daisy in the buttonhole of his khaki blazer and his want to wave his arms around to illustrate his points. Words are never enough for such people, DS Taylor notes, quietly, as King continues, "Often in the dead of night too!"

Farren clears her throat. "Presumably, Mr Drake is worried about his wife. We understand that she went missing, which Mr Drake reported to us some weeks ago. He did not follow up with us as requested, nor did he return any of our telephone calls, so we assumed that she must have returned. It is, thankfully, often the outcome of Missing Persons enquiries."

The couple glance at each other. Her expression doesn't change at all but Derek King leans back in the chair, displaying his Pooh Bear tummy, apparently trying his best not to laugh. "His wife is most definitely not coming back, Sergeant."

"If you know something about her disappearance, please tell us – now." Taylor doesn't do theatricals. In her experience they don't just tell stories with happy endings, they disguise sad truths.

"She's dead." Dorothy King utters the two words as though she were announcing the number and colour of a ball coming to rest on a roulette wheel.

Farren looks from one to the other. "Can you repeat that please Mrs King?"

"No need," Derek King quickly seizes the opportunity to take the lead, "Mrs Drake died at least five years ago."

"Six last Christmas!"

Manifestly not enjoying being interrupted by his wife, he continues; his words slower and more deliberate as if to emphasise his need to convey rather than converse. "There was nothing untoward about it. She'd been suffering from emphysema for some years. Bob told me that she'd never smoked but she'd worked in a pub in North London – that's where he met her in fact – so, secondary smoke and all that!"

"And that's what killed her?" Again, Taylor is struggling

to stick to the script which Drake is so keen to follow.

"A major contributory factor, you might say!" King pauses for dramatic effect, his jowly face betraying too many glasses of red. "She took a turn for the worst in November and went into hospital, then got transferred quite quickly to Redditch."

"Redditch?" Farren is as fed up with going around the houses as her colleague is.

"They have experts in pulmonary conditions at the Alexandra Hospital I believe…"

"And yet she died!"

"Alas, yes. It was too late to save her. She developed pneumonia you see. Drowned in her own fluids as it were."

Dorothy King punctures the ensuing silence in the same monotone voice as before. "Bob gets confused. He often forgets to lock his door or take his milk in or that his wife is dead."

Farren tries to separate the magnitude of such a loss from life's minutiae. She refers to her notes from the previous meeting. "Mr Drake seemed to think that his wife had simply left him and he didn't know when or if she'd be returning."

"Denial. Classic case." Derek King gushes, with an unfortunate wink in Farren's direction. "You can ask him practically anything about Arsenal – Joe Baker and the first European match in 1963, or their first League Cup Final five years later – and he'll give you chapter and verse, often on repeat. But if you ask him about what he did last weekend, he probably wouldn't be able to tell you. Terrible how the mind tends towards fragmentation isn't it?"

"Do you think his stress is because something has sent him over the top about his wife – maybe a memory of her being sparked somehow?"

King leans forward now, in conspiracy mode, his words suitably softened. "I think it has got even worse recently due to the shock."

"Shock? What kind of shock?" Taylor has had enough of her professional time being wasted. She isn't in the mood to dress things up, even if King has rarely enjoyed little else.

"The meeting at Pickerton Lake, I suppose. Sent him into a right old spin."

Farren is marginally more interested in the ending to the story being drawn out. "Bob Drake had a meeting at Pickerton Lake?"

"He did."

"When was this?"

"A couple of nights ago." Dorothy King chips in with a few runs from her flat bat.

"Well, it was a meeting in the broadest sense of the word, darling," King admonishes his wife directly this time, "But not one that Bob initiated or took part in exactly."

Again, the detectives are forced to wait while King

gathers himself for the final, killer delivery. "I think he had heard about the drowning of that poor boy down there, and somehow got it into his head that his wife might have suffered a similar fate. I do know he'd visited the spot a number of times lately, and often at night. Well, on this occasion he saw and heard a very tall man arguing with that gypsy woman who lives down there much of the time. Pretty angry, he said the man was, telling her to 'keep quiet or else.' That's how Bob put it, anyway. The words might have become lost in translation, but he was certainly affected by it. I'd even go as far as saying he was scared for himself, let alone for the woman."

***

"Loved himself a bit too much, didn't he?" Farren accelerates away from Welland, skirting the silent, moody Malvern Hills to her left and heading back towards Worcester.

"Some people love an audience," Taylor looks straight ahead as she replies, "especially when they're putting on an act."

"You don't believe him?"

"I think what he said is plausible enough; people who lose their mind do go wandering, don't they? Searching for the place where they might have left it?"

"Must be awful. As bad if not worse than physical pain I imagine."

"Bob Drake is certainly not a man at peace, but what if this is some kind of elaborate story to cover their tracks?"

"The Kings?"

"We've been surprised before."

"I'd be astonished if she had the wit to do much more than comb her hair in the mornings!"

"Wouldn't matter, though, would it? Derek King probably has enough inventiveness for them both. What if King was having an affair with Drake's wife; got found out by someone and decided to kill her."

"In the lake?"

"May even have been inspired by the accident with the Jones boy."

"What if Bob Drake saw what happened? Maybe he was stalking her – followed them both to Pickerton?"

"Could be, though no stretch of the imagination could render Derek King tall, even if his stories might be."

They both smile but the conversation has left them plenty to dwell on as the miles gradually move behind them.

***

The car door slams in the drive outside – the footsteps make a familiar sound, and not just because it reminds him of the opening sequence to 'Love is the Drug' by Roxy Music. He hears plenty of sirens every day but not that one, not for years now.

It must be Miriam. She's home earlier than usual. He can picture the scene quite clearly: ladies of a certain age in flowery skirts and brightly-covered cardigans, clearing away the top table and then each of the wooden chairs. Stacking and loading them into the small cupboard at the far end of the church hall, ready for the next group to use or abuse.

She's been in the WI pretty much ever since they moved here. He's never been quite sure whether it's the time with them that she enjoys the most, or time away from him.

They've certainly enjoyed some interesting guest speakers over the years: a beekeeper who was sadly allergic to honey; a writer of bestselling children's books who spoke for only five minutes or so, because she was so nervous and preferred to scuttle off into the little world she had created, and a successful pilot who bored them all rigid with his fond memories of Turkmenistan.

He heads downstairs, slowly but deliberately in the darkness. No need to rush. He checks that the front door is locked before heading right into the lounge where, guided by the moonlight flooding through the east-facing window, he carefully places the record arm over the single waiting for him on the turntable. Scratched and a bit pitted from use now, it nevertheless confirms that 'Love will tear us apart, again.'

He considers his own love. Long gone, but surely not yet departed?

CHAPTER TEN

"I wouldn't have described Barbara as shy and retiring." Harcourt takes a left off The Tything and down towards the Flints' house. "Not judging by what DS Farren and DS Flowers told me of her dress sense anyway."

"Oh, I don't know. I've seen so much naked flesh on some of the women I pass these days I feel sure I must have been out with them at some stage!"

Harcourt laughs out loud, even though it isn't that funny, none of it is. He feels more relaxed in Daniel's company than previously, though is still somewhat unnerved when he catches the other man watching him so intently. He continues. "We think that Barbara must have been going to meet up with someone that evening, but we don't know who. Her parents haven't been much use so far, I'm afraid."

"He's a musician you say?"

"In a manner of speaking. They call him 'Top Hat.'

Both men simultaneously begin to sing out loud: 'Top Hat! The indisputable leader of the gang...'

"How did you know that? You're much younger than me?" Daniel is feeling relaxed; the hours he spends away from Charlotte these days are like moments snatched from a relentlessly ticking clock. He feels guilty of course, and not a little concerned as to what she's doing in his absence, but to have something – someone – different to think about for a little while is nevertheless intoxicating.

"I used to babysit Debbie's nephew sometimes," Harcourt grins, "Cartoon Network was a big part of my life!"

They laugh again as Harcourt parks up, instantly adopting his default, serious expression once more. After all, this is a serious matter.

Tommy Flint opens the door to them. He is dressed in dirty, blue jeans that are trying but failing to control a roll of fat that has escaped over the waistline and is now heading down towards the ground. A black tee shirt with cut-off sleeves bears the legend 'Legend.' He stands there just inside the hallway for a little too long after Harcourt has introduced them both. His expression is vacant but both men suspect that, like a computer's disk drive, he is frantically trying to fill in the gaps and make the relevant connections in the background.

"You'd better come in." He motions them past and towards the kitchen. The too-sweet smell of cannabis smoke pervades the entire house. Whether subconsciously or otherwise, Tommy opens the kitchen's skylights, allowing fresh air in and its stale, corrupted neighbours out.

Not planning on them staying for long, Tommy does not offer seating or refreshments, so all three men stand adjacent to the kitchen units. "Valerie's not here." His attitude is not exactly combative, but hard all the same.

"That's quite alright Mr. Flint." Harcourt is relieved that the man is at least speaking. He wonders if the foggy haze has cleared in the man's head since the last time they'd been in his 'presence.' Irrespective of that it would leave an emptiness that cannot be filled (and probably never will be by family or friends). "This is Daniel Reed. He is helping us with our enquiries into Barbara's death."

"Everyone I know says it was an accident. Worcester News confirmed it!"

Harcourt cringes inwardly at the store people still put by newspaper stories.

Daniel is thinking along similar lines, especially remembering some of the aggressive characters he once had to work with; editors who would cut your throat rather than cut the copy you had marked up as being grammatically incorrect as well as often completely incomprehensible.

He looks around the kitchen. Dirty crockery fills the sink, as well as most of the surfaces including the small table that separates them. An array of yellowing plants fills the shelf below the skylight; some just dried up. Others are already dead. Without moving, he can see that many of the plant containers contain ash.

Harcourt changes the subject temporarily. "How is your wife holding up?"

"Like a buttress with a fatal crack in it!"

Both men wait for him to elaborate. Harcourt is unsure whether it is some famous quote that requires no further explanation, or a line from a poem perhaps? He'd have to ask Flowers. Momentarily, he wonders how the young DS, his mum and his brother are faring. So much suffering all around: they seem to be drowning in it. He wonders if Valerie Flint has found it all too much. There isn't much evidence of her having been at home for a while. He'd follow that one up too, with uniformed officers who patrolled the area.

Daniel breaks the silence. "I was wondering if we could look at Barbara's room, Mr. Flint. It might help us to understand better why she went out that night, or who she was planning to meet?"

Tommy responds, but it's as if he is talking in parallel to Daniel, rather than on any kind of perpendicular path where their conversations will inevitably intersect. "Don't judge people by their appearances. Barbara used to walk the talk and look the part, but she was a homely girl underneath it all. I spent more time with her than anyone else – certainly far more than any friends or foes with bad intentions."

'Foes with bad intentions!' Harcourt isn't sure if this is the language of the drug-addled or taken straight from a 1970s 'concept album' (or both). What he'd most like to do is to sit down. Regardless, he allows Daniel to continue as he does seem to be making some kind of progress.

"I get that! I have a similar relationship with my daughter. She still tells me all her secret fears, although I don't imagine that will last for much longer..."

"If that's an intellectual way of trying to find

out what secrets Barbara was harbouring, I'm afraid you're wasting your time. To my certain knowledge, Barbara had no secrets from me – from either of us. Transparency was one of Valerie's big things, you know?"

'Was.' Both men pick up on the passive tense.

"I wasn't trying to pry at all." Daniel remains professionally (or whatever the word is for people with his ability, Harcourt isn't sure) calm as he continues. "But I do know what it is to have the confidence of a daughter. I can't think of any subject that Claire and I wouldn't discuss and it's a precious thing indeed."

"Too precious to lose," Tommy responds in a typically enigmatic fashion. "Barbara was finding it hard to concentrate lately; I will say that."

"Things on her mind?" Harcourt takes Daniel out of the firing line for now, even though he had kept his head down (or held high) remarkably well.

"Always. She was one creative powerhouse. Truly a sui generis."

Harcourt isn't sure what that means but sees Daniel nodding, so he can ask him for a definition later. For now, he sticks to his knitting. "Was there a particular project that was playing on her mind or worrying her in some way – at school, or maybe something you'd been working on musically together?"

"Always. Without chaos, we have no means of valuing perfection – unless they're the same thing of course."

Harcourt feels increasingly like the proverbial square in

a round hole. He notices some A5 leaflets on top of the hob. Tommy follows his gaze. "I'm getting some of the band together again. We're going to do a tribute gig in Barbara's memory – a free concert in the park. A bit like the Stones did, but without the butterflies, obviously."

Again, Harcourt doesn't have any idea what the would-be (or always wanted-to-be) rock star is talking about. It isn't a world he has ever understood. Hunter-Wright sometimes quotes song lyrics which are meaningless to him, or, at least, the real meaning is entirely lost on him. He likes a bit of Abba now again – who doesn't? Beyond that lie the frozen wastes of ignorance (or Finland?).

Daniel notes the confusion on Harcourt's face and rescues him. "May we see Barbara's things, Mr Flint, and her room if that's not too much of an intrusion at a time like this?"

Tommy turns to look at Daniel sharply as if pricked by the same sarcasm that Harcourt had heard. Deciding to rise above any such intention he uses both hands, which have hitherto been leaning on the cream kitchen unit behind him to seemingly prop him up, to propel him forward and back into the room. Wordlessly he leads them both to the foot of the stairs before pointing upwards. "Her room was the one immediately on the left, next to the bathroom. She spent a good deal of time in there too."

They acknowledge the directions, also the distinct lack of humour on the grieving father's face, despite an attempt at it. The stair carpet is grey, like the man, and stained with dark patches representing the memories of spilt drinks – like the man.

Barbara's room is not the untidy – 'creative' – mess Harcourt was expecting. Textbooks with mainly white spines line a shelf above a small desk on which a black laptop lies open – whether sleeping or dead he isn't sure. He remonstrates with himself for using such a word. Respect for others and their property in the face of serious illness or death has always been one of his strong points and a key needle on his moral compass – especially in recent years.

"What did you make of the 'tribute gig?'" he whispers.

"People react to death in so many different ways, don't they? Some just throw themselves into or surround themselves with familiarity, everything they're good at. I've known people to just work to the exclusion of everything else, and I mean everything else. It's a physical compulsion, sure, but it's also about trying to effect a mental repair. As with someone who is autistic, focusing so intently on a single output may make them look or seem strange from the outside, but once you detach them from the one thing that is keeping them going they stop, dead. Tommy may just be looking to make a quick buck or trying to revive a flagging 'career,' but that's a bit heartless don't you think?"

Harcourt does. He also knows plenty about working to the exclusion of everything else, yet it hasn't helped him to move on. Not really. "And je suis generous?"

"Sui generis! It means unique, a class apart."

"Could be a drug reference then." Harcourt isn't impressed by either his ignorance or newly-found education.

Daniel is surveying the tidy room. For some reason, unknown to him yet, he feels that the bed had been made before Barbara had left the room, rather than since. The bedding is plain white with a simple stitched pattern running from (or to) each of the corners of the quilt. It looks quite new, as does the matching white wardrobe and single chest of drawers. Each is closed, nothing half-open; no item of clothing trying to make its escape by exposing itself or trying to hide away. Nothing lies on the carpeted floor other than a slightly faded white fluffy rug: almost certainly a favourite or cherished item that escaped the room's makeover.

Given the untidiness downstairs and the absence of her mother, it feels unlikely to him that either of them would have tidied their late daughter's room. There is 'shrine theory' to be considered though: where relatives and friends seek solace in the perfect order and make-up of a departed entity, whether that was truly borne out in life or not. In this case, however with, again, pots of plants along the windowsill looking the worse for wear – and certainly not having been watered for some time – he senses that the room is exactly as Barbara left it on the night she died.

"Anything?" Harcourt takes in the plain, magnolia walls as he says this. Furthering his confusion over contemporary music, its performers and its fans he had expected floor-to-ceiling posters of pop stars, contemporary idols (male or female) or at the very least the ubiquitous photograph taken by Alberto Korda of "Che" Guevara – cited by some as one of the most famous and iconic images in the world. Perhaps Barbara was all about 'counterculture' (and he isn't referring to shops).

Daniel hasn't moved for several minutes, rotating his head as far as he can (wishing he was an owl as he usually does at moments like these) taking everything in; trying to memorize the scene which is merely a memory now of a fallen star.

Harcourt watches him, his back to the window which is still, mercifully, letting in light and a little warmth from the soupy autumn sunshine, though it can do little to alleviate the coldness within.

"I'm not sure that Barbara was planning to come back."

"Or expecting to come back?"

"I just sense that she knew she was leaving this place for the last time."

And she was right." Harcourt adds grimly and slightly unnecessarily. He must remember that Daniel hears everything and misses very little that he tunes into.

Daniel spies a small transistor radio sitting on a wooden unit to the left of Barbara's desk. Incongruously old and battered, given the otherwise modern décor of the space, he notes that the aerial is extended to what he assumes is its full length. On closer inspection, he sees that the slightly smeared tuning window with its green background is unlit, but also that a tiny red light in the top-right corner is shining back at him, indicating that it must still be plugged in – or fitted with live batteries. He bends down to press the ON/OFF switch and the radio bursts into life. Booming music fills the room. He doesn't notice which station it is being transmitted from, but he does notice the new person in the room, standing silently between him and the police inspector.

Harcourt knows better now than to interrupt Daniel, even as they make their singular way back down the stairs. Tommy comes out of the kitchen to meet them, a single white mug in one hand containing some kind of steaming liquid and fashioned out of not-quite-symmetrical pottery with the words 'Black Sabbath' on its side. It is abundantly clear that no further mugs will be making appearances for their benefit.

"Well?"

Daniel refuses to be put off by either the man's brusqueness or gruff tone in which he has addressed them both. Like Harcourt, he has witnessed plenty of similar cases of distressing behaviour borne out of bereavement.

"Nothing as yet," he stalls the man. "One thing though: did Gary Jones ever visit the house?"

"You've got to be joking! He wouldn't have come down here; he wouldn't have wanted to be seen with the likes of us. Daddy would probably have grounded him as a punishment if he had."

"But they were all friends, weren't they?" Harcourt is curious about both the question and the answer."

"That's as maybe," Tommy continues, staring directly at Daniel and blanking Harcourt completely. "Barbara used to meet up with them in town, at that Janice's place in Pickerton sometimes and down by the lake there. I think Gary Jones might once have held a party at

Malvern Towers, but he certainly never came here."

***

Daniel accompanies Harcourt back to the police station in relative silence. Both men are deep in thought: Daniel regarding the unexpected 'sighting' of Gary Jones; Harcourt, shamefully, considering where to book a meal at the weekend to celebrate – and cement – Debbie's returning home, unscathed.

DS Taylor greets them warmly as they head into Harcourt's office. Daniel notices DS Farren, bent over her computer, seemingly deep in concentration. The two make eye contact but the flicker of recognition on her face is not nearly so welcoming.

"Any news on DS Flowers?" Daniel settles himself in the still-uncomfortable 'comfy' chair to the side of Harcourt's desk.

"Not while we were out. Maybe DS Taylor has an update?"

Taylor, waiting patiently on the threshold, now enters the room. "He 'phoned me from the hospital about an hour ago, sir. It seems that Rob's kidneys are not responding to any treatment. Mrs Flowers has called in the priest so..."

"I didn't realise that they were a religious family, or that she was at least."

"I don't know that they are, but you know Ian. He'd want to do everything by the book."

"It must be serious if it's got to this stage

298

though." Daniel offers. He isn't 'religious' either, sitting uncomfortably in the middle of the science versus nature debate. However, both sides can show signs of what has been and will be, you just have to read them properly.

Taylor nods, her face bowed slightly. "He did say that he thinks Rob is unaware of what's going on, which I suppose is a mercy."

"Must be difficult. You either tell people the truth so that they might somehow come to terms with it - prepare for the inevitable, I suppose - or you want the complete opposite for them. Allow their last few moments to be peaceful and without any kind of fear." Harcourt's voice is barely a whisper as if deferring to the unheard sound of something far greater.

"In Rob's case, it's probably a bit easier, sir." Taylor is at first alarmed by Harcourt's reaction, then actually quite pleased that he has reacted in this way. They each comment from time to time about how dry he is, very 'process driven.' It's good to get a glimpse of the policeman behind the procedure sometimes.

"I assume that Gary Jones didn't have that luxury." Daniel watches as Farren comes to stand in the doorway, studiously looking towards Harcourt rather than him. "I mean, if it was an accident, he'd have had little time to come to terms with what he knew was going to happen – the same if someone was deliberately trying to drown him. His last moments certainly wouldn't have been either peaceful or without fear."

Now Farren does turn to face him. "I didn't think there'd

be any 'either or' in your world Mr. Reed. I mean, you're here to bring certainty, aren't you?"

"Sergeant!" Harcourt has found his big voice again.

"It's fine, Martin, honestly." Daniel remains as calm as ever, entirely unruffled. If he has a volume button attached to his larynx, he has rarely chosen to turn it up or down in their presence. "Certainty is one thing, isn't it? Belief in that certainty is quite another. I wish I could offer - if not Rob - Ian and his mum some degree of certainty going forward, on Rob's behalf if you like. I can't do belief either because, for me, that falls way short of certainty.

Occasionally I am lucky enough to be able to see a shaft of light from the future – like a spotlight being turned on very briefly to illuminate a tiny part of an otherwise dark and empty stage. What I am much more likely to be able to offer, though, is the possibility of finding out what has gone before where your expertise has suggested there are no lights or light operators at all. If that can bring some comfort to those still trying to come to terms with either unexpected or unexplained tragedies in the present, then I think it's worthwhile having a go."

Now Farren does turn towards him. She doesn't say anything, but the unspoken hostility has left her otherwise impassive face.

Taylor sees an opportune moment to speak. "On the subject of shedding light on things from the past, I've been doing some digging into Barry Jones's financial affairs."

Seeing how she has instantly grabbed everyone's attention, she now recognizes the need to manage their expectations and, unfortunately, bring them back down again. How great it must feel to be like Daniel: calm and considered and even emotionally detached. Mind you, she also knows that it will take much more to bring Farren around and extinguish her scepticism completely. Taylor has a much more open mind in some ways – she's needed to just to survive thus far.

"There isn't much. This not being a criminal investigation I seem to have come up against data protection barriers at almost every turn. However, I have gleaned that two of Barry Jones's biggest clients have left him and moved over to other firms – one in London and one in Leeds."

"When was this?" Harcourt is furiously writing notes. They've tried to get him to use Notes on his phone, but that only caused him to leave paper Post-it notes all over his desk, reminding him to make digital notes on his device.

"One was in the spring, sir: a pension fund he was helping to manage for a client based in Austria, but with registered offices in Bermuda."

"Obviously!" The other two offices concur, almost in harmony.

"The second was just three weeks ago. That one was a much bigger client. Some kind of Mutual from California. It seems that Barry Jones was facilitating access for them to European financial markets post-Brexit."

"Please tell me you took that last sentence off of a press release and didn't understand it either!"

They all laugh, Daniel included. Farren's motto in life has always been 'spend wisely but save more wisely still.' It was drilled into her by her mother when she was a child. The wisdom endures, but her current salary makes it difficult to focus on much more than a weekly shop and maybe a couple of nights out each month.

"What it does mean is that one client left before and one after Gary Jones's death." Sensibly, Harcourt summarises: The two events may be completely unconnected of course and the timing might be irrelevant - I imagine these kinds of things happen all the time in the financial services industry. What it does suggest is that big man Barry might not be as clever and comfortable as he'd like the rest of the world – and certainly his remaining clients – to think that he is. I wonder if part of his anger comes from that, although I do not doubt that his grief over Gary's death is also a major contributory factor."

"I have something on that too, sir." Farren this time. "While you were out, I took a call for you from Kate Shelbourne. She and her team seem to be able to get over the privacy barriers much more easily than we can."

"She's like an Olympic hurdler when she's in full flight!" Harcourt tries not to show too much admiration for the journalist. He wouldn't want anyone to get the wrong idea. Besides, Kate can also be equally obstructive to their enquiries – especially when protecting her sources.

"She'd like you to phone her back, but the gist of it is that Gary Jones took out a life assurance policy just a week before he died."

"I wonder who advised him to do that?" Harcourt vocalizes again what each of the police officers is thinking. Daniel, would you mind popping over to see her, please? I know you two have worked together in the past. It might be nothing, but worth following up. What will be worth nothing is my job if I don't fill in the gaps on the monthly budget sheet the DCI left on my desk before we escaped this morning.

***

Kate Shelbourne is waiting just inside the familiar main entrance to Berrow's House and waves as Daniel approaches. He has headed there by foot, enjoying the walk down to and then over the river bridge in the late autumn sunshine which, though it has persisted, only makes guest appearances these days.

How many times did he let himself be carried across the threshold and into a quite different and then unique world? The flat-roofed grey concrete building is showing signs of wear and tear though. He notices some alarming cracks to the left-hand side and weathering has rendered much of the render sporadic at best.

"Hello, stranger!" Kate crosses the foyer to join him, kissing him gently on the cheek. She smells so nice. Dressed in dark jeans and a plain, white top Daniel is reminded – as he is quite often these days – how much nicer it would be if things were just black and white.

"It's been a while."

"Since I've been here?" He returns her warm, easy smile. "Or since we last had a chat?"

"Both I suppose."

"Showing some signs of wear now."

"I hope you're referring to the building!" She watches him process the possibility of an insult before satisfying herself that he does indeed understand her little joke. "We've been on Hylton Road for more than fifty years – well, of course, you'd know that from your time here on the News – but I think we'll be moving out too in the next couple of years or so.

She leads him into a small side room with just one square window, quite high up in the wall so that nobody can see in or out. As he sits down on the plastic chair beside her Daniel can't help thinking about the cells at the police station he departed just over half an hour ago.

"Have you been keeping well?" He enquires genially, immediately hating himself for his blandness.

"Quite well, thank you."

At this, their eyes meet, and they burst out laughing.

"So, that's the Jane Austen formalities over with! How is Charlotte?"

"Thanks for asking. Yes, she's OK. Good days and bad days. On the good days, you'd barely know there was anything the matter with her. When things are less good we tend to lose her completely – sometimes for hours on end."

"That must be tough." She suddenly breaks off, shaking her head. "I'm so sorry Daniel, would you like a drink?"

"No. You're fine, thanks."

"I don't know what's the matter with me sometimes, forgetting my manners like that."

"Really. You're fine."

"I was going to say that it must be impossible to plan things – with Charlotte, I mean – outings and so on, because you don't know how she's going to react. I guess neither of you do."

"A little bit." He knows she is genuinely interested rather than curious; trying to show support – compassion even. She's always been like that. "In some ways – although it makes me feel both sad and bad – it might be better if we had a more definite timeline, but we don't, which makes it so hard."

She places a warm hand over his. Both of them feel better for it. "I suppose knowing what's likely to happen - and when - doesn't always make it easier though. Even if you knew for certain. Well, you'd know all about that!"

"Sometimes." Daniel longs to scratch his nose but knows it is just a reaction to her hand preventing his from moving. Emotional rather than physical. "The uncertainty doesn't just end with us. The medical profession itself is still trying to get its head around this particular variant of dementia. They (and we) learn a lot more with each piece of research - with each new victim of the disease - but we don't yet know how much we still don't know. I sometimes think Charlotte would like to know how things are going to evolve though; on her good days at least. Claire certainly would. She struggles much more with the unknown than I do."

"How about the brother? Fergus isn't it?"

"It is. He's been OK. He phones quite often and occasionally comes to visit. Lucy won't have Charlotte in her house, and therefore that includes me as well."

"Why is that?"

"It's a long story! I know you enjoy those..."

"Especially the prequels!"

"But I won't bore you with it. Suffice to say that Charlotte was quite... outspoken on recent visits to Herefordshire."

"Rude, you mean?"

"I think rudeness implies a certain amount of intent, doesn't it? Charlotte was already ill, but none of us recognized the ailment behind the anger."

"So, this Lucy puts social niceties above her sister-in-law's health?"

"Above Charlotte's and everybody else's including her husband."

"But he has 'his faith.'"

Daniel easily spots the barely concealed doubt. "I'm not sure that gives him much comfort anymore. A couple of weeks ago he told Charlotte that Him having a plan and knowing exactly what should happen where and when must fill Him with despair when man continues to mess everything up. According to Claire, that's a universal problem with all organized religions, not just Fergus's personal take on it all."

"Did Claire fit in OK? I remember you being a bit concerned about the step up to sixth form?"

"She's doing fine, considering all that's going on, or not going on at home. She worries as much about me as her mum, though I do my best to convince her that I'm fine."

"Sounds like you're trying to convince yourself, just a little bit?"

She knows him so well and is adept at reading people. He supposes that it is this that makes her such a good journalist and why people will want to read the words she's gleaned from others, voluntarily or otherwise.

"How about you? What's been going on outside of the paper?"

"Oh, you know. I'm so busy I don't have a lot of downtime. The months and years pass quickly, don't they?" She belatedly withdraws her hand.

Daniel glimpses a momentary sadness in her eyes which, with one blink, disappears. The professional view must be maintained at all costs, he thinks. A discussion for a later date perhaps, when he might be able to support his friend for a change.

"So, I guess Martin has sent you over to chat about the life assurance policy? I must say it's lovely to see you again, but I was expecting one of their officers too."

"They're up to their eyes in stuff. I think they are happy to use me for an extra body, at least when it's someone I know well. I'm sure there will be a follow-up from DS Farren or Taylor."

"Not Flowers though."

"Unlikely for a while."

"I heard the news."

Daniel considers again how wide-reaching and penetrating her sources are. He considers it unlikely that Harcourt would have shared the news of Flowers's brother with her. "I think the endpoint is quite close now – which is another reason why they're flying around a bit."

"Short-staffed? Tell me about it. Anyway, I do have something else to discuss with you as well, so I'm pleased it's just you."

"So, life assurance. Ah, the irony!"

She smiles back, reflecting on the slender thread attaching each of them to the earth for an allocated time. Above it at least. "Barry Jones took out a policy in his son's name when he turned eighteen. Amazingly, this isn't unusual. The premiums are much lower if you start paying them earlier – a bit like pensions. I haven't been able to establish whether Barry was paying the direct debit himself, or whether Gary did. I would have thought the former as Gary didn't have any paid work that I can discover. Not even a paper round."

"The idle rich. Start as they mean to go on."

"A bit callous, Daniel."

"Sorry. Yes, it was, wasn't it."

She moves on, seeing his discomfort. "Again, I haven't yet found out how much Gary's life was assured for, but my source assures me it was for a sum well into six figures."

"And Gary's parents would benefit I assume."

She nods. "Naturally, Gary hadn't made a will so all of his assets and worldly possessions – such as they were – would have been shared between his surviving parents, according to the rules on intestacy for England and Wales, as laid out in the Inheritance and Trustees' Power Act (2014)."

"And the life assurance policy itself: I presume Barry has already claimed on it?"

"Well, there's the rub. Yes, he did – just three days later."

"The price of everything… sorry, I don't know why I'm feeling quite so bitter. DS Taylor had a particularly unpleasant encounter with Barry Jones, and Harcourt didn't fare much better."

"Well, you may all be interested to know that the life insurance company is dragging its feet. Although the coroner had to record a verdict of accidental death in Gary's case, she also made it clear in her accompanying notes that the circumstances of his death were 'insufficiently explained.'"

"I think that would explain why Hunter-Wright was so unhappy about it. He also struggles with the unexplained. They must have been close to an inquest then?"

"If there had been anything at all suspicious about his death then, yes, most definitely. The police offered up no such evidence though."

"Nor did they in the deaths of Zoya Agarwal or Barbara Flint because there was none to be found." Daniel is beginning to understand why all of this has been so frustrating, not least for the parents left behind.

"Three similar 'accidents' in relatively quick succession, though; and all of them resulting in deaths through drowning?"

"I know. I know!" He looks directly at her. Her eyes are wide, and he finds her staring, benign though it is, quite intense. He notes once again how so many people's perceptions of journalists – even those who decry the very noun with no direct knowledge of any of its protagonists – are so negative. True, like estate agents, they may well have brought them on themselves through unprofessional activities (or no activity at all), but the good ones like Kate should surely be valued much more highly.

This woman will stop at very little in seeking out the truth, which will add very little to her life. He feels her loneliness, even as he sits right next to her and continues. "But nor were there any reliable witnesses that would have been able to stand up before a coroner and helped to prove that those deaths too were anything other than unexpected tragedies."

"What if they had been expected, though."

Such background noise as there was in the busy foyer outside their room seems to stop. The silence within goes up several levels.

"Go on."

Her eyes are huge now, almost too big for their allotted sockets. "Suppose there was far more of an inevitability about all of this than mere fate?"

"Kate. We've known each other for quite a long time now, but I've never watched you halt fate in its tracks!"

Those same eyes relax a little, but seriousness has ousted smiles. "Look, would you mind if we take the next bit off the record? We can keep it just between us if you don't think it's worth passing on."

Now he feels a tingle of excitement. A slight trickle of sweat dribbles its way down the contours of his back; unseen and hopefully undetectable by this indefatigable woman. He catches a faint whiff of her perfume and hopes it will provide him with sufficient cover for now. "OK. It's a fair cop." He holds his hands up in mock surrender to whatever it is that she is going to hit him with.

"Except it isn't. Not really." She notes his confusion and resolves to speak plainly. She's normally so good at that – and many interviewees hate her for it – and yet, in Daniel's presence, it's somehow harder. "Let me rephrase that: you and I both know and respect DI Harcourt and all of his team I think?"

Daniel nods a silent accord.

"Except I think that, for some reason, at certain times, he and they may be a little hard on some of the people they get to interview. Yes, I know. I know. Pots and kettles are all black... I've witnessed for myself how they sometimes approach the more 'gentle souls.'"

"I think DS Flowers might take exception to that."

"Yes, yes, I know it's a generalisation, and quite unfair because of that, but you do know what I'm talking about. Flowers is a gentle soul himself, isn't he? An exception to lots of rules."

"I'm sure he's every bit as determined as the rest of them – and you – to get justice for victims of crime. I think he just approaches things differently, which makes that approach all the more effective. People might talk with him and allow themselves to be drawn in a bit more easily than through the more direct approach. I guess you're really talking about Harcourt and possibly DS Farren here. I'd say they were cut from very similar cloth?"

"You remember my friend Nancy? Flowers spoke with her after Zoya's death, but from how she described the interview to me, she could tell that, if not him necessarily but the rest of the team might not take her testament too seriously; especially not when they had that self-righteous woman..."

"Miranda Ann Clackerton."

"The same. Nancy felt that she was having to overturn her 'evidence' in some way: that her version of the 'truth' was somehow inferior to that of a woman whose sole aim in life seemed to be feeding swans. Nancy told me that even Flowers considered her more capable of treason by killing one of them than believing what she saw."

"Therein lies the problem – with the police, not the swans." Daniel sits back in his chair, slightly disappointed that Kate has just told him what he either already knew or had worked out for himself. "Nancy told them she saw Zoya being chased, but nobody else did. Although I sort of dislike the woman by proxy, Miss Clackerton was right there on the riverbank at the exact moment that Zoya went into the river. She saw nobody."

"What if I were to tell you that Nancy also saw Barbara Flint being chased – or followed at least – by the same person?"

So that was it. Daniel sits forward again. "Unless anybody else saw this person too, I'd say it would be dismissed in precisely the same way as before."

***

"It is a bit far-fetched, isn't it?"

"Of course, it is, and yet, the further away from the truth it is, the harder it can be to see." Daniel is in his kitchen, the phone flat to his ear, simultaneously watching Charlotte a few feet away from them in the 'open plan' lounge. She is watching something on the television, even though he hasn't switched it on.

"I'm going to have to keep you well away from DS Flowers when he gets back; I can see that!" Harcourt's voice in his ear is somehow closer.

"Still no news?"

"Supposed to be good when that happens isn't it?"

"Not sure who for. Anyway, I just felt it best to pass it on." He feels slightly awkward about not telling the policeman the whole truth – at least not yet.

"I mean, stranger things have certainly happened. We know that Barry Jones's business may be in difficulties, although this in itself is unproven. We know that he did take out a policy on his son's life just before he died and that he appears to have put a claim in just after he did so. These are facts, not motives. They aren't necessarily connected with Gary's cause of death. There would also be nothing to connect it with the deaths of Zoya and/or Barbara either."

"But you do still think the three deaths are connected?"

"Don't you?"

Daniel nods for no reason. "I do, yes. Coincidences may sometimes come along in quite innocent pairs, but rarely in triplicate."

"It would take a particularly cold-hearted father to even think of killing their son to rescue their business and preserve their image to the outside world. You'd surely spend the rest of your life looking over your shoulder wouldn't you, rather than being looked up to which is so important to Barry Jones?"

"Didn't you mention that a tall man had been seen shouting to that woman by the lake?"

"And Barry Jones is tall – and more than capable of shouting! Yes, but Bob Drake is, how shall I put it, not entirely to be trusted. His mind is…"

Daniel can tell that the DI is reassessing what he was going to say. "It's fine, Martin, you can say it."

"Just that his mind is fractured. As for the Kings, DS Farren was unconvinced by them. She thought they were much more interested in having their fifteen minutes of fame. She and Taylor did briefly consider if there was more to it than that but dismissed it."

Darren recalls his conversation with Kate Harcourt from just a couple of hours earlier. He too feels dismissed. "I agree that it's circumstantial at best. I haven't been of much help yet have I?"

"You're coming in with a fresh eye. That's useful in itself. Making us re-examine everything and everyone. I'll certainly give Jones another call."

"Good luck with that." As he says it, he reflects on the meaning of chance or 'fate' before comforting his wife who is sobbing now like a small child.

***

She watches him replace the telephone in its cradle. It's relatively unusual for them to receive a call on the landline, but that must have been the number he'd given to the police. She assumes he hadn't wanted to be interrupted when mobile.

He turns to face her across the kitchen. She is acutely aware of both the pan of boiling water on the hob and the array of sharp knives she has been using to cut up pancetta and onions for the carbonara. She freezes as he makes his way, slowly but oh so surely, towards her.

"Those people had the audacity to infer that I was somehow behind the death of Gary."

He is towering over her now. It's not just now though – at this precise moment – he has always done so, blocking her view of the outside world: barring her escape route, even if she dared to even attempt to leave.

"Why would they think that? She turns the temperature knob sideways, trying to reduce the heat, as though that will make any difference. She must stay calm. Remember what her mother had always told her: 'Big hearts always outweigh small minds.'

"It appears that someone has told them about the life assurance application." He bends down slowly and deliberately – as he has done pretty much since he went down on his knees for her – not taking his eyes off of her for a single moment (loving the fear it induces in her rather than the love it had once falsely promised). "Now, who do you think that might have been, given that it's a very, very private matter and certainly not in the public domain beyond these four walls?"

He takes hold of her left wrist, gripping it tightly, steering it ever so slowly towards the pan which still bubbles, in defiance of her pathetic attempt to turn down the heat.

"It certainly wasn't me!" She hears a wobble over the last word. They both do. She resolves to make her next sentence sound much more convincing. "I would never do such a thing, even think it!"

He keeps hold of her, turning her round to face him now. She can see the sweat above his top lip, feel the spittle on her cheek as he screams now: "Such a thing! I haven't yet enunciated what their schoolboy – or more likely schoolgirl – theory is. Have I? Have I?"

"No." She has learned that tears are no friends to her at times like this, and she has had plenty of years to learn it well. Hers has been a life of CPD alright" Continuous Personal Despair. And yet, here they come, like a torrent.

"If this ever comes out it will ruin me!" His right hand is now moving upwards, towards her neck, the left still holding her wrist so hard she thinks he'll break it. One of the smaller knives is just behind her but she has little to no chance of reaching it. Helpless she is - always has been – and he has her in his vice.

***

She can hear her grandmother coming down the stairs, presumably woken as she had been a few minutes earlier. The moon is quite bright, casting shadows over the hallway's polished wooden floor.

"Just hang on." She holds the mobile to her chest.

"Janice? Is everything alright?" She can tell by the caller's tone of voice that everything is not 'alright.' It is very much not alright.

"Everything is fine Gran. Just a friend who can't sleep. Worrying about the Mocks. I told her she could 'phone me at any time of day or night. I didn't think she would 'phone in the middle of the night though!" She is trying to make light of it, but darkness is all around her; them.

"I heard you come down?" Daisy enters the kitchen, wrapped up in a tiny, mauve dressing gown and matching slippers.

That hadn't worked then. She had thought they wouldn't be able to hear her if she'd left her bedroom. She'd crept down so carefully, avoiding the obvious stairs that creaked at the slightest depression.

"Would you like a drink? Might help you to get back to sleep again?"

No, thanks though Gran. You get back to bed. I hope I didn't wake Grandad up?"

"Your grandfather sleeps through thunderstorms and people who shout at him. I don't think you need to worry on his part, or mine."

"Thanks, Gran."

"If you're sure you're alright?"

"I am. Thank you again. Sometimes people just need to let it out don't they – things that are worrying them, I mean. Once she's said the words out loud, I think they'll leave her mind alone. Allow her to sleep peacefully."

"How wise you are. I wish I had been blessed with such wisdom at your age."

"You married Grandad! You once told me that was the cleverest thing you ever did."

"I did, didn't I? It must be true then!" She wraps her old,

bony arms around her treasured granddaughter, gives her a hug and what she hopes is a supportive smile, before heading back up towards her shining star.

Janice watches her leave, listens out for the catch of their bedroom door and then creeps softly towards the conservatory. She closes the connecting door gently behind her and sinks into the crumpled cushions of one of the ancient wicker chairs. She is bathed in moonlight now yet feels guilty at how easy her lies had come; at how easy deception has become lately. Surely, she should be hiding away in the darkness, not lit up like the heroine of a nocturnal stage.

"Mocks?"

"Shhh. I had to say something didn't I?"

"Whatever. Look, we've got to get away. It isn't safe here anymore."

"What do you mean? Why?"

"Trust me, Janice. Have I ever let you down?" The caller has not invited a response. "I'll tell you where and when, but it's got to be tonight. Do you understand?"

"Tonight?"

"We can't afford to wait!"

She recalls the last chat she ever had with Barbara. She understands.

CHAPTER ELEVEN

"Who did she say she was?"

"Jean! Jean from next door." Daniel tries his best to keep that frustration out of his voice, though it has been increasingly present even before conversations with his wife – a bit like someone 'getting your back up' before you've even spoken to them again. He's proofreading a 'romantic novel' at the moment with a lot of emotional conflict being described before the main characters inevitably work through it and find harmony once more. But the book is a work of fiction.

"Who?" Charlotte is getting agitated now. She always struggled with things she didn't understand – which is why she was such a good lawyer, anticipating her clients' queries – and never more so than now. Except that now she can't rely on her brain matter or any other external references to provide context to her questions and deliver answers. She and he are just left with endless questions.

"She lives next door. Our neighbour. You and she used to have tea in the garden together sometimes; you'd alternate between hers and ours.

"I think you've got that wrong, Daniel. You seem to be getting a lot of things wrong lately."

There follows a long period of silence during which neither of them sees the point of speaking further. So much for harmony.

Jean smiles in warm encouragement to Daniel. "She'll be fine. I'll keep an eye on her. I thought I might come over and do some pruning if that would be alright?"

"That would be smashing. Thanks again." He surveys the short, neat woman who has proven to be such a friend to Charlotte and, more recently, an unexpected support to them both.

He and Charlotte had often shared a private joke about her dress sense – or lack of it. Today she is dressed in a bright red tracksuit to match the garish scarlet lipstick. When he'd first opened the door to her Daniel had, shamefully, worried that Charlotte might think he'd welcomed a giant strawberry into their home.

No fruit today though. No afternoon tea in the garden.

"Claire will be back mid-morning. She had a sleepover with a friend in Atch Lench last night. Not that they probably call them 'sleepovers' now they're in the sixth form."

Jean laughs knowingly. "How is Claire coping?"

He hopes that she is referring to college work but knows really that she isn't. It hurts him that either of them should now be perceived as having to 'cope' with the woman who has been (is) the sparkling central point in their lives: the planet they've been so happy to orbit for so long. "She's doing fine, thanks. At least there are no exams to worry about for a while." Just daily examinations.

"I'll keep an eye on her. You mustn't worry." Jean is standing a little too close to him; he can smell the peppermint on her breath, disguising who knows what sins. She certainly doesn't do space. "I must say you look very smart."

"Thank you. Needs must!"

"I hope it goes as well as it can do," she leans in conspiratorially, "At least Charlotte is still alive – still with us."

He ponders this as he heads towards the small village of Upton Snodsbury, about six or seven miles east of Worcester. His wife is certainly still alive.

***

Harcourt sits towards the back, on his own for now, taking in the whole scene. Yet another fallen person to go with the fallen leaves, scattered all over the churchyard outside and blowing wildly in the late October breeze.

The piped organ music is respectful and completely unmemorable because of it. There are few mourners gathered today in the presence of their God or their neighbours. Yet another body, he contemplates grimly. Another mother's child taken before its time and for what reason?

He has read that the church is dedicated to Saint Kenelm, son of one of the Kings of Mercia who was brutally murdered by his sister. He remembers seeing his tomb on a visit to nearby Winchcombe Abbey. A fountain had risen from the earth at a place where the boy's body was found and had subsequently been the site of a 'Holy Well' where miracles had been performed. Water: the great creator and even greater destroyer.

He looks up at the stained-glass windows depicting death and other miracles. What a shame, he thinks, that life is usually the other way around. A coldness wraps its arms around him, making him feel less comfortable still. No doubt the size of the anticipated congregation was a deciding factor in the economics of church funerals with the subsequent decision not to turn the heating on.

He understands that many people do find comfort in services like these, held in places like this. The organization running the business is certainly comforted by new customers, if not the manager who, dressed in thin vestments that have almost certainly never included a string vest, looks as cold up in the pulpit as he feels down here on earth.

He hears the vicar utter, almost chant the familiar words from Wordsworth's famous Ode:

'What though the radiance which was once so bright
Be now forever taken from my sight,
Though nothing can bring back the hour
Of splendour in the grass, of glory in the flower;
We will grieve not, rather find
Strength in what remains behind.'

Mrs Flowers begins to visibly shake in the silence that follows. Ian had told him outside that this had been one of Rob's favourite verses. Mortality had duly pulled life's heavy exit door closed, yet what had Rob known about innocently running barefoot across newly mown grass or being able to pick daffodils for his mother himself, or riding a bike along a quiet country lane amid the fresh dew and birdsong of early morning?

The coldness has left him; a band of prickly heat has formed on his neck. He can feel a similar wave breaking across his forehead before surging down his face which now feels as if it's burning. He hasn't experienced this feeling for months but clearly remembers what comes next. There it is: that fainting feeling – probably not uncommon in places like this, at events like these. He's pleased to be sitting down. Even kneeling would be OK in these circumstances.

He tries hard to focus on the case - on the cases. It seems wrong in the circumstances but it's the kind of coping mechanism they'd told him to deploy. Just concentrate on the details and it will pass. He and Daniel are off to the Jones's house in Malvern straight after this funeral service. He at least can move on more easily; Ian has to head off to a private cremation at Astwood in Worcester with just those few family members in attendance. Too many deaths, too many memories of lives unfulfilled.

Sure enough, the burning sensation begins to pass. The swimming sensation has ceased, and he hasn't drowned. It will probably be months before this happens again. Small comfort. He glances over at Daniel, sitting quite alone on the other side of the aisle. He seems to be deep in thought too. Well, he has a lot to think about.

Farren and Taylor are just two pews in front of him.

Even from behind he can tell that Taylor is very upset, but Farren is more resolute: shoulders back and head high. Taylor and Flowers have worked together for a long time now. There is a genuine affection between them beyond any innate respect or team-building premiums. He is concerned about any battles that might ensue over a DI position. Not that concerned though. Neither has yet shown any ambition to break the status quo. Maybe he should be more alarmed by that.

The pallbearers gather behind him, like stuffed crows in their starched, stretched dark suits, flown in on cue from the inevitable yew trees outside. Those trees were supposed to be symbolic of eternity. What do they know of the changing seasons?

Ian acknowledges them with a slight nod as the small party passes by. He looks understandably tired and very pale, almost ghost-like and yet very definitely carrying all the worries of a human world on his slender shoulders.

***

As they leave the next village of Broughton Hackett Daniel looks across at Harcourt. It has been a sombre, almost wordless journey so far, but he senses there is even more to it than the sadness of Rob Flowers's funeral. He spots a road sign on his left and seeks a way past the empty road and into the detective's love of history.

"So why is that village called 'White Ladies Aston?' In all the years I've lived here and driven along this

325

road to Worcester, I've often thought to look it up, but never quite got round to it." His tone is friendly; encouraging, yet he sees hands gripping the steering wheel tightly, deathly white in contrast to the man's crimson face. They are also travelling very slowly, despite having passed the round National Speed Limit marker, depicting the end of the village.

Harcourt takes a few seconds before replying in a strained voice, almost as though he is being strangled. "The White Ladies were named after a foundation of Cistercian nuns in the Thirteenth Century. Their habits were white you see. I think it was the only nunnery to be found in Worcester before the Bishop granted them Aston Manor out here in the middle of the century. The word Aston itself comes from 'East Farm.'

"An Anglo-Saxon word I'm guessing."

"It is." The reply is more Siri than CID. "I forgot that you enjoy seeking out the origins of things too."

Daniel tries a laugh to lighten the atmosphere a little. "I do, but my relationship with history is quite complicated, as you and I can well imagine."

Harcourt continues his thesis as though he hasn't heard a word. "There was another White Ladies priory over in Shropshire too. Charles II stayed there on his escape after the Battle of Worcester, and the farm here remained loyal to the Crown."

"The nuns must have had a better quality of life in the countryside?"

"I don't think the quality of life was in their DNA; only

serving God. Working the fields was probably worse than being in the city, even with all its problems."

Daniel is getting increasingly alarmed, not by the information, but by the way it is being imparted. All the time, Harcourt stares straight ahead but Daniel can tell that he isn't seeing anything. A dirty white van is driving very close to them and had flashed its lights on the previous bend.

"Are you feeling alright Martin?" You seem a bit distant.

The DI turns to him then, slowly, as if hearing him for the first time since his automated assistant answered the previous questions. "I'm fine."

"Only, you seem to be driving very slowly now that we've got a clear road."

Instead of accelerating, Harcourt suddenly brakes and makes a turn to the left, coming to a stop just before a metal gate leading to the nearby field.

Daniel is shaken, though he tries hard not to show it. While he is still gathering his thoughts there is a sudden rapping noise on Harcourt's side window. A large, stubbled face is staring in at them, shouting angrily.

Harcourt barely acknowledges him, but Daniel is out of his side of the car in a flash. The white van driver had also pulled over, just behind them. Stationed half on the road still, the orange hazard lights only add to the sense of emergency.

"Tell your mate he needs to learn to drive properly!" The man bellows at him over the roof of the car. Daniel, adrenaline pumping through his veins, marches around the rear of the car until he is facing the stocky, scruffy man head-on. He ignores the horns and other angry comments from drivers now having to wait behind the van because of oncoming traffic.

"My 'mate' is Detective Inspector Harcourt of Worcester CID. We were driving slowly, waiting for a call, in case we needed to stop quickly." He hears himself shouting back. "Now, if you've nothing better to do, I suggest you get back in your rust bucket right now and stop causing a traffic hold-up and danger to other road users. If you do not do exactly as I say we'll have your car reg through the PNC quicker than you can say greasy burgers and chips, not to mention the intense scrutiny of your service and insurance documents. It's amazing what we can find when others can't."

The man glares at him for at least fifteen seconds, before allowing his brain to override his brawn. He climbs back into his van, crashes the gear stick into first and accelerates away loudly. The other cars quickly follow, many of their near side passengers exhibiting digital warnings that no anti-virus program would contain.

Back in the car, Harcourt seems to have regained full consciousness, even though his head had come into contact with neither person nor object. "I've never seen you so angry!"

"I've never been in this situation before."

Harcourt examines him, looking for hidden meanings to that response, but cannot find them.

Daniel senses a slight forward movement of the car. Realising that the handbrake is not fully engaged, he reaches across to pull the lever sharply upwards, the ratchets protesting their insecurity. As he does so, his right-hand brushes over a small ceramic object in the car's 'accessory tray.' He gently lifts it out while Harcourt looks on, unspeaking.

The figurine features a ballet dancer in a pink leotard and white tutu. The little girl smiles at them but neither of them can return it. Harcourt seems choked up again, while Daniel sees only a child's unmoving face.

***

They draw into the Jones's drive some forty minutes later. Daniel had resolved to give Harcourt as long as necessary to recover from his panic attack. Not only was he concerned for his welfare, but also his own life in Harcourt's hands on the steering wheel.

Eventually, Harcourt had dried his eyes, taken several deep breaths and a long swig of water from the plastic bottle that had hitherto hidden the little figure that lay between them and moved back onto the road. As luck would have it, they had found themselves at the rear of a long convoy of cars following a tractor, which gave him even more time to compose himself.

"I'm so sorry about that," he had begun before Daniel held up his hand as not just a warning sign to slow down but a 'stop' instruction.

"You have nothing to be sorry about. Neither of us was hurt and nor was anybody else. You did the right thing to stop when you did, even if our little friend was upset by somebody else driving a bit erratically for a change!"

Harcourt forces a smile to reappear on his face. "To be honest, it was a surprise to me too. I have episodes like that very rarely, I'm pleased to say. Once they've passed, that's usually it for goodness knows how many months, even a year. Something set it off back there. I'm not sure if it was the candles or the organ music or even the small congregation in a large space. Too much space to fill. I'd felt much better once I'd left the church but then it came over me again, like a second wave.

"Was there a particular case, do you think, that made you so anxious, or is it a culmination of things? I could easily understand why things might have built up in the way that they have." Daniel is keen to offer a sympathetic ear rather than appear to be merely curious. Talking may once have been thought to 'cost lives;' in his experience not doing so has been far more corrosive.

"There is, was, a single event which I can trace all of this back to. As you say though, it's a stressful job and there are only so many bad things that any one person can witness or come to know about."

Daniel waits for details which don't arrive. Harcourt leans over slightly to check his face in the driving mirror, but this is no bonding moment. He is almost as quickly opening his door as closing it behind him with a slam.

Cerys Jones opens the front door and immediately but wordlessly invites them in. Daniel's gaze bounces off the white walls before he and Harcourt are directed into a small, more intimate snug room to the left.

"I hope you don't mind us sitting in here," the lilt in her Welsh voice is endearing but Harcourt is concerned to see her wince as she settles into a well-worn armchair, "I just find it easier somehow. Less formal. Barry rarely comes in here since Gary died so it's become my space now, I suppose."

They sink into a comfy cream armchair at right angles to her, facing a wall-mounted TV screen.

"Gary used to love it in here, watching movies and so on. Called it his 'den.'" She smiles at them but they both know she is far from being relaxed. The memory of her son does not comfort her.

"Thanks for seeing us, Mrs Jones." Harcourt seems his usual self now, or at least the one who hides behind the rules of formality.

"No problem. Probably easier with Barry not here."

"Away on business?" Daniel cringes at the cliché.

"This is Daniel Reed; he's assisting the police on this and other cases."

"Are you to do with accident prevention then?" Her query is straightforward; much harder to answer simply or straightforwardly.

"Not prevention exactly; a more insightful approach though, certainly."

Either she doesn't understand or doesn't believe him; in him. She turns slightly to face Harcourt. Daniel is used to people turning their backs on him. Little do they understand that he can still see their faces – usually from the past but sometimes in the future.

Even from this angle though - and very much in the present - he can see a red line of bruising running across the back of her neck. Fierce and raw, her beige woollen dress with its high neckline does not cover it completely. Had she chosen to wear this because of it, or is she oblivious to the marks?

"So, you've come to ask me about the life assurance policy that Barry took out, are you?" She isn't exactly accusatory, but politeness and friendliness seem to have skipped out of the open door together.

"That's one of the items on our list, yes." Harcourt has probably expected this reaction. "It's part of our due diligence to follow up on such matters."

"Even though Gary's death was accidental?" The last word of her life sentence was delivered more softly, a slight catch in her voice. She'd started well, bravely even, but they can both see how far apart she has fallen. "The premiums on those kinds of policies are structured to be enticingly low in the early days – to encourage young people to at least consider them, or their parents to see them as sensible investments for children who don't yet have the sense to worry about the future."

"You seem very well-informed Mrs. Jones; I guess that's what comes of being married to a financial adviser!" Harcourt did not mean his comment to sound frivolous, more an attempt to lighten the tone a little before they lost her altogether.

Her response is not what either of them had accepted. "I may be what people around here – and especially my husband's friends - call a 'trophy wife' Inspector, but I can assure you that is far from the whole truth. Barry may be the front man, but I trained as an accountant in my own right before I'd even met him."

"You knew all about the life assurance policy all along then: it didn't just come to light when Gary died."

"I advised him to take it out, not Barry. Oh, Barry may well have had plans for the money if it ever materialised. None of us wanted that to happen of course. Not that I'd have seen much of it if it did."

"He would have invested it?" Daniel can see an energy building inside the woman, not from grief, but from anger. Harcourt has opened the funnel wide, and rage is bubbling up from inside, thrilled with the opportunity to finally escape.

"In other women, probably."

Both men sit silently, out of what: respect, pity?

Emboldened by the lack of interruption she has encountered for years, she continues, her voice becoming progressively louder. "Barry had other women before, during and almost certainly after our marriage if I could ever pluck up the courage to end it. I could see similar signs in Gary. I wanted to do something now for the woman (or man I suppose) who fell for the good looks and money as I did.

I wanted to ensure that they would get something for

themselves if anything happened to him. Once married he'd have thrown away the key to any future happiness as Barry did with me. I wanted them to have something to hang on to, especially in later years."

"Did you not read any of those signs in Barry before you married him?" Daniel's voice is gentle, as far as possible from judgemental.

"I was young. I'd been brought up on one of the estates off Tolladine, towards the top of the hill. It wasn't the worst estate in Worcester, but certainly not the nicest of places. We had lovely views of the Malvern Hills, as well as all those lovely houses that weren't like ours. I used to sit at my bedroom window and dream of one day getting out. I thought that Barry would help me to realise that dream, see.

Once we'd left Worcester, I realised that you can't ever really leave your past behind, can you? He made sure of that - when his business associates weren't around that is. Even this house was bought on the bad."

"Please do go on." Harcourt isn't surprised but the as-yet secret still captivates him.

"Barry's father wanted him to buy him out of the company he'd built up from scratch – the family business. They assembled high-quality fabric stuffings of the kind you get in pillows, cushions and even gloves. I think that's where it started, originally. His father – Douglas – wanted to retire and for Barry to take it over and see his colleagues right. Some of them had been with him for over forty years.

Anyway, the deal he forced Douglas to sign gave him

the shares, but at a knock-down price – way below the market price at the time. He then encouraged his well-heeled friends to invest in the company, telling them it was hugely undervalued (which it was) and drove the share price sky high. He then sold the company to an Asian entrepreneur who already had arrangements with many local suppliers of the raw materials the company had been importing. The upshot is that the new owner was able to cut costs and move much of the business to Singapore. Most of Douglas's fellow work colleagues were made redundant. Some were offered work abroad. Well, none of them were likely to do that at their time of life, were they?"

"And the proceeds financed this house."

"Blood money, you could say."

Harcourt could and does, internally.

Cerys Jones hasn't quite finished. "Douglas had his heart set on a little cottage over in Feckenham – just down the road from Hanbury Hall if you know it. Beautiful it was, but he couldn't now afford it. All he could manage was a one-bedroom flat in Pershore. A 'gated community' Barry calls it, but the only gates there are the ones they close in the evenings to prevent the yobs from breaking in and stealing tools from the MOT Centre next door.

Gary had also begun to make snide remarks about him, no matter that he was able to swan around in the luxury house purchased on all that hard work over so many years. He once described his grandfather as a 'has-been' and never visited him. None of us did. We weren't allowed to. No doubt they'd also had me over on one of their 'long walks' together." She shifts in her chair and catches her breath with the pain of it.

"Has your husband ever hurt you physically as well as mentally?" Harcourt has moved closer to the edge of his seat; a move Daniel now recognizes as a call to action.

"Women are hurt by their husbands in many different ways, aren't they Inspector?"

"Would you mind us taking a look in Gary's room please Mrs. Jones? It would help us to get a feel of things." Daniel can see that Harcourt needs help again. He doesn't want to lose him to whatever it was that was so troubling him earlier.

"Of course, providing you never tell Barry that you've done so. If Gary's death was an accident, as you all say it was, he'd want to know why you were bothering to look through his things again. They came before – after he died – and that was bad enough. Barry's a very private man, see."

"He wouldn't want anything to be exposed?" Harcourt's comment is cryptic but instantly understood by the other two people in the room.

Cerys Jones chooses to ignore it – for now. "What sort of thing are you looking for?"

"Just something from which I might be able to get an insight, you might say." Daniel has always been acutely aware from his days at the newspaper that words can so easily be misconstrued, and sensationalised, especially if they're not fully understood. There is a very short pathway between 'psychic' and 'freak.' "The bracelet

Gary wore, for example, might have been useful had it not been buried with him."

"Buried? It wasn't buried. It's upstairs in his desk drawer – the second one down. I hid it there behind a box containing a spare power pack for his laptop. I thought I might go and look at it sometimes when Barry was away, and ask him to forgive me."

"To forgive you?" Harcourt is still angry to be present at the scene of verbal and almost certainly physical domestic violence without really being able to do anything about it unless she asks him to, which seems unlikely.

"When he was little, I saw only his good points. His lovely blonde hair; dimples in his cheeks that you could only really see when he smiled a certain way. His deep blue eyes never seemed to miss anything. Towards the end, I saw only his faults. You could say that imperfection became the rule and I struggled with it. I wish I could change it back. I didn't have the energy, see. That, I can deal with. Not feeling inclined to do so is much harder."

Daniel could understand that in that particular space (if indeed it had been a kind of snug, escape room from family affairs) why there would be no photographs. The hallway outside was used for pieces of classical art, rather than classic family portraits. Presumably, they have been consigned to the family vault. Barry Jones certainly did not want to expose his family. Maybe he wanted to be not only its star but also its entire universe.

As they climb the ornate stairway to the first floor, there is only white space all around them. Gary's room is also devoid of any kind of imagery – not even old football posters, pop art or even 'soft' porn (whatever that might mean).

Harcourt opens the drawer and locates the bracelet, faded and lifeless now. Wordlessly he hands it to Daniel, who takes it from him, also silently. In the past, he has experienced a sensation akin to an electric shock or, at the very least, static electricity. At first, he feels nothing at all.

Aware of Harcourt's eyes boring into him, he turns slightly, towards the window before jumping back in horror. Right in front of him is Gary Jones's face, all bulging eyes and hideously bloated. Deathly white but not dead. Behind him, there is the sudden sound of shoes on the exposed wooden floor, running away from them. He turns to see that the shoes are trainers and that they belong to the spirit of Colin Mills who looks as though he has been scared out of his wits.

***

"You didn't see or hear anything?" Daniel seeks clarification from Harcourt as they head back to Worcester.

"In the boy's bedroom? No. Downstairs, plenty, though she tried to hide it. It's so frustrating to see something so fundamentally bad, and not being the good guy who comes along to sort it out."

"Which is why you joined the police in the first place,

I'm guessing?"

"Something like that. I can't stop thinking about her as a little girl, gazing through a bedroom window and dreaming of something better. Look what's happened since."

"It could be worse;" Daniel replies, darkly, "When I was very small I stood on a little black chair so that I could peep out of my tiny bedroom window. My mum would come upstairs to see if I was OK as I'd been so quiet. I told her about all the people I'd seen, passing by the house, visiting the Post Office opposite and so on. I'd describe their coats and hats or the children's play clothes."

"Doesn't sound so bad!"

"It does if most of those people I'd been describing had died many years earlier."

***

"Penny for them, sir?" Linda Farren is used to long silences from Harcourt, but these are more than pauses for thought. It's as though the police station itself is holding its breath.

Harcourt glances across at her face; sees concern rather than curiosity. "I was just thinking about my visit to Cerys Jones with Daniel Reed."

"You're concerned for her welfare?"

"Of course. Her husband is everything I'd hate to be."

"Money must be good though. I doubt you or I will ever get to live in a place like that, although DS Taylor did say that it was a soulless place."

"And she'd be right about that!" It feels better to talk. Debbie had been out by the time he'd dropped Daniel off and returned home. He hadn't been sure whether he would have discussed his latest panic attack with her (if that's what it was) and was quite glad to have that decision taken away from him.

With Farren, it is strictly business, and she has the makings of a very good detective, though he's heard several unnecessary comments from fellow officers about her pleasing body shape. He finds this and them as repellant as he does Barry Jones.

"We could quietly get in touch with Social Services; ask them to keep an eye on things?"

"That's the problem, though, isn't it? There'd be nothing much to see. He'd make sure of that. Besides, the contact has to come from her. She'd be worse off in practically every way if he was charged, and certainly if he walked. She's lost her only son which might take her years to come to terms with. Losing her husband and most likely her house and income would only compound that."

"At least she'd be safe though. She could start again. People do."

He sees her blush and wonders why. Not for now, though he's made a mental note of it. "Frightening that though isn't it? Especially at her age. Building what you think is going to be a better life, only to have to knock it all down again and find that all you have left is rubble. Old and weathered bricks that had only been held together by long-perished mortar."

"You'll be reading poetry next, sir!"

He laughs out loud. "How is Flowers?"

"DS Taylor spoke with him last night and he didn't seem too bad, considering. He told her he wants to get back to work as soon as possible. Leaving his mother during the day is going to be the hardest part, but at least she has a part-time job at the flower shop in the village, so I guess she'll want to get back too. Some sense of normality."

"Life has to go on, except in some cases it doesn't have to."

"I know you don't believe these deaths to have been accidents, sir. One, maybe, but not three. At the same time, though, do you think they could have been suicides?"

Now he does pause for thought before replying. "I think they probably did take their own lives – without the involvement of anyone else I mean – but I don't believe either of the deaths was entirely voluntary."

"Someone or something pushed them towards it?"

She's good, he muses. The reports on her progress before joining them had fully justified her fast-track status in the Force. "Daniel Reed 'saw' real fear on the face of Colin Mills yesterday; well, a 'version' of him. I don't think he's our protagonist, but fear is undoubtedly a big part of all of this."

Now it's Farren's turn to remain quiet.

Harcourt does intervene this time. "Which bit are you

not yet convinced about: fear or the possibility of better understanding the unknown?"

Her head whips around to face him. Something else has replaced concern. Anger, embarrassment maybe? "Have you been talking to DS Flowers, sir, only our conversation was strictly off the record and…"

"Linda," he gently interrupts her, preventing the outburst from becoming an unwelcome torrent for either of them, "I haven't spoken with Flowers because he hasn't been around. If you told him something in confidence or discussed something that you didn't want to go any further, I can guarantee that he wouldn't have shared it with anybody else. It isn't difficult to spot someone's scepticism, and I'm in no position to judge you on that. Many people would feel precisely the same as you do."

"I'm sorry, sir. I didn't think it would be so obvious."

"Body language gives us the best tip-offs."

She smiles again, relieved, and yet worried now about doing, saying, the right thing to him. "I hope I'm fairly broad-minded, sir. My time so far in this job has already stretched my imagination way beyond what it was; seeing what people can do to each other. Lateral thinking is one of my passions, so I think I am making some progress."

"Except that your experiences – and, let's face it, this applies to most of us – are based on what you see, hear or deduce from earthly matters. The spirit world is, by definition, not part of that."

"Partly. I'm trying to embrace it, I honestly am. It's just that since talking to Ian I've read so many reports of cases – especially in the United States where much of the literature seems to have been written - where people like Mr Reed have been brought in because the police are getting nowhere. And yet, they haven't been any more... successful? High on profile but low on genuine results?"

"I accept that there isn't a great track record for us to refer to and many high-profile failures in this country such as in the 'Yorkshire Ripper' case where an element of desperation led to the willing divergence of key resources at key times. The lateral approach you mention might have been hugely helpful.

I also appreciate why many police forces here and elsewhere are reluctant to involve those with extra-sensory 'gifts' even though the new College of Policing advised that such extra 'help' should not be completely ignored. However, I think that is just as much to do with the bad press they may get as an intrinsic fear of the unknown. When people fear someone or something, one of the most common reactions is ridicule, quickly leading to anger and bullying. It happens from playgrounds to parliaments."

"I accept that when I first heard about us calling in such a person I was surprised, sir. It isn't that I don't like Mr Reed – it's never personal with me - more that I'm not sure how much help he's going to give us. I mean he doesn't seem to have made much progress so far. I suppose it's also a bit galling that we're working all the hours available to get to the bottom of these mysteries while he swans in as though he doesn't have a care in the world."

"Let me put you straight right away there, Sergeant. Mr Reed has many cares: in both this world and the next."

***

Harcourt indicates and turns the car onto the narrow country lane leading down to Pickerton just as his mobile begins to ring. He draws to a halt, checking first in his rearview mirror that there are no other vehicles following them which would have little chance of getting past until he moves on.

"It's Taylor, sir. I've just had a call from Edward Mills. He sounded quite upset so I'm going over there now."

"OK. Do you know what he's upset about?"

"Not yet. The Front Desk took it and passed it straight through to us."

"I'll let the Super know. Take care and stay in touch on any developments?"

"Will do. You too."

Although Daniel is staring straight ahead, Harcourt knows that he is processing information from within, without and further still. "Edward Mills?"

Had he overheard the conversation or not. "The same. He's phoned in. I don't suppose ..."

""I could dial in too! I wish I could, but I'm afraid the spirits don't really do party lines, or does that age me too much?"

Harcourt laughs out loud, incongruous in the

circumstances but a relief nonetheless. "I remember clearly overhearing our neighbour gossiping to her friend about all the goings-on in the neighbourhood."

"I hope she didn't mention you by name."

"Not that I can remember. She'd have probably expected me to bug her house if so, to save me the trouble of lifting the receiver!"

Moments later they turn off the road and head down a sandy track, dried out by the summer sunshine and not yet the quagmire it will no doubt become during the months to come. Although a bit bumpy they soon park up outside of the log cabin they were heading towards. As they are leaving the vehicle a blonde, middle-aged woman dressed in a sort of orange hippy smock approaches them.

Harcourt makes the introductions.

"Let's sit on the deck, though we may need to be cautious if any walkers come along."

It was a summons rather than a suggestion. Hunter-Wright would have been proud thinks Harcourt as he surveys the building. It is in very good condition and not at all as run down and weary as he had thought it and its owner might have been.

"We passed some yellow buoys on the lake; what are they used for?"

Moira Ahern looks back over his shoulder. "They use that part of the lake for wild water swimming. It's much deeper there than it is here. There's a hut further around the bend of the lake with a little jetty where the swimmers congregate. You can't see it from here."

"Do you just live here during the summer months?" Daniel has seated himself in a wicker chair with its back to the cabin wall so that he has a good view of the lake beyond.

"Mainly, yes. I have a small bungalow in Welland but it's so unsettling. The traffic. People shouting. I might as well live in a city as there."

"You prefer the peace and tranquillity of this place?" Harcourt is sitting in an over-size wooden chair which, to his surprise, is actually a rocking chair.

The other two watch him gently bob up and down while trying to remain serious. Their eyes meet and Daniel sees immediately in her faraway look an insight way beyond what the pale blue irises have recorded.

"It brings me peace, most of the time. I can reflect here, and all of life is reflected back at me."

"Your family is not from here." Daniel is stating a fact rather than a question, and certainly not the kind of formal query Harcourt might have addressed to her back in the flat and static comfort of his interview room.

She stares back at him, wondering how he knows perhaps, or trying to process the information recently received by her brain. One key message coming through is that there is nowhere to hide. Not that she wants that now. Not any longer.

"My people are from India originally, Romani people. Our gift has been the ability to travel, to experience what different cultures and races have to offer the world."

"And your gift to the world in return?"

"We have many gifts, Mr Reed. Some of us find the power – the possibilities – a little too unnerving to offer up."

Harcourt continues to rock silently backwards and forwards, unsure of what they are talking about, but trusting Daniel's instinct and a strong sense that he has found some kind of kindred spirit here.

"You preferred to put down roots?"

"From which many fruits have grown, yes. My late father put gold down to buy this lake and the surrounding land back in the 'Fifties. Joe - my husband - helped to build the cabin and develop the site so that others might enjoy its beauty."

"You never thought to make money from it – to recover some of the expense; pay for its upkeep?" Harcourt's question crashes them back into commercial reality, much in the same way that a couple of ducks have seemingly just crash-landed on the lake (albeit in perfect formation).

"He saw it as our refuge should we ever need it? Travellers come up against much hostility, as you will know better than anyone!"

She doesn't exactly target this comment at either one of them, but rather both, and for her different reasons, it seems.

"And your husband – Joe – does he live with you here, or in Welland?" Harcourt isn't in the mood for 'bohemian bonhomie', especially since hearing that Taylor was on her way to the Mills's house.

"Neither, as it happens. When he's in the area he stays in Welland, although he does love to walk beside the lake."

"I'd have thought it would have been the other way round," Daniel wants to linger a little longer, even if Harcourt is determined to cut to the chase, "This seems a peaceful, tranquil place to me."

"Oh, it is. When you've been on the road for a long time, though, you do value creature comforts of the non-wildlife kind more highly."

"He's travelling at present?" Harcourt throws a 'halt' sign at Daniel.

"He is, though I sense that he is on the way back."

"You 'sense' it, but haven't had a letter, or email… or text?"

"None of those is required, Inspector. My messages are borne on the wind. If Joe was in trouble, I'd know; as would he if danger approached me."

"When do you anticipate him being back?" Harcourt cannot completely hide the cynicism in his voice.

"Before the winter sets in," Moira seems to elevate her head to take in the woody smells of autumn as if to confirm her belief, "Though I already know he'll be setting off again before the spring moons push the tides back out again."

"He becomes restless if he stays too long in one place?" Daniel ignores Harcourt's eyes boring into him from the side, even as he reaches each peak in the rocking chair cycle.

"It's in his blood." Moira muses while looking into Daniel's eyes intently. "Mine too, though I've wearied of the unknown."

"You asked us over to tell us about something – or someone – you saw?" Harcourt has had enough and managed to retrieve his notebook and pen without altering the rhythmic, rocking cycle.

"I did!" She takes a deep breath. It hasn't been easy lately, for me or the other people involved."

Both men wait patiently. Daniel can already tell from the way that she tenses and gazes beyond them both again that she has indeed seen someone here - out in the lake - either in her present or in her past.

"Who did you see?" Daniel prompts her now, hoping to provide a shortcut past the preface of her tale.

"I saw the boy who drowned; watched him drown."

"Gary Jones?" Harcourt is scribbling furiously now, excitement colouring his cheeks.

She nods slowly. "He was here with a group of friends. I heard them, laughing and joking, before they came into sight around that bend up there." She points to the far bank of the lake. Both men look in that direction.

"It's deserted now, and quiet. On that evening it was lively; full of life."

They wait for her to continue. A faint mist seems to have come into her eyes, but she still sees what she saw. "I was looking out of the window here. It was a clear night with at least an hour of sunlight left, although it was beginning to fade slightly. One of the boys - I wouldn't have been able to say which one as they both looked very similar – waded into the water. He was heading straight for the cabin here, yet he wouldn't have made it all the way without swimming as the lake is much too deep in the middle. After a minute or so the other boy did the same. I thought he was going to try and race him at first."

"Did he catch up with him - the other boy I mean?" Harcourt is still rocking in the chair, faster than ever now.

She is quiet for what seems much longer than the fifteen or twenty seconds it is. "He did. He grabbed hold of his hair from behind and held him under the water. The other boy was spluttering – you could see the foam on the surface – but his attacker kept lifting his head then plunging it under again."

"Did you hear anything? Did the boy attacking the other say anything?"

"Just: 'Don't you ever do that again.'"

"What happened then, Moira?" Daniel is calm though, in truth, his heart is probably beating equally as fast as Harcourt's.

"Eventually the other boy let go of him and started to head back to the far bank."

"The girls. There were three girls present, weren't there?" Harcourt again, still scribbling.

"There were three others, yes. They seemed to be in shock. I don't think they had expected the other boy to do what he did. I don't remember them saying anything at all before they started screaming."

"Screaming?"

"The boy who was still in the water was struggling to move. He kept disappearing under the surface, despite being all alone. There is a large bed of reeds there. They run along much of the lake's bed, most particularly in the deeper parts, like tentacles from an unseen creature. I could see that his legs had got stuck. No matter how much he struggled, he kept going under."

"Did any of the others try to help him?"

"They all did. All four of them ran into the water and eventually managed to pull him loose and got him over to the bank, keeping his head elevated. When they got there the attacker, who now seemed to be in charge of the rescue, slipped and the other boy's head fell onto one of the large rocks that run alongside the water – making that side so different to this one. Even while the girls continued to shout and scream at him, he tried to give him mouth-to-mouth and what he obviously thought was some kind of CPR, rolling him over and then back again."

"How did he react when he realised that Gary had died?"

"He started to wail. An awful feral noise it was. They all joined in. One of them must have called the emergency services because it wasn't long before blue lights were reflecting in the water."

Harcourt finally brings the rocking chair to a stop, undeterred by the tears pouring down Moira Ahern's face. "Why didn't you tell the police what you saw – either those attending the scene or afterwards?

She shivers and shakes her head. "I know I should have done. I wish every day that I had done."

"You haven't answered my question?" Harcourt persists, urgently, uncompromisingly.

"Because I was frightened of what he'd do to me if I did?"

"Who? The boy who attacked Gary?"

"No. Not him."

"You weren't alone that night, were you Moira?" Daniel is ahead of the detective.

She shakes her head slowly.

"I thought your husband hadn't yet been blown back here by the winds of time?" Harcourt's sarcasm is almost spat out: the distaste of disgust.

"Who was it, Moira?" Daniel remains calm. He needs to be.

"His name is Gordon Clay. He and his wife run a hotel in Malvern. I met him walking around the lake one day. We got talking about the history of the area."

"You got on!" Harcourt appreciates anyone whose guilty secret is a passion for history, at least until proven ignorant.

"We did. Do. He began visiting late at night. Sometimes we'd just walk in the moonlight. I think we were both glad of the company at first."

"He isn't happy in his marriage?" Harcourt finds that he can barely look at the woman, although, of course, he needs to.

"He isn't. I think they may have been happy together once, but people change, don't they? Whether it was the pressure of running the business or just his wife's natural need to be in charge coming out, she became 'insufferably domineering', to quote Gordon."

"He is quieter, gentle." Daniel can see that such a person would find much more of a kindred spirit in Moira Ahern.

"Yes!" She isn't unnerved by his insight; perhaps a little surprised by it though. "His wife perceives that as lacking backbone."

"Meek!" Daniel, in direct contrast to Harcourt, cannot take his eyes off hers.

"Exactly that, but they are going to inherit the earth if you believe what you read in the ancient texts."

"You're not a Christian?"

"I'd be a sinner if I was. I believe in nature, Inspector, and the course it has and will take."

"And you see this as the course of true love?" Harcourt isn't convinced it's much more than a fling, with a delicious hint of danger attached."

"It's just nice to be able to have a free, in-depth conversation on almost any subject without the feeling that you're being attacked rather than challenged. He'd missed that."

Daniel nods, understanding that feeling all too well.

"Gordon was getting increasingly worried though. It wasn't that he wanted to cover up what happened down here exactly, but he told me that if I came to you, it would all have to come out about us and then he'd lose everything: me, his wife, and his livelihood. He can be very persuasive and if that doesn't work, very, very angry – totally different to what he's normally like: a dark side, you might say."

"And yet you did telephone us?"

"When I read about the second girl drowning in Worcester, I knew that I had to. One more death might be coincidental, but two are unlikely not to be connected in some way, are they? Even if you were to believe in God, He's not that mysterious, is He?"

***

"So even in his confused state, if you believe Dorothy and Derek King, it seems that Bob Drake did see Moira Ahern and Gordon Clay arguing; almost certainly about her wanting to contact the police?" Daniel is summarizing his thoughts as Harcourt negotiates the rutted track back to the main road.

"I've asked Farren to check out The Malvern Spring Hotel to see if Clay is there, in which case we'll head over there after calling in on Mr Mills."

"You're not going to be discreet, are you?"

"Moira Ahern turns out to be a key witness in Gary Jones's death and yet not only did Clay say nothing, he also effectively forced her to remain quiet too. Even if I can't get him on perverting the course of justice there's no doubt in my mind that he's a pervert."

***

Taylor's car is parked in the lane outside the Mills' home, but it is a different woman who opens the door to them.

Dressed in light denim dungarees over some kind of black, faded rock t-shirt, her hair is lime green and a stud that might be copper or might just be rusty is lodged in her right-hand nostril.

"Yes?"

"DI Harcourt and Mr Daniel Reed. I believe our colleague DS Taylor may already be on the scene."

"You make it sound like there's been some kind of emergency." She sneers and stands aside to let them pass.

"Hasn't there?" Harcourt is already bristling.

"Not that I'm aware of unless you consider a gross overreaction to non-events by elderly people to be worth your time."

"You didn't contact us then?"

"I did, Inspector." Edward Mills, dressed casually in grey trousers and a brown pullover, strides across the hallway towards them. "You must be Mr Reed? Your sergeant has just been telling us about your involvement with these cases."

"Cases!" The woman's voice is scornful.

He shakes Daniel's hand warmly before ushering them towards the dining room. "I see you've met our daughter, Gina."

The dining room is formal with eight high-backed wooden chairs surrounding a dark oak table.

"I thought we might do better in here as there are a few of us."

Harcourt acknowledges Taylor who is sitting next to a clearly upset Daisy Mills.

Taylor, in turn, briefs them on the turn of events. "Mrs Mills was woken in the night by a noise from downstairs, sir. She came down to investigate but saw nothing untoward other than a light that had been left on in the main lounge so went back to bed and thought nothing more of it until this morning when Mrs Mills went to wake Janice with a cup of tea to find her gone."

"Gone? As in left, bed made, bags packed?" Harcourt hadn't meant for his question to sound so harsh, unsympathetic. The truth is that he is not only angry with Moira Ahern for withholding information but even more so with Gordon Clay who encouraged her to do so. He is itching to get to Malvern to confront the man.

Daniel is also surprised by Harcourt's tone and, after

his eyes briefly meet Taylor's, he seeks to provide some common ground. "We understand that this is upsetting for you both – all three of you."

"It's fine. It's fine." Edward Mills holds his hands up as if he is about to say, 'It's a fair cop, gov.' Thankfully, he doesn't. "We appreciate that this may be something and nothing and no, in answer to your question Inspector, it looks as though Janice has just got up and left. There appears to be no kind of longer-term plan."

"Might she simply have been late for a class or some other kind of engagement?" Daniel can see how trying to get closer to the truth is leading Daisy Mills closer to a reality she can only deny if she is to in any way deal with it.

"That could be true, yes."

"Except you don't believe that to be so, do you, sir." Harcourt is trying harder, his voice softer. He too can see now how stressed Janice's grandmother is becoming. "Otherwise, I venture that you would have waited at least twenty-four hours before contacting us?"

"Quite so. One reads about Missing Persons and how most of them do turn up quite quickly and with quite innocent explanations."

Daniel and both detectives know that this is purely for his wife's benefit. His good intentions do not, however, have the desired effect.

"She would always let me know in advance or leave a note to say where she was going," Daisy Mills blows her nose for the umpteenth time that morning, it seems, "She knows I worry – especially after…"

Gina either hasn't noticed her distress or the despair driving it. "I told you this would happen, didn't I? You keep independent, living beings on a lead and all they want to do is roam, explore."

"For goodness' sake, Gina! This is not at all the same."

"You are Janice's mother I understand?" Daniel's voice is neutral. Harcourt's might not have been.

"Wow. The shrink earns his dough. Yeah, what difference does that make."

"You don't seem overly concerned about your daughter's safety."

"I'm not. She's probably just gone for a walk, or a ramble with friends. It's a nice day out there. Why not?"

"You don't think that three of her friends drowning in recent months would be something to be wary of?" Harcourt is indeed struggling now, really struggling.

"I think being wary of water would be more to the point, don't you? Besides, I thought they were accidents?"

The doorbell rings and Gina nonchalantly leaves the room to answer it.

"I am so sorry, Inspector. Gina left some years ago to 'find herself.' She eventually found herself in some kind of commune in West Wales. She wasn't – isn't – blessed with what you might call maternal instincts. Daisy and I have often wondered if she's on the autistic spectrum. Either way, she doesn't do empathy I'm afraid." Mills is still as polite and well-mannered as he can be. "Neither she nor we have seen her husband – Janice's father – Henry for years now. He left when Janice was very small and Gina soon after. We hadn't seen her for about nine or ten months until she called in, unexpectedly, this morning. So, you see, we've pretty much brought Janice up alone."

"You mentioned that you worry about Janice, Mrs Mills, "Taylor is sitting very close to the elderly lady, her voice gentle, "Especially after… and then you were interrupted. Was it the other drownings you were going to refer to?"

Daisy Mills looks across to her husband, then Daniel, and then directly at Taylor. "Gary Jones had made a pass at her."

"What!" Edward Mills is astounded and must have hitherto been quite oblivious to this news. "Why didn't you tell me?"

"I'm sorry. She was so upset about it and swore me to secrecy. I did want to tell you. It would have made it much easier for me to share such a thing rather than having to keep going back to it on my own."

"When did this happen?" Harcourt watches Gina casually lead DS Farren into the room.

"Some weeks ago – back in the summer. He tried to force himself on her down by the lake one evening."

"But she was going out with Colin Pearson, wasn't she?"

"They were close, yes."

"Did she tell him about this, do you know?"

"I don't know." The woman bursts into tears. Taylor puts her arm around her and Edward Mills immediately walks over and sits on the other side of her.

Harcourt beckons Farren over. "Any news from Malvern?"

"All quiet on the Western Front, sir. Patricia Clay hasn't seen her husband for days."

"I feel as though I've stepped into a life-sized game of Cluedo," Gina Mills's sarcastic observation stops all of them in their tracks, "Maybe you should have called Colonel Mustard for help instead?"

CHAPTER TWELVE

"Splendid to have you back DS Flowers. I'm afraid you might have to hit the ground running though as a situation seems to be developing here." Rupert Hunter-Wright is standing in front of a whiteboard covered in various-coloured scribbles and images of the three people who have died – Gary Jones, Zoya Agarwal and Barbara Flint – as well as Janice Mills who is now missing, if not yet officially.

"Thank you, sir. I would much rather be busy. Too much time on my hands otherwise."

Hunter-Wright briefly recalls the Janis Ian line ... 'Got nothing but time to relieve me.' It hadn't worked for him so far and probably never would for his DS either, acting or otherwise.

"How is your mum coping?" Taylor whispers the question in his ear.

Flowers bends backwards slightly in his chair before whispering his reply, a little more loudly. "She keeps telling me we'll need to move now, as there are too many bedrooms."

Harcourt, sitting on the other side of him, squeezes his hand gently but says nothing. They and DS Farren are sitting in the poky meeting room which smells of stale coffee and ping meals as usual.

"Any news on Gordon Clay?" Hunter-Wright barks the question out of his bloated lips, a shiny band of sweat forming just above them.

"Not yet, sir, but we have put an alert out."

"And this Janice Mills, Harcourt, are we to assume that she is now at risk – from herself as much as anybody else?"

"Difficult to say for certain, sir, which is why we are treading carefully. Edward Mills and his wife are scouring the local area, but keeping it low-key as they don't want to alarm either the neighbours or Janice herself if she doesn't want to be found. They don't want to frighten her off if she is just hiding somewhere nearby for some reason."

"For some reason? You'll have to do better than that, Inspector. Why don't we know of possible reasons why she might go missing? It seems we haven't moved on substantially from the drownings of those two girls, have we? They must have had their reasons too; both of them."

"Indeed, sir. Mr Reed is helping us with our enquiries, as you know, and he does believe that Gary Jones's death is part of this in some way."

"In some way ... for some reason?" Hunter-Wright is very red in the face now. A very bad sign.

"Yes, sir."

'Helping us with our enquiries.' Why does he talk

in such staccato sentences? Before that young man's death, all three girls were alive, not dead or missing. Of course, it's relevant. The key point is whether his drowning was the driver of everything that has happened since, or whether it was the collective result of others' intentions. In which direction should the arrows behind him be slung?

"Do we think this Gordon Clay is something to do with it?"

"Unlikely, sir. We think he was a witness to the Gary Jones death, certainly, but his and Mora Ahern's crimes – if that's what they are – probably represent the sum total of their affair."

"Probably? Since when did the police force deal in such indefinite articles?"

The room is much warmer now than when they all entered it, despite Taylor having turned the heating off at the outset as a pre-emptive strike.

"Some things remain, as yet, unknown, sir. I can assure you, once again, that we are all working hard to throw some light on all aspects of these cases to ascertain who and what and why."

Harcourt remains calm, but his colleagues know that he is struggling. Mercifully, it seems that Daniel Reed hasn't told any of them of his 'difficulties' at Rob Flowers's funeral. Harcourt thinks it will stay that way, though he did confide in Debbie, who showed her considerable concern by asking him every ten minutes or so for the rest of the previous evening if he 'felt OK.' She has continued to ask the same question via text messages throughout the morning.

It is Flowers who tries to diffuse or at least change the atmosphere in some way. Speaking very quietly at first, an almost imperceptible nod of encouragement from Taylor seems to give him the confidence he needs. "It may be nothing, sir."

"Quite possibly." Hunter-Wright's sympathy is only ever short-term.

Flowers is used to it. "I've been thinking – and, as I said earlier, I've had a lot of time to do so in the last few days. What if Zoya and Barbara felt guilty about what happened down at the lake? If Mrs Ahern's account is truthful then they weren't responsible, of course, but what if they felt as if they were?"

"Especially if Colin Pearson tried to somehow convince them – got into their heads - that they were collectively responsible for Gary's death, you know, by not getting to him earlier once he started struggling?" Taylor can already see where Flowers is going with this.

"Or if Pearson swore each of them to silence and then later told them that this made them accessories to the crime because they hadn't come forward to the police – a tactic Gordon Clay may also have tried on Moira Ahern?" Farren too is warming to the theme.

"Except that it appears there was no crime. We can assume that Colin Pearson was trying to teach Gary Jones a lesson after the attack on his girlfriend." Harcourt looks and feels less alone in the room now.

"If that's what she is? I thought you said she might just

be a 'friend'?" Hunter-Wright loves to dot the i's.

"But you'd still be angry if someone attacked your friend, wouldn't you, sir?" Flowers is on a roll now. He takes the senior officer's silence as a signal to continue. "One of Rob's favourite poems was 'The Ancient Mariner.' What if both Zoya and Barbara each hung a metaphorical albatross around their necks, as though they accepted that punishment for their crime? Freedom was all around them apart from in their heads. Nobody could see it, but they felt it, really felt it, every hour of every day since Gary died. I believe this might all be about that sense of misplaced guilt."

There is a sudden, loud knock on the door which then opens, followed by a uniformed constable entering the room. Addressing Hunter-Wright, but loudly enough for them all to hear, he announces: "I'm so very sorry for interrupting the meeting, sir, but thought that you should know this immediately. We've had a telephone call from Mr Edward Mills. He's been searching the old mill race outside his home."

**

As Daniel is driving towards Pickerton to meet Harcourt at the Agarwal family home a medley of Christmas songs comes on the radio. Although he can barely believe that it is just around the corner again, he turns it up, remembering the first time he and Charlotte had sung carols in the church over at Marcombe.

He'd invited her over for a traditional family Christmas. There were just the four of them then. His parents were elderly but had sung with gusto – especially alternate male and female parts in Good King Wenceslas.

They'd attended the Carol concert there three years ago when things were still relatively normal: Charlotte was on edge but not too spiky. Fergus, who was now in charge, was as pious as ever but sang rather quietly. Lucy, his wife, was dressed up in her finery at the front of the church, bitching about the women from the flower-arranging group at the back, as usual. And then there was Claire and him, just singing and looking forward to the festivities back at home.

Mum and Dad are still present, of course, witnessing this latest drama from beyond their graves.

The DJ is introducing the next track from 1962 when it was used as part of a worldwide plea for peace during the Cuban Missile Crisis, apparently, but made famous by Bing Crosby a year later. Daniel is tempted to turn it off. He's never liked *White Christmas* despite it being one of his late mother's absolute favourites. To his surprise, a different song greets him from the car's loudspeakers.

'Do you hear what I hear?

Said the night wind to the little lamb
Do you see what I see?
(Do you see what I see?)
Way up in the sky, little lamb
Do you see what I see?'

Bing croons on as Daniel approaches the M5 flyover. His car is thankfully on some kind of autopilot because Daniel's mind is barely in touch with the road. He has returned to the past, but not with Charlotte this time; it is much more recent than that. Finally, he understands why Nancy said the things she did, and why the police hadn't and probably never would have believed in her.

**

Harcourt is waiting for him outside the Agarwals' cottage.

"Hello Martin," Daniel shakes the policeman's hand warmly while looking for the tell-tale signs of anxiety on his face. "I've had some thoughts about Nancy Gutteridge."

"And there was me thinking you were a happily married man!"

This is not the kind of response he is used to from the DI, but he has also seen something different in his eyes too. Something he has never witnessed before. Excitement?

"Tell me after we've finished here. Just to bring you up-to-date quickly: Edward Mills found a student library card from Worcester Sixth Form College floating on top of the water in the old mill race outside his house. The race is partially blocked at the moment by late summer debris. He hadn't got around to clearing it yet or it would have floated away and joined the Pick further down. Mr Mills spotted the logo immediately, with its blue lower quadrant and white river separating it from the dark grey above."

Daniel is amused by Harcourt's need to describe almost forensically the logo but also intrigued. "Is it Janice's?"

The door before them opens. A kind of hopelessness is etched on Nadin Agarwal's face, yet politeness overcomes the sadness, temporarily at least.

"Good morning inspector. Do you have news?"

The three men head for the tiny sitting room Farren and Taylor had been welcomed into just a short time ago.

"This is Mr Daniel Reed, Mr Agarwal."

"Nadin, please."

"He is looking into several cases, including your daughter's, with a view to understanding better what happened."

"Thank you," the man's voice is gentle, deferential.

"May I first say how very sorry I am for your loss." Daniel sees a man who has given up on the wonder of creation, on life's possibilities. Only good manners are preventing him from crumbling right in front of them, as sure as the fates will destroy the most beautiful of temples.

"My wife and I are still struggling with Zoya's death, I'm afraid."

"I saw your wife just now, down at the mill." Harcourt has also seen how gently he needs to tread.

"Have they... have they found Janice?" The man's trembling voice hangs in the stale air.

"No. No, not as yet."

"Oh. Thank goodness. I mean, not that this is good news of course. It's just that Edward and Daisy were in such a state, I encouraged Oviya to pop down this morning.

Not to intrude, you understand, just to offer some support – moral support if nothing else."

"And I'm sure it is much appreciated." Harcourt can see how much the pain and the fear of the unknown is causing the man, not just in terms of the missing girl's whereabouts, but also forcing him to re-live the final moments when his own daughter was found."

"She must be so worried – Daisy I mean. Janice was more like a daughter than a granddaughter to her and Edward. It was as though Gina had never really been there a lot of the time."

"We understand that was indeed the case: that Gina rarely visited the family."

"I could never really understand that, neither of us could. What daughter would show such disrespect to their parents who had raised them, given them everything."

"Something must have been missing in Gina's case." Daniel is encouraged to hear the man opening up, knowing how much it will help him to do so rather than keeping everything bottled up. "Do you have any idea what it was?"

"None at all. Nobody did. Edward hadn't lived a conventional life. Well, that's not quite true, he lived a very conventional life at first but that was more of his father's making."

"He wanted Edward to become a Civil Servant?" Harcourt again.

"Old money, inspector; he made it happen."

"But this wasn't what Edward wanted to do?"

"Who would?" There is a hint of a smile on the man's face now, as though a ray of sunshine has finally broken through the clouds. Certainly, more relaxed now, he warms to his theme. "Edward told Daisy that he had stuck with it for as long as he could – all the self-important suits fluttering around the demigods of government departments."

Harcourt grimaces in sympathy – for both men. He nods, silently encouraging Nadin Agarwal to continue with his story.

"It transpired that Edward's father had scorned Edward's love of art, even at an early age, instead of encouraging it. He saw frivolity in it as opposed to beauty; thought he'd get mixed up with the 'wrong people.' You could say he did for a while couldn't you, just that they were hidden behind big egos rather than beards!"

"I'm so sorry to have to ask this," Harcourt cuts to the chase - to their real reason for being here, "But did Janice ever appear to be frightened to you? We were wondering if she ever shared her fears with Zoya. I know that you told our officers that Zoya seemed perfectly OK before she died."

"Except that she couldn't have been OK, could she? I always thought that she told us everything, but I must have been wrong, mustn't I?"

Daniel can see that this is still hurting the man more

than anything else. He considers whether he'd feel the same if something serious was troubling Claire and yet she too felt unable to tell him or Charlotte all about it. He knows that he would, but he can't say the same for Charlotte. Not anymore. He recalls another song that was played on the radio journey over here (and usually is at this time of year).

'Love is all around us...'

Substitute that word for 'Loss', he ventures, except that loss goes right through the hearts of us too.

Harcourt is continuing, quite oblivious to Daniel's inner struggles. "Was Colin Pearson around here recently, do you know? I've asked Janice's grandparents of course, but they are much too upset to recall things properly."

"Colin? No, not that I'm aware of. I think he was a bit sweet on Zoya to be truthful, but pretty sure it was never reciprocated. My daughter was just happy to have 'friends' and, at her age, we didn't discourage that. Why do you ask about Colin?"

"No reason other than he and Janice were seeing each other – possibly more than just friends – and we were wondering if he'd been sighted down here."

"I'll ask my wife when she returns if you like?"

"That would be very helpful, thanks."

"I'm so sorry gentlemen, where are my manners? Would you like some refreshment?"

Harcourt is about to refuse politely but catches Daniel's eye again and quickly understands that polite acceptance is required here. "Thank you. Tea please if it's not too much trouble?"

"Not at all and so sorry I didn't offer you anything right away."

Nadin leaves the room quickly; gratefully?

Daniel whispers. "You know how it works these days with groups of teenagers: rapping and raging hormones! What if Colin made a pass at Zoya, as Gary did to Janice?"

"Gary's hardly in a position to teach him a lesson in the same way though, is he?"

"Isn't he?" Daniel's reply is enigmatic enough to pique the policeman's interest. "Hold that thought, I need the toilet."

Daniel also leaves the room, with Harcourt deep in thought. He'd planned to head into the kitchen - where he can hear Nadin making all the noises involved in tea-making - to ask him where the toilet is. Instead, he stops in front of a large, square mirror, gilded in gold leaf possibly, hanging on the wall opposite the room where Harcourt remains seated.

Something is wrong, very wrong. His OCD causes him to reach out to move one corner up slightly to bring the angle back to true. As soon as he touches the piece, he sees a face in the mirror, except it isn't his. It belongs to a young Asian girl. Judging by the fine drawing he'd seen just inside the front door, it is the face of Zoya Agarwal.

Daniel gasps out loud. She is as beautiful in death as she

surely was in life; long dark hair frames her smooth, blemish-free skin. Her dark eyes capture his and won't let go of them. Though her lips remain sealed she is tipping her head slightly. Daniel looks above the mirror and then behind him. He sees nothing (and nobody).

He watches her again, almost hypnotized by the movement. Finally, the penny drops. Zoya is beckoning him inside – to join her in the mirror?

Nadin heads towards him, carrying a tea tray. He sees Daniel, motionless, staring at the mirror. "Is something wrong Mr Reed?"

The smaller man comes and stands beside him, but it is only Zoya that Daniel sees.

"Would you mind if we take the mirror off the wall for a moment?" Daniel replies shakily.

"Of course, if you think it will help. I'll just pop this tray down."

Nadin dives into the living room and almost immediately reappears, accompanied by Harcourt.

"What is it, Daniel?" Harcourt looks in the mirror and sees nothing out of the ordinary.

Daniel is entirely aware of the sensitivity of the situation given the presence of the dead girl's father; equally that the DI's reflection too has failed to materialise in the mirror.

"I just sense that there is something behind the mirror," he manages, lifting it from either side and releasing it from the metal hook that has supported it – the whole family – for so long.

The mirror is hiding nothing at all, only a faded square of wallpaper in contrast with the sheets of its slightly brighter neighbours. The mirror, is, as he had expected, quite heavy so Daniel places it on the floor, being extremely careful not to damage it. Harcourt leans over to look at the mirror's backing panel and there, stuck to it with what looks like sticky tape, is a piece of light-blue writing paper.

Beckoning Nadin closer, the smaller man carefully removes it while Daniel holds the mirror steady before placing it back on its hook. Only his reflection – and those of the other two men – now looks back at him.

"Would you mind if I sit down, please, just for a moment?" Nadin is visibly overwhelmed by the discovery, although the name of the person behind the subterfuge, and the reasoning behind it, are still far from certain.

"Of course," Daniel places his arm around Nadin's shoulders and leads him to a tatty old armchair that must be his refuge from the horrors of the world outside.

Harcourt joins them, note in hand. "Would you like to read this, Mr Agarwal?"

"Nadin, please. No, inspector, I think it would be better if you read it – aloud if you don't mind?"

"Of course. Thank you." He unfolds the paper to reveal one side of beautiful handwriting in black ink, almost certainly from a cartridge pen.

Nadin looks up, blinking in the sunlight now streaming through the front window. That's Zoya's writing. I'd recognise it anywhere. We bought her a new pen for her sixteenth birthday. It was her pride and joy…"

Daniel places a comforting arm on his shoulder as Harcourt reads the note out loud.

'Dear Mummy and Daddy

If you ever move house, I hope that you will find this note and take a little piece of me with you.

I wish I could have told you what was on my mind, but I couldn't bring such shame on our family, especially after Daddy has worked so hard to make this an honourable place for us.

I saw it. I saw what happened to Gary. Colin told us all to keep quiet about it, but I can't do that – not any longer. He is on my mind and in my mind whether I am awake or asleep. I did nothing to help and expect nobody to help me now.

If this message is not found until after you have passed, I will be able to explain it all properly then, as we begin our new journeys. In some ways I would prefer it, knowing that your pain in this life would not be compounded by my misery and my guilt.

For now, thank you for everything and please do not forget me, or that until all of this happened, I tried so hard to make you proud of me.

Your loving daughter

Zoya'

Daniel pours out three cups of tea, after which the three men sit silently, each of them lost in their individually troubling thoughts.

***

The call is put through to DS Farren. "I'm afraid DI Harcourt is out at present; can I help in any way."

"Possibly. This is Lance Pearson."

"Alright."

The caller can tell that she hasn't made the connection so clarifies: "Father of Colin."

Now Farren is alert and attentive. "How can I help you, Mr Pearson?"

"It's probably nothing, but my wife was concerned. Colin didn't sleep here last night."

"I see." Farren unfolds and immediately folds her legs again.

Whether it is the white knuckles or leg movement, Flowers notices and beckons Taylor across the room.

"As I explained to my wife, Colin is eighteen. We shouldn't be so surprised."

"Except?"

"Except that he hasn't ever done this before, or at least not without leaving us some kind of message, be it a note on the fridge or even a text when he's been on his way back. The aspect of this that has so unnerved my wife is that there is nothing: radio silence, which is quite an unusual event in itself, I can assure you."

"When did you last see Colin, Mr Pearson?"

"He was here when I got in yesterday. That would be about five-forty; the traffic was bad, and I was delayed."

"And you physically saw him."

"I physically did, yes. With my own eyes, in fact."

She tries to ignore the sarcasm, but the other detectives note the familiar sigh that accompanies their colleague being patronized in some way. It's worse when the offence is overtly based on sex.

"And did you see him leave, sir?" Again, there is no emphasis on the last word of her sentence, and yet it speaks loudest.

"I did not. Marion came in about two hours later and asked if I'd seen him. I told her that I had. It seems that he had left the house in the intervening period."

"Is there anything else you can tell us? How did he seem? Did he pack any clothes that you are aware of?"

"Do you have teenage children, Sergeant?"

"I'm not married, sir."

"Makes no difference."

"It does to me, sir."

There is an uneasy silence before the doctor gives his assessment. "Colin has perhaps been a little moodier

3

lately. The NHS keeps both of us away for long hours, so Colin is left to his devices much of the time. Judging by the mounds of sweatshirts on his bedroom floor with tell-tale sweat patches all over them I would suggest that he has been doing a lot of running – even more than usual. Sorry, I don't mean to do your job for you, but you did ask."

"So, it would be difficult for you to tell me if clothes had been packed – if he was going away somewhere?"

"It wouldn't be difficult to tell you if I knew the answers to either of those questions. What I can tell you is that his car was parked in the street outside our house yesterday. It has now gone – departed with either him or somebody else at the wheel."

***

They hurry past a blue plaque commemorating Dr Edward Long Fox, a pioneering psychiatrist who, it recorded, had created the therapeutic spa on Knightstone Island to help treat mental health patients. Colin is holding her hand tightly, almost too tightly, his gaze strangely fixed and barely hearing what she is saying (or choosing not to).

"Why are we rushing like this?" Her words fly off into the wind which builds as they head around the rocks.

"Because the sooner we get there, the better. The sooner we'll be safe."

He'd heard her that time.

"I'm frightened, Colin. I need to call my grandparents. They'll be frantic by now."

He tightens his grip. "That's just it; don't you see? We mustn't let them know we're here, or anyone else. We'll only be safe if nobody else interferes with our plan. We need to end this, right here and right now."

"What plan? Has this been planned all along?"

"Not by me."

"Who then?"

He doesn't answer her directly. "We must be very close to the place now: I just know that we are. Trust me!"

***

"Yes, sir. One of our masts pinged Colin Pearson's car just before Junction 21 of the M5, but no motorway sightings beyond that."

"So, he's definitely turned off then?" Hunter-Wright is pacing backwards and forwards behind his desk. This conversation could go either way.

"We believe so, sir, yes. The most likely destination according to Daniel Reed is Weston-super-Mare."

"Has he previously worked for the RAC?"

"Not to my knowledge, sir. Colin Pearson and Gary Jones spent time there on holiday with their families."

"And you – or Mr Reed – believes this to be significant?"

"We both do, sir. Mr Reed believes that this represents a secure place for Colin to visit, one where he and Gary had fun; were happy together. A place where they would have been carefree."

"Do you think he wishes to protect or harm Janice Mills?"

"If he is unstable, we think the former, sir. If Colin is the perpetrator of all of this in some way, not to say similarly unstable, then we do have serious concerns for her well-being."

"They know all about it in Somerset?"

"Avon and Somerset Police have been issued with photographs of both persons, sir."

'Persons?' Who uses words like that? Hunter-Wright stops pacing.

***

"You don't believe that Colin is behind this do you?" Daniel hazards a look at Harcourt, who has his foot on the floor of the car.

"We have to consider all possibilities." Harcourt stares ahead, seemingly oblivious to the two lanes of cars to his left that appear to have parked on the motorway. He is lost in earlier memories of Weston-super-Mare. He and Debbie had spent a long weekend there some five years ago now. He remembers the new 'Grand Pier' – all modernist white walls and glass, with its curved roof that had dared to be so different.

It hadn't seemed like a pier to him at all. Not the scary kind where you can catch glimpses of the frothing sea through slatted wooden boards. When you could hear suspicious creaking noises from the stilts below as the wind turned. While you waited by fishing lines held over the edge by a multitude of small, excited boys supervised by sunburned fathers reliving the long days of summer when they had been able to do the same. Piers got damaged, even washed away, but that replacement had felt as though it had lost its soul.

"But it makes no sense." Daniel's voice has gone up a pitch, startling him and bringing the day's unfolding events back into focus. He suddenly looks very pale.

"Little in this case has done."

"No, I mean, yes, but surely Colin would have led or persuaded - whatever - Janice to drown in the mill race outside her home? Why go to all the trouble of kidnapping her and dragging her as far as Weston to do the same, especially where there are bound to be far more witnesses?"

"Because he's desperate – is close to the end of the line."

"The winning line?"

"This isn't a race, Daniel."

"You could have fooled me." Daniel grips the window handle as they hurtle past the M4 interchange and briefly acknowledge Bristol's docks below.

After a few more hair-raising minutes he tries again, tentatively, remembering Harcourt's attack just a few days earlier. Panic on a country road would equate to carnage here. "Miranda Anne Clackerton didn't see anybody chasing Zoya Agarwal because there was nobody that normal humans would have seen."

"Normal humans? You're not going to get all George

Orwell on me, are you?"

Still, they race on, blue lights flashing in the dank afternoon light.

"No normal human saw anyone chasing Barbara Flint either. You're not telling me that Colin Pearson was involved in both of those deaths, yet nobody saw anything or anyone?"

"It happens, sometimes... wait, are you suggesting that Nancy Gutteridge is somehow abnormal."

Relieved that he's finally been understood, although still unnerved at the speed they are travelling, Daniel feels able to share his theory. "I think that Nancy has a similar gift to me. She may only see dead people from the past but..."

"That's enough."

"I'm sorry?" Now Daniel feels deflated, truly mystified by the response.

"That's enough! Seeing dead people is enough of a 'gift' to have if indeed she does have it."

Words. He has lived and loved them all his life, and still, they can trip him up.

"Yes. Yes. I believe that she can 'see.' She saw Gary Jones chasing Zoya Agarwal on the towpath in Worcester. I believe he was haunting her for not helping to save him when she had the chance. These people were friends; you do anything for your friends don't you – one for all and all that?"

"She was certainly frightened." Mercifully a sleek, dark

blue BMW has ventured out into the overtaking lane and Harcourt has to brake, before hooting loudly and sending the car back into the fast lane where it belongs.

"Fear rather than a steely determination to kill herself, however guilty she felt. I believe that Gary haunted her in the same way as he did Barbara. Remember, Barbara's parents told us she was terribly unsettled – couldn't concentrate on anything. I saw Gary in her bedroom. I believe he lured her down to the canal. She told her mother that she was meeting Colin because she could hardly tell her that she and the ghost of a boy she used to know were off out for a walk together, could she?"

"And Nancy saw this?"

"You can only be otherworldly if you live in a world sometimes inhabited by spirits. She was just in the wrong place at the wrong time."

"Or precisely the right place at the right time! And the fact that the boys looked alike was just a coincidence? Colin was never there, which is why nobody other than Nancy saw anyone?"

"Correct. Each of the victims (who, remember, were haunted by the idea that they'd played a part in his death) thought they heard Gary, saw Gary – a bit like in the Hammersmith Ghost case from more than 200 years ago. I'm certain that this is all about Gary's revenge. It's a tale as old as time (whatever that is). Death by water is the means and, from The Iliad through Hamlet and Heathcliff, revenge on the living is as powerful a motive you're ever likely to detect for characters alive and dead: especially if they're dead."

"Let's hope Colin and Janice are still alive then!"

***

DS Flowers's voice fills the car's interior, even though the speakers on the dashboard are tiny. "I can confirm that we have found Colin Pearson's car, sir. It was parked on the ground floor of the Carlton Street Multi Storey Car Park. Nothing appears to be remiss. There is a ticket stuck to the inside of the windscreen, showing that the car was parked just after midnight this morning. The person paid for 24 hours."

"Nothing else of interest inside the car that you can see?" The adrenaline is racing around Harcourt's body now. The familiar thrill of the chase has kicked in, though it looks as though it might have kicked Daniel into touch.

"Nothing obvious, sir. Response officers are happy to break in, but given this is part of a potential crime scene, I've told them to seal this part of the parking area off for now – in case we need to call in SOCOs."

"Let's hold off for now but good work in preserving the scene. I guess uniform are all over town?"

"They are sir, especially on this south side where the car park is situated. They've cleared the new pier and larger public buildings such as the Winter Gardens."

"Farren and Taylor?"

"On their way towards the Marine Lake, sir."

As Flowers ends the call Daniel cuts in: "She won't be in there! He wouldn't have come all this way to the sea to see Janice drown in a lake."

"Perhaps this is about ending the nightmare for both of them?" Harcourt shoots through yet another set of traffic lights commanding him to stop.

"Two suicides are more than enough. Two more would be unforgivable. Gary may have been leading these young souls to self-destruction, but no charge sheet would have murder as cause of death."

"And neither the public nor the powers above would forgive us if we didn't get there in time."

***

"The white lighthouse out there is on an island called Flat Holm, and that's Barry in South Wales right over to the north – where Gary's mum's family came from originally. On the other side, the Somerset coastline carries on towards Minehead and Exmoor beyond that."

Janice is happy for Colin to act as an unexpected tour guide, recalling all the places he and Gary used to play. Just a few years earlier he'd have been walking along here with a bucket and spade. The time for burials is over now - on land at least. He seems calmer; if not at peace then certainly not at war with himself.

"There it is!" Colin is pointing towards a rusty structure extending from the mainland out into the sea. "That's the Old Pier. Dad told us it was the only one in the country that linked up with an island. It was already closed when we used to come here, but Dad and I once hired a rowing boat and got right up next to it."

Janice shudders at the thought of all those decaying legs

under the water. A sudden flashback reminds her of exactly how all of this began. Even now, she has no idea how it will end.

"I didn't think you spent much time with your dad?"

Colin looks pensive; sad. He takes a deep breath before answering her. "He wasn't always like he is now – tired and cross all the time. He and I would often head off on what he called 'expeditions' together. I don't think that, deep down, he liked Gary much. This was his way of giving us all a bit of space."

"They must have been treasured moments."

Colin looks directly at her now, with an expression on his face she cannot read. "There were too few of them. I didn't understand then that it wouldn't always be like that between us. I'd do anything to spend some quality time with my dad again."

Janice shudders at the very real possibility of never seeing her grandfather again. He's been the only father figure she's ever known.

"And there's the special place! It's still there." Colin points to a large door with peeling red paint. "They used to keep the lifeboat in there, which is why it's at the top of the chute. Do you see?"

He is as excited as Janice has ever seen him, but his next sentence chills her.

"Dad said it would make the perfect hiding place: the last place on earth anyone would ever find us. We'll be safe from Gary there. We need to get over there, quickly!"

Janice remembers reading the sign on the wall as they near the end of the path. It reminded her that the Severn Estuary had the second-highest tidal range in the world within the Estuary's natural funnel shape, making it extremely dangerous to venture out onto the mud flats without referring to the local tide table.

She tries to remind herself that she is in the hands of the one person she would normally do anything for – but not while he's delusional: not like this. "It isn't safe, Colin. We need to stay on dry land."

"No. we need to hide, Janice. This isn't a game where there are any winners."

***

The eight-mile journey would usually have taken around an hour and a half, but they managed it just under an hour. Daniel's stomach can confirm this. They eventually turn off Somerset Avenue and park in a side street close to Anchor Head.

"Farren and Taylor are round by Birnbeck Pier." Harcourt is out of the car and walking up the rocky path within a couple of seconds.

"I thought it got destroyed by fire, must be twenty-odd years ago?"

"No, you're thinking of the other one – the Grand Pier was destroyed but re-opened a few years ago."

"Arson?"

"No, I don't think so. I think it was accidental – something to do with a deep-fat fryer? I do remember that the fire alarms didn't work properly, which is why it spread so quickly."

"Any further updates? On Colin and Janice, not the pier."

"They've seen a couple further down but haven't yet established that it's them."

Daniel has to almost run to keep up. Harcourt doesn't give the appearance of adhering to any kind of fitness regime, but the older man is going to struggle to keep up with the pace he has set, especially as the path leads them uphill.

Seagulls float and wail above them, white against the darkening sky. Daniel feels the salt in the wind, already stinging his face.

Harcourt's radio crackles and Taylor's voice follows: "It is them, sir. We've asked for backup. They're going to come towards us from the other direction so that they can't get away."

"Except by water," Harcourt responds.

"They are standing right on the edge of the cliff, sir. It's a sheer drop down from there, although Colin appears to be pointing at something."

"Has he got hold of Janice?"

"No, they're standing side by side, sir. She does look agitated though, as though they're arguing about something."

"Tread very carefully, Gabby, literally as well as metaphorically."

As they round the point, they can see both police officers cautiously making their way down the cliff edge.

Aware of further movement to their right, Harcourt is pleased to see uniformed officers carefully taking up position, should Colin choose to try and escape from them, if not the boy in his imagination.

"Colin!" Harcourt calls over the heads of Taylor and Farren. "Please come away from the edge."

"I can't. We must hide from Gary."

"Gary's not here, Colin. He grew up and moved away, just as you did. He wouldn't want you to hurt yourself, or Janice."

"I tried to hurt him!"

"Only because you were upset. I'm sure Gary would have understood in time."

Daniel sees three of them. It's as though he's suffering from some kind of concussion. In truth, the boys do look very similar from behind but only one of them is real. Only one of them is really here. He stands just behind the other two, one hand pressing on each of their backs, pushing them closer and closer to the edge.

He understands all of it now. Gary had tried to come between Colin and Janice, yet he had failed because nothing and nobody ever could. Once his best friend, Colin had become a rival to be pitied, looked down on from the golden uplands of Malvern. Gary had moved up, but Colin hadn't, couldn't.

Yes, this was about revenge, but it was also about teaching the usurper a lesson, showing his power even after death over Colin and two of their closest friends. Showing them who was in charge. However, the one thing – the one person – he could not get inside of was Janice. She had promised, was promised. Her grandparents would have been so proud that the family honour was upheld in the noblest of ways. For Gary, therefore, she had to go too.

"Why is he inside my head then?" Colin's voice is pleading now; not quite believing but craving forgiveness.

Daniel can see them swaying. It is only a matter of time before one of them overbalances.

He can hear the waves crashing against unseen rocks below them. "It isn't Gary inside your head, Colin." Daniel's voice is louder than usual, even though the wind does its best to throw his words right back in his face. If he can convince Colin that Gary isn't real, they might stand a chance. What he and Nancy have seen is, for most people, just a fluttering out of the corner of the eye – an uneasy presence.

"You're suffering a form of post-traumatic stress because of everything that happened down at the lake. It's caused each of you to think that there is no escape from it. But there honestly is. Gary isn't chasing you. He isn't seeking you out here or anywhere else. Those days of hiding are long gone. You can finally stop running."

There is a sudden movement. In the blur of colours – blue coat and jeans worn by Colin and Janice's green

Barbour over pink slacks – everything is confused and later nobody will be able to say for certain what happened, but the consensus is that Janice grabbed Colin and threw him to the ground. There is a brief struggle before Farren manages to grab Colin and hold him firmly, while Taylor puts her arm carefully around Janice, leading her away from the abyss.

"Are you OK?" she asks gently.

"Of course; I'm with Colin." Though distressed by the day's events, her words are borne out. She does not seem to be afraid at all.

"I would never hurt her; never." Colin half-whispers. "I love her."

"We know," Farren answers firmly but gently. "We were equally concerned that you might hurt yourself."

"I would have deserved it!" Colin sniffs.

"Nobody deserves to die." Taylor has the last words.

***

They have returned to Worcester, at a considerably slower pace than the journey down to the sea. Farren and Daniel accompanied Harcourt, leaving Taylor to liaise with Flowers and the local police. They haven't arrived back yet.

"What will happen to Colin now, sir?" Farren cradles a steaming mug of tea.

"What happened down at the lake affected him far more than anyone realised. His instinct was to protect Janice and he thought if they could just hide from Gary for long enough, all would be well again. The trauma somehow unbalanced his mind.

When Zoya and Barbara died he must have thought that Janice would be next, and he couldn't have that. Couldn't in any way feel responsible for any harm coming to her too. He might not always have shown his love to Janice, but it was never in doubt. This proved it – to himself and, I think, to her – scary though it must have been at the time.

He'll have to go through a range of psychiatric tests, but he didn't commit any crime. Even if he hadn't withheld information from us, there's no guarantee that either Zoya or Barbara – or both – would still be alive today, such was the power of Gary over them, in death as in life."

"Gordon Clay and Moira Ahern kept quiet too?" Farren isn't one to forgive easily.

"Although they didn't actively waste our time, we could certainly have saved some of it if either of them had come forward earlier." Harcourt acknowledges his sergeant's accusation as well as her tenacity. "Clay's wife might argue that he wasted her life, and I suspect his own life in the Malvern Hills he loved so much is well and truly over. As for Moira Ahern: if her husband is on his way back to the lake, I'd say he'll find there less a sea of tranquillity than the dark side of the moon."

"And the Mills family?"

Farren is relentless, he notes, yet also resentful. "Well, yes, they could make a case for Colin kidnapping their granddaughter, but did he; really? He would say –

and Janice would no doubt confirm – that she went voluntarily and that he never used any force to make her do it. I don't think he'd ever do that to her."

"Agreed." Farren is frozen, even though the station is roasting with a heating system which knows only extremes: not working at all or unseasonably hot (in any season). "Janice seems to be quite in love with him, despite being worried about his behaviour ever since Gary died."

"And he is equally attached to her – by his actions, if not in so many words." Daniel nods his head. "I know boys of that age have wandering eyes, but some do manage to stay where they first settle."

"Did yours?" Farren asks enigmatically.

"They did, and still do."

"Mine too!" Harcourt is happy to play a supporting role.

"Mr. Reed..."

"Daniel!"

"Daniel," Farren begins again, "I'm sorry if I didn't altogether believe in you; in your gift."

"That's fine. It's very difficult sometimes to believe in what you cannot see for yourself."

"Is the Detective Superintendent coming down, sir?" Farren needs to change the subject as soon as possible, embarrassed as she remains about her lack of faith.

"He said he'd be down in a few minutes. Linda, there's also something you need to know about Hunter-

Wright."

Farren holds her hand up. "It's fine, sir. DS Flowers gave me some background."

"Then you'll probably already know that today is the anniversary of his wife's death. Miriam passed away four years ago."

***

Later, Daniel clicks the red cross on his mobile phone, delighted that Claire is going to attempt the sausage casserole that Charlotte would once have so enjoyed preparing for them. He continues down the stairs of the police station before meeting Hunter-Wright, on his way back up.

"As I said in there, excellent work Mr Reed. Thank you so much for helping us – again!"

"You're more than welcome, sir."

"No need for the 'sir,' please do call me Rupert. Actually, I do have one further favour to ask.

"Of course!"

"There are some people here," he lowers his voice, conspiratorially, "Who do not believe. They have lost hope, but I am not one of them. Could you help me to find my son, do you think? He's all I have left."

Daniel sees the man's sadness in his red-rimmed eyes, feels the tired desperation of a lost family member and, even more than that, recognises his honesty and his sincerity before replying firmly: "I can certainly try."

MARKRASDALL

The End

ABOUT THE AUTHOR

Mark Rasdall

 Mark Rasdall was born in Peterborough in 1960 and brought up on the edge of the Cambridgeshire Fens. He is a writer of fiction and history, with a professional background in content creation, curation, and online search in London's advertising sector. He is based in the UK, in a small village on top of a hill in the beautiful Worcestershire countryside. For a few years he ran a sweet shop on Worcester High Street with his wife Michelle.

Now retired, this is the second in his series of Inspector Harcourt crime novels set in a changing rural Worcestershire, nestling between the Malvern Hills to the west and the Cotswolds to the south.

You can visit his website at www.markrasdallwriting.com and follow Mark on Facebook, X and Instagram.

MAILING LIST

If you enjoyed this book please look out for the next title in the series:

Family Fiction

Previous titles:

The Proofreader

Please also join our mailing list for the latest news, including about forthcoming books in the series: https://23e39b8f.sibforms.com/serve/MUIFANz0yGHzWd78toV2l8aQF4W9OEv6OK0gKWoa-Gj_LjT9GSzpHGYX1GZwsXLSNxUGcQezK_H6jsvjgnPYBvhl8ctfHQAvxgVvCJuQNos4F2bRHEYFYH-kgQwGBlyUisLxTZPgufZAQLICtjX5mM83Cf-osZw3dmXqTi-1JvRa9dIBPgcaePmVrm8DnlEhBrWJHSqRbJ9LKKuC

Printed in Great Britain
by Amazon